CW00517007

ORIGIN

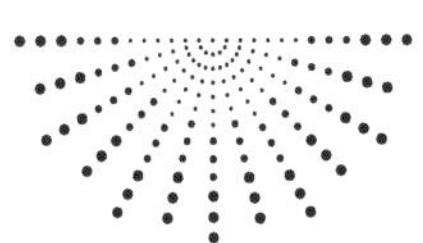

HEROES
VILLAINS
ORIGIN
BESTSELLING AUTHORS
Liza Penn and
Natasha Luxe

1

WATCHER

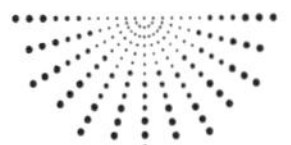

FIVE YEARS PRIOR TO NEMESIS

Pain.

The first thing I feel when I wake up is pain.

The second thing I feel is *annoyed.*

"Keep your cool," I hear a male voice say. Malcolm, leader of Heroes Org.

Memories of the mission we were on flood my mind.

The failed mission. Malcolm as the Hive, leading me and Anthony, in his Steel Soldier suit. It was simple recon, an in-and-out job, but then…

Something happened.

I can't see. *Why can't I see?* Beeping fills my ears—my hearing works at least. Beeping—that's a heart monitor.

"Stay calm," Malcolm says again. This time, his words are laced with power. I feel them wash over me. The beeping slows to a steady rhythm. My flare of panic dies down.

That's his mesmer abilities taking over my mind. I should be pissed—the unbreakable rule of the game is that Heroes don't use their powers against other Heroes, only Villains. But the fog descending over my brain actually helps me to focus on what happened rather than how I feel.

What happened.

What happened?

I search my mind. I was in...Russia. The icy fields of Siberia. We—me,

Malcolm, and Anthony—were following a lead that we hoped would bring us to Elysium, the base of the most powerful Villain of all.

Persephone.

So far, she's eluded not just capture, but also any intel. No one was even sure what she looked like, much less what her goals were, how she was operating, *anything.*

Of us all, Malcolm had the best sense of Persephone. He knew her, once. He was high enough in the ranks at Heroes Org to keep his information classified, but Malcolm was a mesmer—he had powers over others' minds. And that was enough to penetrate whatever abilities Persephone had.

Malcolm's super name was the Hive, and ops with him always made me feel like a worker bee, assigned like a drone to accomplish his tasks. I doubted Anthony felt the same. He wasn't a super; he was born a non-powered human, but his brain adapted to gadgetry in a way that made him valuable to supers. He'd built his own suit, capable of flight and made of bullet-proof material, that turned him into a super in a way few non-powered humans could compete.

He was even part cyborg, with a robotic heart that Heroes Org helped him maintain.

Something about that clicks in my brain.

Anthony's tech skills overlap with biomedical advancements.

Beeping.

A heart monitor.

I can't see—*why can't I see?*

Suddenly, light floods my vision. Except it's not normal light. It's—yellow. I blink.

My vision glitches.

Static fills my eyes, like a television gone haywire, a computer offline.

What the fuck is happening to me?

Siberia. Ice. We were doing recon on another failed mission. Lost a super in that one—Winter Warrior had been scouting the area for Villain activity and came across a nest of low-levels. He had strength, but they had numbers, and when his helicopter went down, we'd lost a good super. His death had rattled Heroes Org. Persephone was stepping up her game, willing to kill Heroes without remorse.

So Malcolm had gone out personally, with Anthony and me as backup. The Villains were supposed to be gone. We were just doing recon.

An attack.

Explosions—I remember explosions. Anthony's suit going into full armor mode. Malcolm—where had he been when I—

When I—

Did I die?

My vision stutters back online.

I blink and sit up. The first thing I see is an enormous machine. It hangs over the bed on a hydraulic arm, positioned over my body. There are little compartments throughout the machine, but whatever instruments inside it are carefully locked behind silver doors. Glass panels reveal scanners with red and yellow lights flashing and some circuitry is exposed, but I can't figure out what this machine *is.*

"He's back." Anthony's voice this time. I turn toward it, the gears in my neck grinding.

Gears?

What the fuck is happening?

Beeping drowns my thoughts.

"He's panicking again. Heart rate up," Anthony says. His voice is too cool, too analytical. I look around the room. There's Malcolm, frowning. This looks like a hospital room. Sterile. White. But Anthony holds a welder in one hand and a wrench in the other.

Like he's working on his suit.

Like he's working on a robot.

But I'm not—

I'm just a person. My superpowers are in healing and strength. A blast like the one in Siberia—it couldn't have actually hurt me, could it have?

"Its eyes are fucking weird," Malcolm says. "Do they have to be that strange yellow? It's like they're watching me."

It. He called me an "it."

I am not an "it."

I am a person.

But...what is my name? Beeping grows louder. My name—my name—what is my name?

...watching me.

I am the Watcher?

No—I am someone else—I am...or, at least, I *was...*

"Turn it off," Malcolm growls.

The world goes black.

2

SCARLET

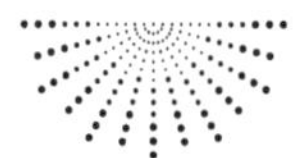

Persephone's harem is packed tonight, and she likes it that way.

I sit cross-legged in a far booth near the bar, nursing my pomegranate cocktail, half focused on the crowd, half focused on the beeping tech in my hand.

The crowd is especially *loud.* Not verbally—mentally. Images flash to me, things each person plans on doing to another or sensations they're currently experiencing. One woman envisions licking another's cunt from root to clit with such startling perfection that my own pussy instantly gets wet.

I squirm, crossing my legs tighter under my slinky ivory dress, grateful when the device in my lap beeps again. I'd have preferred to tuck away into my lab, but on busy nights, Persephone likes me here for a very specific, very *tantalizing* reason. And, honestly, I'm happy to oblige—usually I sit right here, and kick back cocktails, and rub off under the table.

But tonight…*this fucking device…*why is it *beeping?* I've reset it *four times…*

I pop off the back of my transmitter and pick out the circuitry, but the beeping continues, incessant, taunting.

A body slides into the bench across from me.

"Distracted, Scarlet?" Persephone's smooth voice pulls me like a flower seeking the sun. No matter what I'm doing, what I'm focused on—that voice, her attention, those eyes, it instantly yanks me in. All smooth dark skin and the hair of a goddess and huge, tight breasts, she's the reason Villains from all over the world flock here, to Elysium. Sure, getting off in one of these sex scenes is a bonus; but it's really *her*. Her power. Her influence.

Get in with Persephone, and you're protected from Heroes Org.

Get in with Persephone, and you've got access to tech and resources most Villains could never amass on their own.

For a small fee, of course.

I grin at her, eyes shifting through hers for a second, but it's always futile. She never lowers her guard enough for me to read her mind. "Not distracted. Never. Why do you—?"

She cuts her head toward one scene playing out in the far corner.

I don't have to look to know I dropped my focus.

"Shit."

I turn, and sure enough, the couple I'd been holding in a dreamscape is now firmly back in reality. They don't seem to care at all; they're still fucking like animals, his dick thrusting into her pussy so fast I wonder for a second if he's got super speed. To the people watching, the scene looks the same; it's only in the minds of the players that the scene has ended.

That's what I do for Persephone. Aside from tech shit.

I create dreams.

Reading minds is useful, sure. It's how I've earned most of my cash and am able to maintain a few of my own bases around the world.

But creating dreams? That shit's *invaluable*. I can pull anyone into a dreamscape where anything is possible. Want to fly? Go for it. Want to breathe underwater? Sure.

But what people *really* want is to *fuck* in those places.

So I let them.

Persephone takes a cut. And together, we keep most of the world's Villains totally in our thrall.

I turn back to Persephone, who has one perfectly manicured brow arched, her green eyes patient on mine.

I hold up my disassembled transmitter, still softly beeping, mocking me. "Sorry."

One corner of her mouth lifts, as close to a smile as she ever gets. "Scarlet. You need a vacation."

I almost roll my eyes, then remember she's technically my *boss*. "I just took one."

"Going out recruiting doesn't count as a vacation."

"You like Fallon!" I chirp. I knew she would, and I'd told him as much, but he'd still been a nervous wreck. He wasn't sure all his petty robberies would impress the Queen of the Villains, as she's come to be known—but with Persephone, it's less about what you do with your abilities, and more about what *she* can do with your abilities.

The moment he'd snapped out his inky black wings before Persephone's throne, I'd known she was hooked. Ingrained flight ability like his? Lithe muscles, birdlike bones—Persephone recognizes a catch when she sees one.

"I do. And I appreciate your diligence in monitoring supers before Heroes Org can sink their claws in." She taps her green polished nails on the table top, her eyes narrowing at me. I want to look away from her. I never can. "Why do you stay here, Scarlet?"

I pop the transmitter back together and wiggle my eyebrows at her. "Who would want to live anywhere else?"

While most Villains travel from all over the world to occasionally check in—and play—at Elysium, there are some permanent residents. A few low-level Operatives who trade time in the harem for favors; even some humans who swapped their lives so Persephone would alter their body chemistries and make them into supers. She doesn't do that often, but those Operatives are always the most *eager*.

And then there are those of us who keep Persephone's interests running. Me, along with a half dozen others.

Persephone runs her foot up my leg under the table. "You know I love having you here."

My pussy twinges, and I uncross my legs. She goes no higher, though, and I groan.

The thoughts from this room are still insatiable. I'm on the edge of orgasm just listening to these people, their internal pleasure like a pulsating beat in a nightclub.

"I know," I say. "It's the best place for me."

"That's not true, and we both know it."

I frown at her.

Persephone sighs. "You were never destined to stay mine, Scarlet. That was never your place. You know it. I know it. You're meant for more."

"Are you kicking me out?"

She smiles, but it's soft, sad. "At least on a vacation." Then she pulls a folder off of her lap and slides it toward me. "I've booked the trip. Go.

Clear your head. When you come back, I hope you think long and hard about who you are now, and why you're still so sure Elysium is the best place for you."

I stare at the folder. An airline ticket pokes out of the top.

My chest squeezes. With sorrow, maybe? Rejection? But that's not it; I know it isn't. Persephone isn't *rejecting* me. And she's right—I have bases all over the world, decadent homes hidden in gorgeous locations that are mostly unlived in.

And yet I stay here.

Because it's the best place to keep tabs on any Villains who need my tech. Because all my shit is set up here, and moving is a pain in the ass. Because—

I take the folder, my mind thudding with a dozen excuses I know are all lies. "Thanks, Persephone."

She nods once. As she slides out of the booth, her eyes go to the couple I dropped out of their dreamscape. Someone from the crowd has joined them, the woman sucking his cock while her partner still plows into her. They're all glowing now. Like, actually glowing—whoever joined in emits a soft neon green light.

This is why I never leave.

Because out there, in the world, are people who fear supers, who hate us. But in here? We're all just normal. We can be ourselves.

And I don't have to be alone.

"There are many remarkable places in this world," Persephone says. She looks down at me and cups my jaw in her hand. "We just have to be brave enough to look."

She leaves, my malfunctioning transmitter the only thing keeping me company now.

I sigh down at it. "Fuck you, you know that, right?"

It beeps defiantly.

Again, I pry off the back panel. It's easier to focus on this problem than the folder in front of me, the possibility of leaving Elysium, setting out on my own. Tech is always easier than real life shit.

The device isn't short circuiting; it's not glitching; then it must be—

Oh, fuck.

I launch out of the booth—well, I double back, grab the folder, *then* launch out of the booth—and sprint across the room for the rear door.

I give the fucking trio one last glance as I duck out.

They've moved to a bed. One man eats out the woman now while the other has her in his lap, fondling her breasts. Her eyes are closed in sheer ecstasy.

The crowd watching them is going fucking *wild*—in their heads. A few groups are fucking now on their own, one woman bent over a chair while a man thrusts into her; a man blows another.

My whole body quivers, overwhelmed by all this desire, all these thoughts. It's an onslaught of *need*, and the whole reason I never partake in group scenes like this. It's so much just to hear it from people's heads—but to feel it too? I prefer watching.

Then getting myself off later.

The halls of Elysium are, expectedly, empty—at this time of night, everyone's in the dungeon. So I make it to the sub-basement server room in record time.

The rows of monitors and computers all seem in working order, but the moment I step inside, there's a steady beeping from the corner that makes the hairs stand on the back of my neck.

Fuck, fuck, double fuck—why did I think my transmitter was glitching? Of course it wasn't something that dumb—I don't build shit that glitches.

But what the transmitter is signalling just *isn't possible*.

I rush to the back of the room and shake the screens awake. A row of satellites comes up, showing most with bright green signals next to them. Functional. Good. Okay—

My eyes scan the screen, thumbing through Persephone's satellites. The deep space ones are all good. Closer, fine. Closer still—

That one.

What the fuck?

The air bursts out of my lips in a rush.

I run all of Elysium's tech for Persephone. I build anything that needs built, update the security, keep her satellites online, and let her know about any anomalies. In exchange, I have a whole lab two floors up where she lets me tinker with shit.

And this satellite?

It's connected to *all my shit*.

I implant signals in each of my devices to keep track of them. A lot of things are used by other Villains on missions, or sometimes just on loaner—but hell if I trust them to bring them all back. So, I program each one to connect to this satellite, and with a flick of a switch, I can track anything that goes missing.

One thing, in particular, has been missing.

For almost a year.

I destroyed it. It *had* to be destroyed. Cause it never came online, so Heroes Org didn't use it, thank god—which meant it was long gone.

But that satellite—*my* satellite—is flashing, and the code it's feeding is the one I connected to my brain tech. The tech I developed to mimic my own abilities, but on a different scale: implant it in someone's brain, and you could program them to do your bidding.

Even Persephone told me to stop working on it because it was so fucking dangerous. It's one thing for me to be able to read and control people's minds, an ability I was born with—it's another to develop technology that can let anyone do it.

So I'd taken it to one of my remote bases, and I'd trashed the whole thing. *It was destroyed.* I saw it burn.

But I also knew Heroes Org had been tracking me...

And now, as I stare at the flashing icon on the screen, my stomach twists.

Heroes Org got my brain tech.

They've brought it back online.

Which means they can hack someone's mind—just like I can.

3
WATCHER

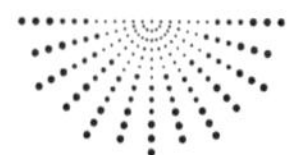

If you had asked me before if I could ever get accustomed to being a cyborg—part human, part robot—I would have laughed at you. I may be a super, but I'm still a man.

Or, at least, I was.

I look down at my hands now. The skin is actually synthetic, the bones beneath are titanium and steel. The blood pumping through plastic tubing is still *my* blood, but is that enough to still call me human?

I don't know any more.

But I find I don't care.

As soon as I was fully conscious—fully *online*—Anthony helped me adapt to my new life as a cyborg. No, "adapt" isn't the right word for it. Because rather than limitations, being a cyborg has presented opportunities. When I have a question, my mind—linked to Heroes Org's database—presents an answer. When I train, my reinforced bones and electro-charged muscles ensure my body can go further than it did before.

It hurts, yes.

Anthony says my body will adjust. Much like sore arms and legs after an intensive day at the gym, but amplified.

My mind hurts, too. There is a constant buzzing in my brain, like a forgotten detail that demands to be remembered but cannot. Anthony says nothing about that, because I have not told him.

I worry about what will happen if I glitch.

There are little moments where my body and my mind don't...they aren't...they aren't *right.* When I saw Malcolm for the first time after truly waking up, the buzzing sound filled my head, my heartrate spiked, and my entire body surged with adrenaline.

I wanted to kill him.

That rage was almost immediately tempered—a beeping sound went off, an alarm Anthony built into my programming—and opposing chemicals flooded my system.

"Normal adjustments," Anthony had said, but his voice had been tight with worry. I do not tell him about the nights when I have nightmares, horrific images of flames and explosions.

My death.

And—sometimes—that strange machine I saw when I first woke up. I'm not even sure if it's real. I cannot seem to recall it when I try.

But I dream about it.

And every time I do, the beeping sound goes off, drowning out the buzzing. Occasionally, Anthony comes into my room, lifting a panel at the base of my skull for "adjustments."

Everything is milder now.

Calmer.

And when Malcolm comes into my room to request me for a mission, the alarm doesn't even go off. Already, I feel whatever cocktail of manufactured programming and chemicals inside my body flood my systems. I see Malcolm, and for a brief moment I see red rage, but then it tempers into solicitude.

"How much do you remember from before you were a cyborg?" Malcolm asks. He speaks in clipped tones. He sounds more like my boss than my friend.

Cyborgs don't have friends.

"Bits and pieces," I answer immediately. "But not much. Not...specifics."

I am Watcher now. I recall having a life before this one, but not well enough to understand it. To miss it.

"Do you remember the mission that turned you into…" Malcolm waves his hand at me.

"Bits and pieces," I answer again, my tone regulated by machinery.

He nods.

"What had been a simple recon mission became far more complex," Malcolm explains. "We uncovered traces of a new Villain in Siberia. One working on a…" Malcolm spreads his hands wide, searching for the right words. "An ultimate weapon," he says finally.

Is that what almost killed me? I wonder, but the thought is idle, distant. Unimportant.

My emotions are tempered now, like the steel that reinforces my body.

"That weapon was a prototype, and we've since destroyed it," Malcolm continues. "But the Villain who made it is still at large. She can make another. And we *must* stop her."

"Is she working with Persephone?" I ask. "I require more information on her background." Already, my brain is running through the data at Heroes Org, accessing whatever cross-referenced information seems relevant.

But there's not much. Persephone is the biggest mystery yet to be solved.

Malcolm narrows his eyes. He's suspicious of me, of my abilities. "She is directly working with Persephone," he answers me. "We think she's a right-hand woman for the leader of Elysium, focused on creating disruptive technology that could damage all of humanity."

"I require more information," I say. My searches have not brought forth anything that would help.

Malcolm heaves a sigh. "Fine."

Tingling washes over my body. It disorients me—I had expected Malcolm to pass me a physical file. Instead, he uses his mesmer abilities to implant an image in my mind.

A beautiful woman with scarlet hair and pale skin and jade-green eyes. The image becomes clearer, vivid and sharp.

"This woman," Malcolm says.

"She's beautiful."

The air grows still around me, and the image of her is yanked from my mind. My yellow gaze darts to Malcolm.

"She is a Villain," he says coldly. "She is not beautiful. And you are a robot. Robots don't have opinions on a woman's fuckability."

Like a morphine drip, the chemicals implanted into my brain burn through my system, calming the rage that flares within me. "I am a cyborg," I relate to Malcolm in even tones. "And while my human genitalia remains intact, I do not consider a woman's 'fuckability' to be influenced by her aesthetic, physical appearance."

"Fucking weird," Malcolm mutters. He was there at my creation, a witness to Anthony's technological wonders, and yet I disgust him.

"Please inform me further of the mission," I say.

"Retrieve the new Villain," Malcolm says. He straightens his collar, adjusts his jacket. This is business. "If we could convert her to Heroes Org, the benefit of having her as an asset would be incalculable. She could use her genius designs to enhance, rather than destroy, humanity."

"Confirmed," I say, logging the mission protocols into my memory banks. A part of me is deeply relieved—this woman *is* beautiful. But she also inspires my humanity in a way I have not felt since becoming a cyborg. I want to be with her—my body hardens at the thought. I want to *be* with her.

"But—" Malcolm pauses. "But should she resist, take her down by any means necessary."

"Standard regulations require me to place Villians under restraint and escort them to holding facilities for formal trial," I say.

"This isn't standard regulations," Malcolm snaps at me. "This woman has the ability to literally *destroy the Earth*. You either take her in or take her down. There will be no restraints or trials. Those are your operations."

"But—" I feel the chemicals releasing in my system again, designed to calm my mind and ease my adrenaline. I override the controls, blocking them. "Sir," I say clearer, "we are not vigilantes. We are not mercenaries. We do not kill like that."

We are the Heroes.

Malcolm frowns, then pulls a palm-sized tablet out of his pocket. He taps on it.

I think of the woman. No files. Only Malcolm, pushing her image into my brain with his powers.

This is all wrong. There is no paper trail. No record of this woman in Heroes Org's databank. And using me for this mission—something is off here.

A small beep from Malcolm's tablet draws my attention. It's the exact same tone as the beeping that sometimes overrides my nightmares.

Quiet placidness settles upon me.

All my worries just…drift away.

Why was I so concerned? Malcolm knows whats best. He always does.

"Do you understand your mission?" Malcolm asks.

"Yes, sir," I say. "Take the target in, or take the target down. She will become a Hero, or I shall eliminate the threat."

There is no doubt in my mind that this is the right thing to do.

4
SCARLET

Persephone booked the vacation for my favorite place: Moscow.

Home.

The hotel she got me is the best in the city. It overlooks the Bolshoi Theater, all lit up in glowing yellow lights against the midnight black sky. The fountains out front bubble and churn as theater guests crowd the stones, the buzz of pre-show anticipation heaving off them in waves. Even from the fifth floor, looking down at them from my balcony, I can hear the wash of their thoughts. Excitement, mostly. Someone is thinking about the date he's on. Someone else is worried about their babysitter and their kids not going to bed on time.

I'm dressed for the opera. The ticket is in my purse.

But I can't make myself leave.

I turn back into the hotel room and shut the balcony doors. My laptop is open on the bed, and I drop onto my stomach in front of it.

The signal's still transmitting. My brain tech is still active, out there somewhere, but I haven't been able to track it anywhere specific, and that just *pisses me off*. First, Heroes Org takes my shit, and now, they have the gaul to wrap it in security that *I can't break?* I'll flay them alive, those arrogant assholes.

I press my face into the bed's feather comforter and let out a frustrated moan.

This is not the relaxing weekend getaway it should be. Maybe the opera is too much for tonight; maybe what I need is just a bubble bath and a raunchy movie and a plate of varenniki dumplings from room service. Good old fashioned self care.

I roll off my bed and head to my suitcase to fish out my bath salts—

But there's a present under my clothes, a box wrapped in shiny purple paper. The card on top says *Scarlet* in Persephone's flowing script.

I grin and tear it open. Did she give me chocolates? Those little ones from Paris with the meringue inside?

What's under the wrapping paper makes me cackle in laughter.

She gave me a *pink dildo.*

A *giant* pink vibrator.

I flip back to the card. The other side says simply, *Enjoy Moscow.*

My pussy tightens, eagerness building. A bath can wait. Maybe *this* is what I need. Not an opera. Not even a trip, really. Just release, plain and simple and easy, to refocus my mind and let go of my frustrations.

Light, operatic music starts to play from the Bolshoi down below as I strip out of my navy silk gown. I leave on my jewelry, diamond earrings and a matching choker, and stand in front of the full length mirror against the far wall. My bright red hair hangs down to my mid-back, delicately curled, and my makeup is absolutely perfect—it's a shame no one will see it, honestly.

I flip on the dildo. It starts vibrating softly in my hand.

I slide it down my body, watching the action in the mirror, and spread my legs wide. I'm wet already; my body knows I need this, too. I tease the tip around my clit, holding the vibrating head right against that bundle of nerves through my red hair. Pleasure winds up through me, warm waves of it building.

When I'm dripping, I glide the dildo up my pussy. It's huge and curved to hit my G-spot, and *god,* does it ever—the vibrating shaft arches through me and perfectly aligns with my wall, making my hips rock.

I'm reminded of the way that trio fucked each other in the harem, and need courses through me. The image of that man licking his woman's clit, his wide tongue stroking that spot over and over—I hold that in my mind as I thrust the dildo in and out, pushing it deeper, deeper, each time hitting my G-spot with lethal precision.

I watch my body writhe in the mirror, one hand thrusting the dildo in and out. The other climbs my stomach, tweaking first one nipple, then the next, before I pinch one between thumb and forefinger and slowly twist, all the while thrusting and thrusting, and *fuck* I wish I had something to put on my clit, an extra hand or mouth. I settle for letting go of my breast and parting my folds to rub in slow, smooth circles.

But my body is tense, wound, the pleasure near to exploding, and the time for slowness is done. I rub harder, matching the dildo's pace, my whole body arching with the growing release—

With a scream, I come, the orgasm rocking through me, making my pussy contract around the dildo and milking out another few waves of ecstasy.

I drop back onto the bed, naked and sweating, the dildo still vibrating in me. Pleasure softens my whole body, makes my mind go blissfully numb. I turn my face towards the balcony doors, happily gasping for breath—

There's a man standing on my balcony.

Shock makes my limbs go stiff.

I sit up, slowly. He doesn't move. He's backlit against the lights of the Bolshoi Theater down below so I can't see his face.

But, weirder still, I can't hear any of his thoughts.

There are only a handful of people who can resist my powers—Persephone among them.

So whoever this is—he's powerful. Or wearing some kind of mesmer-resistant helmet that I can't see.

Either way, it isn't fear that surges through me. Maybe it's from the remnants of my orgasm, but as I sit there, naked, staring at his silhouette, my body tingles with awe.

I cock one leg onto the bed and ease the dildo out of my pussy. It's still vibrating.

I thrust it back in, once, before I pull it out again and shut it off. "Privet," I say in Russian.

The man lifts one hand. He puts it on the balcony door handle and pushes until the door clicks open.

I stay seated, naked, my leg cocked so he has a full view of my wet pussy.

What the fuck am I doing?

Whoever this is clearly came to get *me*. But, try as I might, I can't be afraid.

The man enters my room. He moves carefully, not like someone who was intentionally spying; more like someone who was just walking past and didn't mean to see what he saw. *Five floors in the air.*

Clearly, he's a super with flying powers. He's wearing the standard tight clothing of Heroes Org flyers, red leather clinging to the rise and fall of his lean muscles.

When he turns to shut the door, I get a look at his face in the moonlight.

Soft blond hair hangs wind-blown around his forehead. Yellow eyes flash in a human face, the orbs glowing now, biomechanical prosthetics. I know, because I've built ones just like them.

I fly to my feet. Curiosity overwhelms everything else when the man—cyborg?—faces me, his yellow eyes holding on mine.

"You are Scarlet of Elysium," he says in a mechanical voice.

I cock my head. "Who's asking?"

"Heroes Organization. By order of the—"

Realization floods my body.

No. No fucking *way*.

I whirl to my open laptop and shake it awake, giving Mr. Heroes Org Cyborg a good view of my ass. Being unable to hear his thoughts is fucking *exhilerating*—I have to assume he's distracted by me only because he doesn't finish what he was saying, and he also just lets me access my laptop. If he's here to capture me—which, I'm guessing, he is—he's letting his cock dictate his responses. That, at least, can't be robotic.

Anyway, I don't need long—I have the satellite connection pulled right up. I go to the backend and punch in a new code, then send it out to my brain tech.

It only takes a second. A heartbeat.

Something in the cyborg's head pings softly. A response to the signal I just sent.

My hands start shaking, but I type in another code that immediately hacks the cyborg's tech. Now that I know where it is, it's *mine*.

Fuck you, Heroes Org.

A whole list of directives spreads across my screen. I find the first one —the most vital one—and delete it.

Then I spin back to him, my eyes peeled wide.

Heroes Org sent my brain tech to capture me.

No wonder I didn't fear this man—he isn't entirely a man.

In a way, he's *my* creation.

5
WATCHER

That buzzing—it's been in my brain since I woke up. But now?

"What did you do?" I ask, gaping at the naked woman. Scarlet. Her image matches the one Malcolm gave me.

"Better?" she asks tentatively.

Silence. Sweet, blissful silence.

In my head.

She takes a tentative step toward me. Scarlet is gorgeous in a way I can barely comprehend. Crimson hair curling at the ends. Diamonds glittering in her ears and around her neck. And that sweet wetness between her legs, also glittering. Distracting. Mind-numbingly so.

"How did you—?" I start.

She holds up her hands, stopping me. "First, care to tell me what your 'mission' is again?"

I frown. "Heroes Org sent me to apprehend you."

"Apprehend?" She arches a perfectly lined brow.

"Primary goal is to take you in for questioning and—potentially—recruitment."

"Recruitment?" Her laugh is like tinkling bells. "What makes you think I'm good-girl Hero material?" She drapes herself on a couch, legs splayed, giving me a full display of her pussy, swollen and sensitive from the way she'd been playing with herself. I stare for several long beats, then my eyes drift up to her smile, to the perfectly red lipsticked smirk lingering on her lips. She darts her pink tongue out, licking her bottom lip. Her eyes purposefully dip down to my pants, the erection bursting against my fly.

"I'm not exactly a *Hero*, solnishko," she tells me. My connected brain informs me that she's using the Russian word for 'sunshine.' How odd. "So what happens if I don't come willingly?"

I start to speak, but my throat is dry with desire. I cough, clearing it. "If you don't come with me, I'm to eliminate the threat."

She should be terrified. Instead, she laughs. "Kill me? That's the big plan?"

I nod.

She pulls herself up from the couch, limbs languid as a cat's. She pads over to me, raises one hand, and strokes my flushed cheek. "You feeling better now, without that buzzing in your head?" she asks softly.

I jerk away from her touch. "How did you know?" I demand.

Something flashes in her eyes. "How do you think it got there?" she asks. I shake my head, but she forces my eyes to meet her gaze again. "Seriously. Where did you come from? How do you think you got to be the way you are now?"

"You mean, when did I die?" I growl. "When did I become less than human?"

It's not pity in her eyes—I would have hated that. But...understanding. She understands what I mean when I speak.

"Did you choose to become a cyborg?" she asks. Her eyes rake over me. "I'd need a scanner to be sure, but I'm guessing you're at least seventy-five percent biomechanical now, yes?"

"Seventy-six," I snap.

Her hands slip down my neck, under my shirt. "You feel real enough," she says, her voice a purr. Her hands drift lower, to my pants, the painful erection longing to be freed by her touch. She presses her bare breasts closer to my chest. "You are still a man, even if you're a cyborg."

I snarl, barely able to concentrate, and I step back.

Against the wall.

Scarlet smirks at me, but doesn't approach. "Let me guess," she says. "You 'died' in a mysterious mission that you can't fully recall, correct?"

Tentatively, warily, I nod.

"I thought as much." Despite wearing nothing but jewels, Scarlet walks back to her laptop, bending over it with another decidedly purposeful show of her ass. "There are memory blockers programmed into you. Few people actually *choose* to forget their past. Well..." She pauses, tapping her chin. "I do know of one Villain who made a whole bargain with Persephone just so he could forget his past, but that is clearly not the case with you..."

Focus, Watcher! I shout at myself. This is key intel, exactly the kind of thing Heroes Org needs.

Why...why don't I care more?

"They changed motivation receptors," Scarlet continues, turning back to her laptop. "Wow..." she mutters, then turns back to me. Now there's pity in her eyes. "They really fucked you up, solnishko."

"They? Who is they?" I demand.

"Heroes Org."

"They did not!" My hands bunch into fists. My mind accesses programming on hand-to-hand combat. I could take this woman down.

So why don't I fucking move?

Scarlet's smile is a little sad. "Look, let me play this out for you," she says, sitting on the bed and crossing her legs, but giving me one more glorious look at her delicious cunt. "My tech was stored in Siberia. Well-guarded and hidden. But I'm going to guess you have a mesmer on your side."

Malcolm. Super name: the Hive. Ability: mesmerism.

I nod tightly.

Scarlet's lips press into a thin, sardonic line. "Right. A mesmer would have an easier time at gaining entry into one of my bases. I'll have to remedy that. Meanwhile, you're caught up in all this. You've got...what?" She taps her chin, contemplating me. "Super healing? Enhanced strength and stamina?"

I nod again. Those were the abilities I was born with.

"An ideal candidate for *my* tech." She says that word of possession with obvious emphasis, and the way she looks at me makes me think that she considers me hers as well.

"I'm sorry, solnishko," she says, and her voice drips with sincerity. "But you didn't die in some mission gone wrong. You were killed. And Heroes Org killed you."

"What?" I growl, my knees turning to liquid. "What? No? Holy shit—Malcolm said you'd try to manipulate me, but *holy shit*. Quit fucking with my mind."

"Oh, my darling." Scarlet stands up and reaches for me, but I flinch away. Why can't this damn woman put on some clothes? "I am the first person since you woke up who's *not* fucking with your mind."

That buzzing sound—she made it go away.

My body stills.

"What do you remember?" she asks softly.

"...waking up."

I don't meet her eyes.

"Would you like to remember more?" she says. "My tech has the ability to record even if offline. I could...I could show you what happened."

I stare at her warily. "How?"

Something flashes in her eyes. I get the distinct impression that she could *force* me to see whatever it is she wants me to see, but she's making a point to go slow, to ask permission.

"There's a block on you," she says. "Rudimentary, really, but effective. Heroes Org couldn't delete your memories, but they could block them off from you. I could—remove the block."

I hate how small my voice is when I say, "Will it hurt?"

"Not at all."

I was supposed to take this woman in. I was supposed to kill her if I couldn't.

Instead, I nod in agreement.

And she reaches up and wraps her arms around me. She is so close that it would take just the merest tilt of my head for our lips to meet. A part of me wants that more than the truth—I want to claim her mouth with mine, smear her lipstick, devour her. Her fingers play with the short hairs at the top of my neck, her fingers gliding over my skin—

She knows exactly where my control panel is. With an expert flick of her fingernail, she opens up the little panel, exposing my circuitry. She touches a button—

—and my whole goddamn mind *explodes*.

The mission in Siberia.

It all went sideways.

Anthony hung back. He may have a tech suit worthy of Heroes Org, but he's still a normal, non-powered human.

"Scared?" I asked, laughing. It was a common joke between us. Nothing can hurt me, not for long. Cut my hand off, it'll grow back. Blow me apart, my skin will knit back together. I'm not invincible, but I damn near am.

Anthony doesn't laugh, though.

"I'm sorry, buddy," he says.

There aren't any Villains here.

Just Anthony and Malcolm.

I want to run.

But Malcolm's mesmer powers keep me in check.

I watch as he raises the gun. "Can't implant new tech in a brain that's whole, can we?" he asks.

"Malcolm, wait—" Anthony starts.

Malcolm doesn't turn around as he says, "Would you rather I kill you? I don't think you'd heal as easily, but I don't really care who my test subject is."

Anthony doesn't object as Malcolm kills me.

I SEE IT ALL.

My murder.

Anthony and Malcolm stealing the Villain tech—*Scarlet's* tech—that they uncovered in Siberia. Malcolm forcing Anthony to create a cyborg from my body. Bits of me that could have healed are cut away so stronger material—reinforced bones, synthetic skin, biomechanical organs—could replace my mortal flesh.

It's tortuous to watch.

The scalpel marks match the barely-there scars still on my body.

I see it all.

All the memories that had been locked away.

ONCE, I woke up. My yellow eyes flashed. My enhanced brain processed the entirety of the situation faster than Anthony could turn me off. I knew I had been killed. Murdered. I knew what was happening was wrong.

And I tried to fight back.

"You see?" Malcolm roared as he struggled to control my mind with his mesmer abilities. "We have to wipe his memory! We have to control him!"

"He's our friend," Anthony shouted back. "He's—"

"He's nothing but a robot now," Malcolm screamed. "Do it! Wipe his mind."

AND THAT IS when the buzzing sound started in my head.

I LOOK UP AT SCARLET. There are tears in her eyes.

"I'm sorry," she says. "I never should have made this technology in the first place."

"You made a weapon," I say. "You made *me* a weapon."

She bites her lip.

I shake my head. No. Scarlet didn't make Malcolm turn me into a monster.

He did that, and Anthony.

They made me what I am.

Soulless.

Dead.

"I..." I look down at my hands. "I have to be deactivated," I say hollowly. "Anyone can use me. Program me. Force me to kill..."

I look into Scarlet's eyes. "Can you—can you kill me? For real this time?"

6
SCARLET

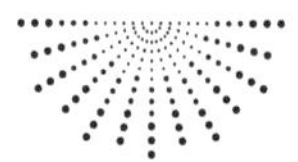

I SIT ON THE BED AND PULL MY COMPUTER INTO MY LAP, HALF IGNORING what the—what *he* said.

"What's your name?" I ask, fingers flying over the keys.

There's a long pause. "Watcher."

I cut him a flat look. "Not your super name."

His mouth drops open. He has soft, pale skin and full lips under wide yellow eyes, and it all serves to give him a perpetually innocent expression. It's damn near impossible to imagine this man as a ruthless Heroes Org super, even less as a cyborg assassin. No wonder he was so easy to hack—nothing about his original intentions lines up with the sheer merciless cruelty it takes to be a mindless killing machine.

"I...I don't know," he admits.

The fuckers took his name, too.

Fury heats my face and I bend back over my laptop. "Well, Watcher, I'm not going to kill you."

He makes a disappointed sound of protest. God save me from noble Heroes—they breed them in droves, don't they?

"I'm not going to kill you," I repeat, "because I can make sure you're never used to hurt anyone. Unless you *want* to hurt them, that is."

Watcher gently lowers to sit on the couch across from me. "How?"

I clench my jaw, scrolling through his code.

Heroes Org might have been able to keep me out of my tech when I couldn't physically locate it, but now? I heave all I've got at their wimpy-ass firewalls.

It takes only seconds for me to access everything. *Everything.*

Fuck you, Malcolm.

I get to it, typing, fueled by rage.

Stealing *my* tech. Implanting it in some unsuspecting, honorable Hero that they murdered to use. Betraying his own people. Turning my creation into a fucking *weapon* and then *sending it to kill me—*

"Scarlet?"

I flinch. I think Watcher's been saying my name for awhile.

"Sorry." I push one more button, hands shaking. "There. You're free."

Watcher blinks at me. "I...feel no different."

"You shouldn't."

"Every time I get a directive from Heroes Org, the sensation is—"

"You felt anything at all from them because they did it ruthlessly. They don't understand my tech. They're a machete. I'm a precision scalpel." I speak through a clenched jaw, all that rage still coursing through me. "And they had no *fucking* business putting any of *my shit* into you."

Watcher's eyes go from me, to my laptop—sitting against my bare thighs, the screen glowing on my breasts—and back up again.

"You just...you just deleted your programming?"

"I cut off all ties to it, yes. No one—*no one*—will be able to program you with commands again."

"Just like that?" There's awe in his voice.

It makes my throat swell. "Yeah. Just like that." I set the laptop on a side table, unable to meet his intense gaze. He can't read my mind—that was never part of my brain tech, and I'd know if he was attempting to do that, anyway—but shit, it sure does feel like he can. "I never should have made that tech in the first place. I tried to destroy it once. Now, I did. In a way." I give him a small smile. "Short of actually killing you. Which, despite your request, I think you prefer?"

Watcher stands. His brows pinch, that awe now written all over his face. "Thank you."

I shrug. "Don't thank me. This is my fault."

"No, Scarlet." He drops to his knees before me.

That position and proximity sends a tingle over my body, reminding me, again, viscerally, that I'm nude.

He seems to remember, too.

Pink stains his cheeks. He runs his tongue over his lips, his eyes firmly on mine, though I have the feeling he wants desperately to look down at my body again. I'd seen—and damn well appreciated—the way he'd looked at me earlier.

"Thank you," he whispers, pleading.

"You're welcome," I relent, matching his tone.

He stays in that position, kneeling, one hand on the bed next to my thigh.

I nod at the balcony doors. "You're free to go. I mean, unless you still want to kill me. But it's your choice now. Whatever you want."

Watcher sips in a breath. "Whatever I want."

My own breath catches. There's a look on his face that I know well. One I see all over Persephone's harem. One that fuels me through my own orgasms.

Sometimes, I need sex so bad that I shut off the incessant flow of mind-noise and fuck in the harem, but half my attention has to stay focused on blocking people, so I'm never fully *there*. Occasionally, Persephone will come out to play, usually when we have special guests at Elysium, and *those* times are sheer magic.

But to fuck a guy whose mind I can't hear? That's a rarity bordering on impossibility.

I sway closer to Watcher, feeling a blush rise across my chest.

"What do you want now?" I ask him, eyelids heavy as I lean closer so that my breasts press together.

He kisses me, quick and gentle, a brief swipe of his tongue between my lips before he pulls back.

It's a question. A bridge.

I cross it, kissing him now, grabbing the back of his head to plunge my tongue into his mouth. He moans against me and crushes the two of us back onto the bed, the full length of his lean body smothering mine into the feather comforter.

I kick my legs free to wrap around him, tugging the buckle of his pants against my pussy.

I'm dripping already. I could take him right now and come within seconds, but this opportunity is too perfect, too rare, to rush.

"Take your clothes off," I order him, voice raspy. "Slowly."

7
WATCHER

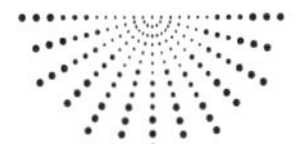

I AM...

Awkward.

As much as Scarlet unblocked her tech, there are pieces of me missing. I suppose that was inevitable. She freed the parts of my mind that are computer instead of brain, she could not replace the bits of me they literally cut away. Those memories are gone. Like my name.

Like...this.

I know the mechanics. My cock is practically pulling me like a dog on a lead, trying to dictate exactly what should happen. This is animal, ingrained in my being, not a thing I need instruction on.

Have I done this before? Have I rutted like a beast? Have I made love like a man?

That, like my name, I do not know.

But I do know that I want this.

And it is that—the wanting, the longing, the sheer *desire*—that moves me forward.

Because ever since I woke up, I have not felt desire. I have only operated, like a good computer, responding to orders. I not only resisted desire; I did not *feel* it.

Not like I do now.

"I want this," I say, marvel in my voice.

Scarlet's slow smile is seductive all in itself. "Then come and take it," she says, voice raspy.

There should be—precautions. But Scarlet just hacked my biomechanics, which I know are clean. And, as I think the thought while looking at her, the computers in my brain activate scanners, showing me that Scarlet is clean and on birth control.

"Undress," she reminds me.

Right. *Slowly*, she'd said.

I tug at the snaps on my red leather flying suit. One pops free. Is this slowly enough? It feels…

Ridiculous.

Laughing deep in her throat, Scarlet hops up from the bed, her breasts bouncing in a mesmerizing way. "Let me help," she says.

She pads across the lush carpet, stalking me.

She meets my gaze, not breaking eye contact as she methodically goes down the line of buttons on my suit collar, undoing each one before slowly tugging down the zipper. There's something sensual in that—of course her touch is hot, but it's her eyes, the way she seems to truly see me…

No one looked me in the eyes at Heroes Org. At least not since my old eyes were replaced with yellow optical receptors.

But then her hand slides beneath the red leather of my flight suit, her touch gliding over my skin, and all thoughts of Heroes Org, of my past, of who I was and who I am—they all flee my mind.

I am here. Now. With her.

Fully.

Instinct takes over. With a growl, I grab her head and kiss her, my tongue claiming her mouth, the brutality of this kiss a form of release, devouring us both. Gasping, my lips tender, I break from the kiss. With the pad of my thumb, I smear Scarlet's lipstick. Her tongue darts out to lick me even as her deft fingers work the rest of the suit free from my body.

Scarlet looks down at my cock, then back at me, eyebrow raised, a smirk on her lips.

She slowly, slowly, lowers her body, getting on her knees in front of me. Before I have time to process how fucking *hot* this position is, she parts her lips and tongues my cock, sliding along the tip before taking the head in her lips, tongue swirling over my senstive skin.

I gasp, shuddering, and I think my legs would have given out then and there, despite my reinforced metallic bones made of titanium, but Scarlet's arms wrap around my thighs as she grabs my ass, pushing me deeper into her throat. She sucks me all the way down, her tongue dancing across my cock, her teeth grazing the skin in a way that makes my whole body shudder with desire.

And when she pulls back, her lipstick all over my cock, my come glazing her lips, I almost lose myself then and there.

With a lustful growl, I bend down before she can take me in her mouth again, scooping her up in one swoop. She giggle-screams in delight at the suddenness of it—I caught her off-guard, and she fucking loves it, I can tell. In three strides, I'm at the bed. I let her body fall onto the soft, downy mattress covered in silk, and she laughs.

It's so pure, her laugh. There's nothing in her body or her voice that demands anything of me. There is only delight, pure and simple.

I love her laugh.

But I'm going to turn it into a moan of ecstatic orgasmic joy if it's the last thing I do.

I climb onto the bed over her. My cock is hot and dripping, and I want to just drive into her, but while that would get me off, I want her to feel this, too, I want her to be with me as we both go over the edge.

She leans up, but my arm is there, pressing her into the mattress. Not hard—she could get away—but she lets me dominate this moment, she lets me push her into the bed with my iron-like forearm.

With my other hand, I trail my fingers from her knee all the way up to her pussy. She's wet and hot, and just running my fingers over the top of her slit has my cock aching.

She giggles again—that sound of joy and sunlight. I plunge my fingers into her, relishing in the way her throat erupts in a gasp, the way her hands twist into the sheets.

She loves the surprise, I think, watching her.

Then that's what I'm going to give her.

I withdraw my fingers slowly, so slowly. Her eyes, wide, go to mine, and her hips buck up, trying to make my touch linger. My grin at her need is cocky, I know it, but if this is what it takes to make her look at me like *that*...

I slide my fingers up, above her slit, higher, swirling over her naval, drawing her wetness over her body. I crawl over her, spreading her legs wide as I position my cock right at her entrance.

Scarlet bites her lip, watching me. I notch my dick on the edge of her, but rather than drive into her as I so want to do, I rub the head over her clit. She gasps and thrusts her hips up, begging me to pound into her.

"Mm-mm," I say in a mocking, chastizing tone. "I'm making you wait for it."

I scoot back on the bed. She's dripping and wet, and I run my tongue all the way up her, root to clit, then suck, hard, on her clit before driving my tongue into her, fucking her with my mouth the way she wanted my cock. Her thighs clamp around my head, her legs pushing me deep into her pussy, and my tongue goes wild, giving her everything I have.

"Oh!" she says, gasping. Her ass is all the way in the air as she tries to push against me.

She's close.

So I pull back.

Scarlet whimpers on the bed. "Please," she begs as I withdraw.

In one smooth movement, I scoot back to my knees, grab her hips, and sheath her over my cock, driving all the way to the hilt. It's so glorious that I yell in triumph.

One thing reinforced bones and enhanced muscles are good for—fucking. I don't feel an ounce of strain as I physically lift Scarlet up and push my cock into her. I bend over backwards, pounding harder. Scarlet's breasts bounce with our fucking, her hair splays around her, she is pure and utter—

"Solnishko," I whisper to her, giving her back the nickname she'd given me.

Her eyes focus on mine.

She's *radiant*, pure sunlight.

I toss her back on the bed, not letting my cock leave her as I move over her body. I prop myself up with one arm and use the other to pet her at the place where we are joined. I meant to make this moment linger, to turn it sweet, but our need is too great, our passions twisted together, and I rub her clit, pushing it against my cock, finding that spot within her were all her need pools. She comes apart beneath me, her body flushing as her orgasm hits her like waves. Her pussy clenches around my cock, her hips driving up into me to meet my touch, and I release into her, melt into her body as we become one.

8

SCARLET

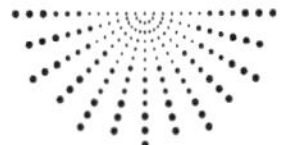

SUNLIGHT MAKES MY EYELIDS FLUTTER OPEN. I LEFT THE BALCONY CURTAINS parted wide last night, and now a brilliant Moscow morning streams in through the glass.

My body is still liquid. I need to get up, pack my things—Watcher's likely halfway back to the nearest Heroes Org base, and even if he somehow doesn't tell them he'd found me, they had to have tracked him still, and they'll know right where I am if they connect the dots between Watcher's newfound ability to resist their influences and his supposedly failed mission.

But I also want to stay here a little longer, and replay last night, over and over—

I roll onto my back and feel a body next to me stir.

He's still here.

He's—

He *stayed*.

I blink at him. He's already awake—does he need to sleep?—and giving me a relaxed half-grin that fizzles all the way down to my belly.

"Good morning," he whispers. He nods at the door behind me. "I called for room service. I figured you'd need sustenance after...last night."

I do. My stomach rumbles, but I don't move, even though I can now smell the food he mentioned—syrupy sweetness and something with cheese—but I stare at him a beat longer.

Then I giggle and tackle him.

His grin widens when I kiss him, my thighs straddling his chest, long waves of my red hair draping around us. The blankets tangle on my legs as I stretch out over him, pressing our naked bodies together.

Watcher runs his hands through my hair, pulling it back in one hand to look at my face. His smile flickers, and instinct has me reaching for his mind—but I can't read his thoughts. Can't see behind the sudden dip of sadness on his face.

I imagine it matches the tight feeling in my own chest: the realization that last night is over.

"Won't Heroes Org wonder why you stayed in one place all night and didn't check in?" I keep my voice light and trail a finger through the dips of his collar bone.

He taps his temple. "I did check in. They're appeased."

"How appeased?" I run my finger lower, down his side, the rises and falls of his ribs and the curve of his hip until I slip between us and grab his cock. He's hard already.

Watcher hisses, but his grin returns, full and bright. "Appeased enough that I think—" He kisses me. "—you should eat breakfast, and then we should shower, and I want you to show me something."

That makes me pause. I pull back to sit on him, head tipped so my hair falls in a curtain. His eyes catch on it, pure wonder, and god, I could lose myself in the way he looks at me.

"Show you what?" I ask.

Watcher cuts his gaze back to mine. He pushes up onto his elbows, stretching the muscles in his chest and tightening his biceps in a way that instantly makes my pussy wet. Fuck, he's sexy, and I don't think Heroes Org's tampering did anything to enhance that. It's all *him*.

"Your abilities," he starts. "You can read minds—and you can handle tech better than anyone at Heroes Org, which doesn't seem naturally derived, but all the same. Both of those abilities, I've seen. There's one other your dossier mentioned that I found particularly... intriguing."

"The dreamscapes," I guess with a smile.

He nods and reaches up to tuck my hair behind my ear, his fingertips lingering on the sensitive skin at the base of my jaw. "It says you can create anyone's perfect fantasy. As I lay awake last night, I wondered—" He sits up now, me on his lap, and closes the space until our lips press together. "—what is *your* fantasy, Scarlet? What does the woman who can create anything fall into?"

I thread my arms around his neck, holding him here, but a veil of seriousness drops over me, weighing down any banter or teasing or drive to fuck. "No one's ever asked me that before."

He pulls back enough to look at me. "Really?"

I nod. My lips part, but my chest is too tight to answer.

What is my fantasy?

What do *I* want?

I've spent the past few years actively ignoring that question, because I knew everything was slowly coming to that answer. What did I want next? Where did I want to go, what did I want to do? I'd still work for Persephone, wherever that was—no one gets out of contracts with her entirely. But I could go *anywhere*. Do...anything.

The only answer that ever came, no matter how hard I resisted thinking about it, was that I just didn't want to be alone again. Before Persephone took me in, I was living in a dingy apartment in this very city, chucked out on my own by a family who feared what I could do. I spent more than two years locked away from everyone out of worry that I'd hurt them or they'd run from me. Until Persephone showed me just how much value a person like me could add to the world.

Still holding Watcher to me, I turn to look out the balcony doors. The Moscow skyline stretches beyond us, highrises and monuments puncturing the blue sky.

"Scarlet?"

Watcher rubs the small of my back.

When I face him again, he must read the weight on my face, how much that question means to me.

He kisses me, but there's a sadness to it. I feel the truth I'm ignoring in every touch:

That last night is over.

That he'll go back to Heroes Org.

That I'll go back to Elysium, and then from there, to one of my half dozen bases. Alone.

I don't want it. I don't want any of it. I want to stay here, right *here*, with this man I hardly know, in this room that isn't mine, in a city I used to call home but now is just another relic of my past.

Our kissing intensifies, softness trading for rough tongues and my teeth on his lip. I close my eyes and reach between us again to guide his cock into me—I'm wet enough that it slides in easily.

Our fucking now isn't fast and needy like it was last night. It's slow, languid, me riding up and down on his dick with my hips gradually gyrating. I clamp my arms around his neck, sensation building with every steady thrust, both of our breaths coming in tight grunts.

"Oh my god," Watcher pants against my ear. "Scarlet—where is this?"

I open my eyes, and my thrusting slows.

I've created a dreamscape for us.

I hadn't even meant to. I didn't even know for sure if I could do one with Watcher and his altered brain.

But my own tangled emotions yanked one out until here my desire lays, spread out before me, undeniable.

We're in a desert, high up on a rocky dune overlooking miles of orange and yellow cliffs that peter off into a sky ravaged by a gold and pink sunset. The air smells of dried-up earth and sweat, and when I look down at Watcher, he's cast in the gilded glow of the setting sun.

"Where is this?" he asks again, his voice tender.

"California," I say. "I have a base there. I—" My breath catches. "I always loved those sunsets the most. The whole sky's on fire."

Watcher grabs my hips and flips us until my back is on the rough desert ground. He bends over me, reaching down to rub my clit in gentle, delicate circles that immediately have me writhing.

He starts thrusting into me, matching the punishing rhythm of his thumb on my clit, his chest pressed to mine, his mouth on my ear alternating between kisses and nips. I can feel the whirring of the machinery Heroes Org used to replace his lungs, but his heart is still human, a steady *thump-thump, thump-thump* that beats in time with mine.

I anchor my heels around him and arch my hips up against his thumb, against his cock. The time for gentleness is over—I want to remember the feel of his body on mine, crushing into me, when all this is over. I need to be able to look back and remember each touch with perfect clarity.

Watcher yanks back off of me, but in seconds, he's on my clit, this time with his tongue. He lifts my hips to his mouth and licks with abandon, circles and swipes that have me sprawling out, arms splayed wide, fingers digging into the rocks and sand. He sucks my clit in between his teeth and flicks it with his tongue, and I come in a screaming cry that echoes over the empty plateaus.

Then he's back in me, plunging his cock against my walls at an angle that hits the same spot as that curved vibrator. My scream intensifies, pleasure ebbing into pleasure in his relentless pursuit of everything that undoes me.

He comes with a sharp curse, his face contorting beautifully, and he collapses against my chest, the two of us sweating and spent as the dreamscape sunset bathes us in the delicate jewel tones of evening.

THERE'S a pair of robes in the hotel room's closet, and I slip one on as Watcher dresses.

I realize, oddly, that it's the first time I've been clothed around him.

I don't like it.

Watcher snaps the collar of his red leather flight suit, facing away from me, his motions stiff.

I chew my bottom lip.

Just say it.

Just fucking *say it,* you coward.

"Don't go back to them." It's out of me like a gunshot and rattles me just as much.

Watcher pauses. He turns slightly towards me, his yellow eyes flashing once, brighter, then dim.

"I have to," he says, but it's weak.

"No, you don't." I point at my laptop. "You're free."

"Where would I go? They still track me."

"I can undo that, too."

"Even if they don't use honing signals or geo-locators, they'll put someone on my tail. And what kind of life would that be? Running from Heroes Org for the rest of my days. They *created* me. They won't give me up so easily."

"Neither will I." Another admission that rattles me so much I feel tears prick my eyes. I step closer to him, letting the robe fall open, but it isn't in seduction—I'm unraveled. "I don't know what this is, but I think you feel it too. This is...*right,* Watcher. You and me. I want to figure out why. I want to—I want *more.* More of this. More of you. Just—stay with me. Please."

His lips quirk, but his eyes are still sad. "Begging doesn't seem a natural state for you."

"With you, it is."

He reaches for me, his hand cupping my jaw, his thumb on my lip.

"They'd chase us," he whispers. "Forever."

"Let them try."

"We'd never be safe."

"I'm not safe *now*, Watcher." I grab his wrist. I know he can see the tears gathering, and I don't care. My dreamscape gave me the answer to my question, an absurd, unimaginable future with this man I just met, locked together in my California base. "Please," I say again, my voice soft and brittle.

He kisses me. I arch up into it, tongue tangling with his, but he breaks it to press his forehead to mine.

"I could not live with myself knowing that my selfishness endangered you," he tells me.

I try to argue. I have a hundred reasons why I could convince him otherwise.

But when he pulls away, I say none of it.

"They'll try to reprogram you," I manage. My voice is level, stronger. "They won't be able to, and they might—fuck, Watcher. I don't know what they'll do when they realize they can't control you anymore."

He takes a step towards the open balcony doors. He doesn't look at me again, and it makes me stumble after him, the edges of the robe brushing my limbs as I move.

"I don't know what they'll do, either," he says over his shoulder. He looks back at me, a long moment of silence where it feels like he's memorizing my face, my body, and I know I must look a mess, all desperation and teary eyes.

I gasp. "Watcher—"

"Goodbye, Scarlet."

He crouches, then bursts upright, and before I can say anything else, he's out the window, gone into the clear blue sky.

9
WATCHER

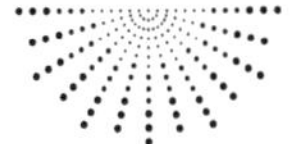

THEY KILLED ME TO MAKE ME.

What would they do to her, if they realized the parts of me she unmade? Unlike my binary coding, I am deeply aware that this situation isn't black and white. Scarlet is not a Villain—or if she is, she is more than that. And I am not a Hero.

Not anymore.

A real Hero would have done the job as ordered by his commander. A real Hero would have obeyed.

I pause midair. Below me, a glacier cracks, the sound barely registering despite how loud it is. Before I was remade, I could not fly, and even if I could, I didn't have every Heroes Org base hardwired into my brain, a honing signal that had me shooting across Russia in a northward arc. I'm not sure if I'm over Greenland or a remote part of Canada, but even as I think the thought, my brain informs me that I'm hovering in the cold air above Greenland, exactly halfway between Moscow and Los Angeles.

Los Angeles. Near the desert ridges that Scarlet loves.

I shake my mind. I'm heading to New York.

And with a clear, focused determination, I blast off toward the city.

. . .

It's late when I land at New York—my flight was quick, but time zone differences mean that my arrival has put me at the Heroes Org base at night. I scan the biometric lock at the rooftop access point and enter the skyscraper.

A part of me means to just get inside and beat Malcolm to death, but there's enough Hero within me still to reject that idea. Besides, even if it was just Malcolm and Anthony who made me into a weapon, the entire organization has no issue using me as one. I need something more than just revenge.

Even at night, the Heroes Org building is not empty. I feel like an imposter as I make my way past Heroes returning from or setting out for missions, Agents gathering and compiling data and handling affairs, and lower workers who keep the whole business of supers running.

No one can see I'm different now. They nod to me—some with fear, some with respect—as I pass. They see my yellow eyes, and they avert their gazes from the most visible aspect of my otherness.

But they don't see that I no longer care about being a Hero.

That I'm no longer *programmed* to care.

I have to use another biometric scan to gain access to the sub-levels of the building, the high-speed elevator making my ears pop as I descend.

This room—the video archives room—is silent and empty. I breathe a little easier, my shoulders dropping a few inches as I step inside. The only noise comes from the hum of computers working.

Before, I would not have known what to do with this many computers.

But I do now.

I hold up my right index finger and bend it backwards at the top knuckle. Rather than a bone breaking, the finger reveals an access port that I plug into the nearest networking system. As the entirety of Heroes Org's database and archives downloads into my mind, I scan the information's code.

There's more here than even my brain can process in one go, but it's clear that I have exactly what I need. I register parts of it, marking them for further inspection.

Like the file on me.

I see my past. My real name.

And then I push that aside, burying the data under other information. I am Watcher now.

This much information takes time to transfer. I'm not finished when the entire room goes dark.

Someone's cut the power. The hum of the computers is silenced, replaced with metallic footsteps crossing the tile. The lights are dark, the room illuminated only by my yellow optic sensors...

And the lights gleaming from Steel Soldier's suit.

"Anthony," I say.

He doesn't lift the mechanical mask.

I have already downloaded the schematics for his suit, the biometric tech putting this non-powered human in the ranks of the supers. A billionaire philanthropist genius, Anthony Stern did not need to dedicate his life's work to developing tech for Heroes Org, much less join the ranks of active supers.

He always said before that he had a lot of bad to make up for.

And I always believed his reasons to be noble.

Besides, he is part cyborg like me. His human heart was replaced with a mechanical one. We are like mirror twins—my human heart is one of the few pieces of me that remains original.

But whatever common ground we share is rapidly slipping away.

"What are you doing?" Anthony asks, the Steel Soldier suit slightly garbling his voice, giving it a mechanical echo.

I know—because my brain is faster than any computer in Heroes Org, because he helped make me so—I *know* how to disable the Steel Soldier suit in three strikes. And I know, thanks to the biomechanical enhancements on my body that he gave me, that I could make those strikes in less than two and a half seconds.

And I know that the overriding code that was supposed to prevent me from ever attacking Steel Soldier or anyone in Heroes Org is gone.

Thanks to Scarlet.

But the way Steel Soldier approaches now—carefully, with his photon lasers locked and loaded, without removing his protective shield—I think he knows that, too.

"What are you doing?" he asks again, a whisper of panic lacing through his voice.

He's scared of what I can do.

Because he knows he's lost control.

I still don't speak.

He fills the silence for me.

"After your check-in, we were blocked from scanning you." He's babbling, nervous. "Malcolm sent me in for a physical check."

I almost snort with bitter laughter. Ah. That's how he knew I was no longer his man. He physically flew to Moscow and saw me and Scarlet fucking. What a voyeur.

I bite back my smile.

I can't wait to tell Scarlet about this. Maybe she'll be into voyeurism. Maybe we'll make a dreamscape with an audience.

If she doesn't hate me forever for leaving her behind.

"I'm out," I say, my voice echoing around the silent room.

The photons in Steel Soldier's fists grow, but he doesn't ignite them at me. I know a blast from him would hurt no more than a bee sting. And it would leave him open for a completely debilitating attack from me.

"You...you can't be," Anthony says. Even though he must have guessed how fully I am in control of myself, how he no longer has any hold over me, he still sounds disbelieving.

"I'm out," I repeat. "And you can't stop me." My laugh is harsh. "You made me into the ultimate weapon. You just didn't realize that I may one day be a weapon against you."

"You were my friend," he says. "I saved your life."

"After you killed me."

He lifts his visor. I see his pleading eyes, full of sorrow.

And confusion.

I scan the records on file for Heroes Org. Ah. Oh.

Shit. Anthony doesn't know that.

My murder has been rewritten in the official files. And Malcolm—he's a mesmer, but his powers have been fading for years.

Although, I can see now, they haven't faded enough. He's used his powers on Anthony. Turning my friend into my maker.

"You're not going to hurt me," I say. It's a statement of fact. Despite the suit, despite the loaded photons, I know Anthony won't fire on me. He's still Anthony to me, not the Steel Soldier.

And he doesn't understand what happened in Russia. What happened to me. He doesn't even understand his role in it. Malcolm's dug his mesmer claws deep into Anthony's brain, and my friend has blocked out his memories of my creation, fabricating a story that's entirely false.

No wonder every time I saw Malcolm, my whole body panicked. No wonder Malcolm had Anthony program in chemical releases to keep me in check.

Malcolm has always been my true enemy.

Even as Anthony and I stand there, my brain's processing the entirety of the data I'd been able to hack into and store. The data I've downloaded shows me just how deep Malcolm's powers can go, how strong he actually is, and how difficult it will be to break his influence over people who've been around him too long. I don't think Anthony could handle the truth right now. I don't know the full extent of Malcolm's control over him, and breaking a mind from mesmer influence can be...tricky.

"When you're ready for the truth," I say, "you're going to need help. And I'm not going to be there to help you. But...I trust that you'll be smart enough to figure it out."

"What do you mean?" Anthony asks, brows furrowing.

I *can't* give him more information—Malcolm will surely hack into his brain and either erase it or kill Anthony to keep his secrets.

"Look to the stars," I say.

"What the fuck does that mean?"

I take a deep steadying breath. I want to tell him everything. But I don't even know everything—the power was cut before I saw it all. Anthony, if he remains here, will be able to uncover whatever it is Malcolm is hiding. But I can't just hand him the information, or Malcolm, with his mesmer abilities, will know.

And...I'm not even sure I can fully trust Anthony. My friend isn't the same person I was training with when I first arrived at Heroes Org. He's changed. Not as much as I have, with a brand new body, but...

Enough that I'm not sure I can tell him everything.

"What are you even trying to get me to find?" Anthony asks. His confusion is bleeding into frustration, anger.

"I can't help you with more," I say sadly. "But there *is* help out there. Others who know the truth. There's one...I think she'll be able to help you the most, actually. But she's safe for now. Hidden. Protected."

Anthony growls, his eyes glaring.

I sympathize. But I *can't* help more. I've probably said too much already. "I want you to find the truth," I say. "And maybe when you do, we can be friends again."

Anthony's gaze darts around the darkened room. Cutting the power was efficient—it ensured my access link to the data was cut off. But I have enough.

"You can't leave," he says.

"You can't stop me," I reply, my voice calm.

"What did you download?" he demands.

"Enough to ensure the safety of myself and anyone I care about," I say. I start to walk forward. Anthony stands his ground, so I pause. "I have just downloaded enough information to take down this entire organization," I say. "I will give it to Elysium. I will leak it to the media. I will do whatever I want with it."

"You—you can't," Anthony stutters.

"I can," I say. "But I won't. As long as you inform Malcolm of this simple fact—if he leaves me alone, I'll leave him alone."

I shoulder past Anthony.

"But—we need you!" he says.

That makes me stop. Without turning, I speak to the darkness. "Here's the question that should be keeping you up at night, Anthony," I say. "Why? Why was I needed? Why did Malcolm turn me into the ultimate weapon?"

My yellow eyes glow. I wait for Anthony to answer me.

He doesn't.

So I leave.

10

SCARLET

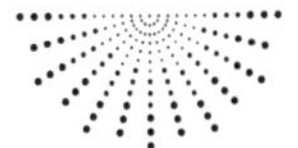

I HEAVE THE LAST BOX ONTO THE DOLLEY AND ROLL IT DOWN THE CARGO plane's ramp. One of the many bonuses of moving with Persephone's blessing: I got all my shit in one go. She'd even offered a full moving crew, but I was too stubborn to accept that. And too emotional. And too...raw.

This is monumental, establishing my official main base here. This whole place has always been mine, but only when I was in the area and needed somewhere to lay low in the California desert. Now, it'll be my *main* base.

All mine.

Just...mine.

I park the dolley and rub the back of my hand across my sweaty forehead. My muscles ache from hauling around these boxes all day, and I still have hours more to go. Behind me, the landing bay doors are still open, showing the pink-gold sky dipping into a sunset.

I should eat. Or shower. Or sit, maybe, and just take a break, but the very thought of stopping too long has my sore muscles seizing in panic.

If I stop, I'll think.

If I think, I'll fall apart.

This is good. Persephone kept telling me that. *This is good, Scarlet. You'll see. You'll be so much happier on your own.*

Will I? I sure as hell don't feel happy *now*.

I kick the dolley and the top box flies off, scattering bath products.

The clatter of shampoo bottles hitting the cement floor echoes off the high bay walls, down the open door that leads into my base's twisting halls. Just empty, ringing noise that fades into utter, maddening silence.

There's no one else here.

Just me.

Forever.

I pick up the next box and throw it with all my strength at the wall. It smashes and rebounds, spewing makeup across the floor, and I curse at myself, but *fuck, I hate this.*

I'm alone.

Again.

Tears sting my eyes, and self-deprecation has me scrubbing my nose and bending to pick up my makeup and bath products.

"Goddamn it, Scarlet," I hiss at myself. "You've done this before, okay? Uspoykoysya, kontrolirovat' sebya—"

"Do you always speak to yourself in Russian?"

Everything in my body goes stiff. One hand is extended toward a runaway tube of mascara, and I do a quick count of the ways I could take out whoever it is. I have a knife strapped to my thigh, but I stupidly left the bay door open. Who could've found me here? Who could've—

That voice processes.

I fly to my feet and whirl around.

Watcher stands between me and the cargo plane. He's in a plain white t-shirt and tight jeans, hands shoved into his pockets, head tipped and eyes bright. His mouth half lifts in a tentative smile, but he doesn't take a step toward me.

Longing surges through me. I almost whimper, but *fuck*, I have more self-respect than that.

I plant my hands on my hips. I'm in a sports bra and tight leggings, hair pulled back, my skin covered in sweat and the gunk of moving all day, but one sweep of his eyes up and down my body, and I feel my chest flush, shoulders pulling back, breasts out.

But anger puts a hard stop on my arousal. "What the fuck are you doing here?"

He flinches. "That's fair. I—" He licks his lips and takes a step closer. When I don't retreat, he takes another. "I wanted to make sure I could keep Heroes Org at bay before I returned to you. I needed to ensure that you would not be threatened."

Another step.

"I can take care of myself," I say.

"I don't doubt that. But I needed to take care of myself, too."

"And have you?"

He's standing right in front of me now. So close I can feel the heat coming off of him, can smell the windswept breeze on his skin.

I look up at him, and when I swallow, he tracks the motion with his eyes, riding the rise and dip of my throat.

"Yes," he tells me. "I had to make sure they wouldn't come after me. I'm sorry I—"

"And they won't come after you?" I cut him off. My heart's racing, and I know his sensors can see it, the uptick in my pulse that I can't deny anymore.

He nods.

"Where are you going to go?" I ask, but my lips lift in a slow grin.

A pause, then his jaw works in a repressed smile, his eyes rolling once. "Oh, I think South America? I was just coming to let you know. Bye, Scarlet."

He turns and takes a full step away before I chirp and grab his arm.

"Brat," I snap and fling myself on him, arms around his neck, lips on his.

"Oh, you're one to talk," he growls into my mouth, and I nearly fall apart at just the tone in his voice, all primal and dark.

He scoops me up, and we stumble back until he deposits me on a metal table near the hallway door.

The kiss is scorching and rough, each bite punishment for his absence these past few days, for leaving me in that hotel room even though I knew, unspeakably, that he'd return to me. I rake my nails down the back of his neck, and he hisses, then his fingers are tugging at my sports bra, peeling it up and off until my breasts hang free between us.

There are no words. We don't need any. He's here, sucking his way down the side of my neck, and I arch into it, giving him room to leave his apology on my skin. And he does—each touch of his tongue on the sensitive skin around my breast is as good as him on his knees, begging for my forgiveness.

And when we move to the floor, our clothes gone, our bodies entwined, the California sun sets through the bay doors, casting us in rays of perfect, gilded scarlet.

EPILOGUE: PERSEPHONE

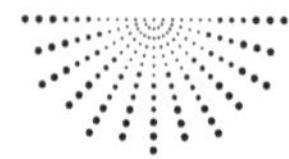

He is called Watcher, but I am the only one who sees it all.

And I am the one who knows that all is working to *my* plan.

They think they are in control. When Scarlet was coming into her powers, it was I who helped her create dreamscapes. When she came back from Moscow, clearly broken-hearted, it was I who pushed her to her remote California base.

It was I who oversaw her technology being developed, and even if I was not the one to implement it and create Watcher—I am not so cruel as that, despite the way the mortals call me a Villain—it was I who ensured Watcher ended up on my side.

The pieces are falling into place.

Scarlet's base is ideally located.

Watcher is safely and firmly away from Heroes Org.

And the technology I need to fight the coming storm…

None of them know what's coming.

Who is coming.

Only I.

But I will protect this little Earth.

I always protect what's mine.

NEMESIS

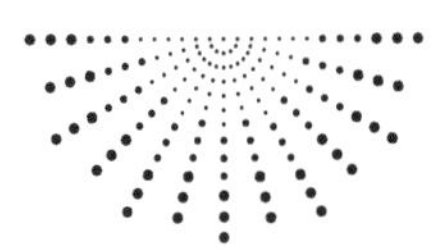

HEROES VILLAINS
NEMESIS
BESTSELLING AUTHORS
Liza Penn and
Natasha Luxe

1

FALLON

"FUCK YOU," I SNARL AT THE SCREEN.

The smiling asshole surrounded by glittering lights does nothing but gleam his shiny whites at me. All-American Man may have super-hearing to go with his super-strength, but even he can't hear me through a television screen. Still, I salute him with my middle finger.

I shouldn't bother with this bullshit. Everyone in the entire world sees Ari Dodgers—better known to his fans as All-American Man—with stars in their eyes. He's the perfect Hero.

And me?

I'm just a Villain.

That's the bullshittiest part of the bullshit. Some people are born Heroes, with bright blue eyes, ashy blonde hair, and an ass that looks good in Spandex.

And some people are born ... me. Which isn't to say my ass doesn't look damn fine in Spandex, too. I just don't show it off as much.

I flex my shoulders, and the feathers on my wings shudder. Raven-black with an oil-like sheen of greenish blue, these are not the wings of an angel.

That's fine.

I'm not an angel.

Not like *All-American Man,* Ari Dodgers. He may not have wings or a halo, but every goddamn person in the country thinks the sun comes out of his ass.

And if, every once in a while, I can cast a shadow over that sun with my wings? All the better.

"While we all know of your heroics from the news," the entertainment reporter says, leaning closer to him, "your new movie will tell your story on the big screen. It releases in just one week—can you tell your adoring fans what making this movie was like?"

That goddamn movie. I have no doubt they've made me look like a slimy piece of shit. It was bankrolled by Heroes Org, after all. Still, morbid curiosity and all that.

"I've got to say, it's a real honor," Ari says, his melodic voice resonating through the hall. "I have only ever wanted to help people—I had no idea this path would lead me to becoming a star!"

Fucking hell, I need a drink. I leave the floor-to-ceiling screen going as I stand and move to the back of my room, where my bar is stocked with the best vodka money can buy. My lair isn't as large and fancy as some Villains's, built into the side of a cliff and accessible only by flight, but while I may sometimes forget to stock the kitchen with staples, I always have vodka on hand.

The reporter laughs, her eyelids fluttering. Her cheeks are flushed, and it couldn't be more apparent that she wants to fuck him. Everyone does.

Hell, even I'd take a turn if I didn't know just how deep the asshole's assholery went.

"And what was the most difficult part of playing yourself in the movie?" she asks him, leaning closer.

Ari laughs. "I was born for this role, I suppose!"

The reporter giggles. The camera man takes this moment to pan around the room—this is Ari's only press junket stop in America, done on stage in front of a movie screen that will show a special audience of Hollywood's elite a preview showing of the movie version of Ari's origin story, a week before the wide release. Everyone in the auditorium is eating out of this prick's hand.

Everyone except *her*.

I pause the replay and zoom in on a woman's face, half-shadowed in the wings.

Creamy skin and a pink snarl barely marring her face. I lick my lips, imagining the fangs this girl has. She hides them well. She wears a crisp linen shirt and a black pencil skirt, her hair done in a neat bun, her eyes attentive. She looks like the picture of calm.

But she fucking hates being there.

"My kind of girl," I say aloud, wondering who she is. I mean—I know of her; I've seen her face on the front page of the tabloids. I thought she was nothing but arm candy. I ignored her, mostly—I don't need to bother with normal humans to exact my revenge on the would-be gods.

Now that I'm looking at her, though, I realize.

She's something *more*.

I hit play again, and the video jumps to life, focusing in again on Ari. His lips are pulled into a model's pout—his version of being serious—and the crowd eats it up.

I chug my vodka, relishing the burn down my throat. I don't know why I bother torturing myself. I'm going to have to punch a *lot* of things to make myself feel better after this.

"Probably the most difficult part of filming the movie," Ari says to the reporter, "is that while I got to play myself, my girlfriend, Lilly, was played by Amelia Hawthorne." Before the audience can react, Ari puts his hands out as if in protest. "Which isn't to say Amy isn't awesome! I adore her! It's just ... the only girl I ever really want to kiss is my Lilly."

They all fucking go wild. The whole auditorium fills with whoops and cheers, and the cameraman does another pan across the crowd—this time focusing right in on my girl in the pencil skirt.

Most girls, I think, would blush at this sort of attention, especially from Mr. All-American himself. But she—Lilly—that's no hot flush that fills her cheeks, no sparkle in her eyes. Oh, she smiles all right. She strides forward and takes Ari's hands.

But that's straight-up ice flowing in her veins.

"You're *furious*," I say to the image of her, my words echoing in the empty room. A grin smears across my face.

Interesting.

I stand up, my wings dragging on the ground as I move toward the screen. The banner across the bottom displays her name:

Lillith Giles, former waitress

. . .

Former waitress? What the actual fuck kind of file does CNN have on this girl? She's absolutely a lot more than a former anything.

Before I can fume more, the camera focuses back on Ari. He looks right through the screen—not at the girl on his arm. She's almost out of frame, and that pisses me off. The one person who seemed to have any personality at all, and they've cut her from the picture.

"These past few years have been intense," Ari says, his brows pinching together in the perfect display of concern. "Not everyone is born with powers, and those of us who are must use them to protect the weak."

At *that,* the fucker pulls the girl, Lilly, closer, wrapping his arms around her. She stands there, spine made of steel, not melting into his touch even though there's a pretty pink smile on her lips.

A cool blast of air hits my back as Ari holds Lilly on the television screen. My wings sometimes have a mind of their own, and they're fully extended now, shadowing the TV, as if they'd like to wrap around the girl in Ari's embrace.

Fuck. My cock has a mind of its own, too. Just seeing her has made me hard with a lust flaring through my core in a way I definitely didn't expect. I want to reach through the screen, toss Ari aside, and show that girl how to fucking *fly.*

Instead, I have to watch the video play out. My jaw clenches as Ari slides into a graceful kneel. The audience goes fucking berserk as Ari gets on one knee, holding out a ring box.

"Lilly—my Lilly—will you be my bride?" Ari asks, holding out a ring with a rock on it the size of a grape.

There's a beat—a single moment—where no one moves.

And right then, I see the doubt in Ari's eyes.

He's All-American Man, the biggest superhero in the entire world, but he's not sure he's got this girl. And that makes my whole fucking week.

She doesn't want him. The realization hits me like a ton of bricks. It's not just that she's uncomfortable being in the spotlight, a hard place to be next to the most popular man in the country. No, she ... she doesn't want him. Even as her hand reaches for the ring and her head nods "yes," I know it's true, I *know* it—

She does not want him.

That ring on her finger? It's a lock on a cage. And when Ari slides it over her knuckle, I *know* she knows it.

I snap my wings out, twisting my neck so it cracks audibly. A few of my black feathers flutter around the room. Oh, girl. If there's one thing I can't stand seeing, it's a caged bird.

It's taken me more than a *year* to recover from my last encounter with Ari Dodgers. All of America thinks he's nothing but a Hero, but I know better. When that psycho clipped my wings—quite literally—he knew what he was doing.

And what's more? He liked it.

I clench my fists, ignoring the quake in my shoulders. I was born with wings; I was meant to fly. And when Heroes Org decided they didn't like the way I flew, they sent Ari after me.

Just like now, it was all about the cameras. They took me down—it took three of those Heroes Org fuckers, *three of them*—but they had an unbreakable net, and they made sure all the best angles of the flying camera drones were on me. The news still posts clips of that day, the day All-American Man took down the Raven.

I thought once I was brought down it was over. But then All-American Man took me alone to a canyon. A desolate, abandoned place where there were no cameras. Just him and me and the hate between us.

When his mask came off, the knives came out.

He dumped me in the bottom of a canyon, broken, and left me there, unable to fly home.

And he's the one they call Hero.

I can fly now, but it's fucking painful. Worth it for the air. But every time I do, I think about how I'm going to hurt the one who hurt me.

"Shouldn't have chickened out," I whisper to the image of Ari laughing and hugging Lilly Giles. He didn't want to kill me, he said. He wanted *nature* to do it, so he just left me to die.

That's not a mistake I'll make.

On television, Lilly looks down at the rock on her finger like she can't quite believe it's there. I don't think she even actually said yes. She just didn't say no, and that's enough for Ari.

I'll be fucked if I let him clip anyone else's wings, literally or metaphorically. But this girl may just be my ticket through Heroes Org's defenses. I flex my fingers, my talons sharp as blades.

This is the opportunity I've been waiting for.

2

LILLY

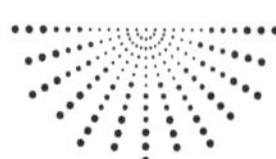

THE ROCK IS HUGE.

That's the only coherent thought that makes it through my shock.

My god, this rock is *huge.*

All the way through the remainder of the press junket. All the way through the parting photos and the "Look this way, Miss Giles! Give us a smile—kiss her, All-American Man! Let's see that ring!"

What do you mean, you can't see it from there?

This rock is *fucking huge.*

I hold my hand up against the light coming in from the hotel room's open balcony doors. The sun's setting just beyond, throwing perfect gilded Santa Monica rays into the room, over the curves and valleys of my fingers as I tip the ring back and forth. The diamond catches the light, glittering, enticing.

It's way too big. Gaudy and cumbersome. How on earth am I supposed to function while wearing this thing? I came in here to change before dinner, and all I could manage was getting my button-down off before the edge of the ring ripped a hole in my skirt. My *favorite* skirt, too.

So now I'm sitting here in my underwear, staring at this ring, if it's fair to call it that, and all I can think is *too huge. It's too huge. My god, it's so huge, all of it, ALL OF IT—*

I couldn't very well have said no, though, could I? On stage. Dozens of cameras in our faces. Ari staring up on me from his knees, and fuck, he knows I can't resist that sight.

But still.

The word had been right on the tip of my tongue. I'd swallowed and parted my lips and heard myself say ... yes.

Yes.

I'm going to marry All-American Man.

Ari, he'd whispered as he'd cradled me through the air, the diner where I'd worked reduced to rubble behind us. *Call me Ari.*

I lower my hand now, eyes going to the view out the window, the sunset over the ocean—

Panic flies up my spine, and I leap to my feet. A body hovers on the edge of the balcony, cloaked in shadow against the bright sunset, and I go scrambling for the decorative blanket draped over the end of the bed. Goddamn paparazzi—this is exactly what they need, isn't it? A photo of All-American Man's petite girlfri- ... *fiancé* in a skimpy lace bra and panties that definitely do *not* fit the Ideal Image that he works so hard to cultivate. Wholesome, family-friendly, demure.

Halfway through flinging the blanket over my body, I get a jolt from a former life. The life before Ari rescued me. The life where I was just a waitress bussing tables to pay my tuition, and I wouldn't have really blinked twice at a photo in a compromising position.

In fact ... I would've liked it.

Even now, a little thrill tangles with my panic, and I go rigid in the process of turning back to the balcony, my heart hammering too fast, belly pulling taut. I know exactly how the photos will look. I know *exactly* how good *I* look, and my hair's already perfectly curled into relaxed brown waves for dinner, make-up subtle but smokey.

I blink, and my eyes focus more fully on the intruder.

All the tension releases.

"Goddamn it, Ari."

It's him hovering on the edge of the balcony railing, using his super flight to stay balanced.

He bounces off the railing. "If that's what you're wearing to dinner, I made reservations at the wrong restaurant."

My chest tightens. But it's not like he can read minds, thank god—so I quickly force a smile and rock my hips back and forth, letting the blanket sway.

"What, Le Haut's dress code isn't a hotel quilt? Damn, it's all I packed."

Ari crosses the room and takes one of my hands. With the other, I keep the blanket pressed to my chest.

"How were your meetings?" I ask.

His lips tighten, and he looks down at my finger. At that ring.

He's quiet for a long moment. He gets so serious, so quickly. And it's in these moments that I see the weight that being All-American Man takes on him. Unlike most of the self-righteous asshats who work for Heroes Org—powered people intent on enforcing other powered people to hold to law and order and not descend into chaos—Ari actually *cares*.

He saves people from buildings set on fire by rogue supers. He rescues victims abducted by media-proclaimed Villains. He fights the bad guys and goes out of his way to help the needy and gives a huge chunk of his income to charities. He takes his job as one of America's protectors seriously.

Maybe too seriously.

It's one of the things that first drew me to him. He's the most genuine person I've ever met.

I pull my hand out of his to cup his cheek and lift his eyes to mine. They're hypnotically blue, the color of the California sky when we landed here this morning, and the sharpness of his jaw only tightens more when he flexes that muscle in my palm.

"What's wrong?" I ask as softly as I can.

His lips part. For a moment, I don't even dare breathe.

But then he smiles, that camera smile, that "Thank you, Citizens, for naming another museum after me" smile.

"Nothing, Lillypad. The meetings were fine," he says and leans in for a kiss.

I put my hand on his chest. "Nothing? Nothing at all? Why the heavy sigh—just getting sick of the California pollution?"

He smirks. "We'll have to tolerate it a bit longer. The movie premiere isn't until next Friday."

I hold. He doesn't expand.

"Ari."

"Lilly?"

"You can talk to me." It comes out in a rush. "I know you met with a few Heroes Org donors, right? What'd they say? There were board members too, I heard—"

Ari stops me with his thumb on my lips, the rest of his hand lightly around my neck. I think he means it to be sexy.

It is.

Damn it.

"That's not for you to worry about," he tells me in a chastising voice.

"Not for me to worry about?"

"It's Heroes Org matters. Not civilian stuff."

"I'm not just a civilian. I can be there for you. *Let me—*"

"It's not that simple, Lilly," he says my name with a sigh of exhaustion. Bone-deep and wrung out because we've had this exact conversation before.

Frustration surges up my throat and nearly tumbles everything out in a scream.

I bite my lips together, hard, but it's too late—my expression changed.

Instantly, Ari goes into Fixer Mode. It's his turn to cup my face.

"You're unhappy," he says, and the guess is so damn accurate that I can't stifle my laugh of shock.

"No. Everything is ... perfect." Because it is. I'm engaged to *Ari Dodgers*. I'm about to have an engagement dinner at the most expensive restaurant in LA. I have a rock the size of a small meteor and, after his movie premiere, we'll go home to a penthouse overlooking Central Park *and everything is fucking perfect.*

Ari nods. And he smiles. Because, on paper, everything *is* perfect, and he knows it. He's very, very good at the on paper stuff. Follow the rules, that's Ari Dodgers, and he knows he's done exactly what a good boyfriend is supposed to.

Only a total bitch would be unhappy.

"Are you excited to start planning?" he asks. His grin widens, two perfect dimples puncturing his cheeks. "Mrs. Dodgers," he adds, and something in me breaks.

I don't want to talk anymore. I don't want to play this game I only just realized we've been playing.

I ask him about anything real.

He deflects.

He asks me if I'm happy.

I deflect.

Shit. We're not happy. *I'm* not happy.

And I just agreed to marry him. On TV. In front of this entire country that *adores him*.

God, I *am* a total bitch.

My stomach bottoms out. I need a distraction. I need to feel not so goddamn *disconnected,* like maybe I can make this work, maybe *we* can make this *work—*

I hike myself up onto my toes and thread my arms around his neck.

He has *really* nice lips—full and soft and gentle.

"I think we should be late to dinner," I tell him.

"Malcolm made these reservations himself—"

"Don't talk about your boss, Ari." Malcolm Odyssey is slick and sleazy and not at all who I want in my head right now.

I drop the blanket and press my body to Ari's.

He goes a little slack against me. "Oh. *Oh.*"

I kiss him, prying his lips apart, tongue darting between his teeth until he relents with a throaty growl that goes straight between my legs.

Ari's hands slide up my waist, find the clasp of my bra, and in one flick, it pops open.

My heart hammers still—I don't think it's stopped since I thought he was paparazzi on the balcony—and I need the pace to match it. I need furious and rough.

I grab the back of his neck and bite on his lip. He stumbles toward me, thrown off balance, and we land on the bed, him between my splayed legs.

He's still in his press junket outfit, and I make quick work of the buttons to yank the shirt down his arms, stopping at his elbows.

It's part genetics from his super-strength, part rigorous daily workouts that make him so—well. The first time I saw him sans-shirt, I was half-delirious on painkillers after he'd saved me. The fight at the diner had ripped his uniform, exposing his chest. In my drug-haze, I'd apparently grabbed his pec and said, in a pathetic attempt at a sultry tone, "*Jacked.*"

But it's the truth. There are entire tabloids dedicated to swooning over his body. And it's worthy of every single article written about him, every photo taken that analyzes what he must look like naked. Not that All-American Man would *ever* submit to nudes. He's got enough pictures of me on his phone to start a porn site; I've got one or two shots of us at the beach, him in trunks.

Ari tries to wriggle the rest of the way out of his shirt, but I hold it in place at his elbows.

"Trapped, All-American Man," I croon. "What are you gonna do about it?"

Ari's eyes darken, his brows dipping in that chastising expression again. "Lilly. Let go."

I don't loosen my hold. I pull my shoulders up, breasts brushing against his chest, and I hear his little intake of breath.

"Come on, Hero," I tease. "Make me."

For a moment, I think he might give in. God, he has *super-strength*—he could toss me across the room and fuck me standing up. He could swoop me into his arms and fly us out into the sky and fuck me in the clouds.

It makes my heart wild to think of that—fucking while flying. The freedom of it, the combo of dangerous and daring ...

But all he does is twist his hands to grab my elbows and, gently, move my arms away.

He slides the rest of the way out of his shirt and sets it to the side. Next go his pants, then boxers, in a neat stack at the end of the bed.

By the time he's back between my legs, all sense of urgency is dead in my chest. But he *is* really hot, painfully so, and the sight of him naked is still enough to make me whimper.

It's not enough to get back that sense of *need,* though.

Ari hooks one thumb in the waistband of my panties and eases them off, eyes on mine all the while.

There really must be something wrong with me. I know Heroes Org has a whole file dedicated to people who have sent me death threats ever since going public about my relationship with Ari. People would literally kill to be here, straddled by All-American Man.

It has to be me. I have to try harder. I have to make this *work*.

I grab his cock. It is, unsurprisingly, as impressive as the rest of him. No need to worry about a condom between our paparazzi-enforced monogamy and my IUD.

I stare up at him as he lowers down on top of me, gently—*gently, again*—easing into me. His size could be punishingly huge. But nothing about Ari Dodgers is punishing.

He threads our fingers and presses our hands above my head, as close as he ever gets to trapping me, and starts thrusting, slow, steady, building in rhythm as the sun dips lower behind us and the tangle of our fingers digs my engagement ring into my skin.

I hook my legs around him and buck up to meet him, rubbing my breasts against him, fighting for stimulation. He makes a startled grunt but doesn't lose pace, thrusting and thrusting until—

He gasps, body tightening, eyes pinching shut. Luckily, I'm not on the edge of orgasm, so going without isn't as frustrating as it usually is.

Right now, it's just ... heartbreaking. All of it.

This is my future. It spreads out in front of me suddenly, a life of nights like this, of press junkets and paparazzi and *Be chaste, Miss Giles—Don't dress that way, Miss Giles—Smile for the camera, Miss Giles—*

"Mrs. Dodgers," Ari whispers and kisses me, such tenderness in his eyes that I feel, again, that part of me break.

I do not love this man.

But I have to marry him.

3

FALLON

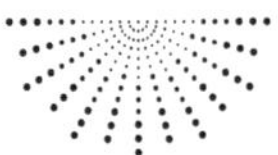

I'M PERCHED ATOP THE WATER TOWER, ACROSS THE STREET FROM THE HOTEL, when Ari Dodgers emerges, Lillith Giles on his arm. The smug prick is so aware of the paparazzi that he makes sure to turn to the light but so oblivious to his fiancé that he doesn't notice how she tries to stay in the shadows.

Or maybe he is aware. Maybe he likes it that way. Ari has never publicly dated a super, only nonpowered humans like Lillith. I'm betting he doesn't like to share the spotlight.

The top is down on the convertible, and Ari holds the door open for Lillith, the picture of grace. He takes his time walking around the front of the car, flashes of cameras glinting like stars over the waxed hood.

Even from here, I can see Lillith's fingers drumming with impatience. I smile. Then a glint of light catches on her ring, and my expression melts away.

This is business.

According to my recon, Ari has reservations at a fancy restaurant. I scoped it earlier—the paps are already there, waiting, not even bothering to hide their cameras. They'd been promised a show. It was likely a set-up from Heroes Org, a way to keep Ari and his lovely romance in the public eye.

But the red Audi doesn't veer left, toward the restaurant. Ari speeds off right, heading to the hills.

I frown, wincing a little as I stretch my injured wings.

I wonder if it will ever not be painful to fly again. One year later, and I'm still not over it.

I keep my eyes on the racing red car as I leap from the tower, swooping north. If Ari is actually doing the decent thing—keeping his fiancé away from the paps and avoiding the Heroes Org plot to exploit their little engagement—that means he'll be going somewhere private.

Somewhere alone.

Which is absolutely fucking perfect. I don't need witnesses to what I'm going to do to him.

Sure enough, the Audi zooms off the main road. I keep high overhead—if they look up, they'll see me. But I've learned long ago that people usually only see what's directly in front of them. Nothing more.

"Where are you going?" I mutter to myself. The air is warm, the sun barely below the horizon. Dusk makes everything golden, but rather than slow down and enjoy the ride, Ari picks up speed. The Audi hugs the curves, and I strain my wings, trying to keep up.

At my best, before Ari clipped my wings, I could fly like the wind. This shouldn't be a struggle, keeping up with one sports car. I grit my teeth, ignoring the pain lancing through my shoulders and back, and tip into the air current, my body a bullet.

Ahead, the road winds. He'll have to slow down there.

But ... he doesn't.

I swoop lower. The top is down on the convertible, Lillith's hair blowing in the wind. Ari is casual, one hand on the steering wheel, the other on Lillith's thigh. But Lillith grips the arm rest, clutching it.

She's scared.

And no wonder. Ari's pushing a hundred as he veers around the first curve of the abandoned road. His tires squeal.

"What the fuck," I mutter, swooping lower. Ari may have super-strength and super-healing—a crash off the side of a mountain won't hurt him at all—but that kind of shit can kill a nonpowered human like Lillith.

I'm close enough now that when Ari rounds the next bend, I can hear Lillith scream—a short burst of pure terror. I squint at Ari. Overhead doesn't give me the best view, but he seems casual, relaxed ...

Distracted.

I may want to rip the asshole limb from limb—he has no wings to break, but I don't mind tearing off his arms and letting him feel that pain—but I don't particularly want to see a girl as fine as Lillith Giles reduced to nothing but blood and bone at the bottom of the mountain.

I dip down more as the next hairpin curve comes up. I don't know what I was thinking of doing—would Ari stop if I landed in front of the car?—but before I can make a decision, the Audi spins out of control, doing a complete three-sixty before crashing through the metal barrier at the edge of the road. Metal screams against metal as the car soars through the air, hanging impossibly over nothing.

And—oh, fuck.

Lillith's seatbelt is off. She's flying through the air, her body tossed from the car, aiming for the rocks and trees below. I spare one glance to Ari, who sits motionless in his seat as the car flies off toward the canyon. He's not going to save her.

Oh, fuck no.

I tuck my wings in tight, plummeting down, arms outstretched. Fuck the car, fuck Ari, fuck everything, I *will* save this girl. Her body is limp as a rag doll as she falls—she's passed out—but if she hits the ground, there's zero doubt she'll die.

I won't make it. I push against the wind, letting my wings beat out, hard. Black feathers fly off me, mixed with blood—I've reopened the old scars, I'm straining too hard, and it's for nothing, nothing, because I can't reach her—

My talons strain harder, reaching, reaching—

I slam into her body.

I brace my arms around her, whirling through the air, totally out of control. I went too hard, too fast, and I can't catch the air again.

All I can do is wrap my wings around my body, around Lillith, and hope to fuck the impact doesn't kill us both.

I cry out as I hit first a tree, then the sheer rock on the side of the mountain. Blood and black feathers burst from my wings, but I don't move them, I don't dare take away the only protection I can give this girl. I roll down the sloping mountain, painfully crashing through rocks and saplings, until I hit another tree with a bone-crunching slam.

I breathe. My heart pounds in my ears; every cell in my body screams in pain. I can smell smoke, dirt, blood. I may have the ability to heal quicker than nonpowered humans, but it still fucking *hurts*.

But inside my embrace, under the darkness of my wings, the soft, fragile body of Lillith Giles is safe.

And that's enough.

I STAND SLOWLY, still holding Lillith, wrapped up in my wings. The car is crashed into the canyon below, smoke billowing up from its broken hood. I can see Ari slumped over the steering wheel.

This is my moment.

He's out now, but he won't be for long. He shouldn't even *be* knocked out, not by something like this. It's fucking weird, but I'm not going to question it because, frankly, it's perfect.

Maybe if I was some sort of Hero with morals, I'd give a rat's ass about the integrity of killing a man passed out, but fuck, I don't care. He's an asshole, and he's injured enough that this will be easy. I don't need a fair fight. I just need him to pay.

Lillith groans in my arms, and instantly I soften my grip on her. I caught her before she landed, but she's still injured. A cut on her head weeps bright red blood. One eye is black, her lip busted. Her shoulder is twisted, maybe dislocated. Her body is still limp, but she'll wake soon. In pain.

I growl in frustration.

I adjust my grip on Lillith, touching the comm unit on my chest. After a beep, an overlay of a map illuminates on the lens in my left eye. The closest safe house with a med unit isn't that far away.

"Good," I mutter. It's Scarlet's unit.

Lillith needs medical aid, and I know fuck all about fixing broken humans. Scarlet, though, is one of the best. I tap in my access code and get the all-clear.

Lillith, still unconscious, moans in my arms. Her head flops forward, nestling in the crook of my neck. Her body is soft, and warm, and ...

I snap my wings out, scoop her legs up so that I can carry her more easily, and soar, leaving my revenge behind but taking the girl.

I FLY SLOWER NOW, my wings aching, but Scarlet's base is close enough. Built into the side of a canyon, almost indistinguishable from the landscape, I'd miss it if I didn't have my locator.

As soon as I land, two people step out, pushing a gurney covered in a white sheet. Scarlet is nothing if not accommodating. I gently place Lillith's broken body on the gurney. The dirt, grime, and blood stand out even more against the crisp white sheet, and my hands form fists, talons digging into my palms.

Another one of Scarlet's people steps out. No—not a person. The Watcher is a cyborg, part human, part robot, and entirely built to be perfectly loyal to Scarlet and meet her *every* need.

"Payment will be expected," the Watcher says.

"I know," I growl. "Now get out of my way."

The Watcher steps aside. He may be more than half robotic, but Scarlet made him so lifelike that it's only his eyes—glowing yellow optic sensors—that really give away that he's not fully human.

This isn't the first time I've had to use one of Scarlet's bases. And payment's a bitch. But at least it's worth it. Her med units are the best of the best, and until it's time to pay up, Scarlet doesn't mind me doing whatever the fuck I want.

And what I want? Is answers.

As soon as I'm in a private room—a room I know is *truly* private, because that's part of what I'm paying for—I take off my optical camera and load it into the processor built into the slick white wall.

I had hoped that the tech would capture me kicking All-American Man's ass. It records everything, and selling the footage of America's golden boy broken and defeated would have made me a pretty penny. Plus, it'd have been fucking hilarious.

But instead of capturing my triumph, the vid feed captured the car crash.

I may have wings, healing, and strength, but even my eyes can't process every second of an unexpected car crash.

The vid feed does, though.

I slow it down, zoom in, and enhance the image of Ari and Lillith inside the Audi just before it veered off the road, crashing down into the valley below.

Lillith looks terrified, but Ari's calm, just as he appeared to me when I was watching from above.

But the thing is—it looks like he purposefully turns into the curve. His hands don't grapple with the steering wheel as the car loses control. On the contrary, he ... he lets the car spin out. He just lifts his palms up placidly.

The car breaks over the barrier, soaring into the air.

I use the controls to make the video image still.

I squint.

No.

No—*why?*

"Enhance," I say, zooming in on the interior of the car as it flies over the edge of the canyon.

Ari didn't just let go of the steering wheel. As soon as the car started crashing, he unclipped Lillith's seatbelt. On purpose. I watch, my mouth dropping open, as the fucker reaches over and releases her buckle.

He was ... he was trying to kill her.

But fucking *why?*

An incoming message interrupts my thoughts—and although I appreciate that Scarlet didn't use her mesmer abilities to break into my mind, I'm still annoyed. "Yes?" I growl.

"And a good morning to you as well." Scarlet's dulcet voice sounds amused.

"It's seven in the evening," I snap.

Scarlet laughs. "Time has no meaning."

"What do you want, Scar?" I ask. I need to figure out what the fuck is going on, why America's most popular superhero just tried to murder his fucking fiancée.

"Turn on the news," Scarlet says, then a soft beep tells me she's logged off the comm system.

I frown. I don't want to stop what I'm doing, but I know Scarlet wouldn't interrupt me if it wasn't necessary.

With a wave of my hand, I dismiss my own video feed and bring up the local news.

A chopper casts shadows over the car crash I just left. Ari is awake, looking rumpled but whole and well, completely uninjured from the car crash he caused.

Then a "Breaking News" graphic interrupts the feed. A solemn reporter fills the frame.

"We interrupt the disturbing tape of the car accident involving All-American Man to show you exclusive footage provided by the Heroes Organization that pertains to this act of violence. Viewers, be advised that this is triggering content."

The video shifts.

"Fuck," I say.

There were cameras on the road. *Why were there cameras on the road?* But either way, they got me. The video shows me stalking the car, swooping closer, my black wings a shadow over the red metal. The car crashes, I dip lower—fuck.

Fuck, fuck, fuck.

This shit's been altered. Smoke and small explosions have been doctored into the footage, making it look like I caused the accident. And when I dive down and grab Lillith's body, the film makes it look like I kidnapped her.

Well. I kind of did kidnap her.

But not like this.

The news shifts to show Ari, looking grave. "The Raven has taken my fiancée after trying to kill me," he says. "I will stop at nothing to save the woman I love."

4

LILLY

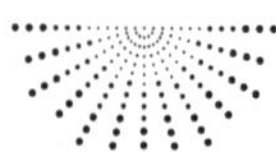

EVERYTHING *HURTS*.

I haven't even opened my eyes yet, but god, I don't want to. My body feels like it was tossed end over end down a rocky ravine—

Shit.

A memory slithers out of my thudding, bruised agony. The car zooming around the canyon's tight curves. Ari, laughing, pressing the pedal faster. Me, in the passenger seat, death-gripping the armrests and shouting at him over the roar of wind through the convertible.

I'd *never* seen him like that. Uninhibited. Deranged. Free.

And until it had crossed the line into outright dangerous, I'd been more attracted to him than I'd ever been before. Where was *this* Ari when we'd been idly fucking in the hotel room an hour ago? Daredevil Ari, Rule-Breaking Ari—

"Nothing life-threatening," a voice says nearby. A woman, low and sultry. "No broken bones, even. She's stupid lucky."

I go rigid, heart ramping up, and something by my head beeps rapidly. A heart monitor.

"What's that?" Another voice this time. Male. Rough and guttural like he's not used to using his voice for normal conversation.

"She's waking up. Give her a few minutes. Christ, Fal, she just fell off a cliff."

"I know. I was there." Each word is dripping with fury. It's not even me he talks to, and I get a little thrill of terror.

"Then ... ugh, fine. Sulk in the corner. What do you even need her for, anyway? She some trophy of yours? You couldn't get All-American Man, so you're taking his girl?"

"I didn't *take* her—"

"Yeah, yeah." A few buttons click. A door opens. "Call me when she wakes up. I'll need to check for a concussion."

The door shuts. A lock beeps.

My whole body is coated in cold sweat. I keep my eyes squeezed together, my jaw clenched tight, wracking my brain for something, *anything* after the crash that could tell me where I am now—but it's all just haze. Flipping. Falling. The wind. Soft darkness holding me. The smell of sweat and cologne, something woodsy and masculine and definitely not what Ari wears.

You couldn't get All-American Man, so you're taking his girl?

Fal. The woman called him Fal.

I scramble through my brain for Ari's enemies. He's got plenty. Nearly every self-professed Villain would love a chance to fuck over All-American Man, and this wouldn't be the first time someone tried to use me to get to him.

It would be the first time they actually *got me,* though.

Fal. Fal. Who the fuck—

It hits me like a gust of wind.

Fallon.

The Raven.

Of course. He's been off the radar for the past year since Ari nearly killed him in a fight not far from LA actually. He was a menace, even as far as Villains go—absolutely no scruples. He'd rob a charity as soon as he'd rob a bank. He held so many state officials ransom that they started calling it *getting Ravened.*

But no one's heard from him since that fight. Since Ari told me, rather vaguely of course, that *the Raven would never be a threat again.*

Well, clearly that was a lie.

I split one eye open. The woman had said he was sulking in the corner, and that's exactly where I see a man-shaped blur.

Only ... he has wings.

I've never seen the Raven in person, and every image I have seen is media portrayals of him spread out against a stormy sky, dark skin and black leather pants and a black shirt matching the full girth of his wide black wings. Like a crow. Like a raven.

"He swooped out of the sky," one trembling vault security officer had said. *"One minute, the sky's clear—then the next, he's there. A phantom."*

The Raven leans in the corner, just next to the door, arms crossed, eyes closed. His wings are folded behind him, but the curves peak over his head, two identical hills of black feathers that trickle down past his arms, all the way to the floor.

I open my other eye and do a quick survey of the room. It's small, nearly bare except for the bed and a table with monitors and medical instruments. Looks like a typical hospital room, but no way he just took me to any random hospital. Am I that lucky?

The assortment of medical instruments is common enough. A cup of pills. A stethoscope. A—

Scalpel.

Next to it is an empty syringe. The label on the side tells me it was some kind of antibiotic, and the thought that the mystery woman injected me with something hits me like a fist to the gut. How long was I out? Long enough that way, way worse things could have happened to me.

Whatever the Raven wants with me, he needs me alive and unharmed.

Did he cause the car crash? Why risk killing me only to nurse me back to health?

The weirdness is even more terrifying, honestly. I'd rather he'd just locked me in a cell to await ransom or rescue.

I cut my gaze back to him. He's still got his eyes shut.

My heart monitor starts pinging again as my pulse flies. Fucking hell—I take a deep breath. Another. The beeps slow.

I ease one arm out from under the rough hospital blanket. I'm still in my engagement dinner dress, a tight ivory number that leaves my shoulders bare and stops mid-thigh. Ari's people have frequently snapped at me for dressing too *immodestly,* but it was *my* engagement dinner. I was going to dress however fucking slutty I wanted.

When I roll the blanket down, I see that the dress is now stained with bits of dirt and blood. My blood.

I shove the thought away and grab the scalpel.

The Raven isn't indestructible like some of the other Villains. He bleeds, too.

In one smooth movement, I fling myself off the bed and launch my body across the room, at the Raven. The blanket flies back; the heart monitor chimes so loud it echoes off the walls; my bare feet slide across the tiled floor, and I arch the scalpel back, then bring it down and forward, aiming for his jugular—

The Raven's eyes burst open.

The blade of the scalpel grazes his skin, and that's when he snaps his arm up and seizes my shoulders. Hands like vices. Hands that stop me mid-motion, the scalpel only barely in his neck, not nearly deep enough to hurt him.

His eyes latch onto mine. They're dark, nearly black, matching everything about him. A shadow. A flash and a thought that vanishes without a trace.

One corner of his lips slides up. It'd be a smile if not for the fury in his eyes, darkness layered under darkness.

Effervescence shoots straight down to my toes. That I realize are not touching the floor. He's holding me in the air, the pads of his hands rough around my arms, the muscles in his chest bulging under his tight black shirt, but not with strain. He looks barely put out at all.

"That's no way to thank your savior," he tells me, a growl.

Most of my heart monitors disconnected in my jump, but if they were still attached, I know the beeping would be deafening. My pulse aches in my veins, thudding in my neck, across my arms; it thunders between my legs too, and I'm embarrassed, suddenly, at the realization that this moment has me on the edge of orgasm.

This moment.

Really?

It's the adrenaline. The holy-shit-I-almost-just-died. The double-holy-*shit*-I'm-now-abducted-by-a-super-Villain.

My body trembles. I know the Raven feels it.

God, let him think it's only fear.

"You have no idea how badly you've fucked up," I spit. "You do know who I am, don't you?"

A muscle in his jaw tics. His dark face is perfectly sculpted, all angular lines and a sharp nose and slanted brow—every detail only makes him more imposing. More of a Villain.

"Lillith Giles," he says my name with a hint of a laugh. How is this funny? "Fiancée to the country's beloved All-American Man."

"He'll kill you. He'll *kill* you for touching me, you fucker."

"Will he? Sounds pretty dark for him. Heroes never actually go the full extra mile. They shy from the kill strike."

The Raven sets me down and I stumble back, my legs gone to jelly. I don't fall only thanks to the bed close by, and when I hit it, the scalpel slips from my limp fingers and clinks against the floor.

My aches and pains, temporarily muted in my attack, roar back to life. Every muscle screams for relief, but there's no way I'll let him know.

"What do you want?" I demand.

A single line of red wells on his neck from the scalpel. Barely a scratch.

"What do *you* want, Lillith?" The Raven looks down at me, and this time, he's smiling. His eyes still have that dark twist to them. Shadows rippling in the night. "Are you aching to go back to your dear fiancé?"

He crosses the room. My thighs are pinned to the bed, and I have to tip my head back to look up at him, chest straining against the low neckline of my engagement dress.

The fact that that's where I'm supposed to be, drinking champagne with Ari, doesn't hurt like it should.

"Of course," I make myself say.

"Was that a pause I heard?"

"Fuck you."

The Raven grins. It's boyish in a way that instantly softens him.

So I punch him.

And I'm still wearing my huge engagement ring.

My fist connects with the side of his face and throws his head back. Blood wells, sprays in the air; my ring ripped skin.

Ah, so a rock that big *is* good for something.

Victory fizzles through me, as effervescent as when he'd held me off the floor. I use the blip of surprise to dive around him, angling for the door—

He grabs my waist and lifts me off the floor again. A twist, a heave, and he slams me onto my back on the hospital bed, using the full weight of his body to pin me down.

His wings cup around us, closing us off from the room. Jagged spots of blood pepper his cheekbone from my ring, a single bead rolling down the side of his face.

A cry bursts between my lips. Only it isn't a cry. It's a moan, velvety with need, and I find myself staring up into the Raven's eyes, breasts heaving with each gasping inhale, his arms still twined around my waist.

He hears the cry that isn't a cry. His eyes turn up, intrigued.

The edge of his jeans presses against my hips.

He's hard. Rock hard.

I'm not the only one turned on by this, and that sends a bolt through me, dizzyingly heady. Did that woman give me painkillers? I'm delirious. I have to be.

"You're not a prisoner, Lillith Giles," he whispers. Then he's bending down to put his lips on my ear. "Unless you want to be."

That echoes through my head like a struck gong.

Unless you want to be.

Do you want to be, Lillith Giles? Say the word. Say no, and this ends now.

What ends? What—

My eyelids flutter. The room goes hazy, and I think maybe I'm just passing out again—god, like *this,* trapped helplessly under the Raven—but that voice in my head. It asks again.

Do you want to be a prisoner? Do you dream of being trapped? Subdued? Taken?

Who is that? The voice is feminine and honey-like. Tempting. Rich. Each word ramps up the sensations in my chest, higher, higher, until I'm nodding, a truth untamed.

Yes, I think. *Yes.*

A low chuckle. *You've got some Villain in you after all, sunshine.*

The haziness lifts. I'm still in the hospital room, trapped under the Raven, but something about it feels ... different. It feels how Ari looked in the car, uninhibited, like a restraint had been peeled back.

Free.

The Raven is so close over me that I don't even notice when I breach that space. My lips grab his, hungry, desperate, and all the terror, all the pain, all the uncertainty spirals through my body. The pent-up desire from my unsatisfying time with Ari. The confusion and guilt and fear. It's all there, making me arch my body up against the Raven, his lips thin and sharp against mine.

He makes a heady groan but doesn't pull away. The opposite—he seems like he was hoping this would happen. His tongue darts between my lips, exploring the inside of my mouth in smooth strokes. God, he knows what he's doing, and those strokes fill my mind with the sudden image of how it'd feel to have that tongue on my clit.

I mewl, reeling, and my hands travel down his chest, all hard planes and rigid lines, until I'm grabbing his belt, peeling it open, reaching down past the band until my hand fills with his cock. He's so hard, and just as big as Ari, if not a little thicker.

The Raven still has one hand around my waist, and his wings unfurl from us, flicking back, then down once, and we lift off the bed, hovering midair in the hospital room. His lips trail along my neck, interspersed with sharp bites of his teeth. Each nip unravels me—god, I *need* him in me, right *now*—

I wriggle my legs apart to hook them around the Raven's hips, the sensation of being weightless in the air only enhancing every other touch. The roughness of his free hand scrambles at the silk of my dress, yanking it down off my breast, and his thumb tracks over my pebbled nipple in a way that has me crying out.

I'm not wearing any underwear, and I guide him towards me, a jerky, desperate pull—

The Raven makes a startled gasp, like he's drowning. It isn't in pleasure—it's ringed with realization, and we drop back onto the bed in a heap.

"*Goddamnit,* Scarlet!" he barks.

It's a curse and a prayer and a death threat all in one.

And the moment he says that name, the spell breaks.

That uninhibited freedom retracts like a window shade rolling up to reveal the true light of day.

I gulp in a strangled breath. Did we just—did *I* just—

The Raven flies back off of me. His dark eyes are wide, fury giving them a reddened edge as he stuffs himself back into his pants and ducks his head away.

My breast is still hanging out of my dress. The hem is hiked over my hips, exposing me to the room.

Slowly, moving through oil, I adjust myself. My throat is swollen with ... not quite horror. Not quite shame.

That was better than I've had in a long, long time.

And we didn't even *fuck*.

I should *not* have had a reaction like this to a *Villain,* let alone one of Ari's worst enemies. I should have been disgusted. I should have kicked him off me and screamed for help.

But, god, I can't get my mouth to spew any of the things I know I should as I curl on the bed, knees to my chest, and stare up at the Raven.

The door opens, revealing the single most breathtaking person I've ever seen. Dense red curls hang down to her mid back, accentuating the curves of her body, all hips and breasts and high heels. She's got a lab coat over a slinky black dress, and she cocks one hip against the door frame to give the Raven a roguish grin.

He looks like he wants to murder her. "What the *fuck* did you—"

"Please." She rolls her eyes. "I asked her permission. Didn't I?"

She looks at me.

And I recognize her voice. It was the one in my head, asking me what I wanted. It's also the voice from earlier, the one who had doctored me. Scarlet.

"I'm a mesmer," Scarlet tells me. "Among other things, I can make people give in to feelings they might otherwise have suppressed. Foolishly suppressed, as it were."

A mesmer?

My thoughts jump to Ari's boss, Malcolm. He had similar powers; he used to be able to affect people's emotions, and when he was younger, his powered name was The Hive due to his ability to make people mass hallucinate. But Ari had told me, in confidence, that Malcolm hadn't been able to use his powers in years—the product of a fight against a powerful Villain that had stripped him to basically a civilian. Which was why Malcolm got his current position as CEO of Heroes Org, all business tasks and front man status.

"And I asked your permission," Scarlet says. "You said yes."

I nod, more in shock than anything. She did. I knew exactly what I was agreeing to, a moment of release.

"See, Fal? She said yes." She turns back to the Raven. "Thought you could both use a little ... reprieve. Why'd you spoil the fun?"

The Raven advances on her, shoulders curled, wings outspread. Scarlet doesn't back down, but some of the teasing joy on her face tightens.

"You going to threaten me, Fallon?" she hisses. "In my home?"

That stops him in his tracks.

"Thought so." She dips her eyes back to me. "Rest up, sunshine. I have a feeling you'll need it."

"Need it?" I push to my feet. But I'm completely liquid from—*everything*, and I instantly sit back down again.

The Raven—Fallon—twists towards me, holds his hand out like he's going to catch me.

What is going *on?*

"What are you going to do to me?" I ask, and it comes out exhausted.

The Raven looks into my eyes, dark, serious. "You're free to go. You're not a prisoner here."

"Then why—"

"Before you leave, though, I think you might be interested in seeing the evidence I have."

His voice is husky. From what we almost did?

"Evidence? Of what? Of your own fuckery?"

The Raven cuts that boyish grin again. "All-American Man tolerated that tongue of yours? Surprising. But no, Lillith Giles." His grin sharpens. "Evidence of your fiancé's attempt at murdering you."

5
FALLON

LILLITH SPUTTERS AT ME. SHIT. I SHOULDN'T JUST DROP A BOMB LIKE "YOUR fiancé tried to murder you" on her, not when she just woke up from the wreck.

Not after we almost ...

Lava rolls up my spine, searing me with a heat I can't deny. Because I would like to deny it. She's Ari's future wife.

She's not mine.

Even if she wants to fuck me, according to Scarlet.

A desire to possess this woman makes me curl my talons into a fist. I relish the pain in my palms. It grounds me, helps me to focus.

"Look, I don't know what game you're trying to play with me, bird-brain," Lillith snarls. "But Ari would never try to murder me."

There's a quake in her voice and fire in her eyes.

It's too much. Too soon.

But the truth is still the truth.

"I'll let you deal with this," Scarlet says in a low voice. She winks at Lillith, then closes the door behind her, giving us privacy.

I cross the small medical room to where Lillith perches on the edge of the bed. My talons are sharp, hooked claws that can rip apart a super's flesh, but my touch on her skin is gentle, the barest whisper. She shivers as I trace my talon from her bare right shoulder, down toward her breasts, stopping just at the edge of her low-cut dress.

Her eyes are liquid, wide as she looks up at me. Unconsciously, she bites her lip. My gaze zeroes in on her mouth, and I go instantly hard, thinking about how she'll look with my cock in her mouth, those teeth grazing over my head ...

Goddammit, focus.

"Where are the seatbelt marks?" I ask, my voice raspy with desire.

Lillith blinks several times, trying to come out of her reverie. "Wait, what?"

I drag my talon back up toward her shoulder, tracing where a seatbelt should have left a welt on her bare skin. My claw is rougher this time, digging into her pale skin just enough to leave a pink mark that fades quickly. She leans into the touch, letting my talon press harder, harder. Fuck me.

"Seatbelt marks." I snatch my hand away, and, when that's not enough, I step back. I don't trust myself to touch her again. "You should have welts there, from your seatbelt during the car crash. Do you remember why you don't?"

Lillith glowers as she considers it. I can practically see the gears turning in her head. The way Ari took those curves so fast.

But then she shakes her head. She's not ready to fully face the truth of what happened. Shock is a hell of a thing, blocking out the stuff her mind's not ready to process. Fine. I can give her time. I'm not a monster.

Not like her fiancé.

"Think about it," I say, tossing the words over my shoulder as I turn to walk out of the room.

I fling the door open and nearly step on the little woman about to enter the room. "Fuck, Edna, sorry," I say, hopping out of her way.

"Yes, yes, whatever." She bustles past me, her arms laden down with a bundle of neatly folded black cloth. I stand for a moment, watching the short woman walk briskly into Lillith's medical room as if she owns the place. Lillith's brows pinch together in confusion. She looks up, meets my eyes, and for a moment, her expression melts in shared amusement.

Then she remembers who she is. Who I am. And she frowns at me, ripping her gaze away from mine.

It shouldn't hurt so much.

But it fucking does.

I step through the door and slam it shut behind me. I want to punch something. Many somethings. But before I can walk more than two paces down the hall, an arm grabs me and pulls me into a room.

"What the fu—?" I start, then realize where I am.

Scarlet releases my arm, a knowing smile on her face. The room is dark, illuminated only by the screens built into the wall.

Each one shows a different angle of Lillith, sitting on the bed of her medical room.

"I thought you'd like to watch," Scarlet says. Her voice is idle, but I know from the spark in her smile that the bitch has been peering a little too closely into my mind.

Because Lillith's right. I'm not a Hero. I don't do *good* things.

I love the stalk.

Watching, from the shadows. A hunter waiting for prey.

And that's what these security cams give me. A way to watch Lillith when she doesn't know she's being watched.

"There's sound, too," Scarlet says, flipping a switch.

On the screen, I hear Edna explain that Scarlet sent her to give Lillith some new clothes.

"Thank god," Lillith says, standing. "I love this dress, but it's not exactly loungewear."

"Neither is this," Edna says, all efficiency.

Lillith takes the black cloth from Edna and unfurls it with a snap. A pair of heavy black pants, the waist trim. Edna passes over a long-sleeved shirt made of some sort of slinky material.

"It's all been bonded with Kevlar," Scarlet says. Bullet-proof material, even if it's thin as silk. Edna's the best.

"Why did Ari try to kill her?" I ask Scarlet, even though my eyes are on the screen.

"Oh, I have no idea," Scarlet says. She sounds bored, but when she catches my eyes, I can tell there's gravity to this discussion. "I can keep you safe here, for now," she says. "But I have to tell Persephone eventually."

"Fuck."

"I know."

"Fuck."

"Yes, yes, I *know*," Scarlet says. "But All-American Man just tried to commit murder, Fal. Of an innocent. Persephone must be told."

She's right, that's the worst of it. But I don't want to get Persephone involved. I don't want to wake that dragon.

I want to pretend that Ari doesn't exist, that Persephone doesn't exist, that there's no one in the fucking world but me and Lillith.

And then I can figure out a way to use her against All-American Man and finally take that smug prick right the fuck down.

"Well, like I said," Scarlet continues, "I can buy you a little time. For now."

She winks as she leaves me alone in the room. The room full of screens.

All displaying Lillith.

Edna leaves Lillith with her new clothes, the door clicking softly behind her. For a moment, Lillith just looks at the pile of black material on the edge of her bed.

I feel myself growing hard. It's wrong, but fuck if I care. Watching her like this ... for once, I'm glad Scar can read my mind just enough to know what I want.

Lillith doesn't reach for the clothes, though. She looks around the room. This is the first time she's been awake and alone. She's not panicked like when she first opened her eyes. She's methodical, analytical.

Lillith goes to the computer first, a laptop on the counter. She taps at the keyboard but doesn't seem to find anything important. I can't tell if she gets past Scarlet's security or just grows bored with trying passwords, but either way, he abandons the laptop. She turns slowly, her eyes taking in everything.

And then her gaze drifts up. She looks right into the camera, and a shiver goes up my spine.

She cocks her eyebrow, a smirk on her lips. The cameras are well hidden in the room, but she's spotted one.

She knows she's being watched.

She looks right at the lens, right at me, and slowly reaches behind her back, unzipping her dress.

Does she know I'm here, watching?

The dress falls off her body, and I can't think another fucking coherent thought. I rip my belt buckle open, practically tearing the material as I work to free myself from my pants. My hand grips my cock, hard, the momentary pain of it helping me to focus.

Lillith stands there, naked in the room, looking curiously up at the camera. She's not noticed the other cameras, though. There's one behind her, showing me her ass. Another to side, so I can see the perfect angle of her breasts, the way her nipples are hard. Another near the door, giving me a closer look at the smirk on her perfect pink lips.

I rub my thumb up and down my hard cock. I've never been affected by someone like this; I've never felt this uncontrollable need.

"Are you watching me, Fal?"

Lillith's voice is almost a whisper, like she's a little afraid to say it out loud. But her eyes don't leave the camera as her hands move over her own body.

Oh, fuck.

I move my own hand, faster and faster, thrusting hard as I watch Lillith's long fingers glide over her nipples, whirling over the hard tips. She licks her lips slowly. I grunt, my body hunching at my need, my hips thrusting the air, wishing that I was pushing into her instead. I throw out my left hand to brace my body against the wall in front of the screens.

Her hands move lower.

I groan, the need filling me. There's only a wall separating us, and right now I feel like I could rip it down to get to her. But I don't.

Not yet.

Her hand splays across her flat belly, then she dips lower, lower. She plays a little, just barely touching herself.

"I want you to watch," she whispers, so low I almost don't hear her. And then she slides her finger through her slit. Her eyes get soft, her lips parting as she rubs herself.

My legs quake as I jerk harder. In the other room, Lillith's hand moves faster, too, her finger gliding deep inside her.

A little moan escapes her lips, and I'm fucking lost. I shout, unable to keep the noise inside as I fully release, my hot load splattering over the screens, dripping.

I pant, my heart racing. She's not quite done yet. Lillith withdraws her finger from herself. Without blinking away from the camera, she lifts her hand to her face, her tongue flicking out, licking her own wetness from her glistening finger.

I already feel myself getting hard again. Fuck, but this girl fills my every fantasy.

As if she knows her power over me, as if she relishes it, Lillith turns slowly, gracefully. She doesn't need to bend over to get the clothes off the bed, but she does, fully showing me her ass and dripping pussy. My hips involuntarily rock forward, longing to ram into her.

She straightens up, holding out the clothes Edna brought her. Too soon she's wrapped up in black cloth. I know Edna's skills; I know this outfit is strong enough that it would be difficult for even my talons to rip through the material.

But god, I want to.

I want to rip every stitch of clothing off her body and tease that girl the way she teased me. I want to bring her to edge of orgasm and then lick her into a puddle of desire and then fuck her right through another orgasm. And I want her to look at me with those seductive eyes and see me, not a camera lens.

Although ... I also am *loving* the idea of fucking All-American Man's girl. I thought to take Ari down with my fists, but it'll hurt him more to see a video of me fucking her. Of her letting me fuck her.

I tuck myself back into my pants and clean up.

I want all those things the way a drowning man wants air.

But first I have to give her the truth, whether she's ready for it or not.

6

LILLY

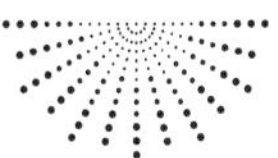

I'M PERCHED BACK ON THE BED, ONE LEG HOOKED OVER THE OTHER, IDLY swinging my foot in the air when the door opens.

It isn't the Raven. It's Scarlet again.

I try not to let my disappointment show.

And then I'm immediately horrified at myself.

Disappointment? What the *fuck* do I have to be disappointed about?

It's only because I so quickly figured out how the Raven ticks. I can seduce him. Distract him. Use that as my way out of ... wherever we are.

But I'm not a prisoner here, according to him. I can leave if I want to.

I push off the bed, the soles of my new shoes squeaking on the tiles. That Edna woman makes good clothes—they fit like a dream and highlight everything I always want highlighted when I'm forced to buy more demure clothes to appease Ari's people. Malcolm, especially, is raucous about modesty—which directly counters the gleam in his eyes when I saunter out to an event in a slinky dress.

The worst part is that Ari always *agrees* with them.

So being freely given clothes that leave very little to the imagination ...

There's a bounce in my step as I cross the room to Scarlet. Well, a bounce that makes me stagger a bit, still reeling from the bruises, the beating of the fall.

Scarlet holds up two small paper cups. One with pills I recognize as ibuprofen, one with water.

"They're safe," she says and extends them to me.

I take them, but cock an eyebrow. "The need for clarification is less reassuring."

She grins. God, a smile like that, *and* the power to get in people's heads, give them what they want? This woman could rule the world.

I hesitate, but end up taking the pills. My body hurts too much to care, and if they wanted me dead or restrained, they've had ample time.

Scarlet takes the empty cups. Then she steps back and nods up the hall to my left.

"There's a door at the end. Go through it if you want answers."

My body tightens. The snug fabric clings to every inch of my skin. "If I don't?"

Scarlet nods to my right. "The hangar's that way. My ... Watcher is there, and he'll arrange transport for you wherever you'd like to go."

"Just that easy?"

"Yep."

I eye the hall, both sides, and look back at Scarlet. "Which would you pick?"

What I mean is, what does she think I should do? I want her to look into my brain again. Look past all the guilt and duty and tell me what I want.

There's that world-ruling smile. "The fact that you have to ask is an answer on its own, isn't it?"

She turns, the clacking of her heels echoing in the empty hallway as she takes a different route off into wherever we are. Some medical base, likely.

And I'm left alone.

Again.

Only I know I'm not alone. I'd clocked the security cameras in my room—*five* of them, good lord, overkill?—and immediately I spot three just outside the hallway. This place is seriously locked down.

And they're just ... letting me walk out.

I take a step into the hall and look to the right, towards the hangar.

"Where are the seatbelt marks?" the Raven had asked. The memory of his talon dragging across my skin sends a delicious shiver over my body.

But the question is valid.

Where *are* the seatbelt marks? The car flew off the cliff, I remember that much. But I don't remember being restrained. I should've slammed back against the seat, gone careening over the hill, strapped to the car. I shouldn't have flown into the air like I remember.

My fingers itch, and I ball them into fists. My eyes lift to the nearest camera again.

The thought of the Raven, on the other side, watching me, heightens that delicious shiver, makes it spread across my chest and down to my slit until I'm practically vibrating with the need to torment him again. How do I even know for sure he's there?

I don't. But I can feel it. Viscerally. An ache that has nothing to do with the car crash.

That ache goes deeper than attraction and need. There's something behind it writhing, a part of me I've kept restrained since Ari swept into my life two years ago. Just being in this place is familiar in a way that terrifies me. These clothes; the way the Raven and Scarlet treat me; the emotions the Raven brings out in me.

It's a taste, and I've been starving. I know I've been starving slowly for these two years, but I tried to tell myself it was normal. That *I* was the problem.

Here, now, for even just this short time ...

Hunger has made me feral.

I grin up at the nearest camera. "Fine. I'll play your game," I say and turn to the left, toward the door at the end of the hall, the one behind which are, apparently, *answers*.

I DON'T KNOCK. The handle twists easily, unlocked, and I saunter into a room with a wall of windows that shows a California canyon beyond. That does nothing to orient me, but I'm relieved we're still on the west coast, that the Raven didn't fly me away to somewhere truly distant and remote.

The other side of the room is given over to computers.

I stop, my jaw going slack. The monitors gleam down at me, showing a dozen different things. Weather reports in various cities and maps with dots moving, tracking certain targets; and television recordings playing news clips, some old, some live.

Everything, *everything*, from the monitors to the keyboards to the holographic tablets in the desktops, is state-of-the-art.

There's that flare of hunger again. The writhing of a part of me I've had to smother in Ari's shadow. Heroes Org never let me near tech beyond my iPhone—which, damn, I have no idea what happened to it—and a simple laptop. Every time I asked to be included in whatever high-tech research they had going on, Ari would laugh, and tuck my hair behind my ear, and tell me I didn't need to worry about stuff like that anymore.

Stuff like that.

Movement near the computers pries me back to reality. The Raven spins around, lounged back in a desk chair, hands behind his head. His wings are tucked up behind him.

We stare at each other for a long moment. It's raw to see him with all these thoughts of my past life tangling up close to the surface, threatening to spill over from where I've kept them submerged for so long. What will happen if I give in to how much anger I've kept stored away too? What will happen if I let this part of me back into the sun?

The Raven's eyes dip down my body. Thank god—that motion shakes some sense back into me.

We're playing a game still. I know how to best him. Don't drop your guard, Giles.

I point at the monitors. "Watch anything good lately?"

And I bite my lip, grinning.

The Raven's cheeks redden.

Gotcha.

My clit throbs. I hadn't finished, too focused on the knowledge that, somewhere, the Raven was watching me, and maybe, just maybe, I was getting to him.

But it had been, again, one of the hottest moments of my life.

I take a step towards him. Another. He doesn't move in the chair, and when I bend next to him, looking closer at a monitor, I know he has a view of my tight ass in these pants.

Sure enough, when I look over my shoulder at him, his crotch is tented.

"You had something to show me?" I whisper, and that question cuts into this heat. Yeah, he has something to show me: proof of my boyfrie—*fiancé's* attempted murder of me.

The Raven clears his throat and swings his arms down. "Are you sure?"

"I came here, didn't I?"

"Still. You've already been through a lot today."

"How long have I been here?"

"Only about two hours."

"And you care?" My voice hardens. Distrust layering over accusation.

The Raven's face spasms with dark amusement. "I'm incapable of *caring*, sweetheart. This is business, and I'm just trying to decide if revealing this to you now is in my best interest."

"And what would be in your best interest?"

"Making All-American Man bleed."

He says it so straightforwardly that I jerk back. But he doesn't apologize. Doesn't try to cover it up.

He wants my fiancé to suffer. That's why I'm here. That's why he took me.

Isn't it?

Then why did he almost let me go?

The Raven pulls a wireless keyboard into his lap and looks up at a screen on the top right. A video is paused, but I recognize the setting instantly. The road. The canyon. There's Ari's car, the two of us minuscule from the camera's viewpoint.

"How—" I think back. There were no helicopters or paparazzi. That's why I'd thought Ari had gone that way—to avoid the crowds.

I turn my confusion to the Raven. Who points at his eye.

"Optical cameras," he says. "I record every flight."

"Why?"

"Proof." His face darkens. "Not that the media gives a shit about how their precious golden Heroes are actually cheats and liars, but it's come in handy sometimes."

I study his eyes, my own flicking between the two. He goes rigid as I put my hands on the armrests of his chair and bend low.

His irises are nearly the same color as his pupils. Black on black. But I can't see the ring of a contact or the telltale luster of a screen.

I let out a huff of shock. "That's incredible. They're nearly invisible. The prototypes I'd seen were *years* away from being so undetectable."

"The prototypes you've seen?" the Raven asks.

I realize, then, how close we are, as close as we'd been in the hospital bed only moments ago. He smells like cologne. Masculine and rich, dark and heady, scents that make my mouth water with wanting to taste it on his skin.

My breathing quickens, breasts heaving under the skin-tight fabric of this shirt.

"Um. Yeah." I don't pull back, still too curious. "I was in my junior year at MIT when ... " I stop. Swallow. "You probably heard."

"An attack in Boston, right? One of Heroes Org's experiments went awry."

"He wasn't an *experiment*. He just couldn't control his powers, and he got out of containment, and—" I shiver, remembering that day. The roar of a beast blasting through the small diner. The screams of patrons and staff alike as the wall exploded, meaty, inhuman fists tearing through the stone like paper.

All-American Man had been dispatched to *contain the asset*.

My jaw works as I look into the Raven's eyes. The field I'd been studying had been biotech—exactly this sort of thing. Combining humans and tech to supplement non-powered people, or to help those with disabilities, or to just generally improve civilian life.

But then, I'd met Ari.

"Anyway, this is incredible." I lift my hand and put my fingertips against the Raven's temples, featherlight. "How do you put them on? How do you charge them? Do you—"

I'm stopped by his wry smile. It's so different from the strain Ari would show, the annoyance bordering on contempt, that I stop talking, my mouth hanging open.

"I had no idea *the* Lillith Giles was into tech," the Raven says. "Is that what you do behind the scenes for All-American Man?"

My cheeks burn. "Hardly."

"Why is that?"

My fingers on his temples drop lower, landing loose around his neck. I suddenly can't look in his eyes.

He reaches up and takes my hands, trapping my wrists in his long fingers. "I didn't mean to—fuck. I shouldn't have pushed that. Keep talking—you light up when you're getting geeky."

That makes me smirk. "*Getting geeky?*"

He really wants me to keep talking? It's been so long since anyone's taken an interest in what interests me.

It leaves me breathless.

The Raven leans closer. "I'll let you in on a secret, though: I'm not wearing the cameras right now. You're welcome to keep searching me if you'd like."

Unsteadiness surges through me. I'd lost myself in curiosity, and I have a dark moment of self-hatred before I glance at the closed door.

"Is that what Scarlet thinks I want? To *search* you?"

His face instantly hardens. "She won't do it again. She crossed a line."

"Like you did while you watched me get dressed?"

He blushes. His tongue darts out, wets his lips, and I remember, vividly the sharpness of it in my mouth.

I bend closer, closer, until I put my lips on his ear. "Don't worry, *sweetheart*," I echo his moniker. "I liked it."

As I pull back, I take the wireless keyboard from his lap and turn to the paused screen. My hands shake—god, how long has it been since I got to ogle over tech shit?

Two years. Almost to the day.

I slam down on the spacebar.

The scene leaps to life. The car zooms along the road, dodging in and out of the Raven's viewpoint as he dips and dives through the sky. The way he flies—it's jerky, panicky. I'd expected smooth and steady and graceful, given the size of his wings and his reputation.

What exactly did Ari do to him a year ago?

But those wonders evaporate as the video zooms in. The car takes a turn—*the* turn—and spirals out.

Another zoom in.

There's Ari, reaching across the space between us, to unclick my seatbelt. I watch my body rocket out of the car and hurtle through empty space over the canyon.

The camera zooms back out, but only because the Raven is now flying towards me, losing altitude, diving, diving—

He smashes into me, and the camera goes dark.

I gasp. My fingers clench the keyboard in a death grip, and I'm typing suddenly, furiously, using the touchpad to pull the video back up, rewinding.

Again, Ari. Reaching over. Unbuckling my seatbelt.

Zoom out. Move over.

His face. His *leer*, joyful darkness, *demented*.

I play the clip again. Again. Each time, I see the same thing.

Ari tried to kill me.

All-American Man tried to kill me.

And he enjoyed it.

I can't breathe. All the air feels like it's been sucked out of the room, walls crushing in, breaking me down.

Hands take my arms and guide me into the chair. The Raven crouches before me and pries the keyboard out of my hands.

He squeezes my wrist. "I'm sorry, Lillith."

A dry laugh slips out of my throat. "No, you're not."

"No. Not entirely. I am sorry, though, that it was you."

"Why?" The question is a knife. It grates on my throat, and tears well, fall down my cheeks. I shove to my feet and the Raven follows me up, pinned between my anger and the computer desk. "Why the fuck do you *care?* Why were you even there?"

His face is open, and he says, simply, "I was going to abduct you."

It makes my body go ice cold. "Why?"

The Raven surges closer to me, chest to chest, his eyes blazing down into mine. "Because you were a way through his armor. I know a caged bird when I see one and you, darling, were *miserable* with him. You would've been the in I needed to bring him down, whether through information you gave me, or maybe I just would've seduced you and rubbed that in his face."

He's breathing too fast. I am, too, and I know we're both thinking of the hospital room, how easily I gave into him; and after, even, how I taunted him with my body in the cameras.

"As though you could seduce me," I whisper, hoarse.

One side of his lips curves up, tantalizing in its slowness. I want to bite that smile, sink my teeth into his lips until he's begging for reprieve.

Him seduce *me*?

Oh, no.

I'd be the one to break him.

"What changed?" I spit. "You still intend to use me to get to him."

"Yes." All honesty from him. No barriers. No changes of subject that leave me frustrated and ignorant.

"You're just going to use me," I say, and my heart aches. "Like he used me."

Hearing the words out loud punctures holes in my lungs. The tension between the Raven and I evaporates, until there is only that video, playing on repeat in my mind.

"He used me," I say again, because I need to hear it. "He took me, and forced me to be a prop in his life, and because he saved me, that somehow entitled him to it? The *fuck*." I rip my hands through my hair, sobbing to the tacky plaid carpet. "What the fuck did I let him do? Oh my god. I gave him *years* of my life. I gave him *everything I was.* I sacrificed all of me, for him, and he goes and—he goes and tries to *kill me.*"

The sobs are too much. The grief, too potent. It's the apex of betrayal, the realization that no matter how perfect of a girlfriend I tried to be for Ari, I never would have been good enough for All-American Man.

I knew. Deep down, I knew. At every press junket and charity event and mayor's ball, I saw the stares. I heard their hatred.

She's not good enough for our Hero. What does he see in her? Common civilian whore.

Just a waitress he'd scooped out of the rubble of a fight, a dime a dozen. Just some nameless, faceless nobody who was supposed to bend to his spotlight and disappear into him. And the sickest part? I *tried* to disappear. I gave up every interest, every goal, every dream. I quit school. I shoved myself into the boxes Heroes Org demanded.

And it wasn't enough.

I stripped myself *raw,* and it *wasn't enough.*

My grief parts enough that I notice the Raven has taken me into his lap on the floor. He cradles me, rocking us slowly, one hand stroking through my hair, the other gripping me to his chest.

I yank back, fingers digging into his biceps, bearing down. He's powered—he can take the pain.

"I want in," I growl, my voice roughened by tears and fury.

The Raven's eyes widen. "Excuse me?"

"I want in. I want to help you destroy All-American Man."

It's the absolute last thing he expected me to say. He goes completely still, those dark eyes staring at me, waiting for me to renege.

When I don't, he exhales a shocked sigh. "I'll only ask you this once. And you can back out any time. But ... are you sure, Lillith? You realize who you'd be allying with." He licks his lips again, this time, predatory. "I believe they like to call me *a Villain.*"

The *yes* is on the tip of my tongue, but I make myself hold back for a second.

Think this through, Giles.

But there really is no thinking. What's my other option? To go to the hangar and fly back to Ari and wait for him to try again? I have no family I can trust. No real friends.

Fuck this. I'm done breaking myself apart for him.

I've had a taste of freedom. And I want more. I want revenge. I want recompense for the years of my life I gave to him.

Maybe I do have some Villain in me after all.

I slide my engagement ring off and present it to the Raven, the rock glittering between us.

"Oh, I'm sure," I tell him. I meet his eyes, and I see a certain kind of hunger there. It matches my own and winds around us, connects us. "Where do we start?"

He plucks the ring out of my fingers and folds it into his palm. His grin is ferocious, tempting, and our closeness changes, files to a razor-sharp point of longing that has my nerves screaming for the release I've been denied.

Use me, I want to say. *Use me until there's nothing left of the woman I've been these last two years.*

But the Raven just touches one of those talons to my collarbone again. He drags it down, puncturing the fabric but not tearing it, and I arch up against it involuntarily.

"We start," he echoes, "with Persephone."

7

FALLON

SHE HAS A PREDATOR'S EYES, AND I THINK THEY MAY JUST DEVOUR ME, BODY and soul.

And I may just let her.

"Who's Persephone?" Lillith asks.

"The best kept secret in the world," I answer.

But god, I don't want to have to contact her. Persephone is head of the Villains, if there is a leader. Each Villain operates alone, but we all of us know of Elysium, the sanctuary where Persephone rules in absolute control, where she can elect whether or not to get involved in larger disputes. Scarlet was right, though—a superhero going rogue is absolutely the kind of shit that would make Persephone sit up. Take notice. Use her considerable powers to *do* something about the holier-than-thou heroes who think they can mandate the rest of us.

But deals with Persephone are dangerous.

She never helps out of the goodness of her own heart.

Because she doesn't have one.

I lift my arm to access the communication link I wear on my tech cuff. Lillith watches with eager eyes, bright and sparking. Former waitress, my ass. All-American Man had a goddamn genius on his arm and all he could look at was her tits. An MIT girl who can find Scarlet's cameras, knows about bio-optics, and looks like she wants to steal my tech cuff just to take it apart and figure out what makes it tick—this is a girl with more to offer than blind Ari could ever see.

She doesn't ask questions—she just watches as I type on the cuff. Her keen eyes are quick enough to see the message I don't try to hide, directed to Persephone: a brief summary of today's events and a copy of the video file.

When I drop my hand, Lillith's eyes meet mine. "Now what?"

"Now we wait," I say. She shifts off my lap, and I stand, stretching my wings. I cannot hide the wince that mars my face.

Lillith is there. "What did he do?" she whispers, peering over my shoulder at the black wings curving down my back. "I know, about a year ago, you faced off. But no one knows what he did. Only that ... " She pauses, her gaze shifting to my eyes. "Only that you disappeared after."

"It takes time to recover," I say bitterly. "Even a super feels pain."

Her delicate fingers trace down my shoulder, to my left wing. I extend it, relishing the feeling of strength in the movement, wincing at the tightening of pain at the old scars.

That I'm alive is a bit of a miracle—my mother had thought me a monster, deformed and hideous at birth. Birds are not beautiful before their feathers grow in. I've seen enough pictures of hatchlings to know that.

But once my wings fully formed and my body caught up with my physique, I grew to love my abilities. I reveled in flight.

That was the worst part of the last year.

Not being able to fly for most of it.

If it wasn't for my super-healing, All-American Man would have grounded me for good. As it is, Scarlet and everyone else I've seen with any healing ability says I'll never fully recover.

"What happened?" Lillith asks again, softly. Her fingers are in my feathers, the feeling delicious, sending heat over my body.

And then they brush against the scars.

The jagged welts are usually hidden by my feathers, but she's found them. She traces them, a roadmap to my pain.

"After he defeated me," I say, "All-American Man drug me over to a rock jutting up from the canyon floor." My voice is hollow and blunt. I've relived this moment over and over again, so much that I tell myself it doesn't hurt anymore even though it does. "He flew into the air and then smashed into my wings feet-first, using the force of his powers and the rock to break them."

"He *curb-stomped* your wings?" Lillith gasps. She looks as if she may vomit at the idea.

"Then he drug me up, above the canyon," I continue in that same dead voice. "He told me to fly, and then he dropped me."

Lillith curses. When I turn around, my wings rustling behind me, I catch wet emotion in her eyes.

"He really is a monster, isn't he?" she says. "How did I not see it before?"

I shrug. "Most people don't."

She looks like she wants to question me further, but I'm done. "Come on," I say gruffly.

"Where are we going?" She follows me into the hall and down the corridor, into the heart of Scarlet's base.

"Persephone doesn't like tech," I say. "She uses it when she has to, and it's the only way for someone like me to reach her, but she'll save her response for the dreamscape."

"Dreamscape?"

I don't bother answering her. Some things have to be seen to be believed.

At the entrance into Scarlet's base—her harem—The Watcher stands. "I'm expecting to meet Persephone soon," I say. "She knows I'm here."

The Watcher's yellow optics flick to Lillith. "The non-powered human, too?"

"Her too," I answer.

"Very well." The Watcher turns, releasing the lock and letting us inside.

Lillith gasps, clutching for my arm. And for good reason. There are dozens of people inside the room, most of them in various states of undress. Some are together in groupings of two or three or more. Some are alone. Their eyes are all glazed over, but their bodies showcase their thoughts, writhing, playing, fucking.

"They can't see us," I say. "They can't hear us."

"What on Earth ..." Lillith looks around, barely aware of me tugging her forward.

"Scarlet is a mesmer," I remind her. "She can tap into people's thoughts and desires. This is her ..." I feel heat tainting my cheeks. Most of the supers labeled as Villains are at least a little more subtle about what they do, but not Scar. "This is her harem," I say.

"Do ... are they happy?" Lillith asks.

"Oh, deeply." Scarlet's voice cuts across the echoing chorus of moans and blissful sighs of the people around us. My eyes shoot to the center of the room, where Scarlet sits upon a white enamel throne raised up on a dais. "Each one is living out their own fantasy in their minds. This is their choice, sunshine. I just help them make it real."

"And she watches," I add. Scarlet sees them not only here, in this harem, but also in the fantasies, her mind divided, finding the pleasure in each scene, lust multiplied dozens of times over.

Lillith's eyes sharpen. She gazes out at the bodies fucking all around her, a den of orgies. A mix of supers and nonpowered people—there's a woman with long blonde hair riding the hips of a man with rainbow scales down his back. Another woman with the power of controlling plants has four different people squirming at her feet, the vines growing from her body tantalizing each one in a different way, plunging in and out of every orifice, sliding over the hot, writhing bodies.

"I don't just watch them here," Scarlet says gently, strolling down the dais to us. She touches Lillith's chin, drawing her attention to her alone. "I watch them here." She shifts her finger to her temple.

Realization hits Lillith, and she gasps. Scarlet is the cinematographer of each visionary dreamscape, creating perfect fantasies for every person in the room. The only price is that she gets to watch each fantasy play out. And, if she taps into their minds for secrets and information they otherwise wouldn't give her ...

Well, we are Villains.

"So these people," Lillith says slowly. Not a single one of the dozens in the room are aware of her voice; they're too wrapped up with living out their fantasies. "They're private, in their mind, but public with their bodies, here. And you watch them?"

"Me, and my Watcher," Scarlet says. From out of nowhere, the cyborg appears, his yellow optics gleaming. "Sometimes we join in, but we like the edges of the fantasies more."

A little muscle in Lillith's neck moves as she swallows. Her tongue darts out, wetting her lips.

She's excited by this, I think. I glance over at Scarlet, who arches an eyebrow. She noticed, too. Lillith is deeply into the idea of being watched.

I feel my body tensing, hardening. I think of all the times I watched her, tracking Ari through his girlfriend.

She was hot then, but add the voyeurism, and she's scorching.

But we also have business to deal with. "Persephone needs a meeting spot," I tell Scarlet.

Scarlet doesn't let her emotions betray her except for a single sharp intake of her breath. "Ah," she says. "You'll need a dreamscape."

I nod. I don't like communicating like this, but it's safe. Technology can be hacked. Scarlet's mind can't. Persephone dislikes putting anything relevant online. After she accepted my vague message, she confirmed only that we'd meet in the dreamscape. She's saving the real business for talking in person.

Or, well, in the dreamscape, which is like being in person. Scar's powers enable her to make a dreamscape that both I and Persephone can access. A totally safe, totally private place to talk—with the exception of Scarlet, but she would never betray us.

"And little miss sunshine, too?" Scarlet asks.

"I go where he goes," Lillith shoots back, and pride burns inside me. This girl is quick to know what she wants and to claim it.

"Very well," Scarlet says. She moves her hands, but before she does, the Watcher speaks.

"I feel like now is a relevant time to mention that I have medically scanned both participants," he says in his perfectly even voice. "Both are clean, and Miss Giles's IUD is functioning perfectly."

I feel heat rising to my cheeks. I mean, yes, thank you, Watcher, but dammit, could he have been more subtle?

Scarlet smirks at me, waves her hands, and everything goes dark.

WHEN I OPEN MY EYES, I'm at the beach. White sands stretch out, fading to blue waves cresting.

And Lillith is there.

Her black outfit has been replaced with a gauzy white thing that blows in the wind, pressing against her skin, leaving nothing to the imagination. I look down—Scarlet's put me in something black and short and not what I'd wear in public.

But this isn't public. This isn't the beach.

We're in a dreamscape.

"Where's this Persephone?" Lillith asks, looking around at the deserted coast.

"She didn't give me a time," I say. "Just orders."

"Sounds like Heroes Org."

"She's not like them," I spit.

I can see the questions on her lips—how would I know? What experience do I have with Heroes Org beyond fighting them?—but before she can ask, I snap my wings out.

In Scarlet's dreamscapes, they never ache. It was the only thing that got me through the last year, escaping into a fantasy where I wasn't injured, permanently marred by a psychotic Hero.

Lillith's eyes scan my wings. "I've always wanted to fly," she whispers.

"Ari can fly," I say. All-American Man uses his powers, not wings, to fly, but he can do it. He could have taken her into the air whenever she wanted.

Lillith presses her mouth tight. "He said it's dangerous. I'm too *fragile*." She spits the word out.

I cross the sands over to her. "You're anything but fragile," I say.

She looks almost like she wants to protest, but I don't give her the chance. I scoop her in my arms, and my wings beat, hard, once, twice, again. And we're soaring over the white-peaked waves of the ocean, flying faster than should be possible. The sandy beach disappears, replaced with nothing at all but water.

Lillith whoops with the sheer joy of flight.

It's the exact same sound my heart makes every time I soar.

And I can't help it—it's the feeling of flight, the feeling of sharing it with her—I twirl in the air, and my lips claim hers.

She doesn't pull back.

She doesn't hesitate.

She wraps her arms around my neck. My wings beat up and up and up, higher and higher, as she deepens the kiss, her tongue flicking into my mouth, her fingers playing with the feathers right at the base of my wings. My arms around her hold her tight against my body, safe, but her legs wrap around my waist.

Scarlet gave her nothing to wear but that gauzy white cover-up. It rides up over her hips, and I feel Lillith, the heat and wet of her body, bare, pressing against my abs.

I groan. We're so high up now that I feel like we could touch the sun.

Lillith pulls away from me, resting her head on my shoulder. We're so close I can feel her heartbeat over top mine. It's almost as sensual as knowing her bare pussy is pressed just above my cock, held tight to me by her legs wrapped around my waist.

"Is she watching?" Lillith asks, her voice a soft kiss on my earlobe.

It takes my brain a moment to figure out speech again. "Scarlet?" I ask. "Absolutely she is." There's nowhere for her to hide—not a cloud in this fake blue sky, not a ship on the ocean. But Scarlet sees all.

A shiver of anticipation goes up Lillith's spine. I was right—my girl is absolutely into voyeurism.

For a moment, I go rigid. *My girl.* When did I start thinking of her as mine, and not Ari's? When did this become about us, and not revenge?

It's still about revenge, I whisper to myself viciously. *This is just an added bonus.*

Lillith leans away from my embrace, looking down, down, to the sparkling sea far below us. Even if we were to crash, nothing would hurt us here. It's in our minds, a shared dream.

The way she leans back pushes her breasts against the thin material. With a growl I dip my head to the cloth and rip it away with my teeth. It comes apart easily, freeing her breasts. Lillith shrugs out of the remains of the gauzy white cover, and it flutters down to the sea, disappearing in the waves.

Lillith laughs as I dip my head down to her chest, licking between her breasts, kissing to one nipple, then the next, letting my teeth graze over the dimpled flesh. Her voice becomes heady and guttural, deep with longing.

"Not fair," she says, gasping as I swirl her nipple around my tongue. "Not ... not fair."

She wriggles down, her pussy sliding over my body, her fingers reaching between us. I think she's going to pleasure herself, but instead, her hand goes lower, to the drawstrings at my waist. In a moment, the knot slips free, and I kick the black cloth away.

My cock is hard, pressing up against her bare ass. For a moment, I forget about everything. My wings still, every ounce of my awareness focused on my cock, her tight ass, how easy it would be to shift her body, to plunge into her wet pussy.

With a gleeful scream, Lillith's hair flies up as we plummet down. With a rush of adrenaline, I spread my wings, catching the warm air and regaining balance.

"I've never fucked while flying," I whisper, my voice ragged with constraint. I wanted her so much that for a moment I forgot to keep us aloft.

Lillith smirks at me. "I've always wanted to join the mile high club."

I bark with laughter at this, but the sound turns into a throaty groan as she shifts, sliding her body down. I grit my teeth, trying to keep my wings pumping as she slides her slick pussy over me.

"Hold me," she whispers, meeting my eyes. "Don't let go."

My arms tighten around her. *Never. I am never letting go of this girl.*

And then her hand snakes between our bodies. She grabs my cock, and my wings give out—just a moment, just a dip—and the thrill of it, the danger, the idea of fucking while flying—it all centers around that sensation, her fingers tight on my cock, pulling down and up, her thumb rubbing over the head, smearing my wetness around.

And then she lifts her hips, using her hand to guide me to her entrance. She looks down—down at my cock rubbing against her clit, down at the sea a mile below us—and then she meets my eyes, looking right into the heart of me as she slides my cock inside her, pressing down with her hips to fully drive me into her.

I shudder, my vision blackening at the pure hotness of it.

And then she moves against me, timing the thrusts with the beat of my wings, and it's so fucking hot, it's more than lust, it's deeper than that, and wind swirls around us, buffeting our rhythm.

She trusts me, absolutely, completely, not just with fucking but with flying. She arches her back, her breasts a feast before me, and with a snarl I claim her nipple with my teeth, tasting that sensuous, sensitive flesh. She gasps, driving herself harder against my cock, faster.

With an arch, I swoop down. Gravity helps me drive into her. We're not falling—we're soaring. My arms shift to her hips, steadying her as I pound into her pussy. The ocean gets closer and closer, but I also feel the coil of lust tightening inside her. Her cunt clenches around me and she falls apart, screaming my name in her orgasm. Just as the waves kiss our hot skin, I beat my wings, hard, and we rise again, higher and higher, every lift matched with a thrust of my heavy cock into her dripping pussy, hard, fast, and then I come apart, my wings fluttering as she clenches around me, drawing every last drip into her.

She's limp in my arms, but she makes no move to pull away from me. "Now that," she says, her voice raw, "is flying."

8

LILLY

I HAVE NEVER BEEN THIS BLISSED OUT.

Fallon and I recline on the white sands, my head on his chest, his arm curved around my waist. My head rises and falls with the cadence of his breath, mimicking the ebb and flow of the waves crashing on the shore. His wings fan around us, warming in the sun, one of them cushioning my body.

My eyelids flutter shut, drift open, my whole body relaxed and content and utterly appeased.

I can't remember the last time I felt *satisfied.*

Fallon's hand traces a line from my elbow to my shoulder, sending goosebumps over my bare skin. "How are you?"

The tentativeness in his voice is adorable.

I rise up and straddle him, bracketing his hips with my thighs, and lower over to press my lips to his. The kiss is slow and decadent, savoring the taste of him, the feel of his tongue in my mouth. My hands roam across his taut chest, the divots and valleys of his muscles, until I dip lower, between us, and grab his cock.

"I'm fantastic," I whisper against his mouth. "And you?"

He moans, almost a purr, and in one fluid motion flips us so it's me on the sand and him bending over me.

"Almost fantastic," he says.

"Almost?" My hand is still around his dick. It's fully erect again and I roll my palm around the head, streaking the wetness down the shaft and back up again until I have him burying his face in my neck, nipping at my shoulder.

He continues that down my collarbone and sucks one peaked nipple into his mouth. When he curls his tongue over the tip, I squirm, vision going dark in ecstasy.

Then his lips are at my ear. "They're watching you, Lillith. Can you feel it? Their desire? You're so fucking hot, and they're on the edge because of you."

My throat swells shut. I swallow, gasping for breath like we're miles under that ocean, consumed with desire. "They?"

"Scarlet. Watcher." Fallon trails his lips down my body again. "Persephone."

"She's here?"

He moans and nods. His lips brush my hips, and he licks a long line down to the top of my slit.

I seize and grab his head. "Fallon—"

He pulls up instantly, looking at me. "We can stop, Lillith. Any time. Do you have a safe word?"

"Safe word?" Just saying that makes me dizzy. No—I never needed a safe word. Not with Ari.

Fallon grins, and it's wicked. God, I'm swept away in him, in *this*—how long has it even been? Only a few hours? Fuck, I'm in trouble.

"Pick one," he whispers, pleading, *begging*.

"Crash," I say.

His grin turns sardonic. "Really?"

"Yes."

"Say it, and I'll stop."

And then he dives, and I really am crashing.

His mouth is on my pussy like he's starving and it's the only nourishment he'll get. He spreads my legs, one over each shoulder, and delves his tongue into my folds, intimately tracing the sharp tip of his tongue over every inch of me.

It isn't enough—it's too much—I grip my hands into his hair and buck under him, trying to guide his mouth to my clit.

"God, Fallon—*Fallon*—"

He rumbles, and that vibration ripples over my pussy. "Begging, sweetheart?"

"Y-yes—*please*—"

That punishing tongue circles my clit once. I'm on the edge, sensations wound up over every nerve.

Fallon rises up, and when I look down at him, he's grinning that devilish grin.

"Give them a good show," he says, and the weight in his voice makes it a command.

The reminder that people are watching sends my head lulling back, ecstasy surging up my body, nearly undone. There are eyes on us. On me. There are bodies responding to my euphoria. I have them in thrall.

This is power. Power I've never known before.

Power I crave the way I crave Fallon's mouth on my pussy.

And when he goes back to his torment, that tongue drawing figure eights around my clit, I fall apart.

The orgasm tears through me like a hurricane, wild and untamed, destructive and beautiful. I scream, body arching and thrashing, every inch of me alive with sensation.

Fallon rides the waves, his hands digging into my thighs, talons sharp but not puncturing as he holds his mouth on my clit and sucks hard.

I drop back into my body like that final descent to this beach—rapid, spiraling, but knowing that Fallon will land me safely. And he does—he licks up and down my pussy, cleaning the aftermath, and kisses his way back up my body. When his lips reunite with mine, I taste myself on him, and all the sensations fly back through me at once.

I'm in trouble, I think again.

There has to be a catch. A single man cannot be this perfect; a *Villain* cannot be this perfect.

But we're only doing this to get revenge on Ari. Fallon and I aren't tangled up in each other solely to enjoy this—it has a purpose.

It has an end.

Panting, I clamp my fingers around the back of Fallon's neck and pull apart. "Is this ... is what Scarlet does recorded somewhere? Are we going to send this to Ari?"

Fallon's whole body stiffens. Every part of him goes rigid, the tension of a moment broken.

For a heartbeat, I think maybe I misunderstood; maybe Fallon is doing this because he *does* just want *me*—

He props on his elbows and the grin he throws at me is icy. "That's why we're meeting with Persephone."

Fallon shoves to his feet. The moment he does, his clothes reappear, the swim trunks Scarlet gave him in this dreamscape.

I look down. My own clothes have popped back up again. Though *clothes* is too strong a word—it's flimsy gauze at best.

I don't mind. At all. It's the same powerful feeling as knowing people were watching Fallon fuck me with his mouth.

He helps me to my feet. "Are you ready to meet her?"

"Fallon—" I touch his arm as he turns. For a beat, he keeps his face to the side, and I see his jaw tighten.

I have the sudden urge to kiss that tension away.

"What did we just do? Why did we do that?" My questions are whispers. Each word ramps up my pulse, and I hang on the precipice of the silence that follows.

Finally, Fallon looks at me. There's something guarded in his eyes, something that wasn't there before.

"Why do you think we fucked like that, Lillith?"

Because I wanted to. Because I needed *to. Because I feel more alive in these few hours I've spent with you than in two years with my boyfriend.*

But I can't get myself to say any of that.

"I mean," my throat is dry, "how are we going to bring down Ari?"

Fallon smirks. He touches his thumb to my cheek and drags his talon along my skin. Not drawing blood. But nearly.

"First, Persephone."

Before I can ask more, he turns again. I follow his gaze.

A woman is standing up the shore. She faces us, the sea wind whipping her braids against her midnight black skin. She's wearing far more clothes than we are, a sharp pantsuit that's buttoned just below her breasts with no shirt underneath.

She's utterly striking, standing against the white sands, all darkness and confidence.

Persephone.

Her eyes are the only spot of color on her. Green like a field in springtime. They go from my face, to my breasts visible through this fabric, to my pussy, and back up again.

She was one of the people who watched us. Who watched *me*.

And by the glint in her eye, she liked what she saw.

I go dizzy with longing. It makes me stand taller, shoulders back, confidence exuding in waves.

Persephone blinks slowly at me. "Your guest put on a nice performance, Fallon," she says to him, but watches me.

Fallon draws a circle on the back of my hand. "Sweet, isn't she?"

"Very."

"Next time, join us," I hear myself say. It zips through my body, and I realize—*yes*. I want that. I want that even more than I want people watching. For others to see, then join in and take the ecstasy higher, push us all over the edge in an uncontrollable race—

My chest rises faster, and I know I'm flushed with longing.

Fallon and Persephone grin, seeing it, knowing how riled I am, and *god* that just spirals me more. I could come from this alone.

Fallon leans closer to me, his lips brushing my ear. "Soon, sweetheart," he whispers and grabs my ass through the gauzy dress, one finger dragging into my slit.

I moan, but he's already turning to Persephone.

Fallon closes the space to her. I follow, the sand soft on my bare feet.

He nods at me. "Meet Lillith Giles. Former fiancé of All-American Man. Lillith, this is Persephone, the leader of Elysium."

"The leader of Elysium?"

Fallon's face is amused. "What you'd call the group of Villains."

I knew a lot of the Villains gathered under a banner similar to Heroes Org, if only to *combat* Heroes Org, but I didn't expect them to be so ... organized. There's order to this meeting, the same way Ari defers to Malcolm.

"Yes." Persephone folds her arms behind her back, stretching her suit jacket almost wide enough to see her chest. I have a feeling she knows exactly how far she's pushing it, and doing it intentionally. "Why did you call me, Fallon? I imagine it has to do with the fact that half the country's looking for you."

My eyebrows peak. "What? Why?"

"The media's spin is that he abducted you. That he caused the crash."

"But I saw the video," I say, though I suddenly wonder—was it doctored? No—it was too raw, too bland. There were no jump cuts.

But all that tech ... could Fallon have edited it?

My eyes slide to him. He's watching me as though he knows exactly what I'm wondering.

He makes no move to confirm or deny my suspicions.

"The media will always tell tales that support Heroes Org," Persephone says. "All of the major news stations are *owned* by Heroes Org. The truth is often ignored entirely."

I remember what Fallon said, about how his optic cameras rarely do him any good, even if they record what really happened.

"So what are we doing here?" My voice rises, panicky suddenly. "Can you actually help us kill Ari?"

Persephone tips her head. "Is that why you called me, Fallon? To kill All-American Man?"

"No," Fallon is quick to say.

I gape at him. "No?"

"We want protection," he tells Persephone. "You know I'm good for that. Just buy us some time with the Heroes Org's manhunt so we can figure out our *own* plan." He says the last words to me, pleading.

I don't get what he's so riled about. *He* summoned Persephone. And all he's getting from her is protection?

"Are you capable of killing All-American Man?" I ask Persephone.

Fallon seizes my arm, his grip tight, but Persephone nods.

"Then *that's* what we want," I say.

"Lillith—*no*." Fallon drags my eyes to his. "I don't know how things operate in Heroes Org, but here, we don't just do things out of the kindness of our hearts. Everything has a price. And for Persephone to help with something as big as killing All-American Man ... you don't want to pay that price. Trust me."

"Maybe I do," I snap at him, my breathing tight and aching. "Maybe that's exactly what I want. To give anything to see him brought down."

Fallon's eyes are wide, his pupils dilated—there's excitement layered under his concern. Is it my anger riling him? Whatever it is, it has me looking at Persephone and nodding.

Persephone's eyebrows go up. "Interesting. Do you first want to know my price for giving you the power to kill All-American Man?"

"Giving *me* the power?"

"That's what I do, Lillith Giles," Persephone says, sultry and low. "I can make supers. But to make you into a super powerful enough to defeat All-American Man, the cost would be *you*. Entirely. After you complete your task, you would be mine, forever." Her lips thin, a smile laced with intention as her eyes dip leisurely down my body again, back up. "In every way."

She isn't even touching me, but that gaze sets off all my nerves.

In every way.

Fallon's grip on me digs deeper, his talons extended, and I realize it's in my defense.

He doesn't want me to agree to this.

I'm utterly raw, though. From the crash. From this dreamscape. From the reality that Ari tried to *kill me,* and I have no other way to exact revenge on the world's strongest superhero.

"All right," I say.

"Lillith!" Fallon takes my other arm. To Persephone, "Just—give us time to consider it. Please. Let her think it through. She's been through a lot today, and it isn't—"

Persephone steps closer. She gives Fallon a sharp look and after a long beat, he relents, stepping back.

That's a difference, then. In Heroes Org, Malcolm had the last say. He was a dictator. But Persephone is letting me make my own mind up. It's a choice.

Then Persephone has my face in her hands. She stares down at me, and I'm silenced by the peace in her, the green depths of her eyes utterly serene, calm and sure.

She bends forward and presses her lips to mine. It's not like with Fallon, all sharp angles and peaked need. It's slow and soft, lying in the sunshine, basking in warmth that spreads across my body with every swipe of her tongue on my lips.

"I'll give you one day to consider," she says into my mouth. "I like my pets willing, after all."

She steps back, and I stagger in her absence.

"I'll be in contact," she tells Fallon.

In a flash, Persephone vanishes, and Fallon and I are again alone on the beach. The wind whips at us, and where the sky had been unhindered blue before, now the sun is setting, though I have no idea what time it really is.

I have a feeling the sunset is more a reflection of my mind's sudden hesitation and anxiety. A wound-up battering of the past few hours busting through my ecstasy with reality's sharp fingers.

"Lillith." Fallon's voice is rough. "You can't do this. I have enough money to pay for Persephone's protection—that's all we need. You and I can figure out a way to bring down All-American Man without needing such drastic measures."

My jaw tenses. "Drastic measures? He tried to *kill me,* Fallon."

"So you'll throw your life away because of it? This isn't how it should've—" He stops. Runs his hands through his hair, making the black strands stick up.

"Let's just get some sleep," he amends, flat. "We've both had a long day."

Before I can demand he finish what he was really going to say, Fallon tips his head back to look at the sky. His wings relax around him, the tendons in his neck contracting.

He vanishes from the dreamscape.

Unease traps a breath in my lungs.

I turn and kick at the sand, sending it spewing in a wave of white particles. It does nothing to alleviate my building anxiety, my fear, my *rage*.

I want Ari to suffer. I want the power to take him *out*.

But Fallon does have a point. I'd be giving my life over to Persephone. What would that even look like?

And then there's that video. And the way Fallon said *This isn't how it should've—*

This isn't how it should've *what*? What plan did he have for me?

I just would've seduced you, he'd said, *and rubbed that in his face.*

He didn't truly stop me from talking to Persephone. If he didn't want me to make such a deal, he could have fought harder.

But this way, even if I sacrifice myself, he still gets All-American Man destroyed.

My mind goes back to the video I played, over and over, of the crash, Ari unclicking my seatbelt. It'd *looked* real.

But was it? What if Fallon actually *caused* the crash to abduct me just like he said, and he edited that video clip to get me willingly turned against Ari? And I took it to the extreme by initiating that deal with Persephone, better than he could've ever imagined.

My unease plummets into my gut like a rock.

I have to get another look at that video. I need to see the raw code, to see if it was *real,* or if I've played right into a Villain's hands. I can't commit to Persephone's deal without knowing that Ari really *did* try to kill me.

"Scarlet?" I look up at the sky. I'm suddenly struck with the thought: can she hear everything in my head?

The dreamscape dissolves around me. I'm left standing in Scarlet's harem. The change is gradual, like rising out of a pool. Only a few couples remain, still enthralled in each other, their eyes glazed over as though they're all looking at something hidden beyond a veil, just out of sight.

Scarlet and Fallon are nowhere to be seen.

It's Watcher who faces me. "If you'll follow me, Miss Giles. I'm to show you to your room."

"The hospital room?"

He smiles, kind. "Of course not. We provide proper lodging here for our guests. This way."

"Wait." I hold out my hand. Watcher turns back to me. "How does it ... work? Scarlet's power. Does she hear everyone's thoughts all the time?"

Watcher lifts one perfect eyebrow. He's incredibly handsome for a ... whatever he is. Maybe a cyborg? I can't quite tell. There's no way he's entirely robotic, not with that expression, those soft lips.

And I realize, with a jolt of electricity, that he watched Fallon and I fuck too.

I bite my lip.

But Watcher's all business now. He pulls a small device out of his pocket, a round metal disk with a button in the center.

"Scarlet goes to great lengths to ensure her clients are never taken advantage of," he says. "But if you ever fear Scarlet is overstepping, or you would just like a sign of good faith in her, you can press this button. It emits a signal that disrupts any mesmer's powers."

I instantly take the device. "Thank you."

He bows his head and holds out his arm, motioning me to follow.

"Where's Fallon?"

Watcher keeps a brisk pace out of the room and leads me down a few twisting halls.

"As I said," Watcher tells me, "we provide proper accommodation. He will contact you tomorrow, I imagine."

"Right." Anger flares through me. I'm just supposed to wait in some stuffy room until Fallon decides he's ready to see me?

Watcher opens a door for me and steps back.

Beyond it is a room that is anything but stuffy.

Opulent red walls surround a canopy bed piled in pillows and silk blankets. A separate door leads to a bathroom, and I can see a massive claw foot tub from here. The far wall is entirely windows, showing the night-drenched canyon beyond, stars speckled across the sky.

"If you require anything, ring this bell." Watcher points to a button on the wall. "Goodnight, Miss Giles."

He leaves, shutting the door silently.

I wait a few beats, then turn the knob.

It's unlocked.

I'm not a prisoner. Fallon isn't holding me here against my will. And that's the difference—I'm *letting* him use me, where Ari used me whether I wanted to or not.

But is the reason why I'm such a willing toy with Fallon based on truth? Did Ari really try to kill me—or was it Fallon all along?

I should've asked Watcher where this room is in relation to the rest of the base. Is that computer room nearby?

I start to reach for the button, to ask—

My hand shakes. Exhaustion creeps up over me in a wave, every inch of my body aching with some kind of pain or pleasure or both, a mix of the accident and fucking.

Before I do anything, I need to sleep.

I sink onto the bed, still in that black outfit from Edna. I should find something to change into—there's a bureau in the corner—

But sleep claims me.

9
FALLON

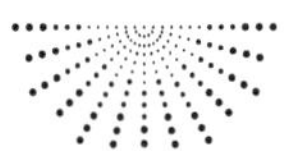

I PACE MY ROOM.

None of this is working as I'd plan.

Right, I think. *What even was the fucking plan, Fallon?*

All-American Man robbed me of flight. For a year. I *still* can't fly without pain. And ... despite the propaganda, I *know* that fucker's not a Hero. He's a psychopath. What he was going to do with Lillith—that proves he needs to go down.

I wore the video gear. I stalked him. And yeah—given the chance, I wanted to kick his ass. Even if I know he's fucking stronger. There's a reason why Ari Dodgers is the fucking golden boy of Heroes Org.

And seeing Lillith? A caged bird, ready to fly away?

Some revenge sex had seemed like just the ticket. If I can't beat him, at least I can fuck his girl.

Bile rises in my throat.

They're all right. I am a disgusting Villain.

I don't want to just use Lillith.

I don't want her to be hurt—by Ari *or* by me.

I don't want her to sacrifice herself to Persephone.

"Then what do you want?" I growl at my reflection in the window. My gaze shifts through the glass, toward the red rocks of the canyon.

I've avoided the canyons ever since Ari broke my wings. They were too painful to look at, and they all look the same anyway.

But when I look out over the desert landscape now?

All I can see in my mind's eye is Lillith.

Saving her. Fucking her.

Fuck.

The truth hits me sharp, hard.

I want to protect Lillith more than I want my revenge against Ari.

I collapse on my bed. The problem? I may be too late for either.

Lillith doesn't know. She can't know; she's not powered, and she's never seen Persephone in action.

I take a deep breath, imagining Lillith in front of me.

I go hard.

"Not *now*," I growl at my cock.

I close my eyes, picturing her. "Lillith, you've got to understand," I say, my voice echoing in the empty room. "Persephone is like a nuclear bomb. Sure, you'll take out Ari. But you're going to get radiation poisoning and die, slower, but still dead."

I open my eyes to my vacant room.

That's not going to work. It's the truth—I've seen it happen before—but it won't convince Lillith of a goddamn thing.

Because I've been where she is now. I've seen others be in the same spot.

Revenge like that burns you up from the inside, just like Persephone's powers would do.

And Persephone meant what she said, where the deal would make Lillith hers forever.

I growl, digging my talons into my palms. The idea that Lillith would *belong* to someone else... Bad enough when Ari claimed her, but Lilith was still free then. If Persephone took her...

I would never have a chance to be with Lillith again.

She doesn't understand the full implications of the deal Persephone is offering her. She can't—she's blinded by her need for revenge.

But I also know that explaining this to her now—it would just do no good.

Because I wanted that deal, before.

It was after I was injured. I damn sure called Persephone for help then. I was willing to do whatever it took to get my revenge and to get my wings.

Once it became clear that I'd never fully recover from All-American Man's injuries, I came here, using Scarlet to reach Persephone. I begged that bitch to give me the powers to take him out. I offered her everything, body and soul.

And she fucking laughed at me, then.

"No," she told me, the word so resonant that I still feel it in my chest. "You are being a child, sad because you lost a fight. That revenge is not worth the bargain."

So, what changed?

I really had hoped that Persephone would see the video of All-American Man going full dark into murdering an innocent and ... well, I'd kind of hoped that killing innocents would make her see Ari as a problem she could deal with herself. And if not, yeah, protection. Something.

I hadn't expected her to make a deal with Lillith.

Lillith, who has *no fucking clue* what it means to be burned up from the inside with a power like Persephone's.

My girl is strong, but no one can survive Persephone.

Not without losing who they were in the process.

10
LILLITH

THE SMELL OF BLUEBERRIES AND CINNAMON PULLS ME OUT OF THE DEEPEST sleep I've ever had.

I roll onto my side with a groan to get away from the haze of morning sunlight streaming through the windows. The smell only grows stronger, and when I slit one eye open, I see a table set next to my bed.

Memories of yesterday surge through me in a warm rush, tingling from the tips of my fingers to the pit of my belly. The car crash; Fallon saving me; waking up here at this Villain fortress somewhere in the California canyons; the video of Ari trying to kill me.

And being entwined with Fallon in Scarlet's dreamscape.

That memory beats most strongly as I sit up, the silk sheets pooling in my lap. A small table has been unfolded next to my bed, set with a vase holding a single purple lily so dark it's almost black. A plate of scones sits next to it, along with a bowl of cream and jam, and a silver coffee pot steaming out the neck over a porcelain cup. A small paper container of ibuprofen is there as well.

I grin, biting my lip, and reach for the coffee pot.

There's a note folded next to it with my name scrawled in delicate cursive.

Lillith.

I pluck it from the table and spread it open.

I didn't want to wake you. Please take as much time as you need. Persephone can wait—

The mention of Persephone jolts through me, equal parts fear and thrill.

—and you need to heal. When you're ready, call Watcher, and he'll find me.

It's signed, simply, *Fallon.*

I refold the note and hold it to my lips, grinning like a fool. How could one note send me reeling? And this breakfast spread, the gorgeous flower—

My joy dims.

I look at the note again.

When you're ready, call Watcher, and he'll find me.

Ready to face Persephone? Ready to discuss mine and Fallon's plans for taking down Ari again?

I won't be ready.

Not until I check that video of Ari trying to kill me.

But first ...

I grab a scone, and coffee, and cream, and fall back into the pillows, letting myself enjoy this utterly indulgent wake-up.

AFTER A QUICK SHOWER and a fresh set of clothes, presumably courtesy of Edna again, I slip out into the hall. It looks identical to the others, metal flooring and nondescript white walls. No portraits or art or anything to differentiate where I am, I at least see the number 7 scrawled on my door. Okay, room 7. I can remember that.

I pick a direction and start walking.

There are no security cameras here at least. This must be the wing for *guests* that Watcher mentioned, affording a bit more privacy than the hospital wing. I wander for a good ten minutes, taking turns that look like they're leading me towards utilitarian areas—more piping in the ceiling, the sounds of people moving about—before I come to a turn that leads to a set of sliding doors and a helipad beyond.

This must be where Fallon brought me in. Medical equipment is stacked near the door, a stretcher and first aid kit and other necessities at the ready.

My gut twists.

I press on, shoulders level. If that's where I came in, then the medical area has to be nearby, and the computer room was just off of it—

Aha.

I hit an intersection I recognize instantly. There is the door to the hospital room I was in. Which means—I turn, and find the door to the computer room.

A quick glance up tells me I'm in view of the security cameras, but I don't care. I've found the computer room. I only need a few minutes to dissect that video, and I can even try to erase any footage of me snooping while I'm there.

If I'm the only one in the room.

I twist the knob and open it slowly, my breath held, heart hammering against my ribs—god, even this is exciting though, charged with electricity at the thought of Fallon being in there, catching me. What would he do if he found me poking around where I'm not supposed to be?

I'm almost disappointed when the room is empty.

I close the door behind me and rush over to the computer station. The wireless keyboard is just where Fallon left it after he pried it out of my grip.

I wake up a screen and get to work.

There's a password, of course. But this is a computer system in Scarlet's own home, so the security isn't as high as something beyond her protective walls might be. A few moments of rudimentary hacking from my MIT days, and I'm in.

The video files are easy enough to find. I'm surprised to see others pop up, as though Fallon downloaded all his flights to this terminal. Maybe this is his back up? Why would it be at Scarlet's house?

I make a mental note to figure out more about the relationship between Fallon and Scarlet. Not that it matters—an attractive Villain like Scarlet, madame of a dreamscape sex harem? Of course Fallon's slept with her. Hell, *I'd* sleep with her.

But the thought of the two of them being something *more* almost makes me miss the video I'm looking for.

I didn't even stop to think yesterday whether Fallon was involved with anyone or not. I was too concerned with my own newly single status to ask if *he* is even single. But if he is with Scarlet, surely she wouldn't have so willingly let us fuck like that? Unless she gets off to it too.

Shit. I really need more information.

I shake my head and refocus on at least *this* information. First things first: figure out if Ari really did try to kill me, or if Fallon doctored this video.

I find the video I'm looking for, the most recent flight on Fallon's drive.

My specialty at MIT was never computer engineering, but I knew enough to apply it to my true passion: bioengineering. So many aspects of tech go hand in hand, braiding together in a weave of give-and-take.

I pull up the code for the video. The raw data.

My lip aches, and I realize I'm biting it again.

Get yourself together, Giles. It's fine. If this file is doctored, I'll just shoot a message to Ari, and he'll come save me.

Do I want to be saved?

I flinch at my own shitty question. If it turns out Ari *didn't* try to kill me? Hell yes, I want to be saved. I can't stay trapped here with a supervillain who staged an attack.

No matter how good the sex is.

Focus, dammit.

My hands shake as I scroll through the code. Lines of text stretch out, and I scan through it all.

I do it again. Three times.

It's real.

Fallon didn't edit this video. It came straight from his optical camera. Unmarred.

He didn't lie to me.

This ... whatever *this* is that I'm doing here ... is real.

I blow out a breath and drop back in the computer chair. Relief gushes into my chest, buckets of it, and I laugh at myself, how tense I'd gotten. I have to be out of my goddamn mind to be *relieved* that my former fiancé did, in fact, *try to kill me.*

Better him than Fallon.

My fingers slip on the keyboard and the video starts playing.

Ari takes the turn.

He reaches down.

Unfastens my seatbelt.

I go flying.

My eyes catch on something I hadn't seen the first time. Or rather, I didn't know to look for it.

I pause the video and bend forward. A few clicks, and it rewinds to the moment Ari takes the turn.

The car flies along the road, unhinged.

But Ari's face ...

I zoom in, but the angle is mostly Ari's back. The video starts playing at its slowest speed, frame by frame, until—there.

I pause. Zoom closer.

Ari's facing video-me, his body twisted in the seat. The angle of Fallon's camera catches most of his face, and his eyes especially. They're ... unfocused. He's grinning maniacally but he isn't looking at *me,* though he should be from that angle. He isn't looking at the car or the road or the canyon.

He looks almost like the people in Scarlet's sex harem. Eyes glazed over, lost in their own minds.

My heart rate skyrockets.

Fucking hell, did *Scarlet* mesmer Ari to crash the car?

"Of course not."

The voice makes me whip around, crashing back against the computer table.

Scarlet stands in the room, facing me, her arms folded under her breasts. Her tight red dress hugs every curve and stops mid-thigh, showing the way those muscles are perfectly sculpted in her don't-fuck-with-me stance.

I don't want to fuck with her.

Only I kind of do.

My fingers go to my pocket, where I tucked the device Watcher gave me. If he works for Scarlet, though, is this device even real?

I whip it out and press the button, hard.

Scarlet flinches immediately and sighs. "I told you, I didn't affect All-American Man."

"Forgive me if I don't take your word for it, since you plucked that worry right out of my head."

"Fair enough. But you're the one sneaking around one of *my* computer labs, so maybe let's just call it even?"

"One of?"

"You don't think this piddly little office is the extent of my security, do you?" Scarlet cocks an eyebrow, and something about the combination of the sarcasm on her face and the fact that she thinks this high-tech spread is still *piddly* makes my legs tremble.

"There's more?" I ask, hungry. I can't believe how quickly this side of me has sprung back to life. It's aching for nourishment, for tech and info and to experiment with various integrations of bio-adaptations and new developments—

Scarlet nods, grinning. "Maybe I'll show it to you later. If you're a good girl."

Oh, god, that's not even fair.

"How do I know you're telling the truth? About Ari." I point at the screen.

"Because I didn't even know All-American Man was in the area, let alone care to take him down. Fallon has the beef with him; not me. I've got my own demons, and while I may care about Fallon, there's a code in Elysium: we don't take responsibility for each other's enemies. You want to take down your nemesis? You gotta do that shit on your own. Don't make someone else bear your grudges."

I frown at her, doubtful, and she shrugs.

"If you still don't believe me, you can ask Persephone. She'd bring down all hell on anyone caught breaking one of the few rules Elysium has."

"So maybe you did it, but you don't want to get caught."

"Persephone has ways of getting the truth out, believe me. There's no *not getting caught* here. I'm not dumb enough to help Fallon on his revenge quest, and he wouldn't ask it anyway." She points at the screen. "Your boyfriend tried to kill you all on his own, sunshine. You know that now. So how about we put away my toys?"

Scarlet crosses the room to me and eases the keyboard out of my hands. Her fingers trail across the front of my shirt, grazing my nipple through the thin fabric, and my pussy instantly spasms.

She did that on purpose. I can see the glint in her eye.

I triggered the signal that interrupts her mesmer abilities, so I know this attraction I feel is entirely from me. *I* want her. But not in the same way I want Fallon—this feels more raw, a purely primal attraction. Scarlet emits this air of sexuality with a firm line drawn in the sand. She's not for a relationship; she's just *sex*.

Her fingers fly across the keyboard and it takes me a full five seconds to remember to breathe again.

I glance up at the screen to see Fallon's flight videos disappearing. "Wait!"

Scarlet stops, but her look tells me she's only doing it because she *chose* to obey. "This is where I let Fallon upload shit when he needs a west coast base. I don't think he'd take kindly to you poking through his personal things."

"No, I mean—well, yeah, I think he probably wouldn't like it either, but—bring the videos back."

There's a long pause. I think Scarlet might protest.

But she hits a button, and the videos pop back up.

"That one," I say. "That's—he kept that video?"

Scarlet chews the inside of her cheek. "I really don't think he'd like me showing that to you."

My throat goes dry. The date of that video ...

That's the day Ari almost killed him. The fight where All-American Man broke the Raven's wings and left him for dead in a canyon not far from here.

"Scarlet." I look at her, something dark and anxious welling in my gut. "How bad is it? What Ari did to him."

She props her hip on the table next to me. After a long moment of consideration, her blue eyes flashing over my face, she squints and types out something on the keyboard.

The videos vanish again, but in their place pops up a series of X-rays.

All the breath whooshes out of my lungs. They're wings. Fallon's wings. Well, his left one—the right suffered mostly just cuts and scrapes, so there's only one close up of it. But that left wing has X-rays from a dozen different angles, spread out over a number of weeks. Months, even.

"He recovered here," Scarlet tells me, but I can't bring myself to look away from the screen. "All-American Man shredded the tendons attaching his left wing to his spine. He's lucky he can even walk, let alone fly as well as he does. I tried everything—surgery, therapy, surgery again. But what All-American Man did isn't just unfixable. It's—"

"Cruel," I finish. My fingers are in fists on the computer desk, shoulders hunched and temperature rising with every rasping inhale.

Ari did this.

Ari did this.

And suddenly, it doesn't matter whether he was affected by something during the car crash. Because *he* inflicted this pain on Fallon, a pain that goes beyond just self-defense. This was premeditated. Intentional. And he knew damn well he'd done it—I remember how he'd acted after that fight. Forlorn, in a resigned way, as though it had to be done; and also smug. He and his boss, Malcolm, had shared grins any time someone mentioned the Raven.

"That bird won't be flying anymore," Malcolm had said, and Ari had *laughed.*

I'd snuck into this room to confirm if I should make this deal with Persephone, to do whatever it takes to become enough to bring Ari down.

This is confirmation enough. He needs to be *stopped.* He needs to pay for what he did to Fallon, and to me, and to whoever else he's hurt in the name of Heroes Org justice.

For once, though, I take a beat, and actually think about what it would look like if I let Persephone make me into a super. Someone who could kill All-American Man.

I'd fight him. I'd murder him.

And the country would still mourn their favorite Hero, their golden boy, their savior. His movie premiere next week is testament enough to their love of him—they'd immediately take his side and paint me the Villain, and even if I was bound to Persephone after this, I'd still forever be an enemy of *goodness* and everything Ari supposedly stood for.

Maybe Fallon is right. This isn't the way to bring Ari down.

To destroy a god, you don't just kill him. You make him bleed, and let everyone see that he's no god at all.

I touch the computer screen, my finger on Fallon's X-ray, the severed tendons making me ache.

"I have an idea," I whisper to the computer. "Two ideas, actually."

Scarlet makes a soft moan of interest. "Oh?"

When I look at her, she must see the change in me. One corner of her lips lifts, but she stays silent.

"First ..." I wave at the computer stuff. "What do you have in the way of biomechanical equipment?"

She laughs. Sharp and loud. "You're joking, right? Have you seen Watcher?"

Hope floats through me. "I think I—we, if you'll help—can make a brace for Fallon." I point at the X-ray where his tendon should connect to his spine. "It won't heal—you've established that. I can create something that simulates his own tendon, but supplements for the muscle and tissue damage. For one of my projects at MIT, I was on a team responsible for developing and testing prosthetic limbs. It'd be like that, only smaller scale, more localized. Not a whole wing. Just—" I trace my finger around the affected area. "—these muscles, these tendons, a bone or two."

Scarlet leans in, her face gone serious, and she's even more beautiful all studious and focused.

"Well, shit," she hisses at the screen. "A full year I've been trying to rehabilitate him, and you come in and solve it in a day." She flicks her eyes to me and grins. "No wonder he's so smitten with you."

"Smitten?" But my pulse races.

"Smitten. Enamored by. Totally obsessed with fucking. Pick your descriptor." Scarlet leans back. "What's your other idea?"

"Ah." Now all my hope and arousal twists sharply. "When does Persephone get here?"

Scarlet drops the keyboard onto the desk. "Twenty minutes ago."

"I—she's *here*? Already? Like in the flesh or waiting in a dreamscape?"

"Oh, she came herself, for something as big as a mortal making a deal with her. Why do you think I was looking for you? You can't sneak around in a mesmer's house, by the way. Not without activating *that*." She points at the device in my pocket. "Which you didn't until very recently."

Anxiety overtakes everything else. Sweat slicks my back and I run my hand through my hair, dried from my shower now and falling in soft waves around me.

"All right. And Fallon?"

"With her in my harem."

"*What?*"

"Not *with her*—Christ, you gotta chill." She winks at me. "Especially if you keep catering those naughty thoughts about me. How can you expect him to not get turned on by other people, too?"

I don't expect that. I don't *want* that. I just ... I don't know what I want.

But I do know what to do about Ari.

"Take me to them?" I ask. "And after ... help me with that brace for Fallon?"

Scarlet's face darkens. "If you're going to agree to Persephone's deal, sunshine, I'm not sure there will be an *after*."

"Don't worry," I say, but I'm anything but *not worried* myself. "I know what we need to do."

11
FALLON

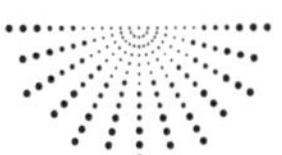

Persephone reclines on Scarlet's throne. The harem is empty now, save for the two of us. Persephone seems perfectly at ease, but my entire body is tense.

I wanted to talk to Lillith before Persephone got here. I wanted to—fuck, I don't know. Beg her to call off the deal. Do whatever it took to make her see that this revenge wasn't worth it.

The irony twists me up. A year ago, no one could convince me *my* revenge wasn't worth it.

Not until I realized I had far more to lose than myself.

"Ah," Persephone says idly. A second later, the door to the harem opens. Lillith strides in first, determined. Her eyes skim over Persephone, landing on me, and even from here I see the secret smile playing on her lips. Scarlet strolls in after, an appreciative leer smeared across her face as she watches Lillith's ass. Her expression turns into a scowl when she sees Persephone draped over her seat, but Scarlet doesn't object as she approaches.

"I have been patient with you, mortal," Persephone tells Lillith. "But I expect a decision." There's an implied *"now"* in her voice.

Lillith nods and lets out a shaky breath. She had walked with such forceful determination, but now that she's in front of Persephone, she seems a little scared.

"Lillith, you don't have to—" I start, but my words die as Lillith glares at me. My mouth closes with such force that my teeth clack together.

This is between her and Persephone.

I may want to swoop down and fly Lillith off somewhere safe, where neither Persephone nor Ari can make a claim on her, but ...

It's not my place.

It's *her* decision. Her choice.

And I have to let her make it.

Persephone's smile spills across her face, red lips curving salaciously, her eyelids drooping with anticipated pleasure. "My dear Lillith," she says, "are you going to be, truly, *mine?* I'll give you everything you want."

At the cost of her soul.

Lillith squares her shoulders. My heart beats so loud in my chest that I almost can't hear her answer:

"No."

Persephone cocks an eyebrow. "No?" she asks, drawling out the word.

Lillith says it again, clear. "No. I don't want to take the deal."

Persephone's gaze sharpens. "You no longer burn with revenge," she says, a statement, not a question.

I whip my head around to Lillith. What changed in one evening to shift her so dramatically?

"I don't," Lillith confesses. "At least ... not against Ari."

"You don't want to kill the man who tried to kill you?" I say, unable to bite back my words.

"This is a good thing," Scarlet says, cutting her eyes at me. "Remember? We don't want your little sex toy to burn up from the inside in an all-consuming rage of self-destructive violent revenge. Or at least, I thought that was the goal?"

"I'm not a sex toy!" Lillith snaps.

"And I don't want her enslaved for revenge," I say, my voice rising at Scarlet. I turn to Lillith. "But what changed?"

"I think Ari ... I think he's being controlled."

"Controlled how?"

"Like with powers similar to Scarlet's. By a mesmer. Not her, but someone ..."

"Those powers are rare," I say. Not unheard of, but not common.

Lillith's eyes are alight with possibilities. "I know, but that look on Ari's face when he unfastened my seatbelt ... he wasn't in full control. And I think—"

She cuts herself off, but from the look in her eyes, the way her gaze flicks to my wings, I can guess her thoughts. Does she think maybe someone forced Ari to break my wings? Fury boils in my chest. No. I saw the malicious glint in Ari's face. I saw the way he reveled in my destruction.

No, that fucker is still going to pay. Besides ...

"A mesmer cannot *fully* control another person," Scarlet says. "No mesmer is that powerful. They only amplify desire."

"Which means," I growl, "Ari may not have been in complete control, but he had to at least be going along with whatever puppet master it was that took over him and tried to kill you."

Lillith frowns, processing this. Ari may not have ever actually acted on his darker rages—my wings, her death—had he not been influenced by a mesmer. But he at least had to have wanted her out of his life.

"Why did he propose?" Lillith asks quietly. "He could have just broken up with me." She shakes her head again, trying to clear her mind.

But fuck—she's right. There's something ... off ... about the whole thing. Something's not adding up.

Ari's still a fucking asshole, though, that much is for sure.

But if these doubts keep Lillith from binding herself to Persephone, it's enough for me.

I look over at Persephone. Ever since Lillith started talking about a possible mesmer, she's been silent. Her eyes are narrow, sharp. Her painted lips are tight; her jaw is clenched. Lillith's words have an impact on her, that much is clear. I watch as Persephone takes her bottom lip in her white teeth, biting it in concentration.

Something's not right here ... I think again. Persephone's powers are among the strongest in Elysium, and she's been around as long as I can remember. She knows more than she's letting on.

"But also," Lillith continues, and my attention diverts to her. "I do still want vengeance for all this. I don't want to kill Ari, not if he wasn't actually in control of his actions and was at the mercy of someone else. But you're right—he has done some horrible things, and he keeps getting away with it because everyone in the world sees him as some golden-boy superhero."

"So what's the plan, sunshine?" Scarlet asks.

Lillith meets my eyes, and there's fire there, a passion unquenchable that fills me with lust. "I think Fallon is right. We have to get him where it hurts. Ruin his rep. He's spreading this tale about how I'm a victim of

Fallon. Let's let the whole world see how very much I enjoy being with him."

"I'm not exactly the kind of guy to go to fancy dinner parties and use you as a trophy," I say.

Lillith blushes, and fuck—I didn't mean to imply she was nothing but a trophy to Ari. I open my mouth to apologize, but she shakes her head. She's mad at him, not me, at least.

"No, I don't plan to be paraded around like a thing," she says.

Scarlet's lips curl up. "I like where this is going."

"What about a sex tape? Of Fallon fucking me to oblivion, proving that I'm not some kidnapped victim?"

Oh, this is a plan I love.

"It would be hard to release it wide," Scarlet says. "Any film evidence with a Hero in Heroes Org gets *quickly* taken down." She shoots me a look —we both know that Heroes Org does *everything* to protect the reps of their people. I've tried to get proof to the public of Ari being a psychopath for more than a year.

"So we don't release it to the world," Lillith says. "We hack the movie premiere next week, so Ari sees it instead of some bloviating propaganda film he's made to tell lies about how awesome he is."

I can't keep my low whistle of appreciation from escaping. All-American Man loves his image as being crystal clean and above reproach, but he also loves the idea of everyone being in love with him. Proving that Lillith left him of her own free will for dick far superior to his own is the perfect twist of a knife straight into his image.

"I'm in," I say, my voice already raspy with desire.

"You can use my dreamscapes to practice," Scarlet adds, her lips curling up. "I assume you'll need rather a lot of practice before your major film debut."

"And I," Persephone says, her voice dripping with power, "am not amused."

We all whip around to her, fear settling over us at her chilly tones.

"I came all the way from Elysium for this deal," Persephone says, standing up from the chair on the raised dais. She strolls down the steps toward Lillith. "I am not leaving empty handed."

Lillith's eyes are wide with fear, but Scarlet smirks at me. Lillith isn't used to Persephone's raw power. I stride forward, slipping my arm around Lillith. "Don't worry," I say, the words low, just for her.

I turn to Persephone. "I believe we could find a way to make it worth your time," I tell her. My hand slips down Lillith's arm, my thumb over her racing pulse. "Persephone is ... energized by high emotions," I tell her. "Do you think the two of us could, perhaps, help her have some *very* high ... sensations ... as thanks for offering her services?"

Understanding alights in Lillith's eyes. She starts to nod, and Scarlet smiles.

A moment later, Lillith, Persephone, and I are in a dreamscape.

"Scarlet does know what I like," Persephone says, looking around. This dreamscape is designed for Persephone's pleasure—it resembles a room at Elysium. Dark stone flickers with firelight from the enormous hearth. A puffy white fur is spread out in front of the flames. Nearby, a golden chair stands regally by a window, through which stars and moonlight shine. This could be a medieval castle.

And Persephone is, no doubt, the queen of it. Her long hair is piled up on her head, a golden crown encircling her braids. She wears a long emerald gown made of silk that clings to her skin. With graceful, easy steps, she drapes herself across the throne.

Her eyelids are heavy with expectation as she waves her hand at Lillith and me.

We are to begin.

She is to watch.

I cross over to Lillith. Her gown is far simpler than Persephone's, but it's white, edged in gold, cut so low that her breasts are in danger of spilling out of them. I glance down at myself—Scarlet's never been that great with male clothing, and my plain black pants don't quite fit the scene.

Best to just get rid of them.

But first, Lillith. She's trembling—with anticipation, not fear. I step closer to her. "Persephone is right there," I whisper, loving the way my low voice makes goosebumps prickle on her bare arms. "And Scarlet's watching, too." We cannot see the mesmer, but I know she's there.

"We better get all the practice we can get," Lillith says. "Rehearsals start now, and we need to give the people quality entertainment."

"Mm."

A wicked smile lights up her whole face.

"But remember—our safe word works here, too," I say. I make sure she meets my eyes. "Persephone wants a show, but only if you want to give one."

"I do," Lillith says, and as soon as the words are out of her mouth, I grab the white gown at her shoulders and rip it down. The material shreds easily, parting down the middle and wafting off her body like dandelion fluff.

Lillith shivers.

"You like this, don't you?" I say, drawing her closer to me. "You love that there are others watching. You want the whole fucking world to watch."

Her arms go around my body, her fingers playing in the downy feathers at the base of my wings. I go blind with desire for a moment, the pants far too constraining. With a growl, I yank them off—at least Scarlet makes clothes easy to dispose of.

My cock springs forward, already dripping with desire. Lillith slides a hand from my back, around my hip, gripping my cock, rubbing a thumb over the head. I groan, wanting nothing more than to plunge into the sweet warmth of her, but no. No.

We have a show to put on.

I lean down and swoop my arm under Lillith's knees, easily lifting her and turning to the huge white rug in front of the fireplace. I see Persephone, watching from the shadows. I spread Lillith out in front of her, like an offering, her legs splayed so that Persephone has full view of Lillith's cunt, wet and aching to be filled.

Instead of fucking her with my cock, I slide down Lillith's body. "Fallon," she gasps, leaning up, but I've already plunged my face down, tonguing her clit with the force of my desire. It's not gentle kisses; I do not build up the pleasure. I work her clit around my tongue with the urgency that I have felt all night long, sucking and swirling, bringing her right to the edge of orgasm immediately.

She screams my name, fingers clawing at the white fur. I should do this slowly, I know I should, but her passion makes me move faster. I prop one elbow up and use my other hand to explore her depths, pushing two fingers deep inside her. Her body clenches around me, tight, and my cock vibrates with need.

Before I can do anything else, I feel long, cool fingers gliding down my back, in the spot between my wings.

Persephone has come to play.

I don't stop fucking Lillith with my tongue. Her hips buck, her legs clench, and she gasps with pleasure.

Persephone's hands glide over my ass. I feel her settle down behind me, her palms sliding down my legs, back up, moving up my thighs. She straddles one of my legs. Her gown is gone—I feel her wet pussy on my leg as she grinds into me.

I moan, the sound vibrating up Lillith's clit, as Persephone reaches through my legs and grabs my dripping cock. I fuck Lillith with my fingers hard, my strokes matching Persephone's as she pumps me. Lillith writhes on the fur, screaming from pleasure, and it drives me even harder. I withdraw my fingers, using both my hands to lift her hips up to my lips and feasting upon the hot sweetness of her.

And then I feel Persephone shift, slipping under me. Her lips go around my cock and I lose my goddamn mind. I roar with desire, tonguing Lillith so hard that her entire body spasms with desire fulfilled. She turns to liquid in my hands, her body satiated, but I'm not done.

Persephone glides her tongue around my cock, swirling along the head. I glance down at her—I'm straddling her, my balls bumping against her bare, luscious breasts. Her eyes are hungry as she sucks harder, urging me to thrust into her throat.

Lillith gets to her knees, watching as Persephone sucks. My body is rigid, hard as my cock, but I don't want to get off, not yet.

Lillith crawls over to me, breasts swinging, her eyes limpid and heady with want. She moves down Persephone's body, and I arch backward, straining to see what my girl is doing.

Lillith crouches between Persephone's legs, flicking her tongue out and drawing it up in one long stroke right up Persephone's slit.

Beneath me, Persephone coils up tightly. Her teeth brush the sensitive skin of my cock, and I almost lose it right there.

And then she *hums*. Persephone makes a throaty noise, deep inside her, vibrating up my cock and through her as Lillith lovingly and carefully licks her pussy. I can't focus on anything more than Persephone's lips on my cock, but Lillith's lips are on her cunt, and the mere *idea* of it drives me fucking wild.

And not just me. Persephone stops sucking me, too pleased to think of anything but the need coiling inside her. I watch her, my cum dripping off her red lips. My cock is still rock hard, ringed with her red lipstick, and that is so fucking hot. Persephone's lips are gasping in hot, heady moans, her shoulders sliding across the white fur, her hair splayed out in front of her.

I carefully lift up off her, using my wings to steady myself. Persephone writhes, her dark nipples taut, her fingers clawing at the white fur as

Lillith's hands glide up her flat stomach, gripping her hips for a better angle at her pussy.

My girl is so fucking *eager*. She's on her knees, bent over Persephone's cunt, her ass straight up in the air as she licks with vigor.

An effort that good deserves a reward.

I move around to Lillith's back, grabbing her hips with my hands. She leans into my touch as I thrust into her cunt, ramming into her with such a strong force that her face buries into Persephone's pussy. I see Lillith's fingers tighten on Persephone's hips, but she doesn't stop—she licks just as hard, matching my strokes into her.

But this time, it's Lillith who gives way to pleasure as I drive into her, right to the hilt. Her whole body coils with want, and I give it to her. I pound into her, hard, her hair flying. She's screaming again, gasping my name, already starting to fall—

And then Persephone languidly turns to her. She reaches up between us both, cupping my balls a moment before gliding a finger around the base of my cock, slippery with Lillith's wetness.

Persephone doesn't stop. Her fingers move up Lillith, gliding through her delicate folds to find her pulsing clit. I pound into Lillith as Persephone's gentle, cool fingers swirl her clit around.

Lillith cannot keep her orgasm in check. Her entire body clenches around mine. She sobs into Persephone's shoulder as her body releases, and still Persephone works her clit, her fingers riding that wave of pleasure.

Spent, I look down at them. Lillith, now sated, goes limp in Persephone's arms. She's dripping, Persephone on her lips, me in her cunt. And when she looks up at me, eyelids heavy, she looks completely and utterly *satisfied.*

12
LILLITH

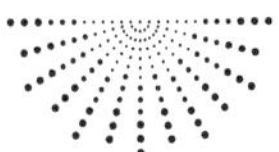

I WAKE UP BACK IN THE ROOM WATCHER GAVE ME. FOR A MOMENT, I LAY still, reveling in the last beats of the singularly most amazing dream I've ever had—

Until I feel an arm around my waist, and I realize I'm naked on these silk sheets.

It wasn't a dream.

I turn, honestly not sure who I'll find with me—and *god,* my pussy instantly cinches at that. It makes me feel untamed in a relentless way, freedom incarnate. Who is in my bed? Persephone? Fallon?

I roll over to find Fallon asleep, one arm crooked under his pillow, his chest rising and falling in a kind of deep, soundless sleep that makes him look utterly peaceful.

A grin cuts across my face and I press my hands to my lips, holding in a squeal. I should be focused and firm—I'm here to bring down Ari. But, god, I feel more *me* than I have in years, and I can't not be elated by that.

I press a kiss to Fallon's cheek and slip out of bed, careful not to disturb him. After a quick shower—my body is battered still, from the car crash and now the subsequent, glorious fucking—and another new set of those black clothes from Edna, I scribble a quick note to Fallon.

With Scarlet. Find me when you're awake.

Last night was fucking mind-blowing. Wanna do it again?

Lilly

I pause.

Then I scratch out *Lilly* and write *Lillith.*

I'M ONLY a few steps out of my room when Scarlet comes sauntering down the hall toward me.

"This way," she says and angles her head for me to jog alongside her.

"Where are we going? I was hoping we could start on Fallon's brace for—"

"Why do you think I came to get you, sunshine?" Scarlet grins at me.

I touch the mesmer interrupting device in my pocket. I haven't pushed it yet. But if we're going to work together, build this mechanism for Fallon, it might be easier if she can, actually, read my mind.

Scarlet leads me through her twisting labyrinth of a home, deeper than I've been in it yet. This whole place extends well into the side of the canyon, with occasional glass panels showing the cut stone just for artistic flare. We even pass an indoor waterfall, cascades of water flowing over smooth red stone before vanishing into the floor.

We reach a set of metal doors that Scarlet opens with a quick swipe of a bracelet on her wrist. Beyond it is ... utopia.

Fucking *utopia,* Christ god almighty, I need to sit down—

Rows and rows of tables hold computers, holograms, robots, gadgetry —everything tech, an R&D playground that has me standing there, mouth agape.

"Holy *shit,* Scarlet."

"You like it?"

"Holy *SHIT,* Scarlet!"

She beams at me and snatches a tablet from a table. A few other people are at various places throughout the room, doing their own experiments, but they pay little attention to us.

"I've downloaded Fallon's X-rays and medical records," she tells me, all business. "The worst damage is where the tendons connect to his T4 vertebrae."

I stumble towards the table I now see is spread with the sorts of things we'll need. Biotech targeted to medical purposes, prosthetic limbs and braces mostly.

My mind shifts. Refocuses. And suddenly I'm back at MIT, thoroughly enamored with my degree, my classes, this thrill of figuring out how to make science work for humanity in a way that will actually improve lives.

I grab the tablet from Scarlet and get started.

I HAVE no idea how much time passes. Watcher brings Scarlet and me food, steaming bowls of some kind of chicken soup that's so good I ask for more.

Eventually, I stop only to stretch my shoulders. I'd been bent over the prototype of Fallon's brace, testing the recoil of a different metal spring—and I see Fallon, sitting in the corner of Scarlet's lab, watching me with a weird glint in his eyes.

I instantly flush. Scarlet's busy muttering to herself as she types an endless string of the code that'll go in the brace.

I slip out from behind our table and cross the room to Fallon.

"How long have you been here?" I ask.

"Long enough to be completely confused."

"Did Scarlet tell you what we're doing?" Heat rises up my neck. I realize—*I* hadn't even told him. I hadn't really intended for it to be a surprise, but if it doesn't work, I don't want to get his hopes up.

Even so, he should be part of this. It's his body, after all.

"No, but that's not what I'm confused about. I mean, don't try to explain the mechanics to me, I beg of you." Fallon holds up his hands in surrender. "Confused about why the *fuck* you haven't been doing this all along? About why you ever quit?"

I tuck my hair behind my ears just for something to do. Fallon must sense my nervousness—he jumps to his feet and takes my hands, his lean fingers threading with mine.

"I shouldn't have," I whisper. "I see that now. I shouldn't have let him take this from me." It hurts too much, still, to think about the time I lost to Ari. But I smile up at Fallon. "Come here and see what we're working on."

Fallon follows me to the table where Scarlet furiously clacks away on the keys.

"Not done yet," she chirps. "You'll have to come back later for the test run."

"Test run?" He eyes me, and his trepidation is so fucking adorable that I kiss him.

"Don't trust me, Raven?" I whisper against his mouth.

He grows, a low rumble, and hooks his finger into the belt of my pants.

"Save it for later," Scarlet says and thwacks my shoulder with a pencil.

"We're making a brace for you," I tell Fallon.

He pulls back a beat, honest confusion passing over his face.

"Scarlet's tech is *amazing*," I say. "Light years ahead of even the stuff at MIT. And we've come up with a brace that should simulate the muscles and tendons that Ari damaged."

I wave my hand at the absurd looking contraption on the table. It vaguely resembles the shape of a wing, with spindly extensions and movable joints that'll support his damaged ones. It's light, due to the alloys Scarlet had—he shouldn't even feel it once it's on.

Fallon's eyes are huge. He stares at the brace before flipping his attention back to me.

"You designed that? For me?"

My throat swells. Is he pleased? Horrified? Did I embarrass him by assuming he'd want his girl—am I his girl?—to help him? Ari would've been disappointed, but it honestly didn't even occur to me that Fallon would be anything but happy.

I rethink everything in the seconds that stretch between us.

Then he dives at me, scooping my face in his hands, kissing me so deeply that I arch backwards, mewling into his mouth.

"Fuck, Lillith," he whispers into me. "What did I do to deserve you?"

"You like it?" I hate how small my voice is, but I can't fully get rid of my unease.

"Like it?" He kisses me again. "Yes. *Yes*. I just—*yes*."

I throw my arms around his neck. He grabs onto my ass, and I think he's about to sit me on the table, fuck me right here in this laboratory, when Scarlet loudly clears her throat.

"If you're going to do *that*, maybe take it to my harem, hm?" She's half eyeing us, half working still.

I twist towards her while Fallon nips down the side of my neck. God, I'm spinning, and every inch of me is ready to tear his clothes off.

"You're—you—ah, fuck—you're going to keep working?" I manage.

Scarlet grins. "Just because I'm not in the harem to give you dreamscapes doesn't mean you can't still have fun there."

"Or your room," Fallon says into my ear. "Your body, splayed out on that bed—"

"Who else is in the harem right now?" I ask Scarlet.

She cocks an eyebrow. "A few couples. People still like to use its toys even when I'm not there, like I said. Watcher provides other ... arrangements."

I turn to face Fallon. "We need to practice, don't we?" I bite his ear. "We need to make our fucking look as goddamn believable as possible."

We only have four days until Ari's movie premiere. That's something else Scarlet and I need to work on: hacking the premiere's screen to broadcast Fallon fucking me to everyone in that theater.

Heroes Org. Ari's boss, Malcolm. Every spineless yes-man who let Ari strip me down to nothing over the years and watched as I became less and less of a person. All of their eyes fixed on me, writhing under the Villain Ari supposedly defeated a year ago.

And Ari, at the center of it, knowing with just one look that his girl willingly left him to fuck his nemesis.

A tingle of need rushes through me. Sweet and succulent and so visceral I stroke Fallon's hard cock through his jeans.

He moans. "What are you suggesting, sweetheart?"

"I want you to fuck me, in the harem, in front of everyone," I tell him. "*Now*."

THE HAREM LOOKS THE SAME, but it's definitely got a different vibe.

The booths and alcoves still hold couples enthralled in one another, but now, everyone is very aware of the fact that they're *here*. A man with a glowing orb in the center of his chest leans back in a velvet chair while a woman sucks his cock. A different man holds himself and two other people suspended in mid-air, the three of them fully dressed but pulsating to a slow beat emanating from overhead speakers. Other couples sit at tables, nursing drinks from the bar at the back of the room, but the thing that draws my focus the most is the display of toys now propped in the middle of the room where Scarlet's throne once was.

Handcuffs. Whips. Chains. Dildos. Cockrings. A whole array of every kind of sex toy imaginable, with Watcher next to the display, handing out toys as people approach him. He has a tablet in one hand, and he checks things off on a screen before directing people to a hall behind him.

I walk up to him, my chest wound tight, Fallon's hand in mine.

"Fallon and I—"

"A room, Miss Giles?" Watcher looks at his tablet.

"A—room? I have a room already—"

"No. Here." He nods over his shoulder to the hall.

I glance at Fallon, who squeezes my hand, pulling it closer to run over his hard cock.

"For privacy," he tells me, but the gleam in his eyes says he knows exactly what I'm going to ask Watcher.

"Watcher." I turn back to him. "What if we wanted ... an audience?"

I gesture at the man getting a blow job in plain view.

Watcher gives a small smile and waves at the room, the booths, the chairs and lounges. "We are at your disposal, Miss Giles."

I tug Fallon for the nearest free set up: a few padded chairs next to the bar. Three people sit at that bar, martinis in hand, and when I push Fallon down onto a chair, their attention swivels to me.

My pussy is instantly wet. My whole body feels electrified, knowing what will happen, how many eyes will be on me—and, even better than the dreamscape, knowing that I'll be able to *see* these eyes on me.

Fallon's wings drape over the back of the chair. He reaches up to me, fingers tugging at my belt buckle. "Lillith, your word."

"Crash." I hesitate. "What's yours? We never—"

He grins, feral. "Let's go with *catch*."

I bend to kiss him, tongue shooting into his mouth, tangling with his.

When I stand, I hike off my shirt, letting my breasts hang free.

The room silences, save for the steady pulsing music. Watcher lives up to his name, his yellow eyes fixed on me. The people at the counter twist in their bar stools for a better view. The man getting a blow job has finished, the woman reclined in a chair, and he sits with his chin in one hand, watching from behind tinted glasses. The trio of dancing people has descended, and they sit entwined at a booth now.

All eyes on me.

The sensation is too much. So taut and wrung out that I can't breathe—not with fear, but just with *feeling*, so much all at once—

Fallon reaches up to touch my face. "Lillith. Look at me."

My eyes drop to his.

And he smiles. "I'm here, sweetheart."

That's all I need. All I want.

No matter what happens, I know he'll catch me.

I strip until I'm naked in this harem room. Then Fallon's clothes are gone, too, and I straddle him on the chair. We're not in a dreamscape, but I momentarily wish we could go airborne again—once his brace works, we will. Maybe even for the sex tape—we'll fly through the California sky, fucking right over Ari's head.

That shouldn't thrill me as much as it does.

I grip the back of Fallon's chair. His back is to the room, which gives me the best view; I can see every eye on me. Every appreciative lip bite. One woman at the bar has her legs spread, her fingers playing with her own pussy as she watches me.

Fuck, *fuck*—

I grab Fallon's cock and slide down onto it, slowly, achingly, taking each inch at a time.

"Lillith," Fallon pants my name, his hands digging into my hips, trying to push me faster.

"I'm in charge," I tell him, but my eyes are on the woman fingering herself. At a booth across from me, the man from the dancing trio has his cock out, and one of the women strokes it, up and down.

I match those strokes. Slow, rhythmic, my eyes locked with that man's, and I can see the exertion on his face, the restraint and building ecstasy.

I grip Fallon's hair and tug his head back to kiss him, my breasts rubbing against him. He pulls away to suck one nipple into his mouth, gently grazing his teeth over the tip, his hand plucking at my other one, twisting it, squeezing.

The man getting stroked—the woman with her fingers deep in her own pussy—they watch, and gasp, sweat beading. The man reaches down the shirt of the woman stroking him, freeing her breast from her low cut neckline, and he circles his thumb around her round, pink nipple until her eyes roll back in desire—exactly matching what Fallon does to me. The woman fingering herself peels the strap of her dress down to expose her own breasts, and I choke to see clamps on her nipples already, toys from Watcher's display. She tugs on one and moans so loudly I almost come right then.

It's like my own sensations feed theirs, and vice versa. It's like we're all part of this, tangled together in bliss, and every nerve is on fire, every inch of me *alive*—I feel like I could explode through my skin, rocket around this room, light up the sky.

My breathing is too hard, too fast. I thrust up and down, up and down—

Fallon lifts his head to look at me. "Lillith?"

"Fallon—"

"Are you all right?"

How can he tell? Just looking down at him centers me, and I kiss him, our tongues mingling.

"Yes. Yes, I'm—*fuck*." I can't put words to it.

It's so *right*.

It's everything.

He is everything.

And suddenly, even though the room is packed, even though I'm attuned to the growing releases of everyone here, all that matters is Fallon. The way his dark eyes snap onto mine makes my chest well with longing for him, for more of this, more of that pureness when he'd kissed me in the lab, more of ... *him.*

I kiss him again, and when he slips his fingers between us to pinch my clit between thumb and finger, I immediately come undone in his lap, crying out as the orgasm rips through me, head to toe. Fallon follows me over the edge, and moments later I hear the woman at the bar come in a shrieking fit; the man in the booth grunts and curses.

Fallon, sweat drenched, his lips in a blissful grin, takes the back of my neck and keeps my lips on his. "Lillith," is all he says, and it's all he needs to say for me to be utterly his.

13

FALLON

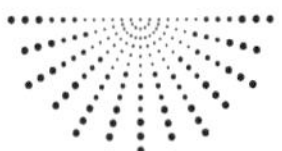

"We do have one problem, though," I say as Lillith curls next to me, her fingers twirling through the dark hair trailing down to my cock, up and down, just like the strokes she made, hard and fast. Shit. I can't think straight like this. I reach down and grab her hand, pulling her focus to my eyes instead.

"Problem?" she asks idly, her voice liquid.

"This tape we're making," I tell her. "You're right—this is going to hurt Ari more than me smashing his face in."

Her grin is wicked.

"But also?" I add. "We're going to need to do that one in private."

Her grin turns to a pout, and I want nothing more than to suck that lower lip of her into mine, nibble it until she's gasping and scrambling to ride me again.

"If this is going to hurt him," I say, my voice lower, "we've got to make him think that all you want is me."

It was hot as fuck, the way Lillith brought those other strangers into our fucking with nothing but their eyes on her. But I want Ari Dodgers to see Lillith with a hundred percent focus on me.

I want him to know, without a doubt, that it's my cock that makes his girl wet. That it's my fucking that makes her scream. And it's my body she worships.

Even if ... even if, when this is over, there's every chance she'll leave me.

Ari held her down for too long. I knew from the start Lillith was a caged bird who longed to fly free.

Of course, I won't lock her up.

But by god, I want to fuck her while I can.

From the slow, languid smile playing on her lips, I think Lillith likes the idea of hurting Ari almost as much as she likes the idea of getting other people off when they watch her. She stands slowly, pulling me up, and my cock is already hard again just at her look.

Our clothes are rumpled on the floor, but when Lillith bends to pick them up, I tug her closer to me.

"But," she says.

"We're at Scarlet's base," I say, grinning. "Clothes are always optional." Not just here in the harem, but everywhere.

Heat rises on her body, a natural instinct to cover fighting with her base desire to be seen. She nods, biting her lip, and fuck if I don't get even harder.

We don't run or try to hide. Lillith and I walk out of the harem, completely nude, as if it's a perfectly normal thing to do. But when her hand slides up my back, her delicate fingers playing with the downy feathers at the base of my wings, I almost grab her and fuck her against the wall.

But I don't.

I want her all to myself. At least this once.

I walk faster, and Lillith giggles. She knows exactly what she's goddamn doing. I slam into my room, grabbing her by the hips and pulling her inside before kicking the door closed.

She's flushed, her skin hot with longing, but the cool air of the base has her nipples hard enough to cut glass. I know they're extra sensitive, but I'm not gentle—my girl doesn't want gentle. I bite down, more pressure than a nibble, not hard enough to draw blood.

"Fallon," Lillith gasps, tilting her head back.

My name. She's gasping *my* name like it means something to her, and even if I know it doesn't I can pretend. My teeth move to her other nipple, and she cocks a leg over my hip.

She's *dripping* with want. I can feel her sliding over my skin, the heat of her. With a growl, I throw her on the bed, my super-strength easily lifting her and tossing her to the silken sheets. She lands, legs splayed, laughing with the joy of it all, her eyes on me.

I spread my wings and soar over to her. Just a short burst of flight, designed to drive me with extra force right into her. Her gasp of surprise turns into a longing moan of desire as my cock fills her right to the hilt.

I lean back, relishing the feeling. It is a triumph.

Without withdrawing, I let my hands drift down to the place where we are joined. My hard cock is wrapped up in her soft warmth, but I find the little button of pleasure coiling within her. Her clit is hard and when I just graze over the surface of it with my fingers she gasps and her body clenches around mine.

I pull out—not all the way, just enough to comfortably stroke her clit, swirling into a circle, then drive into her again, hard, timing my rhythm between soft and slow and hard, sweet pressure. Lillith grinds her hips up, begging me for more, and I press down on her clit as I push into her. My orgasm is quick and draining, but she clenches around me, pulling every last hot drop into her, sighing as if I've delivered a feast right into her cunt.

I trace my hands from her hips, brushing over her skin, around her nipples, and she shudders, her whole body, from the top of her head right down to her pussy.

"Fallon," she says again, her eyes on me, only me. Her lip is red and swollen from how hard she's bitten it, and I drop a kiss on her, soft and sweet.

"Just like that," I say.

Her eyes show confusion.

"On the tape. Just like that. It will drive Ari fucking insane to see what I can do to you."

Her eyes shutter, hiding her emotion, and she pulls away from me. "Yeah," she mutters.

At that moment, the door opens.

"Scarlet, goddamn," I say, scrambling up and reaching for the sheets.

Scarlet, standing in the doorway, cocks an eyebrow at me. "What? You're getting shy now? Come on."

"Now?" I ask. I stride across the room to the closet, pulling out pants and a shirt. I glance back at Lillith. We left her clothes in the harem. Rather than be shy in front of Scarlet's smirking gaze, Lillith is grinning, her nipples hard again. I have no doubt she could go for another round right now. Instead, I pass her a shirt. My pants are going to be too large for her, but my shirt reaches almost down to her knees. She lets it fall over her shoulders and scoots off the bed.

No panties. Just my shirt. If she bent over, it would expose all of her.

Fuck, I'm getting hard again. I very much regret containing myself in these pants at all.

"It can wait for just a bit," Scarlet says, not needing to read my mind to know what I want.

"Fine," I growl. "What's so important?"

"I finished," Scarlet says, turning on her heel and heading deeper into her base.

I'm so focused on sex, all I can think of is to equate finishing with orgasming. But Lillith is smarter than me. "The brace?" she asks.

"Your plans were simple, and the foundation was solid. I set some of my biomechanical robotics up to speed the process."

An automatic door opens, and Scarlet steps inside her lab.

On the table in the center is a brace. A metallic skeleton outline of my wing, with tiny biomechanical enhancements to make up for the tendons All-American Man irrevocably ripped apart.

Lillith crosses the room, nodding in approval. She's in full-science mode, her brilliant brain calculating each element. "May I?" she asks Scarlet before touching the brace.

"Of course, it's your design."

Lillith lifts it up, then motions for me to turn around. Her touch on my back is light, and the brace itself weighs no more than a few feathers. I feel her fingers sliding over my skin, through my wings' feathers, but once adjusted, I don't really notice the brace at all.

But I notice the way it feels.

"Try it," Lillith whispers, stepping back. And I do. I throw my wings out, and they don't hurt.

They don't fucking hurt.

Across the room, a small motor whirrs as Scarlet uses a remote control to fully open the gallery windows. I take off running, heading straight for the open space, my wings tossed out.

I hurtle myself into the empty air.

And my wings catch me.

I *soar.*

I catch an updraft, my body rocketing up into the blue. *This* is what flight is, this is glorious, this is *everything*. I dip down, relishing the way the air glides over my body, my feathers.

It doesn't hurt.

Nothing hurts.

I whirl mid-air, looking back to Scarlet's base. There's Lillith, standing right on the edge of the open window, watching me, a huge grin plastered across her face. Her eyes are alight, her skin is glowing, she's a goddamn angel, even if I'm the one with wings.

Oh my fucking god, I think as my heart swoops, looking at her. *I'm falling in love with her.*

I kick up in the air, flying high, higher, an Icarus seeking the sun. Love? I can't *love* her.

But the emotions inside me now, they're well beyond mere fucking. I don't care about revenge.

I only care about her.

14
LILLITH

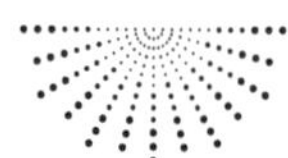

There are still a few tweaks Scarlet and I have to make to Fallon's brace—the read out tells us it doesn't respond as well as it should when he glides and dips left—but overall, it's perfect.

I can tell how perfect it is when Fallon lands back inside the lab. He's winded and panting, his face alight in the biggest smile I've seen from him yet. He looks years younger suddenly, unburdened by pain or revenge or—

That's it, I realize with a jolt.

He doesn't have that glint in his eye anymore. The one I knew meant he was always half stewing over how to destroy Ari.

Fallon just looks *free*.

I tentatively touch his wing, reaching through the feathers to disconnect the brace.

"How did it feel?" I ask, but I can already see the answer.

He waits until I set the brace back on the table before he grabs me under the arms and swings me in a wide circle. His euphoria soaks into me until I'm giggling right along with him, and when he stops, he catches my mouth on his.

"Thank you," he whispers into my lips, and I twine my arms around his neck to push my whole body into the kiss.

Thank you, I want to say. Thank you for letting me do this for you. Thank you for bringing me back. Thank you for saving me, not just from the car crash, but from my old life, that cage I didn't even really know I was in. I'm alive again, and it's because of you.

Fallon sets me down. "This calls for a celebration. Scarlet—I'm commandeering your kitchen."

From her computer, Scarlet whips a look up at Fallon and says, flat, "No."

"That wasn't a question."

"For Christ's sake, this time *clean up your shit,* Fal."

But Fallon's already halfway to the doors. "Can't hear you over the sound of the fresh fettuccine alfredo I'm gonna make."

"*You're* going to make?" I ask. I stay next to the worktable, but Fallon looks back at me with a wink.

"I think my girl deserves a special dinner," he says.

It connects, then. "Wait—*you* made those scones you left me?"

"Of course."

My legs go jelly-like and I drop onto a chair, Fallon's shirt hiking so my bare ass hits the seat. A final grin, and Fallon darts into the hall.

My god. On top of everything else, he cooks too.

Scarlet snaps her fingers in front of my face. "*Hello?* Shit, you've got it bad. Did you hear anything I said?"

I wince at her. "No. Sorry. I'm just—" I bite my lip.

But Scarlet gives me a look that says she understands.

"I *said.*" She points to the brace. "If you could plug it back into the terminal, I'll start coding the updates to—"

She stops talking mid-sentence.

Her eyes drift out, staring at something I can't see, a look of utter confusion scrunching her face.

Unease immediately washes through me and I fly to my feet. "Scarlet? What is—"

"We need to speak, Lillith Giles."

I whirl around.

Persephone stands in the middle of the lab. She's wearing the same severe black suit as before, but instead of emitting an air of allure, now she only looks fierce, every bit the Villain Queen Fallon alluded to.

My mouth goes dry. I'm suddenly very aware that I'm in nothing but Fallon's t-shirt, and even though I shouldn't feel self-conscious at all around Persephone, I find myself wishing I was more ... prepared?

Something about this feels intense.

Scarlet shoves out of her chair. She stands alongside me, maybe sensing I need some support.

"Should Fallon be—" I start to ask when Persephone shakes her head.

"It's you I need to speak with," she says, those all-seeing eyes on me. "When I was last here, you mentioned that you believed All-American Man had been influenced by someone to crash the car and kill you."

Is that a question? I nod either way.

"The accusation, had it been true, would have meant someone within Elysium had gone against our most cardinal rule."

I nod again. "Scarlet told me about that. No Villain can help another exact revenge."

Persephone nods. Her eyes flick around the lab, and she sighs, looking suddenly ... worried.

Oh, fuck.

"It was not one of my people who affected All-American Man," Persephone tells me. "It was, unfortunately, someone far worse. Someone I am unable to dole out punishment to."

"What?" Every muscle in my body clenches tight. "How—how do you know?"

She gives me a cold smile. "Do not underestimate my skill in tracing a super's powers. They emit signature trails, as your electronic devices do." She nods at the equipment behind Scarlet and me. "And this particular signature, when I knew to look for it ..." Her eyes snap to mine. "What do you know of Malcolm Odyssey?"

The name throws me back a full step. "Ari's boss? He's the CEO of Heroes Org. But he's basically a civilian. His powers—"

Persephone lifts one eyebrow, and that's all the contradiction I need.

I put a hand to my mouth, shock ripping through my whole body.

Malcolm Odyssey, in his prime, was one of the strongest Heroes in the world. His mesmer powers were so famed—and so feared—that just saying his super name, *The Hive,* was enough to send most Villains fleeing.

But the story at Heroes Org was that there was an attack. An unknown super with similar powers went up against him, leaving him stripped of his abilities, which was why he became the administrative head of Heroes Org instead of an active Hero.

Persephone looks away again, but not before I see the sudden wateriness in her eyes, the way she bites the inside of her cheek. "I never thought I'd pick up that trail again," she says, half a whisper.

"You," I gasp the word. "You were the super who defeated him."

Persephone looks at me side long, again not needing to say a word to give me a full answer.

Of course. She's the only super powerful enough to go against a mesmer of his reported strength.

But clearly, it wasn't enough.

"How?" I look at Scarlet, who has gone pale. "He doesn't have powers. Did they heal? How did he—"

"I'm still investigating," Persephone said. "I fear Malcolm's machinations run deeper than any have predicted. The implications of him reigning unchecked for these years ..."

She shakes her head, and I recognize the motion as self-deprecation; she blames herself for whatever Malcolm might have done. There's more to this story, and I'm overwhelmed by the need to ask her what, exactly, happened between her and Malcolm, how she fought him, what she did to strip him of his powers—or at least what she *thought* she did to strip him of his powers—

But Persephone fixes her gaze back on me. "I have much work to do. But I wanted you to know that your suspicions were correct. All-American Man was not in complete control of his body the day he tried to kill you. It is likely he has been at Malcolm's mercy more often than not. You, too, may have been affected during your time with Heroes Org."

I feel all the tension give way in my body. It's like a tap draining out, shock trading for horror.

Ari wasn't himself when he tried to kill me. But even so, a small part of him had to *want* to be rid of me. How small? Was he just regretting our engagement as much as I was? If Malcolm had gotten in my head, could he have twisted my doubts that much to make me try to kill Ari?

Are all of Ari's monstrous acts really Malcolm's fault?

Shit. He doesn't even *know*. He trusts Malcolm with his life, with his reputation, with his career, with *everything*.

"Thank you," I manage.

Persephone nods.

Then she's gone.

Scarlet instantly swings in front of me. "Hey? Are you all right?"

I blow air through my nose. "Oh, fantastic."

She squints. Is she really trying to read my mind right now? I reach for my pocket, but I left the mesmer device with my clothes in the harem.

She backs up. "Sorry. I just—don't do what you're thinking of doing, all right?"

"I'm not thinking of doing anything."

"Sure." She frowns at me. "I'm getting Fallon. He needs to hear this."

"Will it change things?"

My question stops her halfway to the door.

"It does, doesn't it?" I hear my voice go soft. "Ari isn't a vengeful murderer. He isn't ... evil."

Scarlet gives a sad smile. "Nothing is that black and white, sunshine. Wait here."

She brushes out the door, leaving me alone in the lab with my stewing thoughts and the soft whirring of the computer next to me.

My eyes go to that computer.

I think Fallon is already over his need for revenge against Ari. Giving him his flight back seemed to have healed him in ways no amount of destroying All-American Man's reputation could. And I'm healed, too, watching Fallon's joy, being here with him and getting to reawaken this side of me—it's enough. It really is.

Can we put aside our revenge plot? Can Fallon and I really just be *here*, the two of us, content with each other?

I sit in front of Scarlet's computer before I can talk myself out of it. The first thing I pull up is the local news—the headline proclaims *All-American Man's Fiancé Still Missing; Nation in Mourning as Hunt for The Raven Continues.*

My heart rate spikes. I tap my heel on the cold tiles, lip caught between my teeth.

Ari won't stop looking for me. Fallon and I won't be able to be together until he's not a fugitive and I'm not All-American Man's Fiancé.

And Ari won't really stop looking for me until he knows the truth.

I tear through Scarlet's files, hoping they link up to the downloaded videos of Fallon's flights. Luckily, they're all right here, along with his X-rays and medical records—she must've pulled everything into this system to help us with his brace.

I find the video of the car crash.

Then I use my rudimentary hacking skills to set up a secure email.

It isn't what you think, I type. *Do you even remember doing this to me?*

This isn't you. It's Malcolm.

Don't come looking for me, Ari. I'm finally free.

I attach the video and, fingers shaking, hit send.

15

FALLON

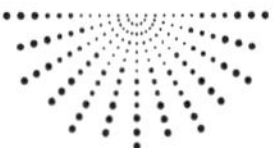

"WALNUTS, WALNUTS," I MUTTER, PEERING INTO THE CABINET.

"You looking for notes?"

Scarlet's voice is so unexpected that I thwack my head on the cabinet door. Cursing, I rub my bruised temple. "Do you have any?"

Scarlet narrows her eyes. "You are not violating fettuccine alfredo by adding *nuts*."

"It's a good combo!"

"No." There's a definitive quality to her voice, but then I see a package of raw walnuts near the back. I grab the bag and head to the stove. I hate that I don't have the right flour to make my own pasta, but at least the sauce is going to make up for the dried stuff. Parmesan, butter, cream—

"So, Persephone was here," Scarlet says.

"Fuck!" I say, jumping back. "You need to start with that, Scar!"

"And it looks like your arch-nemesis was being mind-controlled by none other than Malcolm Odyssey himself."

"What the—" I start. I shake my head, trying to clear it. "The Hive was decommissioned."

Scarlet arches an eyebrow at me. "You doubt Persephone."

"No—just. Whoa."

"Yeah." She leans over the counter. "Whoa. Also, by the way, pretty sure your girl is going to contact her old lover and tell him everything."

"Christ, Scarlet, what next?" I exclaim.

"She still thinks there's a chance there's good to him."

Fuck.

All-American Man really is the golden boy. And now that it's clear he's not secretly some psychopath, Lillith's going to choose him.

Why would she choose me, next to him?

I'm nothing.

Broken.

Rageful.

"You're spiraling," Scarlet says idly.

"Fuck, wouldn't you?"

"No." She sits on the counter, her ass too close to my butter. I swat her away, but I don't exactly feel like carbs right now. "I just program my men to be perfect. Much simpler that way."

Focus, Fallon, I think. *One thing at a time. Pasta first. Then I figure out what to do if ...*

If Lillith doesn't want me anymore.

What was I thinking, anyway? This has *only* ever been about getting revenge on Ari. Now that Lillith doesn't care about that much anymore, what's the point? She's going to walk right out the door, and I'll never see her again.

Except on his arm.

"Spiraling still," Scarlet says idly.

"Not all of us have cyborgs programmed to love us," I growl.

She pauses. "You could."

"Could what?"

"Could have Lillith programmed." She twirls her fingers. "She likes you, you know. It would be easy for me to ... *suggest* ... that she stay with you."

A part of me wants that. I just want her to be *mine*. Body and soul.

But that would make me Persephone.

And I'm not her.

"No," I say, spitting the word out. "No. She makes her own choices. It's ... it's what I want."

"Really?" Scarlet's expression is unreadable.

"Yes." No. I don't know. But the only thing I'm certain of—as much as I want Lillith to be fucking *mine*, forever, I want her to *choose* me. I don't want her in a cage, not in real life, not in her own mind. I want her free, and I want her mine. And if she doesn't choose me, well, at least I'll know that I never took away her choice.

If she wants Ari, she can have him.

If she wants no one, she can do that, too.

But if she wants me, I'll burn down the fucking world to have her.

Meanwhile, I'm not going to burn the food.

I slam a pan down on the gas flame. Scarlet makes no comment on the way I abuse her kitchen. But once the water's boiling for the pasta, she casually says, "It's not like that. With Watcher and me."

"I know," I growl. I do. Scarlet and Watcher are a pair—and Watcher's not some mindless robot there to do her will. I glance at her. "Sorry."

She nods, accepting my apology. "But also, the offer stands. Lillith could become a problem if she goes back to Heroes Org with All-American Man."

Fucking fuck. "Maybe I need an alliance. Someone to help me fight this."

"Not very Elysium of you."

She's right. I never would have thought of an alliance before, but now, with everything on the line, maybe I should. One final showdown to just fucking end it all, and leave Ari permanently behind us. Me. Us. "The Winter Warrior hates All-American Man, too, and he may ..."

"Good luck tracking him down."

I heave a sigh. "I don't know what to do, then, Scar, okay? Happy? If Lillith chooses to walk out the door right now, I'm not going to *force* her to stay. Not even if Persephone herself came down and tried to make me."

"All right, all right," Scarlet says, hopping off the counter as the water boils over the side of the pot. Steam hisses, and I curse, reaching for a cloth to sop up the mess.

"But you know where I am," she says. "When you change your mind, when you decide you want her no matter what the cost ... know that I could make her want that, too. And my deals? They're much better than Persephone's."

I spin around, whisk in hand, but she's already gone.

Across the room, a television clicks on. Scarlet's parting shot: a news segment. "Fuck you," I snarl at the picture of All-American Man standing in front of a podium.

"It's been days," he says, his voice deep and rich, "but I have not lost hope. Lilly, my love, I *will* save you!"

Ari Dodger's eyes plead with the camera. It's a touching moment, or it would be if it wasn't bullshit.

The live feed switches over to a reporter. While the doctored footage of the crash plays in the corner, the reporter gravely states the "facts."

That I'm a monster.

That I stole Lillith.

That I must pay, no matter the cost.

Everyone in the fucking country wants my blood.

16
LILLITH

I MAKE MY WAY BACK TO MY ROOM AND FIND MY CLOTHES FROM THE HAREM neatly folded on my bed. But when I go to put them on, I stop, and pivot to the armoire in the corner. Surely there's something a bit ... *nicer* in here than the skin-tight black shirts and pants.

My chest flutters like a hundred butterflies have taken flight. Something about this dinner with Fallon feels *big*. I want it to be big.

I want to ask him to let me stay. With him. I want to ask him to give up this revenge quest against Ari and just be with me.

I find a slinky red dress shoved into the back of the armoire. It's perfect—low-cut with a one-shoulder strap and a thigh-high slit that leaves the skirt floating around my calves. There's a pair of silver heels alongside some more basic shoes.

In no time at all, I'm dressed, my hair and makeup is done, and I'm a complete nervous wreck. Can Scarlet feel how terrified I am wherever she is in the base?

Yes, comes a monotone response. *Keep it down if you don't mind; I'm trying to fuck Watcher.*

That makes me burst laughter before I shuffle for the mesmer device in my old clothes.

"Will it work on you, wherever you are?" I ask the room.

Don't worry about it. I have my own ways of shutting up the particularly loud minds in my home, she tells me. *By the way, have fun tonight. You don't need to be nervous.*

I tuck the mesmer device down my cleavage. And pause. "What did he say? When you talked to him."

Ah-ah, nope, not getting in the middle of this, she says, but her tone indicates she *has,* somehow, already gotten in the middle of this. She's Fallon's friend first—I can respect that.

"Fine, fine. Go ahead and block my mind, cuz I'm going to stew some more."

Thanks for the warning.

Silence follows, so I assume Scarlet's raised some kind of block around me. All the better—I want to be clear headed.

If that's possible.

I leave my room, worrying my lip as I take the turns Scarlet told me earlier lead to the kitchen. Did I overdress? Probably. But I know I look hot as hell, which will help my argument that Fallon should give up his year-long revenge plot.

Only ... I don't want to have to *argue* with him. I want him to *want* to give it up, for me. I want to be enough for him.

Shit. What if I'm *not* enough for him? What if I've completely misread this whole situation, and he's only been in it for the sex and the revenge? I was the one who got to come out of my shell and fall back in love with a missing piece of myself—Fallon got a fuck-buddy and a wing brace.

I stop outside the kitchen door. There's a small port-hole window—through it, I can see Fallon bent over two plates of fettuccine, adding finishing sprinkles of what looks like parsley.

Every breath feels raw. Scraping my lungs like sandpaper. My stomach twists, watching him, seeing him in this totally innocent, domestic element.

I want this. I want him.

I'm putting so much of myself on the line here, in a way I've never felt before. What is this? Not just anxiety, not just nerves—

Fuck.

It's love.

I reach for the doorknob, but my chest contracts. I need to breathe. I need—I need *air*—

I stumble back up the hall, to where that helipad landing area was. The sliding doors swish open for me and a burst of evening air hits me, smelling of clay and summer's baked-in heat.

Get it together, Giles. You've been in love before.

Haven't you?

Fuck. Fuck, no I haven't. Not really. Not like this.

Oh my god.

Oh my *god.*

I've fallen in love with a Villain. And I have no idea how he feels about me.

I walk into the center of the helipad and tip my head back, breathing in as much air as I can. Okay. There's only one way I can end this torment, right? Just back in there and—

A *whoosh.*

A thump.

I whirl around, the itching sensation of being watched grabbing onto me before I can make sense of the shape that just landed on the helipad.

He rises up from his landing crouch, his vivid red cape a stark contrast to the orange canyons that rim the helipad, set aflame in the evening sun. His suit is red too, mixed with a patch of silver across his chest and a giant blue star right in the center. Patriotic colors for the most patriotic Hero.

Ari looks at me.

And smiles, his eyes tearing.

"Lillypad," he says, arms out like he expects me to run to him. "I knew you were alive."

I couldn't breathe before.

But I'm positively *choking* now.

I shake my head once, twice, and Ari closes the space between us to take me into his arms.

"My smart girl," he says into my hair. "How did you hack a Villain's system? You're so brave, Lilly. I'm so proud of you. But it's over now. I'm taking you home."

"Home?" I pull back to look up at him. "What? Ari—"

He finally seems to notice my dress. "What happened to you, Lilly?" His face darkens. "What did the Raven do to you?"

"Ari—"

"No, don't tell me. It's over now. It doesn't matter. We're leaving."

"Ari!" I shove against him. Again. He doesn't release me, and panic bundles into a tight knot in my stomach.

Scarlet—*Scarlet*—

But she blocked me. She won't hear me, and Ari isn't inside her base to trigger any alerts—

I punch at him, but he's looking at the sky. Nothing I can do would hurt him, anyway, and my panic grows claws, hacks through my body on a relentless tear.

"Ari! Ari, *stop—*"

Before I can do anything, before he even thinks to *hear me,* Ari has me lifted off the ground. We rocket into the sunset, Scarlet's base a pinprick beneath us, my screams muffled in the roaring wind.

17
FALLON

SOMETHING'S WRONG.

I put the fettuccine under a warming light—Scarlet's kitchen may as well be a restaurant's—and go looking for Lillith.

Her room, empty.

My room, empty.

The lab—not empty, but she's not there.

The harem—even less empty, but neither Scarlet nor Lillith are there. And neither is Watcher. Okay, then. Fine.

I go to the security room. Scanning the footage shows me that Scarlet and Watcher went to their own private suite, no doubt for some alone time. She enjoys shows and displays, but she's also selfish when it comes to her and Watcher, and the deep connection they share.

But where's Lillith?

Her rooms are empty now, but I rewind the controls. Scarlet has strict rules about letting people be private when they want to be private, so the fact that there are cameras on inside Lillith's bedroom mean that she's given permission to Scarlet for that to be the case. And little wonder, my girl likes to be seen.

I stop when I get to less than an hour ago—Lillith, in her room, changing clothes. She takes off the shirt I'd given her, pulling it over her head, exposing her bare body. I go instantly hard, and I want to get off to this image, but not yet. Not yet.

She must have forgotten about the cameras. She moves about the room unconsciously, and that just works to make me even harder. I know she'd get off on it too, if she knew. It's the secret, unknown eyes that excite her.

I'm hard again, and I long to release, but I have to focus.

I GASP and clutch the wall, curling my hand into a fist. Just seeing her practically gets me off. Christ, I have it bad for this girl.

I trace her movements through the screen—after she got dressed, she went in the corridor ... to the kitchen. She lingers by the door. From another screen, I see myself, waiting.

I zoom in on Lillith's face.

She looks like she's ... sad? Nervous? She opens her mouth to speak, but then she closes it. Walks away.

Up…

To the helipad.

There aren't any cameras out there—they're offline, I need to tell Scarlet that—but I scan the feeds from the other outdoor cameras.

And I see—

All-American Man, flying away. His red cape billows, but I still see Lillith—Lilly—in his arms.

"Fuck," I say, gutted.

I gave her a choice.

And she chose him.

EVENTUALLY, I stumble my way to Scarlet's private rooms. Few people know about her hidden suite, but Scar and I go way back, before Elysium.

The door's locked.

Go away, Scarlet's voice says in my mind. My skin grows flushed; my dick gets hard. Scarlet's inches away from orgasming in her private suites with Watcher, and that feeling infects her mesmer talk with me. I feel what she feels—aroused, hungry.

But I want Lillith, not this second-hand orgasm. The thought pushes the lust from my blood. "Scarlet!" I shout with both my voice and my mind.

"What?" The door to the suite opens. Scarlet rides Watcher, the cresting wave of desire broken by the distraction of my presence, but she doesn't stop the slow, steady rhythm. "What on Earth is so important you have to interrupt *now?*" she asks, glaring, not stopping her fucking.

"Lillith is gone," I say.

Scarlet pauses, but she doesn't get off Watcher's dick. She wiggles down, and the cyborg groans in pleasure. "Where?" she asks.

"She left with All-American Man," I say.

This gets Scarlet up. "What?" she snaps. She leaps off Watcher, off the bed, and grabs a silk robe, wrapping it loosely around her bare body. It does absolutely nothing to hide anything more than part of her shoulders and back.

"He came for her. Here. She must have told him to save her. And he did."

"She said nothing of the fucking sort," Scarlet snaps. Watcher—knowing what she needs without saying a thing—leaps to attention and grabs a control data pad from the table by the wall. Scarlet quickly scans through the feeds.

"You don't understand," I say. "I told her it was just about the fucking, the revenge. But it's not like I can compete with Ari Fucking Dodgers ..."

"Fal," Scarlet says, "shut up."

"She's gone, Scar."

"She's not."

"I saw her go!" I shout. "I saw All-American Man take her away!"

"Then *he* kidnapped her!" Scarlet screams at me. "Because that girl is head-over-heels in *love* with you, dumbass!"

I blink several times.

Scarlet uses my silence to turn to Watcher. "Contact Persephone. My security's been breached."

"On it, mistress," Watcher says, and he's gone.

Scarlet turns to me. "Listen, Fall. I know the truth, whether it's on security cams or not. She loves *you*. Not him. And she was going to tell you. If All-American Man took her, I guaran-fucking-tee it wasn't her going willingly."

My mind races to process this. I was so *sure* that I wasn't good enough for Lillith—fuck, I still know I'm not good enough for her, she's way out of my league—but if she loved me anyway ... if Ari came and just took her ...

"I have to save her," I whisper.

"Damn straight you do," Scarlet says. "Now, come on."

. . .

In Scarlet's lab, she quickly attaches my brace back over my left wing. "This is more than ready for you," she says. "Watcher's been running sims, and he's faster and more reliable than any computer."

"Thank you," I say.

"Don't thank me. Thank Lillith. When you get her back."

I nod tightly.

"Now, here's the real shitty part," Scarlet says, moving around the lab table to a glass case. "If Persephone is right—and she's *always* right—then that asshole in charge of Heroes Org is a super still. The Hive."

The Hive.

A name I never thought I'd hear again.

I don't even know how to counter someone like him.

"Fortunately, I do," Scarlet says, reading my mind.

She lifts out a helmet. It's fashioned almost like a Viking headband, with wings at the temple, but a thin, silver material stretches over the skullcap.

I lift it over my head.

And—silence.

I hadn't realized how much white noise existed in Scarlet's base, but this is true, utter silence.

"I can't hear you; you can't hear me," Scarlet says.

"I heard that."

"In your *mind,* smart ass." She taps the metal covering my head. "This blocks a mesmer's powers. It's not perfect, and it's not done, but this is short notice, so it'll have to work."

"Where did you even get it?" I ask.

"A loaner from a god."

"A god?!" I say.

Scarlet waves her hands dismissively. Sure, there are supers. May as well be gods, too.

Scarlet taps my head, reminding me of my eye tech, and she pre-loads in a GPS locator. "This is where Ari is?" I growl, glaring at the blinking red dot.

"It's where the red dress Lillith was wearing is," Scarlet says. She's wearing an Edna gown—they can be tracked. But it's not like we have GPS to everyone on the planet.

But if the dress is taken off ... Fuck. I'll lose her. I have to get to her as quickly as possible.

"Go, go," Scarlet says. She doesn't even push me to the door—she lowers the window to the lab. I take off, spreading my wings before the glass is all the way down, soaring out into the unknown.

Who would have guessed—the Villain is flying off to save the girl from the Hero.

I don't care how twisted this is, though.

I'm going to save her.

18
LILLITH

Despite what he said, Ari doesn't fly us *home*, to New York, thank god—he takes us to the Heroes Org branch in LA, the top dozen floors of the tallest building in the city. A wide balcony serves as a landing pad for any flying Heroes, and as the sun fully sets behind us, glowing over the Pacific Ocean in the distance, Ari touches down.

I immediately scramble out of his arms. My skin is wind-burned from flying—why the *fuck* did he fly so fast?—and my insides feel just as raw, scraped and bleeding as I stumble to put space between me and Ari.

He cocks his head at me. "Lillypad—"

"Don't call me that."

He holds his hands out, surrender. "I've seen this before. You've been through a trauma. Let's just get inside, and we can—"

"I didn't *ask* to be saved!" I scream.

Ari frowns. "Sweetheart—"

"Did you even read my message? I *told* you not to come for me!"

"What message?"

The confusion on his face is so real that I trip over it.

"My—the message," I say. "The email I sent you. With the video of the crash."

He shakes his head.

"Then ... wait. How did you even find me?"

Ari nods at the glass doors behind me. "Malcolm picked up a signal that matched the tech that the Raven had used in the past. He said—"

I whirl around. I can't see anyone standing in the lobby beyond the doors, but my skin tightens, every muscle contracting, panic setting in.

Fallon wasn't using any of his tech. *I* was using *Scarlet's* tech.

Malcolm intercepted my email. He saw what I meant for Ari to see.

He knows that I know what he's been doing.

"Malcolm is here?" My voice is rough.

"Lilly—what's this about?" Ari comes closer behind me and puts his hands on my arms, tries to rub up to my shoulders.

I jerk away from him. "Ari, take me away from here. Now."

"What? Lilly—"

"Take me *back*!" I scream, the word shaking off into the sky. Tears gather, prick across my eyes, and I beat at his chest with my fists. "I didn't want you to save me! I sent you a message telling you I was fine. That I didn't want you to come for me. I was with Fallon because I *wanted* to be, Ari. I didn't—" I stop, gasping, tears streaming down my face. "I didn't want to come back to you."

Ari's whole face contorts, confusion sharpening to understanding. "You ... you wanted to stay? With a *Villain?*"

"He's not a Villain, Ari. I mean, he is, but it's not—"

"He tried to kill you! He abducted you!"

"No, Ari—*you* tried to kill me!" My anger flares. "Malcolm used his mesmer powers on you. That was the video I sent you. *You* swerving the car. *You* unbuckling my seatbelt. Malcolm may have controlled you, but a part of you didn't want me in your life anymore, and that's what he fed on. You don't love me anymore than I love you. Do you?"

I stop, and in the silence, I realize I could be wrong about everything.

But the way Ari doesn't immediately respond. The way he stands there, hands splayed, eyes wide, tells me I was right.

A cold wash of dread flies through me.

"Did you know?" I whisper. "Did you know that Malcolm still has his powers?"

Ari hesitates. Then nods. "I knew he was gaining back some small abilities. But, Lilly, he'd never use his powers on his Heroes. He doesn't need to. He only controls Villains."

"Ari."

He shakes his head. "You don't love me? Why did you say yes?"

My thumb goes to my ring finger. The engagement ring I took off—and gave to Fallon.

"We can talk about this later," I plead. "Right now—we need to leave."

I grab his arm and try to pull him to the edge of the landing pad. He doesn't budge.

When I look up at him, Ari is staring straight ahead. His eyes are glazed over in a now recognizable fog.

Every hair on my body stands on end. I turn, slowly, to see Malcolm Odyssey framed between the two massive open doors.

In his fifties, trim and sleek, even now he's wearing a suit that costs more than most cars, his gray hair styled in a controlled wave across his head. He tucks his hands behind his back and cocks an eyebrow, surveying me first, then Ari.

"Ari." I pull on his arm. He doesn't look at me, doesn't move. *"Ari—"*

"Oh, he can't hear you, Miss Giles," Malcolm says, his voice honey-smooth.

"Let him go," I try.

He laughs. "I don't think so. You and I need to have a chat."

"Fuck off."

He takes a step closer to me. I back up, but there's nowhere to go. The edge of the landing pad stretches over the city below.

I'm trapped.

It's likely the only reason Malcolm hasn't used his mesmer powers on me yet, too. That, or none of my desires line up with what he wants to force me to do.

My heart thunders in my chest, sweat beading down my spine. Can I get around him and make it inside the building? I've never seen Malcolm in a fight, but I doubt I could take him long enough to get past him and away.

"Miss Giles," he starts. "You've become a problem. Didn't I give you everything? Fame, fortune, the arm of the most influential and powerful man in the country. And how do you repay me? By surviving."

I flinch. "Surviving?"

"You ran your course. It was becoming more and more apparent that you had no intention of adapting to the requirements necessary to be All-American Man's fiancé, let alone, god forbid, his wife." Malcolm turns, surveying the higher floors above us. "Of course, he couldn't *break up* with you, no—and you certainly could not be allowed to break up with him. I told him proposing to you was a fool's idea, but our Hero is nothing if not a romantic. He believed a ring on your finger would be enough to get you to thoroughly ... behave."

I bare my teeth. "So your solution was just to kill me? Did Ari know that?"

"Of course not. He has to be blameless, our Hero." Malcolm gets close enough to Ari that he pats his cheek. Ari, still frozen, doesn't react. He doesn't even flinch. "I simply enhanced his own feelings of doubt and let him run his own course. Amazing what the mind can do when it's unhinged."

My arms shake. The need to get away is overwhelming, and I swallow, hard, forcing myself to stay steady, to buy time until—until what? Fallon has no idea where I am. He can't save me.

I inhale, breathing deep—

And feel something pinch between my breasts.

Scarlet's mesmer device. The signal that interrupts any mesmer's powers.

"So why did you let him get me?" I snap at Malcolm. My fear tangles with rage. I need to get him talking. I need him to not look at me for the five seconds it'll take to free the device and hit the button. I know he'll only give me one shot at this. "Why not just tell the world that I was dead and be rid of me?"

"Only to have you pop back up on the arm of a *Villain?* Oh, no, dear. When I intercepted that email from you, I realized what a unique opportunity you had presented to Heroes Org. Quite the PR feast, actually. Our Hero," Malcolm pats Ari's shoulder, "saves you from the vicious Raven, only for the Raven to race back in a violent rage. In the crossfire, you are, unfortunately, killed. Our Hero then avenges you by killing the Raven, as he should have done a year ago, and though the nation mourns our Hero's pain of losing his fiancé, they rejoice knowing he is, and always will be, righteous in their eyes."

He's going to kill me—I knew that.

But Fallon?

He's going to kill Fallon, too.

Nausea knots my stomach. "No. I won't let you. *No!*"

I grab for the device, subtlety be damned.

But Malcolm is close. Close enough to seize my wrist and wrench my arm so hard I see stars.

With his other hand, he pats my waist, searching for the weapon he thought I was reaching for. When he finds none, he grins at me, menace and evil.

The device is safe.

But I can't get to it now.

"You don't have a choice, Miss Giles," he tells me. He lifts a finger, places it on my temple, and the whole world goes dark.

19

FALLON

JUST MY FUCKING LUCK.

Lillith's dress is located at the Heroes Org base in LA. I mean, at least it's not New York or out of the States entirely, but of fucking course Ari would take her to the closest place crawling with goody-two-shoes dumbass *Heroes*. At least it's late enough at night that—hopefully—no one else will be around.

I slow as I approach, even though it basically kills me to do so, but I need to be careful here. Ari could enlist any of his buddies to help. Worst damn part of Heroes Org—with Elysium, each person takes care of their own shit. Heroes fucking team up all the goddamn time, and for no good reason. All Ari has to say is that he wants to kick my ass, and every Hero in the building will be riding my tail, just clamoring to get a punch in.

Except it's not a whole team of Heroes that slams into me.

It's just All-American Man.

And it's enough to almost take me out with one hit.

He attacks from above, an elbow in the center of my back with enough force to bow my body backwards. Ari is holding nothing back as he slams into me; the blow is enough to have permanently damaged the spine of a normal human.

Fortunately for me, I'm not normal.

I twist around, using gravity to aid my wings as I whirl first down and then around him. Dodging another blow, I swerve to the left, swoop to the right.

All-American Man, red cape billowing, tries to cut me off, corner me.

And here's the thing.

If I fucking cared about him, I have the advantage in the air. He's stronger, but I'm a better flyer. I could take him here. I know I could.

But I *don't* fucking care about him, not anymore. I only care about Lillith.

Fuck revenge. I want *her.*

So rather than stick around for the futile pissing contest All-American Man so clearly has planned, I swoop low, catch an updraft on the side of the skyscraper, and glide up to the top of the building.

I expected to have to fight my way to Lillith.

But she's right there.

Along with dozens of cameras.

"Lillith?" I say as I land. I eye the cameras. They're all drones; no operators. Trained on me. Heroes Org must have wanted to film All-American Man kicking my ass and use it for promo.

They can't win the game if I don't play.

Smirking, I stride over to her. "Lillith, come on," I say. She's not bound or tied down.

But she doesn't move.

To my left, All-American Man lands on the roof, even doing that stupid Hero-kneel landing. What a tool.

"Lilly," Ari says, his voice hollow. "Come here."

And ...

She does.

Lillith—*my* Lillith—walks across the roof, one graceful foot after the other, the red dress flitting through the rooftop winds. Her hair blows into her face, a halo obscuring my last site of him as she heads straight into his arms.

I hear the cameras whirr as the lenses all zoom in on the touching reunion.

"Lillith," I say, my voice breaking.

Not like this, I think. *Don't let her finish with me like this, with a knife in my back and another in my heart.*

"She's mine," All-American Man says. There's triumph in his look, all caught on camera.

"She's not anyone's!" I shout. "She's her own person!"

"And she chooses me."

"No, I don't."

I almost don't hear her. Each word is a struggled whisper, and she doesn't move away.

"What?" I ask.

"I belong to no one." It *is* Lillith—she still doesn't move away from Ari, but it's her voice, her defiance.

All-American Man moves, arms around Lillith, toward the door. Their steps are shuffled. Lillith doesn't try to break free, but I know I heard her. I lunge forward. If she wanted the asshole, she could have had him, but I'll be damned if I'm not going to make abso-fucking-lutely sure that's what she wants.

I move like lightning, using my wings and the wind on the rooftop to throw myself between them and rip Lillith from Ari's hold.

And I see her eyes. They *scream* with pain. Her body is limp, a puppet whose strings can be pulled, but her eyes—her eyes are desperately trying to tell me that this isn't right, something's not right—

The Hive.

Malcolm is controlling Lillith. She can't fight, but she's trying to tell me—

A fist connects with my jaw as Ari shifts into attack mode. As I go—literally—head over heels, wings over ass—I try to look into All-American Man's eyes, really look. There's a chance they're glazed over, too, maybe this isn't the fucking asshole.

Although, I remind myself, *he couldn't be so easily controlled if he didn't at least a little want to do this, to* be *this.*

Fine.

Maybe I'll play their game a little.

Bunching my hands into fists, I *fly* at All-American Man. I catch his smirk—this is what he wants. *No,* I think, *this is what The Hive wants.*

At the last minute, I veer away from All-American Man, ducking under his blowing cape, off the side of the building, and catching air with my wings as I whirl around mid-air, scanning the rooftop.

The Hive doesn't have to be on the rooftop to control us, but I'm guessing Malcolm doesn't want to miss any part of the show. Sure enough, I see him, hidden in the shadows of the water tower on the roof.

I can fight All-American Man until my wings fall off, but it'll do nothing at all if I don't take down the Hive.

I scan the roof.

Lillith is by the door—she can't escape because she's in the thrall of the Hive, more powerful than solid metal chains. But she's safe enough there, not at the edge.

All-American Man is gathering his power, ready to totally take me down. I wheel around in the air, making it look like I'm dive bombing toward him.

Instead, I swoosh past him and head straight to the water tower. I feel a buzzing in my head—thank goodness for Scarlet's weird god-helmet protecting me from the Hive's mind control.

I *slam* into the Hive. He may be older than most Heroes—god only knows how old—but he's built like a fucking rock. Hitting his body was like hitting the cliffside of a mountain, but I have the force of flight and my own rage fueling me. I knock the Hive down, and we skid across the asphalt, right to the edge of the building. His suit shreds on the harsh concrete, and he curses me as I hold him over the side.

"Let me go," the Hive says. Power laces through his voice.

"Can't make me," I taunt. I see his eyes flick to the silver helmet.

I heft his body over to the edge and hold his neck off the side of the building. It's twenty stories down to the ground.

"You may be able to control minds," I growl, "but you can't fly."

I pick him up, holding him over my head.

Heroes hesitate.

Villains don't.

I throw the Hive off the side of the fucking building and peer over the ledge to watch him die.

Except—

All-American Man shoots out from behind me, dives into the air, and snatches him about three seconds before the Hive splatters across the parking lot.

"Fucking fuck," I growl. Well, fuck this shit. I don't have to win. I just have to save Lillith.

I spin on my heel and race to her. She's still motionless by the door. She may be able to resist the Hive a little, but—even though he was thrown off the top of the building—he still has her in his thrall.

I'll fly her off. Take her across the world. We'll break this connection and—

With a breathless gasp of pain, I'm flattened against the concrete. All-American Man has dropped the Hive off safely behind the cameras, and then kicked me in the back, in the same spot as he attacked before.

But this time, rather than roll off me and fight, he grabs *something*.

A handful of feathers—and the brace. The brace Lillith made for me. He *rips* it off my back, snapping it in half as if it was nothing more than a toothpick.

Pain lances up my back, down my wing.

It's not just that the brace is gone. It's that *Lillith's* brace is gone. She made it for *me.* For us.

All-American Man stands, heels on my spine. And then he *slams* his boot right into my wing, bending the delicate bones, snapping my feathers. I scream in pain.

This is the canyon all over again.

Except—

Through the tears I can't hold back as All-American Man grinds his steel boot into my torn tendons, I see Lillith.

This is the canyon all over again.

Except this time, I'm not just going to lose my wings.

I'm going to lose *everything.*

20
LILLITH

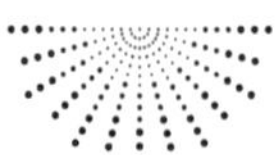

FEAR.

That's the emotion Malcolm taps into, the one that he gets to overcome all of my other senses and fall prey to his mesmer abilities.

Blood-freezing, muscle-gripping *fear*.

It's primal, fight-or-flight but taken to the extreme. Malcolm's control is all oil and grease where Scarlet's was a calm breeze. It's all I can do to just stay standing and not collapse in a dead faint.

I'm frozen on the roof, my heart hammering, as my eyes shift over the scene in front of me, only enhancing my terror:

Ari, ripping the brace off of Fallon's wing.

Fallon, screaming, *screaming*, as Ari stomps down on his wing hard enough that I hear bones pop, the pain visceral and raw on Fallon's face.

Move, damn it, Giles! Fight back! Do something—

This is every moment of the last two years all at once.

Helpless. Useless. Motionless. *Nothing*.

Ari reaches down and tears a helmet off Fallon's head. The moment he does, Fallon looks up at me, his eyes wide with apology—

Then his body goes rigid. His gaze goes blank, the same glaze that coats Ari.

My eyes flick to Malcolm, panting and wincing, off to the side, his suit shredded, his normally pristine hair mussed and a bruise on his cheek.

"Kill her," he growls.

Ari backs away, his arms limp.

The drone cameras swivel to Fallon.

Fuck. *Fuck, no—*

Malcolm isn't going to kill me.

He's going to make *Fallon* kill me.

Only Fallon won't do it. He doesn't want to, not the way Ari did—

Fallon rises to his feet. But he takes no step toward me, doesn't even look at me.

"Kill her!" Malcolm screeches.

Fallon's whole body trembles. Sweat beads down his face, the muscles in his neck straining as he fights Malcolm's hold on his mind, those invasive powers tearing through every thought, every emotion, looking for one he can latch onto, one he can enhance to get his puppet to kill me.

A cry, and Fallon drops to his knees. Blood drips from his nose.

"Kill her!" Malcolm's desperation piques—he has his hands outstretched, fingers clawed, channeling all of his power at Fallon.

He's so focused on Fallon.

So *desperate* to break him.

He's almost forgotten about me.

I take a breath. Another. My fear is still raging, still threatening to make me black out in shock, but the tips of my fingers tingle.

I reach up, grab the mesmer device from my cleavage, and hit the button.

Everyone on the roof stiffens.

The cameras drop, clanking against the cement, some shattering.

Fallon is the first to move. He collapses forward onto his forearms, wheezing with a cry, and I dive for him, released, too, from Malcolm's hold.

"Fallon!" I grab his shoulders and draw him upright, my hands on his face, making him look at me. His eyes are clear.

He blinks at me once, twice, before he gasps. "Lillith."

A breath surges out of my lungs and I throw my arms around his neck.

Over his shoulder, I see Malcolm stumble forward. His eyes lock on me, livid, before shifting to the device in my hand.

"You!" he snarls. "You *bitch*!"

He makes it one step towards me.

And suddenly, he's in the air.

Ari has Malcolm by the neck. The look on his face is one I've never seen, utter rage, raw grief mixed with fury.

"By the power of Heroes Organization," Ari growls through a clenched jaw, "I am placing you under arrest."

Malcolm sputters, clawing at Ari's grip. "Ari—you don't —understand—"

"Oh, I *do* understand," he spits. "I understand *everything* you made me do. Everything you brought out in me." For a moment, Ari looks like he might cry. "You're finished."

He braces, preparing to take flight with Malcolm in his grip—

"Ari!"

He stops.

I hold up the mesmer device. "It's what's stopping his powers."

When I toss it, Ari catches it easily, but he still won't look into my eyes.

Fallon and I pull apart. Fallon tries to stand, but one wing hangs shattered off his body and he falls back to his knees with a shout.

Ari turns his head away. "You're free to go," he says, his voice rough.

I keep my hold on Fallon's arms, tears threatening to unravel me. "Ari—"

He finally looks at me. His eyes are watery and unblinking.

"Does he need a medic?" Ari asks.

It's Fallon who groans, "Scarlet's coming."

I shake my head at Ari. "Thank you," I manage. It's all I can think to say.

Ari nods, every inch All-American Man, the Hero he always believed he was.

What will it do to him, dealing with Malcolm's betrayal? He seems aware of the things Malcolm made him do. That kind of guilt could crush a person.

But Ari isn't just any person.

He takes off, launching from the roof, Malcolm pinned in his grip. He banks, angling down for the balcony landing pad of Heroes Org. Gone.

I scan the horizon until I spot a small, sleek jet angling for us. Has to be Scarlet.

"She's coming," I tell Fallon. "Scarlet will help—oh, fuck, Fallon." Tears grab my throat. Now that we're alone, all the emotions bubble up, the remnants of fear Malcolm stirred mixing with watching Fallon at Ari's mercy.

He still has blood drying on his mouth.

"You fought him," I gasp through tears. I press my thumb to his lips.

Fallon, somehow, smiles, though I know he's in debilitating pain. "Of course." His eyes tighten, sharpen, focusing on me with a renewed passion. "There was nothing in me he could use to turn me against you. I ... fuck, I'm in love with you, Lillith."

And then I'm kissing him as gently as I can, sobbing as Scarlet's jet lowers beside us and the full weight of these past few days evaporates off my shoulders.

My Villain saved me.

And we get to go home.

ONLY IT'S TECHNICALLY *SCARLET'S* home, but Fallon's in no condition to go to his actual home, one I haven't even seen yet.

"I should start charging you two rent," Scarlet mumbles as she types away at her computer. Her lab is empty except for the two of us. I prefer it that way—no excess distractions. Just her and I in perfect sync, mostly due to her mind-reading abilities, the two of us whipping through these tests with ease.

"You love us," I say and bump her with my hip.

"I'm just saying. First it was you. Now it's Fal. And as much as you keep *saying* you'll leave when we finish this—"

"We will."

"—I have my doubts about your abilities to stay in one piece. Plus, you like my harem too much."

I bite my lip at the memory of Fallon and I fucking in front of the crowd, our bodies writhing in tandem with the other harem guests.

Soon, when he's healed enough, we'll have a repeat of that before we leave. Because we *will* leave. We really have overstayed our welcome here.

"You got this?" I say, finishing up one last tweak on Fallon's Brace 2.0.

Scarlet nods and bats me away. "Go check on our patient. Tell him if he's even a *millimeter* out of bed, I'm gonna fulfill all those fantasies you've had of me. *Without* letting him watch."

I bark laughter. "Scarlet!" But, hell, I'm flushing like crazy, and I kind of hope he's being the horrible patient he's proven to be.

She cuts me a smirk.

I leave the lab, jogging through the twisting halls of Scarlet's home to get to the medical wing, and push into Fallon's room.

Sure enough, he's standing, trying to look backwards at his wing, still mostly in a medical brace and bandages.

I sigh over-dramatically. "Naughty."

He flinches and spins around, which only makes him wince and drop to sit on the bed. "Fuck."

"Yeah. Especially when you learn what Scarlet threatened you with."

"Going to have her way with you, is she?"

I hold a hand to my heart. "As if I could be so easily seduced."

Fallon grins and reaches for me. I kick the door shut behind me and hurry to him, letting him pull my hips against his crotch, my hands around his neck, fingers trailing through his hair.

"Only a few more days in here," I tell him. "And just a few weeks after that with the bandages. The new brace is coming along well. It'll be ready and waiting for you, and you won't have—"

"Lillith." Fallon squeezes my ass. "I'm okay. Really."

Two weeks since Ari nearly snapped his wing off. Two weeks since Malcolm's mesmer abilities were finally defeated, and his true betrayal sent shockwaves through Heroes Org. The news outlets have been running updates nonstop—a new CEO stepped in, a retired Hero known as the Magician who promises to root out the full extent of Malcolm's corruption in a top-to-bottom shake down of the company.

All-American Man, it's reported, has taken a leave of absence.

I trace Fallon's jaw. "I know. I just—" My voice wavers.

I almost lost you.

I almost lost you before I really got you.

He leans into my palm. "I know, sweetheart."

Fallon takes my wrist and presses a kiss to the inside of my hand. His kisses creep higher, higher, until he brushes his lips across the front of my shirt, grazing my breasts.

My breath catches. "You are *so* not medically cleared for that."

"Are you sure? Won't know until we try."

"Oh, I'm sure." I push on his shoulders until he releases me, and I step back, my chest tightening at the way he pouts.

"*You're* not cleared," I echo and suck my bottom lip between my teeth. "But I'm just fine."

I unbutton the front of my pants.

Fallon grins at me and starts to stand when I push his chest until he lowers back down.

"Oh, no," I say, a purr. "You only get to watch."

"Evil."

"What can I say? You're rubbing off on me."

"I'd *like* to be rubbing off on—"

But then I strip my pants off and kick them and my shoes to the side. Fallon shuts up with a startled hiss, hands fisting in his bed's sheet.

Shirt next. Bra, underwear; it all comes off until I'm naked before him. I can see his cock erect, lifting against the medical gown, and the heart monitors he's attached to start going crazy.

I lean over him, breasts hanging between us, and catch his mouth with mine.

"Remember everything I do," I whisper into his mouth. "I want your fingers and tongue to touch me exactly like this later."

"Fuck, Lillith." He presses his mouth to mine, but his hands stay on the bed, obedient, for once.

I grin against him. God, I'm putty with this man.

I kiss him again, and again, each touch setting me on fire, making me feel like I'm the one with wings.

ALTER EGO

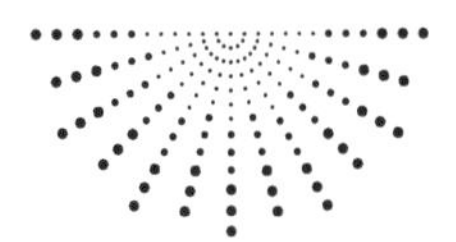

1

PIPER

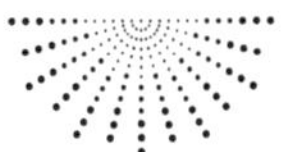

I CAREFULLY OUTLINE MY LIPS IN MY CLASSIC RED LACQUER. I WATCH MYSELF in the mirror even though I've done this a million times.

Heroes Org is all about the *image*. I know that. And I have done everything I can over the past decade to accurately present the "proper" image. I lost those ten extra pounds when human resources wrote me up. I wear the classic pencil skirts, even if they're not comfortable. I button the top button of every white silk blouse. I wear my hair pinned back, neat and tucked away, even if it takes me an extra hour every morning to tame my curls.

But I don't care how many times a higher-up has commented on my lipstick. I *will* have this one form of self expression.

And after all I went through to claw my way through the ranks of this company, a classic red isn't going to kill my career.

Besides, I need it.

It's the only armor a civilian like me has in a corporation full of supers.

I check my lips in the mirror, then twist the gold tube down and tuck it into my purse. I straighten my skirt, square my shoulders.

Time to meet the new boss.

"Agent Carson, good to see you."

I turn at the sound of my name as I exit the restroom. "Hello, Phil," I say. "I mean, Agent Cole. How was Tahiti?"

Agent Cole doesn't have much of a tan to match his month long vacation, but his smile is blissful. "Loved it," he says. "Didn't expect to come back to such a mess, though."

I grimace. That's putting it lightly.

Before his trip, Agent Cole left the department with everything neatly prepared for our best quarter yet. Our prime Hero, a super beloved by the country so much that his moniker All-American Man was used without a hint of irony, was riding a wave of popularity that was bolstered by a publicized romance and an upcoming feature film. We had several other Heroes lined up to hit the spotlight next, creating a successive and increasingly bigger series of promotions.

It was all perfect. We even had some huge corporate sponsors in the works, and the media was eating out of the palm of our hands.

And then All-American Man went rogue. Worse, the CEO of Heroes Org, the man in charge of, well, *everything*—turned out to be corrupt. The depths of his depravity were, for the most part, effectively hushed up, thanks in big part to the new CEO.

And the new CEO wants to see me.

Personally.

"I've got to go," I tell Phil. "Catch me up on the vacation later?"

"Definitely!" he calls, waving as I turned the corner and headed to the elevator.

Agents—non-super-powered humans working within Heroes Org to help handle the organization's assets—work on the lower levels of the main base in LA. My ears pop as I head up to the top floor.

It's rare that I go this far up, literally. Usually my assignments are handed down from middle management.

But the new CEO is taking a personal approach.

As soon as I step off the elevator, I can tell that I'm not working with the old boss any more. Chrome has been replaced with bronze; shiny white walls have been painted emerald green. A woman in a blazer without a blouse on, much less one buttoned up to the neck, greets me as I step off the elevator. "Agent Carson?" she enquires from her desk without consulting her laptop.

"Yes," I say. I pat my hair; not a pin out of place.

"Follow me." She stands and turns without looking behind her as she leads me down the corridor.

I trail behind. Her hips sway, and her heels clack on the tile floor, mesmerizing me.

"Mm, yes, I find her entrancing as well," a deep voice says when we stop outside a glass door. I blush at being so obviously caught staring at the assistant, but she winks at me.

My eyes move up and meet the intense gaze of the new man in charge of everything. Lucas Gardson, code name: the Magician.

Some say he's not a super at all, but a god. He's not like most of the other supers. All-American Man may have the bulging muscles and perfect tight ass that makes him a classic hero in the country's eyes, but the Magician is different. Slender build but with biceps carefully emphasized by the cut of his coat such a dark green that it's almost black. Slick black hair over clear jade eyes. And there's no winning smile made for photo ops. Nope—the Magician has a smirk twisting his lips, and a sparkle in his eye that makes him seem almost as if he's actually a Villain, not a Hero at all.

"Thank you, darling," the Magician says to the woman who escorted me. She practically purrs in response, then slinks away, like a cat satiated with rich cream.

We both watch her go.

Then the Magician turns to me. *Mr. Gardson,* I think. He's not a super in this role; he's my boss. *I should call him by his name, not his codename.* But I absolutely cannot think of him by something as mundane as a mortal name. He's *the Magician.*

His eyes rake over me, a slight frown marring his perfect face as he starts at my sensible low heels, skims over my tucked-in and buttoned-up blouse, and lingers on my red-painted lips. Ah—finally, a smile.

"Agent Carson," he says.

"Yes, um, sir?" I hate the question in my voice, but I don't realize until this moment that I'm not sure how to address him. Regardless of how I think of him, I need to use whichever name he prefers.

He smiles, white teeth gleaming, and despite my discomfort and questioning tone, he doesn't enlighten me. Fine. The Magician it is.

"Yes," he says, nodding in satisfaction as he looks at me. "Yes, I was right to select you, Agent Carson."

I open my mouth, but I have no idea how to respond. What have I even been selected for?

The Magician's grin widens, crinkling at his eyes. He leads me deeper into his office, then shuts the door so we're alone. For one moment, my mouth goes dry at my thoughts—the Magician is heart-stoppingly *intriguing*, and the door's soft click as it closes reverberates up my spine.

No way, Carson, I tell myself. *You know from experience not to play with anyone on the job.*

That never *works out.*

I learned my lesson long ago.

I smooth over my blouse, feeling the silk under my palms and reminding myself that it's going to stay tucked in no matter what.

As if he can read my thoughts, the Magician arches a brow at me but, thankfully, makes no comment.

"I have a special mission for you," the Magician says. He raises his hands, swirling his fingers, and an image appears in his palm.

I move forward for a better look, intrigued. Green, wispy smoke rises around a perfect, three-dimensional miniature of All-American Man.

My heart clenches.

Ari Dodgers.

My first assignment.

My first failure.

Well, failure isn't a fair assessment. Ari went on after I recruited him to become Heroes Org's top super. But things didn't exactly turn out as I'd hoped...

My eyes drift up to the Magician's. The wispy image of Ari disappears from his palm, green smoke dissipating between us.

"Oh, I was right about you," the Magician says. "You're the one who's going to bring All-American Man back to Heroes Org."

"I—sir, I *can't.*" My voice breaks over the last word.

He arches a perfect eyebrow. "And why not?"

"We. . .have a history."

The Magician's face twists into a knowing smirk. And then, as I watch, his face melts further, the jaw growing fuller, the eyes darker, the nose narrower, the lips fuller. He transforms before me.

He becomes Ari.

My heartbeat thrums violently, and black dots dance before my eyes. I've been with Heroes Org for a decade, and I've been able to, for the most part, avoid facing Ari directly. He made it clear that he chose the organization over what we had, and I respected that decision. I believed in it. Heroes Org does important work. I could put aside my heart and my desires so he could be the hero we all need.

But I couldn't do it if I had to look him in the eyes.

When the Magician—in Ari's face—speaks, he also has Ari's deep, resonant voice. "Come find me, Piper," he says. "I need you to save me."

"Don't," I snarl, turning away. The Magician is a master of illusion—little images like the tiny form he had in his palm, but also perfect disguises. He wouldn't have Ari's powers in this form, but he would look like Ari, sound like him.

When the Magician touches my shoulder, it feels like Ari's touch.

I melt.

"You're perfect," he says, in his voice, not Ari's.

I turn around. The Magician is himself again and he seems to have a note of sympathy in his face now, or perhaps just curiosity. "Agent Carson, I am aware of your history with All-American Man. And so I know you understand me when I tell you to bring him back to the fold by any means necessary."

"Sir…" I take a deep, shaky breath. "I do know Ari."

"Intimately."

A blush claws its way up my cheeks, but I refuse to acknowledge it. "This recent... departure of his. It's unlike him. I can tell you that he's probably gone to Brooklyn. There's a place there—I can give you the address. I know he kept the lease; it reminded him of home. He's a New Yorker at heart. I'll tell you everything I know, and you can send another agent in my place…"

My words die on my lips at the Magician's look. He arches his eyebrow—honestly, the man has to know what that does to us mere mortals—and leans in closer. For just a moment, I see Ari's blue eyes instead of the Magician's green ones.

"Agent Carson, your mission is vital. You are to bring Ari Dodgers back to Heroes Org by *any* means necessary."

2

ARI

THE WORST PART ABOUT BEING SUPER IS THAT I CAN'T GET DRUNK, BUT THAT sure doesn't stop me from trying.

The dozen empty whiskey bottles spread around this tiny kitchen clatter when I trudge through them. I scramble across the counter, grab my glass, and down the remainder of my dinner in one go.

No food on my stomach. Nothing but aged whiskey for two days straight.

And still, I've only managed a slight buzz, a bit of a fog that has my vision slightly jumbled. But nothing like the knock-out, drag-out *drunk* I want to be, the kind of eviscerating blackness I've heard people rave about.

To not feel anything.

To dissolve in a lack of sensation.

I *want* that. I want it so bad that I tell my growling stomach to shut up as I grab for another whiskey bottle.

Only there aren't any.

When did I last hit the store? Three days ago?

I went through my whole whiskey supply in three days.

Which was the whole store's whiskey supply, actually. They'd thought I was having a party.

Something about that makes me laugh. A bursting, rumbling laugh that echoes in my small, empty apartment, banging off the water-stained walls, the cracked window that shows the view of the narrow alley and the opposite building. I know that view so well. I'd stare out the window and count the bricks until my mom stumbled home, drunk, but actually drunk, *human* drunk, and then I'd watch her, blankly, as she tried to make something resembling dinner. Usually cold hot dogs and boxed mac 'n' cheese.

My stomach grumbles again.

"Fine." I grab my wallet and shove it into my jean's pocket. My shirt is... clean? I give it a sniff. Enough for a trip to the store to get boxed mac and more whiskey.

But as I turn, my eyes catch on the note I stuck to the fridge. The number that's been haunting me for the full two months I've been holed up here.

I have no idea who it goes to, only that it's a breadcrumb on the trail to contact *her*.

The *her* that Heroes Org would've killed to access: Persephone. Leader of the Villains. The evil queen herself.

Take her down, the whole pyramid crumbles. Take her down, and Heroes Org would've been *rolling* in profits.

So why didn't I turn that phone number over the moment I plucked it off a Villain? Why did I even *take* it? The Villain who gave it to me—and I don't even *remember their name*—had pressed it to my chest and said, "When you're sick of this golden boy image, call her."

Right before the Heroes Org cameras had caught up to me, and I'd punched the Villain's lights out.

Guilt, I've decided, is a vine. It sprouted the moment I woke up from Malcolm's mesmer spell, and it's been growing ever since, tangled roots digging deep into my soul and unfurling limbs stretching up with each memory I unearth, each person I hurt, each second I vividly remember being *aware* of Malcolm's power but *not doing anything about it.*

I knew he was doing something to me.

And I felt so powerful, I didn't care.

He let me be uninhibited. For the first time in more than a decade, I'd felt *free* as All-American Man. I could breathe under the shackles of my perfect image, the stringent requirements, and the soul-numbing censoring that made every smile fake. My boss used his mesmer powers to get me to do his dirty bidding—but only because a small part of me wanted it.

I only felt free because I was hurting people.

I only felt uninhibited because Malcolm took away my guilt, my empathy, and unleashed the selfish, mutilating beast inside.

The beast is shackled now. I've spent these past two months beating him senseless.

And all the guilt I didn't feel while under Malcolm's spell is growing, growing, each breath, *growing.*

I pop the note off the fridge and stare at the numbers. I've memorized them by now, and it's good I have; my hand shakes so hard that I have trouble seeing the paper. Or maybe I am, finally, *drunk.*

That's gotta be it.

That's gotta be the reason I pull out the cheap burner phone I bought —mostly to order take-out—and type the number into a text message.

Persephone, we need to talk. Meet at Callahan's Bar in Brooklyn. Tonight. 10PM.—All-American Man

I imagine the message shooting off as I hit send. I imagine it getting, somehow, to Persephone. I imagine her appearing in the little dive bar at the base of my building, a Queen of Villains, and I imagine myself stumbling to my knees at her feet.

How many of her Villains did I hurt? How many of them did I *kill*?

One face immediately flashes into my mind. Well, two:

The Raven, his mouth open in a scream.

And Lilly, horror in her eyes, disgust at the way I'd nearly snapped off her new boyfriend's wing.

I shake so hard I drop my phone on the counter. That shaking doesn't stop—it creeps up my shoulders, down my chest, until every inch of me is trembling, and I stumble for the sink and vomit up the whiskey in a heave.

I can still remember how it felt having the Raven's wing in my fingers. So delicate. So bare. I could've ripped the whole thing off.

I wanted to.

But I didn't.

Why didn't I?

Because of Lilly, I think. I knew what I'd done to her, how I'd willingly let Malcolm use me to try to *kill her,* and that reality had finally caught up to me just as she'd used the device to block Malcolm's signal.

I gag again, eyes pinched shut, but the shaking spell has stopped, thankfully.

They're getting more frequent.

I don't know how to stop them. I don't know what I'll do when the guilt growing in me has nowhere else to go, and I just explode with agony at all the terrible things I did, all the horrific acts I can't undo.

I need to atone.

I have no idea how to do that.

My phone buzzes.

There's a dingy rag over the faucet. I slurp a handful of water and wipe my face before grabbing the phone.

There's only one word on the screen:

Confirmed.

Well. Okay then.

I laugh again, deprecating, and something like a weight lifts from my shoulders.

I have no idea how to atone.

But meeting with the Queen of the Villains. Begging her forgiveness.

It's a start.

VOMITING the whiskey only made me realize how painfully hungry I am. I have enough savings that I'll never have to work again—and the world would be infinitely better off, I've realized—but so far, I've only been buying the necessities: booze. Delivery pizza. The occasional take-out Chinese.

Now, I make myself go to the actual grocery store. Progress, right?

As I peruse the aisles, head bent under sunglasses and a baseball cap, I grab every gross bit of junk food I can find. Heroes Org's strict diet never let me have things like—

What is this? Flamin' Hot Cheetos? What on earth—into the cart it goes.

Cheese? In a can? What monstrosity—I grab two.

I round the next aisle, stomach growling so loud a passing old woman looks at me, askance. I need to hurry up and finish so I can get home and eat—I should just check out now, then eat—

I pause. Why should I wait? All-American Man would've waited. But whoever I am now?

I grab the bag of Flamin' Hot Cheetos, rip it open, and shove a handful in my mouth.

Holy *heaven.*

This is *amazing.* I mean, absolutely disgusting and chemically-induced, but somehow the best thing I've ever eaten.

I push the cart with my hips as I stuff handful after handful of these neon orange horrors into my mouth. Damn, why did I believe Heroes Org when they said carrot sticks and celery were the best snacks?

Another person is coming up the aisle, and I duck my head out of instinct, shame coursing through me. But, no, screw that—I'm a rule breaker now.

I keep eating.

The person stops directly in front of my cart.

Shoulders tense, I slowly peek up, sure it's a manager, and that the next news reel will show All-American Man discovered shoplifting in Brooklyn. Heroes Org would *love* that.

But it isn't a manager.

The woman cocks her hip, a ghost of a smile stretching across her red lips. "Hello, Ari."

My whole body freezes so solid I think, for second, that it's some kind of ice or memory Villain.

Because that *cannot* be Piper Carson standing in front of me.

I open my mouth.

It's full of Flamin' Hot Cheetos.

So I swallow, quickly, and stuff the rest of the bag back into my cart.

"Piper?" I say, a question.

She looks... good.

No.

She looks *gorgeous.*

Her curly brown hair is free from her usual tightly-pinned bun, and those ringlets only remind my fingers of what it felt like to be buried in them. She has a loose jacket on, fitting the cooler weather, but instead of her agent dress code outfit, she's in skinny jeans and a tight tank that shows her perky nipples beneath.

I remember what those nipples felt like, too. Under my fingers. In my mouth.

An image from a lifetime ago flies through my head: Piper under me. Another person I haven't seen in years behind me. The three of us, writhing, sweating, *fucking*—

Stop it. What is *wrong* with me? After everything I did to Piper, she deserves better than for me to gawk at her and relive our better days.

I drop my face into my hands and rub my temples. "I'm drunk."

"Are you? How much alcohol did it take?"

"Eight... no... nine bottles. A dozen? But—" I look up at her. Suspicion washes through me. "Heroes Org sent you. You aren't usually at the New York office."

Last I heard, she was climbing the ranks of the agents.

I tried not to ask for updates on her too often. It was part of the terms of my own promotion. Best for both of us to not be tied together.

Still, I'd see her at events. Or in company-wide meetings.

Or at the press junket for my movie, when I proposed to Lilly, and Piper was in the third row, fourth seat over, with a few other agents, and it'd taken everything in me not to look directly at her as I'd pulled out that ring.

Piper turns away, her eyes cresting over the rows of breakfast cereal around us. "This is my hometown, too, Ari. You think they'd stick me with playing your babysitter? I've climbed higher than that. I'm here to visit my mom."

I hang my head again. "I'm sorry. I didn't mean—"

"Yes, you did." She shifts around the cart to stand closer to me. I get a waft of her perfume. Roses.

She loves roses.

I go rigid, arms folded over the cart handle, Piper's image in shadows. I lower my sunglasses to really look at her.

She looks this amazing, smells this good, and I haven't showered in four days.

"It's nice to see you." I whisper the admission before I can make myself shut up.

She stays silent for a long beat.

Then she cocks her head. "Come on."

"What?"

"You're staying in your old place, right?" she asks over her shoulder. I follow, spinning my cart, but she wrinkles her nose. "Leave it. I got this one."

"Got this one?"

She stops. When she faces me again, she pushes so close I can feel heat pulsing off her, all sugary rose warmth and red lipstick.

I lick my lips, fighting hard not to admit the roiling feelings thrashing to life in my chest. No way is she feeling anything even remotely similar to what I'm feeling.

I need to get a hold of myself. Now.

She touches one finger to my cheek. Even that small contact has me getting hard, cock straining against my jeans.

"I heard what happened," she says, her voice hoarse. A façade has dropped—this tone is more the real her, the her I knew a lifetime ago. "And I'll be damned if I let you wallow in boxed mac and whiskey, Ari."

I exhale, chest deflating, leaning closer to her. "Why?"

Why, when she's one of the people I hurt most?

Only I can't put that blame on Malcolm. No—when I hurt her and... I can't even think his name. When I hurt *them*, that was all me.

But Piper smiles. It doesn't reach her eyes. "Come on."

BACK AT MY APARTMENT, I suddenly realize how *depressing* it is here.

The furniture is the same battered hand-me-downs my mom scavenged. She's been dead for years, but I still kept paying for this place even though I now have a penthouse in Manhattan, as if this apartment protected some part of my past I've never been willing to let go.

Turns out, a sleazy apartment in Brooklyn makes the best wallowing lair.

Piper dumps her haul on my counter, deftly shoving empty whiskey bottles and dirty cups into the sink. Seeing her in this kitchen is a stark contrast: my depression-filthy trash strewn about, and her, pristine, confident.

You shouldn't be here, I almost say. *You should go. I don't deserve you anywhere near me.*

"Go shower," she tells me. "I'll make dinner."

"Pipes—"

The moniker slips out totally unbidden. Horror courses through me.

We both go stiff.

"Shower," I repeat, because I desperately need something to do. "Right. On it."

I get halfway to the hall.

"Thank you," I add.

I hear her start banging around the sparse kitchen as I get to the one bedroom and start the shower.

I check the clock.

A little after eight.

Plenty of time until I have to meet Persephone.

Plenty of time for... what? Reconciliation? I'm still not entirely sure why Piper's here. Why she cares at all about someone who ruthlessly chose his career over her.

Maybe I am imagining her.

Maybe I've finally snapped, my guilt warping into full-on hallucinations.

Has she forgiven me? She shouldn't have. Even if she did, she definitely shouldn't be *here*, taking care of me, like I'm still the same awkward teenage boy she rescued all those years ago.

I was—am?—All-American Man. The nation's greatest superhero. Impeccable reputation. The guiding beacon every red-blooded American male aspires to be like.

Only that was all a lie.

And now, Piper's in my kitchen, making *me* dinner, when she should be the one being wined and dined and taken care of.

I'm absolutely pathetic.

The shower steams. I strip and slide in, ignoring the mildew.

The water cascades over my shoulders, battering every muscle. I haven't kept up with my workout routine, but that hasn't deterred my super physique—I'm still cumbersomely huge, and I knock the shampoo bottle out of the curtain.

I bend out to grab it—

And freeze.

Piper stands in the bathroom doorway.

With one hand I hold the shampoo bottle, with the other I brace myself on the towel rack.

I have absolutely no response to why she's standing in the doorway, looking at me like she once did.

There's no way she should still be able to look at me like *that*.

"The Magician," I guess, disappointment souring in my mouth. "This is an illusion." I glare at the not-Piper. "Reveal yourself, Lucas. You can't stoop to such cheap tricks to get me to come back to Heroes Org."

Piper flinches like I slapped her. The sheer disgust on her face floods me with horror—that she'd be that offended, that *I* was the cause of it.

Either Lucas trained to get really, really good acting as Piper.

Or...

She shakes her head. "It's *really* me."

"Then—"

"Can you just shut up, Ari?"

"No. Not really. You shouldn't be in here."

"Why not? It's not like I haven't seen it before."

I stand up and shove the curtain aside. The water still sprays down on me, dripping over my pecs, down my groin, highlighting my hardening cock.

I growl, and *damn it,* my chest *opens.* Anger comes pouring out, that same blind fury that Malcolm helped me give into. The parts of me that did bad things.

And it feels *good.*

"Because you deserve better than to be here. After everything I did—you aren't safe with me. I'm not the man I used to be, and even *that* man hurt you. Now? I'm dangerous, Piper."

"Yes," she agrees. She steps closer. "You are."

I frown. Can't she see what she's doing? What beast she's poking?

"Piper." The way I say her name is all threat. "Why are you here?"

"I told you. I was in town visiting my mom."

"Then why aren't you *there,* with her? Why buy my groceries and offer to make me dinner? You have way more self respect than to be scraping my sorry ass off the floor."

She stops, finally. She's only about a foot away from me, her hands behind her back, pulling her tank top taut across her breasts. My eyes get caught there, and when I look back up at her, she isn't smiling. She looks as angry as I feel, only her anger is righteous where mine's selfish.

Her being here is awakening even more of my guilt, filling me up with grief. But this guilt just makes me fucking *furious.* I'm dealing with enough shit right now—why does she have to be here? Why *now*?

I hurt her. I *gutted* her *and* Bryce.

Fuck. His name. His name rings in my head and I have to close my eyes to get a grip on myself.

"Tell me to leave," she says, rough.

My jaw dips open. The water's still steaming, fogging up the bathroom with humidity that has her hair sticking to her cheeks, her tank plastering to her curves with sweat.

She should go.

I should *make* her to go.

"I hurt you," is what I manage to say. "We should talk about—"

She steps even closer, her breasts rubbing against my bare chest, and I hiss, fully erect, pulled in a dozen different directions.

Push her away.

Pull her in.

Run out the door.

Fuck her against the wall.

"You're still so goddamn honorable. I don't want to *talk*." Her voice is fire. "Yeah, you hurt me. And it's eating you up, isn't it? That's what all this is about. You feeling sorry for yourself."

"I don't—"

"Yes, you do. You want to actually do something about it?" Piper rises onto her toes, eyes level with me, and balances with her hands on my forearms, her fingernails painted a vivid red. "Show me how sorry you are, Ari. Beg for my forgiveness."

3
PIPER

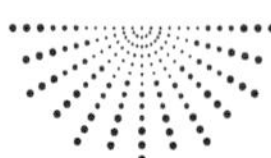

Except—I don't want his forgiveness. Because if he asks for it, that means we both have to acknowledge that these past ten years happened. That there is more between us than the hot humidity from his shower.

So when Ari opens his mouth, I rush to him, silencing the words I don't truly want to hear.

I don't want to question this.

I don't want to question *us.*

I don't want to *feel* anything—not guilt, not doubt.

Just him.

And when my hand trails down his hard abs and to his harder cock, the growl in the back of his throat makes me know that he feels the same.

His kiss *devours* me. His tongue claims my mouth as his own; his arms pull my body to his. We stagger back, into the shower, and water soaks through my clothes.

I laugh at the ridiculousness of it—me, clothed, in the shower. Him, All-American Man, bare-ass naked and looking positively *feral.*

But Ari's not laughing.

There's a darkness to his eyes, as if he's charging down a path that he knows will end at a cliffside, and he has no intent of slowing. He reaches out and rather than pull my clothes off me, he *shreds* the thin material of my tank top, reducing the cloth to rags. I stagger at the force of it—that's Agent Training 101, that even when a super looks human, never *ever* forget that they're not. Ari holds back his strength, but that doesn't mean it's not there.

As evidenced by the way his thick fingers slide into the waistband of my jeans, and he rips the thick denim from my body in one small tug, exerting no more effort than if my pants had been made of wet paper.

I shiver, and that is what makes Ari pause. His eyes search mine, and he's here with me, fully present, fully worried.

I shake my head, water droplets flying. "Not with me," I say. "Don't you dare hold back with me. I know you could crush me, Ari, and I know you won't."

It's like a shutter goes over his face as he pushes aside the fear that made him pause, the fear of hurting me. But he grunts out, "Safe word?"

"Shield," I say.

A flash—not of fear this time, but of vulnerability. *Shit.* I used the same word that I used to use with him, before, when I was a new agent, and Ari wasn't yet All-American Man.

But I see him nod, mentally shoving aside the past for the *now.* "Shield," he repeats, a promise. If either of us say that word, we both stop, entirely, no questions asked.

I lean forward, the shower water running over my head and down his shoulders. "There," I say. "I'm safe with that word, and you're safe from hurting me. And we both know..." I pause. I hate to bring it up, but... "We both know our files." Heroes Org requires regular testing for any diseases, and safe birth control is protocol for any agent who's had a past with supers.

Safe words, safe files.

I sigh. "I don't want to think about *safe,*" I mutter.

"Neither do I," Ari says, a growl in his voice. He grabs me by the hips, swinging me up. Instinctively, I wrap my legs around his waist.

Ari is strong enough that I don't have to worry about him being able to hold me up.

I can feel him already, the hard length of him pressing against my thigh. I have had to watch Ari for the past decade as he sculpted himself into All-American Man. I have seen him hesitate before even shaking hands with someone else. I witnessed the way he held back with his fiancée, as if she were made of glass.

And even though he knows me, he knows we have the safe word and the trust and experience to go with it—I can see him now, holding back.

And that just won't do.

I push up with my legs, reaching between us to grasp his dick and position it, then I slam my body down on it, impaling myself with his hard cock. I arch my back and gasp as I fully take him into me, driving him all the way to the hilt. It's almost painful; my eyes water, and I'm panting, my body barely able to keep up with the full girth of him.

But my move was effective at reminding him that we are *not* gentle souls in danger of cracking at the merest touch.

The throaty growl that emits from him fills my belly with fire, and I clench my inner muscles around his cock, then shift, just a little. His hands go to my hips, strong as iron bands, and he holds me firmly against his body. Whirling in the shower, Ari slams me into the tiled wall, sliding out and then driving back into me.

Pinned against the wet wall, Ari thrusts into me like a drowning man gasping for water.

My head drapes over his shoulder, my body shuddering with every violent thrust.

It's not enough.

I twine my arms around his neck, using the leverage to lift my lips to his ear. I nibble on his lobe, then bite down, hard enough to draw a hiss from him. "Don't hold back," I growl.

He roars at me, an animal breaking free of its cage. One arm goes around the back of my shoulders, propping me up. I arch back, and Ari claims my nipple with his teeth, biting down on the sensitive nub at the same time his other arm snakes between us, finding the place where his body fills mine.

"Ari!" I scream as his fingers slip into the wet warmth between us, gliding over my swollen clitoris. He fully supports my entire weight with his left arm as his right hand works my clit in a way that can only be called *artistic*. His whole body thrums with the rhythm, thrusting into me with his cock, pushing me down with his arm, grinding against my clit in a way that dances on the edge of pain, but in a sweet, delicious way.

My orgasm is shattering. I come apart in his arms, my whole body going limp around him as he pumps into me—once, twice, a third time, hard shoves into my body, as if he wants to drive into the core of me. I feel my tension building again, cresting. Helpless, I ride him into his release, my pussy clenching around him, drawing every last hot drip inside of me.

Spent, he sinks to the floor of the shower. Water drums down on our sweating bodies. My clothes are wet rags on the floor.

But he is still inside me, his cock large enough to stay in me even after he's released.

My phone buzzes.

I bat at my pants, a wet pile of denim.

Ari snorts in laughter, his head bent over my shoulder. I shift, intending to take my phone and pitch it across the room, but my movement makes him stir.

I cock an eyebrow at him. "Again? Already?"

Ari leans back, reclining fully on the tile floor of the ample shower. He thrusts up into me, his hips bucking, and his cock is, most definitely, ready to go again.

I ride him, slow and easy, gliding my drenched pussy over his cock. He's content to lie there and let me wring my pleasure from him, use him like a tool, but he's so much better than any vibrator I've ever had. The shower water is cold now, but I don't mind; it stings on my back, a sharp contrast to the heat building in my core. My hands glide over my own body, tweaking my nipples.

Ari watches me, eyes dark with desire, lids heavy but gaze intent. I don't break my eyes from him as my hands go lower, lower. I reach between us, fingertips grazing his balls, before I press into my clit, adding pressure as I clench around his cock, my body drawing him in.

The urgency from before is gone. This is almost lazy in how easy it is. Ari's hips roll, adding to the pressure as I grind down on him. A smile bursts on my lips even as I gasp his name, another orgasm washing over me. I lean down, my breasts pressed into his pecs, my back straining as I finally release. Ari's arms wrap around me, warm and strong and—

Safe.

My phone buzzes again.

Ari snorts. "You're quite the important one," he says, reaching past me, to my pants. The phone—water-proof and smash-resistant standard-issue from Heroes Org—lights up as Ari pulls it from my ripped pants' pocket.

He intends to just hand the phone to me.

But we both see the message lit up on the screen.

The Magician: Remember.
Bring in AMM by any means necessary.
Do not fail in your mission.

Ari's eyes go from the screen to mine. And all I can think is: *Fuck.*

4
ARI

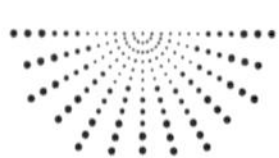

I KNEW IT.

I fucking *knew it.*

But I let it happen anyway.

She's still straddling me, my cock inside of her, but the two of us go absolutely immobile, both staring at her phone.

I shove it into her hands. She has the decency to scramble off me, but she stays in the tub, crouched over my legs.

"You lied to me," I say.

No hesitation from her. No cowering or trying to make excuses. "Yes."

It should hurt. But I have no right for it to hurt. She can do whatever she wants to me, and it'd be no less than I deserve.

I reach behind her to crank off the water. As my hands trail around her, grazing her shoulders, I have the sudden, disconnected feeling that this space is too empty.

Someone else is meant to be here, with us.

His face flashes in my head. I wonder if she was thinking about him, too, while we were fucking.

I wonder if she misses him as much as I do.

"You have to come back," she tells me. Her voice is flat. If she's feeling anything, she doesn't betray it— ever the perfect Agent. "Things are different now. Really. The Magician is overhauling everything Malcolm corrupted, and—"

"*Me.*" I lurch towards her, eyes wide, teeth in a snarl. "*I'm* one of the things he corrupted."

She doesn't flinch.

"How can you not be afraid of me?" I hate that my voice breaks. "Didn't they let you read the files before they sent you on this doomed mission? The things I *really* did, the shit Malcolm covered up? Don't you know how much blood is on my hands?"

"No. Not your hands. *Malcolm's* hands," Piper says with the certainty that hooked me when I was younger. That no-nonsense, no-bullshit focus that she'd used when she'd sauntered into this very apartment and told nineteen-year-old me that there was a future for someone like me, someone who couldn't touch anything—or anyone—without breaking it.

It was the first time I'd ever imagined a different life. Because of *her*.

And now, she leans forward, and I swear I see her hands tremble as she reaches for my jaw. Her fingers are soft on my skin.

"Come back," she pleads. "Let us help you. You're not in this alone, Ari."

She says my name, and I remember how euphoric it'd felt to hear her scream it when she came. It's been *years* since someone got off to me. The girls and guys I've fucked in the past ten years either said nothing at all or shouted *All-American Man*, because *that* was who they were fucking. Not *me*. Not Ari Dodgers.

Even with Lilly, it was tame. So careful. I tried to make what I had with her real, but from the start, it was always a publicity stunt, and that bled into whatever heat we might've had in the bedroom. She'd wanted me to push my limits with her, but Malcolm had drilled into my head how the image of our relationship trumped all else. She couldn't have a scratch on her. Not a bruise. Not a hickey. *Nothing*.

But with Piper.

With Piper...

Her confidence. Her certainty. Her strength.

I fell in love with her ten years ago.

And I haven't stopped loving her since.

I heave myself off the tiles. "I have somewhere I need to be."

"Ari!" She climbs out of the shower after me, grabbing her soaked clothes into a ball against her chest.

In her hand, her phone buzzes again.

"Tell Lucas I'm not coming back," I snap over my shoulder. My bedroom is sparse, but I find an extra t-shirt and gym shorts, and I chuck them at her. "You can wear these out. Hell, stay if you want. I won't be coming back here, either."

I scramble for my own clothes and dress as fast as possible.

"What's your plan, then?" There's ice in Piper's voice. "What is the almighty Ari going to do? You're just going to go back to being a recluse?"

She knows exactly what she's doing when she asks me that.

She knows exactly how deep that question goes, cutting me right to the center of my soul.

I stare straight at her, and for a second, I want to show her just how bad she's hurt me.

But I don't.

I can't.

All I see suddenly are the tears in her eyes when I'd broken things off. The glimpses of her over the years, sadness morphing to anger morphing to indifference.

I bow my head, jaw working. "I have somewhere I need to be," I repeat, and I walk out the door.

IT WAS A BRILLIANT PLAN, really, getting Piper to seduce me back in. I gotta hand it to Lucas—he's even more ruthless than Malcolm.

Which is double the incentive to go nowhere near Heroes Org again.

I sprint down the stairs of the apartment building, going as fast as I dare in case civilians are around. Not civilians, damn it—just *people*. I'm one of them now.

Again.

But am I? Really? Could I ever be anything but this fucked-up shell of a super who utterly eviscerates everything he touches? *Civilians* aren't like that. *Civilians* aren't walking weapons of mass destruction.

I hit a landing and stumble into the wall, catching my breath, but not from the run. From the knowledge that Piper's still up in my room, and she'll probably wait there for me even though I have no intention of going back.

My cock throbs at the thought of her splayed naked on my beaten-up mattress.

Some part of me had known exactly why she was here the moment she found me in the store. But it wasn't for *me* that I'd let her come to my apartment, not entirely—I'd give her anything she wants. Anything except going back to Heroes Org. And if that meant fucking her in the shower? Living with the agony of remembering how *good* it felt to be lodged in her pussy, knowing I'll never have that sensation again, no matter how many people I fuck?

I punch the wall, too hard, and leave a gaping hole in the drywall.

Shit.

Another thing I'll have to write a check for.

I push back and continue down the stairs, eyes blurring.

Piper initiated the sex. She could've tried a hundred different ways to get me to come back, but she picked fucking, drudging up our old connection instead of playing on my ties to Heroes Org, the good I could do there, my duty to the country, and all the other bullshit propaganda.

So it wasn't entirely about getting me to go back. It sure as hell wasn't about forgiveness, though. There's nothing mended between us.

But something feels different now. Resolved, maybe? Like closure.

Like penance.

That's what it was. Her inflicting on me just a fraction of the pain I'd cause her.

I fix my baseball hat tighter on my head as I duck out of the building, into the night. The street is littered with people heading for bars or restaurants, but I turn sharply to cut into the bar attached to this building.

There's a weight in my chest now, a realization growing stronger as my eyes adjust to the dive bar's low lighting. A bar stretches along the left wall while shaded booths fill the right. A pool table and a few pinging arcade games sit in the back. The whole place smells like cheap booze and piss and there's a handful of people here, most nursing drinks alone. This isn't a place you go to socialize. This is a place you go to wallow.

I slide up to the bar and check my phone. Nearly ten, but there's nothing from Persephone.

My thumb twitches. I still remember Piper's number.

No, *fuck*. I paid my penance to her. We're done now, really. She's free of me.

She's better off.

I order a double whiskey and, because I still haven't eaten, some nachos. I'm not at all hungry anymore, though. I'm too focused on that idea spinning through my brain.

Penance.

I can't undo anything I've done, but is there really a way I can make up for it?

The bartender drops a napkin in front of me. I take it, frowning at him, but he looks like he's seen a ghost.

Immediately, the hairs on the back of my neck stand on end. My senses sharpen, honed from years of training, and all my muscles tighten.

The napkin has writing scrawled on it.

Farthest booth.

Do I recognize that writing? I squint, but the lights are too low.

I stand slowly, eyes zipping to the rear booth. A man sits with his back to the bulk of the room. Stupid—he has no view of anyone approaching him.

Maybe he doesn't need it.

A chill creeps up my arms as I cross the bar. I stop just behind the man. The booths around us are empty, and so is the back part of the bar. Like everyone can sense the general *do-not-fuck-with-me* aura this guy emits.

"I expected to meet Persephone," I say, voice low.

The man takes a sip of his drink. "You think the Queen of Elysium would debase herself by coming to a Brooklyn bar?"

I squint. I was on edge already, but something about his voice...

My skin feels too tight. My pulse slows.

I *know* that voice.

Familiarity circles me, a predator I can't see, and it heightens every single fight-or-flight drive I have. And when that happens, I hurt people. I break things.

Calm down. Calm the fuck down.

I manage a strangled breath and slide into the bench opposite the man.

He's wearing a baseball cap, too, his head tipped down. The moment I sit, he slowly raises his chin, until the light from the dingy yellow lamp over our heads shines on his face.

That square jaw. Those gray eyes. That brown stubble against his pale skin and the way it felt under my lips, rough, painful, but so fucking right.

Every wound muscle releases. Every arch of tension. *Everything.*

I'm a ghost sitting here. I have to be.

Because *he* is.

"Bryce?" I whisper his name. I can't speak too loudly, or he'll disappear.

One corner of his mouth lifts. He shakes his head, looking truly dazed. "Wow. I haven't heard that name in awhile."

"What the—*how are you here?*" I claw my fingers into the table, the wood cracking, but it's the only thing keeping me from tearing across the top and grabbing him, touching him, making sure he *is* real.

Bryce cocks an eyebrow. "You texted me."

"I texted—I texted *Persephone*. I—"

"I know."

"How are you here? What the *fuck*, Bryce?"

He blinks. "I didn't think All-American Man could cuss."

"I'm—" It's a shout. The bar freezes; a few eyes turn toward us. I calm down, though it takes all of my strength to do so.

"It's good to see you, Ari," Bryce says before I can speak again.

Is it? I huff a brittle laugh, eyes moving through his. He doesn't renege on it. His face is open and honest, beseeching, almost, like he really is happy to see me.

"What are you doing here?" I manage.

Bryce sets down his drink. The ice clinks. "Persephone wants me to bring you to her."

"You... you work for Persephone?"

He nods once.

I run a hand down my face. Am I dreaming? Did all that alcohol I ingest actually slip me into a coma?

"We can go now," Bryce says. He juts his chin at the emergency exit behind me.

"This can't be—just, give me a second."

I duck my head down, hands on the back of my neck, trying to fucking *think*.

Bryce is my contact with Persephone.

Bryce who Piper recruited from the floor above mine. Bryce who had super strength, too, only he'd learned early on how to control his, while I was always just the gawky kid who hid at home out of fear of hurting anyone. Bryce who used to train with me at Heroes Org, who fell for Piper just as hard as I did, only it wasn't *just* her I'd dream about, and by some twist of fate, some fucking *miracle* of heaven, the three of us collapsed into each other in a madcap tangle of bliss.

And then...

And then Malcolm, and a contract I'd have been an idiot to refuse. A morality clause that strictly stipulated my public appearance and how the face of Heroes Org was expected to act.

One word from that clause still throbs in my brain.

Monogamy.

I'd thought Piper and Bryce would still have each other, that I could extricate myself from our relationship and leave them intact. They were so much more suited to each other, anyway—both ripe with confidence, both absolutely sure of who they were and what they wanted out of life.

But the minute I broke things off, I saw the reality of what we'd been. What we'd had.

It was all of us, or nothing.

I broke us.

I chose my career over the two of them.

So years later, when a routine mission went sour Bryce had been on solo, Piper and I couldn't even mourn together. We were both at Bryce's memorial, and I'd wanted to go to her, to just talk—but she'd turned on her heel and walked away, and I'd known then how badly I'd fucked everything up. It was my fault we didn't get any more time together. It was my fault that Bryce had died, because if we'd stayed together, if I'd rejected Heroes Org's contract and just stayed a low-level super, then maybe he'd have been safe, too. I could've had his back on the mission.

Regret wells up. That goddamn guilt grows another vine, choking me, and I dig the heels of my palms into my eyes.

When I look back at Bryce, his expression hasn't changed. Openness. Patience.

He's not mad at me?

He should be. He has to be. There's absolutely nothing else he could feel toward me anymore.

I have no right to ask him what happened. He's working with Persephone now? He left Heroes Org to join up with the Villains without giving me a single notice that he was still alive? That's his prerogative. That's all his choices, and he owes me not a damn word of explanation.

I nod. "Let's go."

But when I slide out of the booth, Piper's there.

She has her hands on her hips, my t-shirt and gym shorts too baggy on her, the fabric swimming around her body. Her hair hangs in wet curls on her shoulders, but her customary red lipstick is vivid and perfect.

She glares from me to my boothmate and back.

Whatever retort she'd had for me vanishes. I actually see it drop out of her mouth, anger fading into shock.

Piper stares down at Bryce. The look of absolute heartbreak on her face makes my chest crack, and instead of grief, *anger* flares up.

I get why Bryce didn't contact me. But he didn't even let *Piper* know he was still alive?

I reach across the booth and grab Bryce's collar, hauling him bodily out of the booth and slamming his ass onto the table. He lets me—he was always stronger than me—and the little smirk on his lips is infuriating.

There's barely an inch of space between our faces. In this moment, it may as well be ten years ago, my hands knotted in his shirt, moments away from ripping it off his tight chest.

My dick swells, pressing against my jeans.

"What the *hell?*" I snarl down at him.

The few remaining bar occupants scatter out the door. This place isn't a virgin to bar fights, and the patrons know what to do—get out of the way *fast*.

Bryce grabs my wrists. His fingers are too cold, frigid, and hard—

I look down.

One of his arms is metal all the way to his shoulder. A biomechanical prosthetic.

My small spurt of anger peters out.

Bryce reads that opening, that weakness, and moves.

He flips us, landing me on the floor, his thighs bracketing my hips. He plants that metal arm across my collarbone and bends down, using all his weight, all his strength, to keep me planted.

When we sparred during training sessions, back before, at Heroes Org, sometimes I could dislodge him.

But with that arm, the extra weight and strength it provides him, I'm trapped. Utterly. Completely.

My cock goes completely hard. Rock solid.

One touch from this man, and I'm as good as gone.

I grab his arm, neck bent back, my eyes on his.

He looks like he's in pain.

Of course he is. *I'm* the reason for it.

Fuck.

But...

I can feel his dick against my stomach. It's hard, too.

"Bryce," I gasp.

Behind us, Piper yanks at his shoulders. "Bryce—what the fuck? Get off him! Oh my god—"

Bryce obeys. He staggers to his feet, staring down at me with his head slightly crooked, like he's hearing his name being called down a long tunnel.

Before I can chase that look, before I can get him to tell me what *the fuck happened,* he nods at the back door again.

"Persephone's waiting."

5
PIPER

It's not easy being a non-powered human in charge of training and wrangling supers. Now, Heroes Org has some supers in the Agent department, ones adept at breaking up sparring matches that go too far or who can restrain a super when they lose control.

But I've never had that luxury, and I have never let it stop me.

I put my body between the boys—*my* boys—and stand firm. "Look, I don't know what the fuck is happening," I say, glaring first at Ari and then Bryce. "You—" I snarl, pointing at Ari, "—need to come back with me. And you—" I add, spinning around to Bryce. "... you..."

My words sputter out to silence. Because the first thing that comes to mind is *"You're supposed to be dead."*

He is.

I went to his funeral.

I may have cried my eyes out, but I didn't break. Not all the way.

I mourned for Bryce's death, and I saw goddamn All-American Man, and I didn't break.

Not then.

But I might now.

Something melts on Bryce's face, some whisper of emotion peeking through.

Ari grunts and pushes himself off the dirty bar floor.

"And where do you think you're going?" I demand, whirling back around to him.

"To get cleaned up," he says. There's anger in his voice but defeat as well. I watch as he heads to the men's room.

Bryce sits down at the booth as if none of this is earth-shatteringly *weird.*

"So," I say, sitting down across from him.

His eyebrow quirks up. "Hello, Piper."

I lick my lips over my red lipstick. I never stopped wearing it, not after he told me once that he loved it. I have three tubes at home, even though I never thought he'd see me in the color again.

"Where have you been?" I ask. Then I shake my head. The answer is in front of me. "You've been with Persephone. At Elysium?" The doubt in my voice is real—Bryce *never* seemed like the kind of Hero to go dark.

But he nods.

I see the pieces fall in place, slowly, sifting through my still-shocked mind. After Ari broke up our Triad, because a polyamorous throuple didn't exactly fit the image of *All-American Man,* I stayed on at Heroes Org. My skill set made me the perfect Agent, but it's not like I could apply those skills to any other organization.

A girl needs a job.

But while Ari shot up the ranks of Heroes, Bryce... dropped off. His missions became further and further away. I haven't looked at his file since he "died," but I know he did deep undercover work in Russia, something else in Greenland—places that were cold and snowy and remote.

Places where they'd never send golden boy All-American Man.

When Bryce "died," all that came back was pieces of him. The funeral had been closed-casket.

An arm, I think. *All that had been left of him after the explosion when his mission went south was his arm.*

My eyes drift to the biomechanical arm. It starts at his shoulder, all the way down to his fingers, drumming on the table between us.

Ari broke up our Triad.

Not Bryce.

Not me.

I reach across the table. "I've missed you," I say. *I've missed* us, I want to say.

But I don't.

Bryce smiles at me sadly, but it doesn't meet his eyes.

I frown. "Can you tell me what happened?" I ask. I look to his arm, but I mean more than that.

Because... Bryce is different now. Something's... off.

"Accident," he grunts. "Lost a fight; lost my arm."

"Why didn't you come back to Heroes Org?" We have this same type of tech; we could have helped fix his body. Hell, Anthony Stern himself works for us, and he may be a huge playboy, but the billionaire has brains, I'll give him that. If Anthony can make himself an artificial heart, an arm would have been a cinch.

Bryce shakes his head.

It wasn't just his body that needed fixing after Ari broke us.

"Elysium isn't what you think it is," Bryce says, somewhat ominously. "Heroes Org has it all wrong."

My whole body bucks up in rejection of this idea, triggering an adrenaline surge I have to struggle to keep in check. I've dedicated my whole *life* to Heroes Org, and our greatest mission is stopping Elysium.

"Things are easier there," he continues, not noticing or not caring about the emotions I'm grappling with. "You don't have to dwell in darkness at Elysium. Unless you're into that, I guess. But it helps. I couldn't move on after Ari and you and me... Persephone helped me with that."

Under the table, my hand curls into a fist.

What a fucking luxury it must be, to be a super and have the ability to just fly off and pretend like the heartbreak of your life doesn't exist. I don't know what has happened to Bryce since the days of our tangled mess, but it's clear he's been able to move on. He's not emotionally connected to me, to Ari... to anything.

Must be fucking nice.

I don't have a Persephone and Elysium to distract *me* from my pain.

When Ari broke my heart and Bryce left us, I didn't have any way to escape my life.

I just had to live it.

One long day after the other.

Alone.

Ari stomps up to the booth. He's splashed cold water over his red eyes, but if he thought retreating to the bathroom would help him "clean up," he's wrong. He's never looked more disheveled and just *messed up* than now.

"Right," Ari says, meeting neither my nor Bryce's eyes. "Let's go then."

Bryce moves to get out of the booth, but I grab his metal arm. My strength is laughably nothing, certainly not enough to keep him still, but he pauses at my touch nonetheless.

"Ari's *not* going to Elysium," I say.

There's not that much Heroes Org has on file about Elysium, the den of thieves and criminals that the worst Villain of all, Persephone, runs. We've lost more than one Hero to her wiles, but we don't know where her base is, nor how she maintains control of the Villains. Attempts at infiltrating Elysium have almost always led to lost Heroes who fall to her, or else mind-altering blank spaces in the few Heroes who come back.

All I know, without a doubt in my soul, is that Persephone is both heartless and powerful.

And that's not a trap I want either of my boys falling into.

"You don't get to tell me what to do, Piper," Ari says. He sounds so fucking tired that it breaks my heart.

I open my mouth to shout at him, but my words die as I feel the smooth, cold metal of Bryce's biomechanical fingers rub over my knuckles, drawing my attention.

"Elysium isn't what you think it is," he repeats. "And Ari can make up his own mind."

I glower at him. The pressure on my hand increases—not painful, but I know that if I tried to jerk free, it would hurt. I frown. Is this a threat? Or is Bryce trying to tell me something with his touch?

Goddamnit, I used to know him so well that I could read him like a book. I could tell what Bryce was thinking just by looking at him.

But the thoughts behind his ice-cold eyes now are utterly silent.

The pressure releases, and I snatch my hand back before I turn to glare at Ari. "At least know what you're getting into," I snarl, throwing my hand out to Bryce. "What are the parameters of the deal?"

Ari blinks a few times.

"I mostly figured I'd just go to Elysium and let Persephone decide how I should be punished," he says.

"Punished?" I stand up, my voice rising to nearly a shout. I don't care. "You don't deserve *punishment*, Ari!"

He drops his eyes. "Yes, I do."

"If you could quit being a goddamn victim for five seconds, you could actually *do* something useful," I growl.

Ari looks at me like I stabbed him in the heart. I glance back at Bryce, whose lips are pressed shut. He shakes his head at me, and despite his cold front, even I can see the meaning behind this look. *Wrong move, Piper.*

"*This* is what I can do," Ari says, turning away from me to fully focus on Bryce. "Take me to Elysium. I need a judge. I need to pay penance." There's so much defeat in his voice that I almost think, if Bryce were to try to kill him, Ari would let him.

It breaks my heart.

But when Bryce stands, nodding, and starts to lead Ari to the door, I race after them.

My heart may be shattered glass at this point, but my spine is made of fucking steel, and there's no way I'm letting *my* boys get in trouble without me.

6

ARI

Instead of opening the back door, Bryce puts a device on it. Some kind of keypad.

He punches in numbers, and when he notices me watching over his shoulder, he cuts a glare that's so lethal I instantly step back.

What happened to him?

The device beeps, and Bryce surveys the bar behind us. It's still empty —even the bartender ducked out.

Those cold eyes meet mine. For a long beat, he's silent, just staring at me, and my lips part. My chest knots with longing to do *something*—touch him. Kiss him, just to see if it feels the same, if the brush of his mouth on mine still feels as much like home as Piper's.

But Bryce opens the door and shoves me out into the alley behind the bar.

Only... it isn't the alley.

The world shifts. Something like electricity sizzles across every inch of my skin, and then I'm collapsing to the floor in what my eyes instantly recognize as a throne room but my brain can't make any sense of.

I go rigid on my knees, fight-or-flight activated again, prepared to go full All-American Man on wherever this place is—

But I stop.

Hold onto myself.

Breathe.

The long, cavernous room is all dark gothic stone and decor to match. A maroon runner leads to an honest to god throne at the end, held up on a dais constructed of jagged black obsidian. On either side of the runner are clusters of chairs, lounges, chaises, couches, stages—I even see a bed. Some clusters are cut off with curtains; most are open to a full view of the room.

And the people filling those spaces are all fucking. In couples, in whole groups—with each other, with toys. I see one woman plunging her cunt up and down on a dildo sticking out of a horse saddle while a group watches her, stroking themselves. Two men fuck while one blows a third. A woman has her wrists bound in restraints against a wall while another woman alternates between licking her clit and twisting a vibrating dildo into her pussy.

I dig my fingers into my thighs, still on my knees, every muscle in my body gone to stone.

Most, if not all, of these people are supers.

One man is glowing green. Another has horns growing from his head that a woman uses as an anchor. A woman levitates and her partner fucks her with a tongue that grows as long as my arm.

My eyes peel open wide. A breath tangles in my throat, sweat breaking out across my skin, every nerve vividly alive and sensitive. My cock instantly hardens against my jeans, driven to the edge by the sights and sounds of moaning and the shock of going from that bar to *here*.

I recognize many of these people just from their powers.

I've *fought* many of these people. Ruthlessly. For Heroes Org cameras where I left them in bleeding heaps to slink off back to whatever lair they called home.

Panic seizes me, my brain quickly calculating my odds.

I'm not even sure I *can* die, but if all these Villains recognize me, I don't stand a chance of getting out of here alive.

What did I expect, though, when I reached out to the leader of Elysium? These are the very people I need to atone to. The very people I need to pay penance.

Bryce steps beside me where I still kneel on the floor. I look up at him, then back at the door we came through. On this side, it's some kind of portal.

"What the fuck?" I gasp.

One corner of his lips lifts. "Persephone's means of traveling are far superior to whatever last-decade tech Heroes Org uses."

"I wouldn't know what Heroes Org uses anymore, honestly," I say.

Bryce looks down at me.

My body jolts with the familiarity of this position.

Me, on my knees.

Him, towering over me.

My mouth waters, remembering how his cock tasted. How it felt making him come—pulling him to the cusp of orgasm only to tease him back, dragging it out until I had him shaking, writhing, *pleading* at my mercy.

I look away. I have to. The urge to relive those memories is too strong, drowning out everything else.

Like why I'm really here.

"Where's Persephone?" I ask as I come to my feet, not exactly steadily.

Bryce starts to answer when both of us whirl around at the sound of a delicate feminine gasp.

Piper stands on this side of the portal.

I lunge for her, but Bryce gets to her first.

True panic flashes across his face, and he grabs her arm. "What the fuck do you think you're doing? This isn't for you."

She glares at him, seething. "Whatever you two idiots are getting yourselves into, I'm coming, too. You'll likely just get yourself killed, *again*, and fuck, Bryce—I just got you back."

Her last words are soft. My heart breaks.

Her eyes slide to me and I hear those words again. *I just got you back.*

I look away, jaw working.

"You have no idea what you're doing, Piper," Bryce says to her. He's pleading, gentle almost. "I'll come talk to you later, I swear. Just go back to New York."

He pulls her towards the portal. She drops her heels into the maroon runner, tugs against his grip on her—

Around us, some of the orgies have stopped. People watch. I can't read their expressions. Expectancy?

Do they recognize me?

"Bryce," I hiss. "Hey—"

"Stop."

The voice booms across the chamber. The portal immediately vanishes, showing the rest of the room beyond, still more clusters of furniture with people fucking.

I turn, slowly, veins throbbing with every beat of my heart.

In the center of the runner stands a woman who has to be Persephone.

I've never seen her. Never even seen a photo. Heroes Org knew nothing about her other than her name, even though Malcolm swore he knew her once. It was like no one could hold onto details about her unless she wanted them to.

I drink her in now. She's almost as tall as I am, with rich black skin and her hair done in dozens of perfect braids that hang past her breasts, the ends tipped with gold clasps. Her gown is a deep, dark midnight blue, cut all the way to her navel, the fabric so sheer I can see her taut nipples beneath, the apex of her pussy when she takes a step closer to me.

My mouth hangs open. I can't help it.

She's fucking gorgeous. No wonder everyone calls her the Villain Queen. Even without knowing what kind of super she is, I don't doubt that her powers are awe-inspiring and desperately destructive.

Her emerald green eyes lock on mine. She smiles, but it's calculating, and a shiver of anticipation rushes over my body.

"Ari Dodgers," she purrs. "All-American Man. How good of you to come visit."

Bryce and Piper are motionless behind me. But when Persephone cuts her gaze to Piper, I dive in between them, hands out.

"This is about me," I say fast. "Let her go. She's an innocent."

"An innocent Heroes Org Agent?" Persephone tuts. "No such thing."

Shit. She knows who Piper is.

"But you are quite right, Ari Dodgers." Persephone puts a finger on her chin, eyeing me, head to toe. "This is about you."

I swallow. The whole of the chamber is fixed on us now.

I'm likely the first Hero to ever set foot... wherever we are.

And now every single one of these Villains knows exactly who I am.

They don't attack. Likely they're just waiting for Persephone's order.

A strange kind of calm descends over me. I lower back to my knees, head bowed to Persephone.

"Ari!" Piper whispers behind me. "Ari, don't—"

"Persephone," I start. "I come to atone for the sins I committed against Elysium."

The crowd gasps. Murmurs ripple through the people around us.

Persephone says nothing.

I peek up at her. She's watching me, thoughtful, silent, her eyes narrow, her face entirely emotionless.

"I have wronged you," I say. I look at one side of the room; the other. "I committed heinous acts against Villains at the control of my superiors. I wish to make things right, in whatever way you see fit."

I'm signing my goddamn death certificate.

But I don't back down. I don't shake or stutter or feel at all afraid.

This is the rightest thing I've done in a long, long time.

"If you'll have me." I look back at Persephone, deep into her green eyes. "I am yours."

The chamber goes silent. Dozens of people, all frozen in shock. I can hear Piper gasping behind me, but I can't look back at her. Can't look back at Bryce.

Persephone steps forward. She puts her hand on my jaw, her thumb brushing against my bottom lip.

My cock throbs unbidden.

"A promise to me," she says, a breathy whisper, "is forever, Ari Dodgers."

My chest grips. *Forever.*

I need only glance around the room again to feel the weight of that word. One, two, three, seven, twelve—there are more than a dozen people here that I've hurt. Some beyond repair, like the damage I did to the Raven's wing when I damn near ripped it off in my fury. There's likely more that I don't even recognize, adding insult to my injury.

The day Malcolm dropped his hold on me was the day Ari Dodgers died.

I nod in Persephone's grip. "I understand."

"Ari!" Piper shrieks.

Bryce has been utterly silent. Not a moan of agreement or protest.

Why does that hurt?

"But let her go." I cut my head at Piper. "She's not part of this."

"Mm." Persephone looks past me, at Piper. "I think she should be the one to make that decision. Piper Carson—do you wish to leave?"

"Not without Ari," she says instantly.

"Goddamnit, Piper—" I start to turn, but Persephone tightens her grip on my face, holding me towards her.

"Then it's settled." Persephone looks back down at me. "You both will stay. Piper, until she amends the requirements of her departure; and you. Ari Dodgers. You will stay forever—or until you have atoned for your sins. Whichever comes first."

That echoes through me. I feel something heady and effervescent loop around my chest, tugging me towards Persephone, an invisible tie.

My heartbeat quickens. Something in her powers has bound me to her.

The urge to buck away is strong, but I grit my jaw, breathing deep. I agreed to this. This is what I want.

Persephone snaps the fingers of her other hand. "Doctor—show Miss Carson to one of our villas. Arrange for her to leave whenever she chooses. You'll be quite safe," Persephone tells her. "No one does a thing on this island without my knowing. Not a single one of my... *Villains...* will touch you." She smirks. "Unless you want them to."

My mouth goes dry. Can Piper trust her? She should leave. She should get the fuck out of this place.

But I know she's too damn stubborn to leave without me.

A man moves out from the side of the hall. He's one of the few people other than us who's fully clothed, wearing a black suit under a flowing red cape with a collar that rises past his ears. His sharp eyes assess me languidly, tauntingly, and I feel a jolt of tension, knowing I'm at this man's mercy as much as Persephone's now.

And because I recognize him.

Doctor Steve Rare. Brilliant surgeon turned raving Villain after he discovered he had the power to manipulate time and space.

I broke his arm. Twice. Blew up one of his mansions. Chased him underground. Which was, apparently, *here*.

Doctor turns away from me with a scowl and faces Piper. "If you'll follow me."

There's a pause. Finally, Piper relents, trudging after Doctor, ferocity in her eyes as she passes Persephone.

She throws one last look down at me. Utter fury.

She's here because of *me*.

But she doesn't get it. This is where I'm supposed to be. Not Heroes Org.

She'll realize that. Eventually.

When Piper's gone, I start to stand.

Persephone pushes my shoulder. "Did I say you could get up?"

I drop back onto my knees. My heart hasn't slowed down, and it ramps up even higher, something tense winding through me.

Excitement, I realize.

I want to be here, on my knees before her. I can even feel Bryce's eyes on my back, and fuck, that just drives me hotter, though nothing about this should be hot at all.

"You swore yourself to me," Persephone says. "To atone for your sins. What a stupidly open-ended contract you've entered into, Ari Dodgers."

I exhale in a hard puff.

"Ordinarily," she continues before I can say anything, "I'd never agree to such a self-flagellating request. But." She puts her thumb back on my lip, pushes until it's in my mouth. She tastes like jasmine and orange blossoms. "It isn't death that you desire. Your desires are far more in line with Elysium than you've even admitted to yourself. And I think, All-American Man, that we can make this arrangement mutually beneficial."

I can't say anything, even if I wanted to. She moves her thumb back and forth in my mouth, and when her eyes lift behind me, to Bryce, everything in my body tenses.

"We'll start easy," she says. "The safe word here is *afterlife*. Say it at any time, for any reason, and everything stops immediately, no questions asked. Disobedience results in immediate and permanent expulsion, at the minimum. Do you understand?"

I still have a choice, even now?

Fuck, my vision starts to cloud, desire warping with eagerness. I nod. "'Afterlife.' I understand."

"Good. Now, you wronged my Winter Warrior. You will begin the long, slow process of making it up to him by—" She tips her head in a moment of silence, her eyes narrowing until she smiles. "Pick something, Warrior."

Winter Warrior. She means Bryce. That's his name here.

It's also clear Persephone is talking to him somehow. I still can't turn to look at him. Can't even begin to process what she's implying.

She wants me to... do *something...* to Bryce.

"Pick," Persephone repeats, her voice icy, "or use the safe word. Choose neither, and I'll give him to Caldera."

All the blood in my body drains straight to my cock. Caldera—he's here? He isn't even from this world. An outer space Villain who rampaged across multiple countries in eastern Europe at the behest of *His Master*.

We never did find out who that was.

But, fuck, Caldera does *not like me.*

And the thought of being *given* to him. The look in Persephone's eyes, the implications in all her words—my dick knows exactly what she's saying.

I hate how much I want it.

No, *want* isn't strong enough.

I *need* it. My body craves to be used by these Villains the same way my soul aches for absolution. The very idea has me moaning softly around Persephone's thumb.

She smiles at me. "Excited, are we?" She bends down, removes her thumb from my mouth, and kisses me.

Her tongue shoots between my lips, going deep, and I taste all of her, mint and dizzying sweetness.

"Suck his cock," she says into my mouth, and I stagger, catching myself on my hands.

Did she just say—

I look over my shoulder at Bryce.

His face is stony. But I can see his pulse throbbing in his neck. And when he meets my eyes, his lips part, and I see the Bryce I used to know, the one who first kissed me when we were dumb teenagers in Brooklyn.

He picked a blow job. He could've used the safe word, opted out of all of this—but he didn't.

He *wants* this. Wants me.

I need no further incentive. I want that look to stay on his face. I want his dick in my mouth, for us to connect over that like we used to.

I crawl across the floor between us. Every eye in this place is still drilled into me, but I couldn't care less. I owe Bryce this. I owe him as much as I owe anyone here.

More.

I rise up, balancing on my heels, and lift my hands to his belt. It comes apart easily; then his fly; and I guide his pants and boxers down until his cock springs free.

It's already hard, the tip glistening with pre-cum, and I suck in a breath at the sight of it, proof of his arousal.

I look up into his eyes as I curl my fingers around his shaft.

His brows pinch together, strain; his hands ball in fists at his sides, the metal fingers on his left hand clinking delicately.

A single stroke. Testing him. It's not too late to back out of this.

I wait for him to say it. *Afterlife.* For him to walk away and decide he is well and truly done with me.

But, still holding my eyes, he nods. He looks like he's in pain, but a delirious kind of pain, the twisted, aching, writhing *need* that has taken root in me.

That nod unleashes me, and I dive, plunging his cock into my mouth, all the way in my throat.

Bryce gasps, head throwing back to the ceiling.

I anchor myself on his hips, fingers digging into his ass, and start to move, slow pulls, my tongue wrapping around the head and back down until I find a rhythm. It's like no time has passed at all. The taste of him, salty and rich; the feel of him in my mouth and under my hands as his whole body clenches, building tension.

My own cock is throbbing, achingly hard, but I don't dare touch myself. This is for Bryce.

I want to make it last, tease him out like I used to; but I also want to hear him scream my name and know that it was me who made him feel this sensation. I fuck him with my mouth, taking him to the hilt and back again, over and over, faster and faster.

He starts to rock, thrusting against my motion, and fuck, I'm undone. How have I gone almost ten years without this? Without the feel of him, the taste of him?

Then he comes, his load shooting into my throat.

He doesn't say my name. But the cry he releases is raw and all but makes me come right there, hearing the pleasure in it.

I suck down the last quakes of his orgasm, wanting to linger in this moment, *feel* this more—

But Persephone pulls me to my feet.

"Strip," she tells me.

I'm woozy, my lips raw, but I obey. My eyes go to Bryce as I undress. He's tucking himself back into his pants, his cheeks stained pink with exertion, and fuck, I want to kiss him there, take his mouth in mine so he can taste himself in me.

I'm so lost in these thoughts, what I just did, how I never in my wildest dreams thought I'd get to do that again, that I don't even really process that I'm standing naked before all the Villains of Elysium until Persephone grabs my stiff cock.

I hiss in surprise.

Her green eyes turn up at the edges, a small smile. "Every time I see you, I want you like this," she tells me.

I nod, too aware of her hand on my cock, the slow, gentle strokes she's making.

"And every time a Villain summons you," she tells me, stroking, *stroking*, "I want you like this, too. Naked. Ready. Willing."

I nod again, trembling, and my eyes cut around the room. The looks on the faces in the crowd have shifted now. Anger and hatred to something like eagerness. Arousal.

They want this.

They want to fuck me.

Oh, god. I want them to fuck me, too.

Persephone presses her lips to my ear. "Now show them what they have to look forward to. Come."

The word is a command that shoots straight down to my dick, and I come with a rocking shout that echoes off the high walls. Pleasure washes through me in wave after wave, and on the last one, my eyes lock on Bryce.

He's biting his lip, a new hunger in his eyes. Something deep and dark and newly awoken, and I wonder if it matches my own hunger.

All-American Man is well and truly dead. Whoever I am now—a sex toy in a Villain's sex dungeon—is as far from that perfectly sculpted Heroes Org image as possible.

And I couldn't be more enthralled.

7
PIPER

The digs Persephone gives me are really amazing, far more than I had dreamed of. I don't know exactly what I expected as I dove through that portal in Brooklyn after my boys, but I didn't anticipate a tropical paradise, that's for sure.

But that's what this is.

The private villa really does seem truly private. Outside the door, I can feel the hum of... something. Not exactly mesmer powers, not really like anything I know at all, but when I step outside, I can *feel* Persephone's presence. It's true—she's blocked herself off from my villa. But I think if I stepped out the door and just *whispered* her name, hell, just *thought* it, she'd appear instantly.

If that didn't work, though, I do find a panic button in the main room of the house. It's discrete but clearly labeled. The panic button gives me more confidence than ever that I'm truly private in this villa—Persephone won't come unless I press it. And until I do, I'm left with...

Silence.

In my head.

In my heart.

It's almost lonely.

A low whistle draws my attention, and I look up as Bryce steps inside. "She's being nice to you," he says, something like awe in his voice.

I stand and move over to him. "Was she…" I hesitate, not wanting to fully ask the question. "Was she not nice to you?"

His face goes blank.

"Why are you here, Bryce?" I demand. He faked his own death to avoid us; there's no reason for him to seek me out now.

When he meets my eyes, I see confusion and—something else—warring inside him. He was always the quiet one. But this is something different. I cannot fully temper the anger that flares inside of me, but I feel more than just rage at the past. And I want answers.

I cross the room to him, my footsteps silent on the lush white carpet. The faint scents of jasmine waft around us; the air is warm and inviting. But when I touch his biomechanical arm, I feel only cold; I smell only metal.

"What happened, Bryce?" I ask him gently.

His eyes meet mine, and something inside him seems to melt. "I'm not supposed to remember," he says, the words slipping out.

My blood turns to ice. "Not... *supposed* to?" I ask, more of a demand than a question.

Bryce nods, once, tightly. "That was my deal with her. I was fucking *done*, Piper. I couldn't get him or you out of my head. Every time I turned around, there was another reminder of everything we had lost."

Each other.

We had lost each other.

I remember the fight Malcolm had with Ari about it. I wasn't supposed to overhear—I was pretty low on the ranks in the Agency—but then again, maybe Malcolm had wanted me to hear him rage against his golden boy.

"Be straight, be gay, we don't care," he'd said. "But polyamory? You really think the American public is going to accept a national super hero who's in a Triad like that? You're going to be a laughingstock."

Ari had said something, but I couldn't hear his response. But Malcom's words are scarred into me, a brand upon my chest.

"So think about that Agent you're fucking, and the other boy, the Hero. They're not you. You keep fucking them, they'll never *rise up in Heroes Org. They'll be mired in nepotism. That Agent? She's done. She'll be fired. And the super you're fucking, too? He's not as strong as you. He's... disposable."*

. . .

After hearing that, I had wanted to burst into the conference room and punch Malcolm's lights out. I'd wanted to grab Ari and run.

But I hadn't.

"Malcolm was a mesmer," I say aloud, only fully realizing the consequences now that I'm telling Bryce. "He could control minds."

"A mesmer can only heavily influence a mind," Bryce's words are full of vitriol and spite. "Whatever he convinced Ari to be and do, a part of Ari wanted it."

I shake my head. Ari had high aspirations, that's true. But a part of him had wanted to drop me and Bryce, just for a chance to be the top hero at Heroes Org?

A part of me was willing to let him break us, so I could continue being an Agent?

Shame flushes over me.

"You were the only one true," I whisper, looking up at Bryce. And look at what it cost him. His arm. His life.

But he's shaking his head, dark brown locks dropping into his eyes. "No, it's not like that," he says. "The whole of Heroes Org is fucked up. It messes with your head, even if there's not a mesmer pulling the strings."

Maybe.

Following the mission is what led me back to Ari, to Brooklyn.

But following my heart is what brought me here, now, to Bryce and Persephone and this villa and this moment.

"What happened?" I ask Bryce again, softer. "What's been happening? Are you and Persephone…?"

He laughs hollowly. "We're not a couple. I mean, I'm not a saint, but it's not like that." He catches my look. "I'm clean, by the way. Persephone keeps everything safe. And our old rules apply. My safe word is 'sword.'"

"Shield," I say, reminding him of mine, but my eyes slide away. That's not what I'm really asking. I want to know why, from the beginning.

And he knows that.

He takes a deep, shaky breath. "When I was injured, I had a choice. Call Heroes Org, or call Persephone. I called her."

I don't press for details. I can feel that this moment is fragile, and I don't want to break it. I wait for Bryce to continue.

"She brought me here, through a portal. Fixed me up. I think I could have just left after I was healed…Elysium doesn't work with payment and debt like Heroes Org does. Don't get me wrong, things aren't free, but it is different."

"But you wanted to stay," I whisper, heart breaking.

Bryce nods, his eyes slipping away from mine. "She offered to suppress my memories," he says, a confession. "Heal not just my body, but my mind. If I would work for her, she would take away the painful memories."

I reach up with trembling fingers and touch his temple. So that's why he was so cold before, why he barely seemed to register any emotion at seeing us again.

How many times over the past decade had I wanted to do the same? How many times had I looked at the obituary for Bryce or the smiling photo of Ari on a billboard and wished I could just excise the pain that lanced through me?

If Persephone had offered me that deal, would I have taken it?

"No," I whisper aloud. I raise my eyes to Bryce, wait until he meets my gaze. "No, I wouldn't want to lose my memories. Not when they were all I had left of you."

Bryce nods slowly. "I realized that, too," he says. "I asked Persephone to break the spell."

My brows furrow in confusion.

"She's lifted the block," Bryce continues. "It's been... slow. Like water dripping through melting ice. When we got the call from Ari, Persephone sent me because I asked her to. Now, being around him, you—it's coming back quicker. The memories of what we used to be. I feel like…" He raises his hands—both his metal one and the one he was born with—to his face. "I feel like I'm becoming *me* again, being around you both."

My heart twists with pain. I had almost thought it had been easy. Ari had made it look so. When he left us, he didn't look back. And when Bryce had gotten so cold and distant...

"It doesn't hurt as much," he says. "It's not as raw before."

"Time does that, too," I whisper. "You didn't need a mind-controlling Villain to get to that point."

"It's a bit like grief, isn't it?" he says. "Mourning a life you could never have."

"We did have it," I say. "For a little while. And maybe…"

Maybe we could again.

"But you left me, too," I say. The words come out with more anger than I meant, but I don't want to take any of them back. Ari broke us, but Bryce left me to pick up the pieces of myself alone.

He reaches out and takes my hand. Without meaning to, it's balled into a fist. He runs his metallic fingers over mine until I release it.

"I fucked up, too," he says. "Ari and I both exploded, in different ways. And you were caught in the blast radius of both of us."

"It *hurt*," I say, my voice breaking over the word.

Something cracks across the cool, emotionless calm that Bryce usually views the world with. It's like ice shattering behind his eyes.

He dips his head to mine. My hand is steady this time as I reach up to him, brushing the hair out of his eyes. His hand clamps over mine, pressing my fingers into his face, leaning into the touch. His eyelids flutter closed, concentration furrowing on his brow, as if he is trying to imprint my touch into his mind.

And then his eyes fly open, and he's staring into mine.

"Piper," he whispers, his voice aching. "I can't change the past."

"Are you going to be here for the future?" I demand.

He has the grace to flush, but he doesn't break eye contact as he says, "I don't know."

At least he's honest this time.

The rage inside me breaks and falls away.

When Ari left us, I held onto the past. My memories sustained me when they were all I had left.

But Bryce learned to hold onto the present. This moment is all he has; there is no past, no future.

There is only now.

It's not the same, not without Ari. We both still love him, even if he's an ass hat too dense to see it. We're a Triad, nothing less.

But we're also people.

Bryce lowers his face to mine, slowly, slowly. Giving me plenty of time to back away, to stop this, to put up the walls that he sold his soul to erect.

I step forward.

I claim his lips with mine in a kiss that burns away the past.

His arms go around my body, pressing closer into me, closer. His kiss isn't just hungry, it's starving. His tongue plunges into me, claiming possession.

I am his.

And I am his.

My shirt—Ari's shirt, because I'm still in that dumb oversized t-shirt monstrosity—rips easily under Bryce's strong grip, the cloth coming away in shreds.

I almost laugh, thinking of how Ari ripped my tank top. Between the two of them, I won't have any clothes left.

But then my body flushes with heat, and the impact of the words hits me fully. Between the two of them and with no clothing at all is *exactly* where I want to be.

I stumble backwards as Bryce's kissing grows with urgency. My feet move from lush white carpet to smooth hardwood until the backs of my legs thump into a wide, expansive lounging couch. I tumble down onto the soft cushions, putting me at eye-level with the bulge behind Bryce's pants.

I reach for his belt, but Bryce beats me to it, yanking the buckle loose and ripping the fly down so violently that I think he broke the zipper. I wriggle out of the remains of my own clothes as Bryce kicks his pants off.

He looks down at my body, drinking it in. I think, perhaps, that I should be ashamed—it's been a decade, and while the Agency keeps me trim and fit, well... it's been a decade. But I don't feel an ounce of anything but love and desire for this man, and the look on his face tells me the same is true for him.

We are done with words, with explanations, with excuses. He moves over top my body on the wide cushion, his knees sinking down into the velvety soft material, and there is no need for words.

We lose ourselves within each other.

He moves slowly, methodically, as if we both may break. His head lowers to mine, his too-long brown hair tickling my forehead as he kisses me, long and deep and slow. His hand trails along the side of my face, down my neck, over to my breast.

He's not teasing or ramping me up; he's just relishing in the glory of my body.

Bryce's touch is firm but soft as rubs over my breast, then down my stomach, lower, lower. His fingers play a bit, gliding over the soft mound at the entrance to me, barely dipping down into the wetness. I mewl with desire, and he swallows the sound, but I feel the little, deep laugh welling in his throat.

Bryce breaks off the kiss, looking down at me. We're both—we're both *smiling*. When did that last happen—a smile, a real one, lingering on my lips after a kiss?

His eyes don't leave mine as he shifts his body, positioning himself right at the entrance of me. His hands move to my hips, holding me firmly as his full, hard cock slides deep inside me.

We don't look away, even as a desperate gasp leaves my body. To feel him again, to feel him inside me—

And then he *moves*. His grip on my hips is erotically seductive, grounding my body into this moment, keeping me from drifting away in bliss. No—I'm here, now, and so is he, *now*, and we're together, now, in this very moment, neither of us looking away, neither of us losing ourselves, both of us longing to just *be.*

Bryce slides out, but not fully, then pushes deep into me again. The thrust is hard and slow and forceful and it fills me up inside. Intuitively, I push my hips against his firm grip, grinding my pussy against his cock, urging him to go all the way to the hilt.

And then it's *on*. His motions become harder, deeper, more urgent. His hands slip from my hips to the side of the couch, seeking leverage so he can pound into me. Little gasps escaping from my lips turn into moans, demands, more, more, more.

And then he lifts one hand, going to the place where we're joined. Even as his cock fills me, there's room for him to dip a finger against me, his cold metal hand adding delicious tingling as he grinds it into my clit. Stars flash before my eyes, and I scream his name as he matches the pressure on my clit to the rhythm of his cock in me. My pussy clenches around him, my legs go up around his hips, holding him in me, demanding his body serve mine. My back arches, giving me room to take even more of him in, and he releases, pulsing into me, a roar of triumph erupting from his lips.

Hot and sweating, Bryce collapses beside me, keeping me safe between his body and the couch's cushions. My gaze is filled with him.

And his eyes are not dim, not distant.

Whatever hold Persephone had on him is breaking.

Bryce trails a finger—the same one that had held my clit in rapture—down my side, delicate and hot. I feel my body responding.

It had always been like that with him, with us. All three of us. Each ready to meet the others' needs, always ready to go again.

"We have to save him, Bryce," I whisper.

His gaze focuses on mine. There's determination there.

"We have to save us," I continue. "All three of us."

I mean him, too. A full break from Persephone. And me. A full break from Heroes Org.

There is only us.

We have to save Ari from whatever deal he's bargaining for. And we have to save Bryce. And we have to save me.

8

ARI

PERSEPHONE DISMISSES ME AFTER MY... *PERFORMANCE*... WITH BRYCE.

"My Operatives will be rested and taken care of," she tells me.

That's what I'm called now, I guess. One of her *Operatives*.

There are more like me. I scan the throne room again, but I can't pick out who's submissive, and who's here to be served.

Before I can ask, Doctor Rare returns to lead me away.

He says nothing as he walks me through the castle's winding halls. We go up two sets of stairs, and he punches a keypad outside of a door in a long, nondescript hallway.

"The moment I leave, it'll prompt you to reset the keycode," he tells me. "No one will hack it. You will be safe. No one disobeys Persephone here."

I nod. "Thanks."

"Don't thank me. This is standard procedure for Operatives." He waves at the other doors around me.

Now that Doctor's facing me, I'm reminded that I'm naked.

He seems to suddenly recall that detail as well.

His eyes land on my dick. When he snaps them up to me, he gives a feral grin.

"I'll be seeing you tomorrow, All-American Man," he says, and there's a promise in the croon of his words, one that wakes my flacid cock against my better judgment.

Doctor leaves, his cape brushing against my bare legs.

The room is more than just a place to sleep. I'm given a whole tidy apartment larger than my one in Brooklyn. A kitchenette, living space, and bedroom, with a second-floor window that shows a white sand beach backlit by torches against the late hour.

I see a series of small villas across the way, lining the edge of the shore. The lighting's bad, but I think that's... that's Bryce, walking out of one. The door frames someone else, a silhouette I'd know anywhere. Piper.

Persephone gave me a room that directly faces Piper's villa.

And Bryce has gone out to her.

Why did I think he'd come see me?

Of course he wouldn't. I've only begun atoning to him. And none of that atoning will happen in the dark, when it's just us, private and serene. No—this needs to be seen by everyone. Public actions to counter my public sins.

I shut the blinds, though it fucking kills me, thinking of them together, without me.

But it's what I wanted all those years ago, for the two of them to continue on together, happy, after I pulled out.

Before I can let myself spiral or wallow so deep into self-pity that I forget the whole reason I'm here, I drop onto the bed and force myself to sleep.

~

The kitchenette's fully stocked, and I make myself eat a bowl of oatmeal before there's a knock on the door the next morning. I actually managed to shower, too, which is more than my depression's let me do in weeks.

I head for the door before I realize I'm wearing the gym shorts I'd found in the bedroom's bureau. There wasn't a huge wardrobe, unsurprisingly, but it felt weird walking around this apartment nude with no one to see.

But I strip before I answer the door. After all, that's what Persephone demanded of me. To always be ready.

On the other side stands a woman whose skin is entirely *pink*.

I clamp my jaw shut. I've seen people like her before. They're from a planet called Simril, and most of Earth has no idea they exist because it'd freak the fuck out of a normal human. Hell, it had freaked the fuck out of *me* when a group of Simrilians had tried to steal a nuclear reactor two years ago.

I locked most of them in Heroes Org's prison.

Clearly one got out, or she came here from Simril separately.

She has her hands folded at her back, her breasts nearly bursting out of her tight, shiny white sundress. She cocks her head at me.

"The Mistress has summoned you," she says in a high, clear voice.

There's no accusation in her tone. Maybe she isn't one of the Simrilians I arrested.

I nod at her. She turns on her heel, barefoot, and beckons me to follow with two fingers.

I take a moment, fingers gripping the doorframe, and breathe deep.

Day one of my penance begins.

THE THRONE ROOM isn't as full as last night, but there are a few groups engaged in early-morning play. It has a different feel to it, not the heavy, desire-laden energy of last night.

I ball my fists at my sides as the Simrilian leads me to Persephone's throne.

She's seated, back rigid, hands relaxed on the armrests. Her ruby red gown leaves her shoulders bare, the edge tight across her cleavage. "Everything is to your liking, Ari Dodgers?"

The way she says my full name every time shouldn't be as erotic as it is. I nod. "Thank you."

She tips her head. "You have little experience with settings of this nature." She waves at the throne room.

"You mean, did I spend a lot of time in sex dungeons while I was employed at Heroes Org? No, not really."

It's meant as a joke. Because *obviously*, with Heroes Org's morality clauses, I couldn't fucking walk past a strip club, let alone partake in orgies.

But Persephone gives a cold smile that shuts me up.

"Quite a mouth you seem willing to have," she says, "given your circumstances."

I get the unwavering feeling I just fucked up.

"Forgive me," I say.

"That's the whole point, isn't it? But I'm not someone you have wronged, Ari Dodgers. At least, not to that extent." Persephone beckons someone behind me.

I don't turn. The rules aren't exactly clear, but I'm catching on: obey Persephone. Don't be a smart ass. Use the safe word if I want out, but otherwise, submit.

So I don't look until whoever it is stops alongside me.

It's exactly who I expected.

Doctor Rare.

I swallow, my eyes on his blue ones, sweat slicking down my back. At his side is the Simrilian woman, her focus flitting between us. Her chest is flushed with excitement.

"Steve has reserved you first," Persephone tells me. "He will be a good test of your willingness. Remember, Ari Dodgers," and she waits until I look back at her, "*afterlife*."

It feels like a test suddenly. Daring me to use the word. To tap out.

I'm not here for that.

I'm here for *this*.

I turn to Doctor.

He heads for a cluster of chairs on a low stage against a wall.

On that wall hangs two leather manacles.

All the blood churns through my body, hot, heady, dizzying, when Doctor looks back at me and points at the manacles.

"Go," is all he says.

I stumble toward it. The Simrilian woman is there, and she gently takes one wrist, attaches it, and then the other, until I'm cuffed to the wall, facing the room. The height of the manacles makes me have to crouch a little, eye level with her.

"This is Yava," Doctor says. He takes a seat facing me. "You're going to let her get off on you."

I release a little huff of breath, and my eyes drop back to Yava's. "All right."

"Excuse me?"

"All right—" I take a guess. "—sir?"

Doctor smirks and leans back in the chair. "Don't fucking forget it, All-American Man. And don't," he frowns, "come until I tell you. Do you understand?"

"Yes. Sir."

We're attracting a crowd by now. The other few groups stop, turn towards our stage, eyes wide with interest, a few smug grins at All-American Man's first public fucking. Well, aside from Bryce's blow job, which hadn't been quite this... new.

Even Persephone watches from her throne, chin in her hands, eyes dark and glistening.

Yava giggles and turns to Doctor, kisses him deeply, before spinning back to me.

My cock is already completely hard. The cuffs are more decorative than anything; I could easily snap them off. But the thought of it. The *play* of it. I'm on the edge, and fuck, it's going to be damn near impossible not to go off until Doctor tells me.

Which, I realize, might not be at all.

Yava approaches me. She slowly unzips the front of her dress and lets it drop to the floor behind her, revealing perky pink breasts and hard brown nipples and a tuft of dark hair over her pussy.

She trails her hand down the flat planes of my abs. "Do you remember me, All-American Man?"

"Should—" My breath hitches when she grabs my cock. "Should I?"

"Yes. You put me in prison. For a full year."

Fuck. "I— yeah, I recognize you."

"Do you?" She pumps her hand, her eyes all mischief. She's not going to make this easy. "I don't think you do remember me. I think you're lying."

She drops to her knees and takes me in her mouth. She's not gentle about it, her teeth grazing my head, and I slam my body back against the wall, panting loudly.

A door opens across the room.

Piper's here.

With Bryce.

The two of them walk down the runner, and they both stop, simultaneously, when they see me.

I expect Piper, at least, to be furious.

But she glances at Bryce, then at Persephone, and at Bryce's prodding, they sit, facing me, watching.

Desire surges up.

I bite down on my tongue, hard, as Yava keeps up her torment.

Finally, Yava stops. She stands, and the height of the manacles puts me at the perfect level for her as she spreads her legs and steps closer to me, one hand fisting my cock.

She rubs the tip against her clit. She doesn't move to take me inside her, which is both better and so, so much worse. Yava just keeps up that steady motion, circling the tip of my cock on her clit, and soon her eyes glaze over, her own desire rising.

Fuck, this is how she's gonna get off. The sensation's almost too much, sensitivity building, building, until my head lulls back, and I whimper, and *fuck* I need her to *come.*

I drop my head down and catch one of her tight nipples in my mouth. She moans and arches up, offering both fully, and I strain against the manacles, wanting to touch her, *aching* to touch her. But I settle for sucking on her breasts, running my tongue around her piqued nipples and nipping at the sensitive flesh there, urging her cries higher.

Still, she keeps my cock working, her hips writhing as the tip moves, her own personal dildo. The thought courses pleasure through me but *fuck,* no, don't you dare come—I throw my head back, taking a breath, biting my tongue, literally anything to get my mind off what's happening.

But the motion pulls my eyes back to Piper and Bryce.

I can see Bryce's erection from here.

Piper's eyes are wide, her cheeks red, and *fuck,* I know she's aroused too.

Fuck this. Fuck *all of this.*

"Fuck," I groan. "Fuck, *fuck—*"

A shadow falls over me. "Having trouble, All-American Man?"

It's Doctor. I'm sweating buckets as his girl writhes on my cock, giggling and gasping with pleasure equally.

He traces a finger down her shoulder blade. "Yava, come," he tells her, and a beat later, she cries out, her whole body shuddering and shaking on my cock with such vicious perfection that I have to close my eyes, focus on my breathing, my own orgasm is *right fucking there.*

Yava presses a kiss to my cheek. "Thanks, All-American Man."

"Yeah," is all I can gasp. Every muscle is strung taut. Every nerve is wound.

I feel her back away.

Doctor is still next to me.

His breath brushes my neck. "You took a lot away from me," he whispers.

"I—I know."

He strokes a single finger down my still-hard cock, stopping at the very tip, the area rubbed sensitive by Yava's clit.

"Aren't you going to ask how you can make it up to me?" he asks, and his tongue grabs my earlobe. He bites down, hard enough to send a rocket of electricity through me.

My eyes fly open. I look straight at Piper and Bryce.

Bryce is gripping the armrests of his chair, his pants still tented. Piper is bent forward, her chest heaving, eyes on mine.

"How can I make it up to you, sir?" The question is barely audible. Fuck, I'm one touch away from spilling my load all over Doctor's polished shoes.

"You can watch," he tells me, "as my girl sucks your cock."

Yava's sitting in the chair he vacated, naked still, but too far away to reach me. She grins at me and waggles her eyebrows.

I whimper.

"Oh, none of that. You're All-American Man! You can handle this." And Doctor flares his hand over my dick.

A portal opens around my cock. The sizzle of power tingles across my groin, and I see nothing but sparks around it, dark energy—

But then I feel a *mouth*.

I flick my eyes up to Yava, who's sitting in front of a separate small portal, her head bobbing in time with the things I'm feeling.

"Oh my—*fuck*," I groan.

Doctor is having his girl blow me *through a fucking portal*.

I fight the urge to throw my head back again, to look away. *Watch,* that was my order, so I do, I do even though each brush of her tiny mouth and her murderous tongue on my cock is pleasure bordering on pain.

Doctor stays bent close to me, watching me watch her, occasionally nipping at my ear or fingering my chest.

Finally, he leans in again, his lips on my ear. "Now come, All-American Man."

I don't need to be told twice.

I let go, and the orgasm rips through me, ten times stronger than anything I've had in years. Wave after wave comes as Yava sucks me down, pulling out every last ounce of pleasure until I'm so overcome that I drop to the ground, ripping out of the handcuffs, collapsing on my forearms.

Doctor kneels down next to me. To my surprise, he helps me up and guides me into a chair. Yava crawls into my lap and presses a kiss to my cheek.

"You're forgiven," she says and snuggles her head under my chin.

I'm too liquified to wonder at it.

Bleary-eyed, I manage to sight Piper and Bryce again. They're still seated, but Persephone's with them now.

She says something that has them both look at me.

Well. That can't be good.

A rogue wave of pleasure makes me shiver. Behind me, Doctor kneads my shoulders, and now I do have enough sense to give him a *what the fuck* look.

He returns it, his eyebrows cocked. "We're not monsters here, Dodgers. You thought we'd just use you and chuck you out to the next Villain?"

"Well... kind of, yeah."

Doctor laughs. It's deep and rattling. He keeps working at my shoulders, and fuck me, it feels so good that I don't even argue.

"You have a lot to learn about Elysium," he whispers, and my eyes go to Persephone.

Yeah. I'm starting to think I do.

9
PIPER

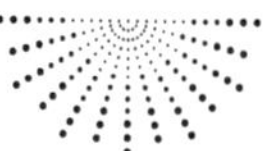

I'M SO STRUNG OUT I'M PRACTICALLY VIBRATING. SEEING ARI UP ON STAGE, used in that way—I know he could have gotten out of it. His safe word would put everything to a stop. But much like Malcolm's mesmer powers, a part of him must want this, on some level, and I don't begrudge him that.

But I also don't want to watch it again.

Ari on stage reminds me too much of Bryce when he first walked into that Brooklyn bar. Cold. Detached.

What he just did? Yeah, it was hot. I can't deny that. Everyone in the entire dungeon was getting off to it, me included.

But I also know it's not all Ari's capable of. He's capable of *real* emotion, true emotion, and there's a very real part of me that doesn't care about anything until I can have that back.

Sometimes sex is just sex, and that's fine. We're human, super or not.

I glance up at the pink lady, now giggling by a booth. Well, most of us are human. Human enough, anyway.

Persephone pulls Bryce aside, deep in conversation. I don't quite know what to think of her. She healed Bryce—physically, at least. I haven't yet decided how good it was for him to suppress his emotions for so long, but it seems as if he's healing mentally as well now.

Get it together, Carson, I remind myself sharply. *She's a Villain. She's THE Villain.*

I look around the expansive room. The sex dungeon slash throne room is built almost like a small theater off Broadway that I used to love. The center of the room has a large stage, with booths built around the perimeter and cleverly hidden rooms and doors that lead elsewhere.

Persephone is the top Villain of all of Elysium. And I'm in the heart of her base.

I'm an Agent. One of the fucking best.

Time to do my job.

My skimpy white crop top and flowing gold skirt is nothing at all like my usual Agent uniform, but that's fine. I've been undercover before.

That attitude fills my spine with steel. It's always been like this. When you're a non-powered human dealing with supers, you have to wear a mask of confidence. You're *always* undercover, pretending to be on the same playing ground as them.

I look around the room again, this time analytically, like I've been trained. I suspect that I'm the only non-powered human in the room, maybe the whole building. Any single person here could break me like a twig.

I roll my shoulders.

The trick is to first acknowledge that—the weakness.

And then to push it aside.

Some people, they pretend like they're not weak. Big mistake. If you just don't look at your own weaknesses, your own flaws, that doesn't make them go away. You have to look the darkest part of you in the eye before you can fight it.

That's the difference between me and Bryce.

Nope, no, absolutely not going to think about that right now. I'm going to get deeper into this castle and find *something* useful for Heroes Org. And also find a way to communicate it all to the Magician back at HQ.

First step: Mask on. Some supers wear masks when they fight for Heroes Org. Being an agent is no different. It's just that my mask is one of a charming smile lined with red lipstick.

Second step: Confidence. I stride across the room as if I own it, as if I neither realize nor care that the booth I walk past is full of the darkest Villains I've ever heard about. When I reach a door at the far wall, I reach for the handle, and I force my body not to jump with surprise when it opens automatically.

I walk right through.

The stone corridor is well lit, with doors interspaced throughout. I walk down the hall, ignoring the doors. It's unlikely that anything good will be found on a level where seemingly everyone has easy access. I need to find stairs that will take me to the more secure parts of this castle.

When I read the scant files on Elysium, back at the office, I'd gotten the impression that Persephone was a puppet master, pulling the strings on a coalition of Villains from a base of operations with connections world-wide.

But while Persephone can open a portal to anywhere in the world—I assume, I mean, she did at least open up a portal in a bar in Brooklyn, or maybe that was Doctor Rare—I can't get a bead on why she does what she does.

Just as I can't figure out why Ari seems so hell-bent on self destruction as a form of penance. Not that his performance with the pink girl and Doctor Rare actually seemed all that punishing...

At the end of the hall, I risk opening one of the closed doors.

The room inside looks like an office, but there are alarm bells ringing in my mind—something is off. Sure enough, when I open the drawers of the heavy mahogany desk, I don't find files—I find handcuffs. The large cabinet against the wall holds a plethora of toys—whips, chains, silk ties, dildos, strap-ons.

This isn't an office. It's a playroom.

All roads lead to sex, at least here.

She feeds off high emotions, Bryce had said.

Which, I guess, explains all the sex stuff? Maybe also Villains are just more okay with it all. Heroes Org had a standard to uphold. Supers like Ari got the brunt of it—strict regulations of appearances, to the point where handlers chose every outfit, dictated perimeters of what was publicly stated, and even manipulated his love life. But as a non-powered human Agent, I'm pretty low on the ladder, even if I've been at Heroes Org for awhile. And still, there were morality clauses in my contract that stipulated how easy it would be for Heroes Org to fire me if I didn't toe the line.

I hear a bump in the room next to me, and even though the walls are thick, there's a keening moan of sexual bliss coming from whatever playroom is next door.

I feel my body grow hot, and my breath comes out shuddering. For a moment, I imagine Ari and Bryce here, in this room, just the three of us. No stage.

A bit of role play would be... nice. I could be the commanding Agent again, training up these two young bucks, whipping them into shape to be Heroes.

My hand splays across a flogger. I would make both boys get on their knees, beg forgiveness of me.

Oh god, I want *that*. Need lances through me.

Focus, Carson, goddammit. I'm a fucking Agent.

Right. I stride out of the room, almost bumping into someone. The person—male, I think, but I can't be sure—is entirely clothed in leather, except for a metallic mask obscuring his face. I'm so disorientated that I'm not sure if this is another sex thing or a Villain's costume. Is this person on the way to a playroom or a mission?

He barely notices me as I scurry past him, and even though I rush now, I move with pretend purpose. If I look like I know where I'm going, no one will stop me.

I hope.

I dare not glance behind me, even if I hear the man in leather's footsteps on the floor.

I don't pause when I hear a door zip open, and the man steps inside.

My heartbeat races, thundering in my chest as I finally, *finally* find a door that leads to a stairwell.

Up or down?

Down. This is a Villain's lair.

All the good stuff will be down.

I race down the empty stairwell, bypassing levels until I reach a sub-basement deep underground. It's cooler here, the smell of stone and earth refreshingly crisp and damp.

I push through the door and step into a computer server area. Wires and hard drives and CPUs are everywhere, accompanied by the soft beeping and gentle flashing lights to indicate that the computers are working.

"Shit," I mutter. I'm more of a boots-on-the-ground kind of Agent, not a tech head like some of my colleagues.

But I'm not an idiot. I can make this work.

Right. First I scan for people—no one. This area is not that well protected. Which means I've either not found something worth finding, or Persephone just assumes she's safe in her own base.

Persephone wouldn't do that. She's a top Villain for a reason.

This must not be that important of an area.

But that doesn't mean I can't use it.

Computers mean networks. Networks mean communication. If nothing else, I can maybe open an access to the outside world, find a link to communicate with the Magician back at headquarters.

I walk deeper into the computer server area. This many machines working at one time means that the room is hot—hotter than the cool sub-basement level would imply. I'm grateful for the skimpy clothes Persephone provided me in the villa.

I need an access point. This much computing power is useless to me if I can't get to it.

There—built into the wall of a little alcove, interspersed with file servers. I step over cluttered wires and head to a wide touchscreen monitor. It's not locked—this screen is linked in with a continually processing unit. I scan the data flashing across it.

"What is this?" I mutter aloud.

I've seen something similar to it before—a radio spectrometer read-out. The text at the bottom of the screen tells me that this is processing data from an extrasolar space-telescope that's off the grid.

Why is Persephone scanning *space*?

Sure, Heroes Org has been contacted by some aliens. And so has Elysium—that pink woman was clearly a Simril. But this space telescope is pointing at dead air…

But those readings are *definitely* picking up... something.

"What's out there?" I wonder. And why does Persephone have an entire sub-basement full of computers just to watch it?

I check the clock on the screen—I've been gone for too long. Someone is going to notice the one rogue Agent at Elysium's base has gone missing. I need to be quick about this. I need to appear innocuous so I have a chance to come back, really figure this shit out.

As far as I can tell, this entire network server is focused only on the space telescope monitoring the radio waves. I'm not skilled enough to hack my way into it and have it rebound a message to Heroes Org. But I soak in all I can, memorizing every detail.

I don't know what this means.

But I'll find a way to make it useful.

10

ARI

Persephone's Operatives have a whole wing of the castle, it turns out. A floor below my apartment holds a fully-equipped gym, a cafeteria with a rotating calendar of visiting chefs, a movie theater, a bowling alley, and an indoor-outdoor lap pool.

I'm here to atone. I'm here to pay penance.

But *fuck,* this is the nicest vacation I've had in a decade.

My performance with Doctor pleased Persephone enough that she gave me free time until my next appointment. I don't ask who's *reserved* me next—the thrill of not knowing is almost as delicious as reliving Yava's mouth on my cock, the way she rubbed my head on her clit.

I find swim trunks in my apartment and head to the pool. I haven't worked out regularly in a few weeks, so I know I'll be sore if I dive into weights too fast, but a few laps shouldn't hurt.

The indoor side of the pool is empty when I get there. The water is perfectly warmed from the sun outside, and I start a slow breaststroke in the farthest lane. The wash of the water over my skin, the flash of scorching sunlight when I cut outside—it clears my head. Centers me.

I'd hoped Piper would decide during the night to head back to Heroes Org and call her mission a failure. But I *know* her—she'd won't tap out any more than I will. The longer she stays here, though, the more I worry about her getting caught up in Persephone's games, too. It's one thing for me to make this deal with Persephone; I owe it. But Piper? She's free.

Unless she's staying for Bryce now, too. Unless the combination of the three of us here has her tethered by our past.

I should go to her. Convince her to leave, or ask what I can do to make things right with her once and for all.

But I don't trust myself around her. Not alone, in that villa.

It's best if I just wait her out.

We're both so damn stubborn.

I hit the edge of the outdoor pool, but instead of flipping and shooting back up the lane again, I brace my arms on the side to pull myself up.

Halfway out of the water, I realize someone's watching me.

Bryce sits on a pool chair, elbows on his knees, sunglasses hiding his eyes from me. He's in a tight black t-shirt and black jeans that tuck into his boots, more outfitted for a mission than for poolside lounging. But he's definitely watching me, every muscle in my chest contracting with the effort of climbing out of the pool. I may not have worked out in awhile, but I still look amazing, and I can feel him take me in the same way I felt his eyes on me in the throne room.

I twist and sit on the pool's edge, my back to him. "I thought this was for Operatives only."

"It is."

There's a long beat.

I look back at him, realization dawning. "You're an Operative."

He grins. "Technically."

I'm hit by the image of Bryce in any of the positions I've been in these past hours. On his knees, blowing someone. Chained to a wall, letting someone get off on him.

The thoughts are enough to get me rock hard again.

Bryce stands. I slide back into the pool to hide my erection, pressing my chest to the side, arms folded on the rough stone walkway.

He crouches in front of me, the heat of the sun pelting us both so I can see sweat beading on his temples, dripping down his neck into the little V of his collarbone.

"It's not your fault," he says.

I jerk back. I don't know what I expected him to say, but that's not it.

"What happened to me on that mission," he adds. He lowers to one knee, balancing just above me. I can see myself reflected in his sunglasses. "I fucked up. *Me.* I let it go south, because I'd started to doubt every single tenet Heroes Org drilled into us. I got in my own head. But you wanna know the funny thing?" Bryce slides his glasses off. When he looks at me now, it's just him, those gray eyes I know so well, that smirk. "Before the chopper went down, all I could think was *God, I bet this is how Ari's head sounds all the time, all this constant overthinking and self-doubt.*"

I want to laugh. I think he expects me to.

I can't move. My knuckles white-grip the side of the pool as I look up at him.

"If I hadn't signed that contract," I say, "I'd have been there. I'd have pulled you out."

"Would you have?" Bryce clicks his tongue and his jaw works. "Or would you have gone down with me? Or, even worse, would you have been disgusted by the anti-Heroes Org thoughts I was having? You were a loyal soldier right from the start, Ari."

"What are you saying?" I drop my gaze. I can't keep looking at him, not while he's reminding me of who I used to be, the starry-eyed kid who thought Heroes Org would save the world with me at the helm.

Bryce takes my jaw in his hand. The contact instantly shoots down to my dick, his calloused fingers somehow gentle on my face. He pulls me up to look at him, and I rise higher with it, lifting myself up out of the water with a small burst of flight until I'm eye level with him.

I don't know why I do it.

I don't know why that knot in my chest pushes me closer to him, a magnet drawing me in.

"I'm saying," he licks his lips, "that everything happened exactly as it should have. I have no regrets."

Now I do laugh. "You liar. No regrets? Did Persephone wipe your memories of what I did to you?"

"Yes."

I flinch. His honesty is raw.

"Yes, she did," he repeats. "But she gave them back right before I met with you. I needed that distance—because I see it all now, Ari. We're supposed to be here. Together. The three of us. I know you don't see it yet, but you will."

He leans forward, closing the space between us, but he doesn't kiss me. He keeps his lips just off of mine, maddening. I don't meet him there, don't move a muscle.

How can he be so sure of himself? How can he have dealt with everything that happened when he spent the past ten years not even *knowing* what happened until Persephone gave him his memories back? He doesn't understand. He can't. That's the only solution—he doesn't really remember how much I fucked up.

But my arms tremble, my heart rocketing against my ribs, and all my usual self-berating just falls flat in my head.

That look in Bryce's eyes.

That's forgiveness.

"Your next shift starts in half an hour," he tells me, then he stands and leaves.

11

PIPER

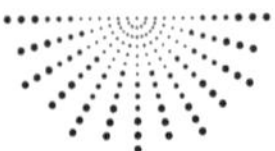

I SPEND MAYBE TWO HOURS, TOTAL, SEARCHING THE BASE. AFTER THE SUB-basement, I try the next level up. The security there is higher than I can break through, and I definitely don't have the ability to shape-shift or bluff my way inside those rooms. Higher up, I find a communications hub, but it's buzzing with activity, far too crowded for me to infiltrate.

I make my way back to Persephone's sex dungeon at the heart of her base, my mind reeling from what I've seen. My recon was simple scouting, but I definitely have a better feel for the lay of the land. The sex stuff here is a distraction—or maybe there is something to what Bryce said, about how high emotions feed Persephone's powers—but there's more going on than I thought. That space-telescope pointing to dead air but picking up radio waves has me staggering with the implications. I need to report back to the Magician.

This is bigger than Ari; this is...

This is...

I blink, unable to focus.

Because as I cross the audience area of the sex dungeon, my eyes land on a stage.

That's Ari, in the center, on all fours, completely nude except for a collar and chain around his neck. And that's Bryce mounting the steps toward him.

Ari looks up at him with an expression on his face that both breaks my heart and sets it racing.

Bryce doesn't speak, undressing as he approaches Ari. He yanks Ari's hips into position.

A pang of longing and pain shoots through me. I shouldn't feel this envy—I've fucked both Ari and Bryce in the last forty-eight hours—but seeing them together, without me...

It is my loneliness, amplified by a million.

It is my deepest fear, up on center stage.

Because I am just a human, non-powered, unimportant. Ari and Bryce were always higher up than me, sometimes literally, considering how Ari can fly. I'm nothing compared to them. Every moment of our relationship, I would marvel that I was lucky enough to be a part of the Triad, but... I'm not a part of it now. Now, Bryce and Ari are together, without me, and—

Gutted, I turn away.

And bump right into Persephone.

She arches an eyebrow at me. "You could join them," she says placidly.

My heart stutters. I turn back to the stage, this time sweeping the entire dungeon. Ari and Bryce aren't just fucking—they're fucking with an audience. An audience that's loving this. Villains litter the booths, some of them touching themselves, some touching others, some outright fucking in the same rhythm as Bryce and Ari.

"It's all a show," I say aloud, my voice low.

"It's not." Persephone steps closer to me. Our words are private. I have one moment of panic—I'm having a conversation in a sex dungeon with the greatest mastermind Villain of all time—but I quell my racing heart.

Persephone licks her lips, watching the thrumming heartbeat in my jugular. There is something feral about the look.

She feeds off emotions, I remind myself. Sex happens all around us, and those high emotions must be a feast to her. But my panicked, adrenaline-filled fight-or-flight response to her, to this—it's a taste of emotion that's strong enough to satisfy her insatiable appetite, I'm sure.

"I know what you're thinking," Persephone says.

My eyes go wide.

"No, not like that." She chuckles. "I'm not capable of reading minds. You're just very... obvious."

A blush spreads up my neck, over my cheeks. My skin burns, and when she reaches out and trails her fingers along my bare arm, I'm surprised she's not scorched by the heat.

"You've been pinned up in an Agent's blazer for too long," Persephone mutters. "I'm getting a clearer picture of you." Her eyes flick to the stage. "Of the three of you."

I wrap my arms around my body, feeble armor. I'm not in an Agent's clothing now—all I could find in the villa's closet for me was that white sleeveless top and skirt. I focus on what she said. "There is no *three of us*." Not anymore.

She arches a perfectly sculpted eyebrow. "Really?" she says as if she already knows the answer.

"Really." My voice breaks. My eyes go to Ari and Bryce.

Ari is on all fours, ass up as Bryce slowly fucks him, drawing out the pleasure in that bittersweet way he has. Ari is always so manic, so determined to do everything all at once, but Bryce always takes his time, pulling every last droplet of pleasure from his partner.

It reminds me of the way he fucked me, in the villa, carefully, not as if we would break, but as if he was re-learning me.

As if he wanted to savor me.

I startle as I feel arms go around me, over me, threading through my protective stance, pulling me apart. Persephone has shifted to be behind me, her touch breaking me. As my arms fall to my sides, her hands rove up my stomach, not hesitating as she cups my breasts. The pressure makes me step backwards, deeper into her embrace.

Her lips drop to my ear. I feel her tongue slide over the lobe, then up, around the shell of my ear, delicate little nips biting at my sensitive skin. I gasp as her hands focus on my breasts, fingers rolling over the hard nubs of my nipples. The sleeveless top slides down, exposing my bare breasts to anyone who would want to see, even if everyone's attention is on Ari and Bryce on the stage. The cold air hits me, prickling my skin.

"Do you want me to stop?" she asks from behind me. "The safe word here is 'afterlife.'"

I gasp as she pinches my nipples, the pain sending pleasure straight between my legs.

"No," I'm able to stutter out.

No—I don't want her to stop. Not when I hear the throaty chuckle in the back of her voice, vibrating up and down my spine. Not when her lips drop to my neck, licking and biting me.

Not when her hands drift back down my stomach, over the slinky gold material of my skirt. She draws the cloth up, bracing one hand on my hip and sliding her other between my legs.

"You like this," she says against my throat as her finger dips into my wetness. "You like watching them." She slides inside me, and my gasp comes out in shudders. "You like feeling me."

I can't answer, but I throw my head back against her, letting her claim me with her fingers. My eyes are glued on Bryce, fucking Ari on the stage. Persephone's fingers match his rhythm, slow and steady, a force unwilling to be denied.

"You can join them," she whispers in my ear. Her thumb has found my clit, and she rolls across the top of that sensitive nub. My legs are jelly, but her firm grasp on my hip grounds me.

"I—can't—" I gasp. Not on stage.

In one smooth, fluid motion, Persephone's touch glides from from my clit up inside me, then back to my clit. "You can," she says. "You obviously want to."

She releases her hand on my hip, and I almost fall, but she grabs my head from behind, forcing my gaze to go to the Villains in the booths around the stage. "My people would love to watch an Agent fuck a fallen hero," she says. "And they would love to see a Villain fuck an Agent."

My emotions are at war, and I try to think through the haze of lust Persephone is pulling from my pussy as she works my clit with agonizing, slow, burning pleasure. It would definitely go against the cultured image of an agent to expose myself in a sex dungeon of a Villain, to fuck and be fucked... but it is undeniable that I want it. I want Ari. I want Bryce.

I want us.

By any means necessary, the Magician had said.

Maybe, if I remind Ari of our Triad, maybe then he'll come back. If not to Heroes Org, to me and Bryce.

And if the only way to have them is on a stage, well...

At least I'll have them.

12

ARI

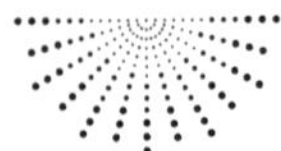

Bryce is the one who reserved me tonight.

It feels like a dream. Each thrust of his cock inside me, gentle, slow, torturously teasing—it's a dream warping into a nightmare and back again.

I want this. I need him inside of me; I don't *deserve* him inside of me—only I do, in the worst way, and I have to actively keep my mind on the bite of the stage under my knees or the jagged stone walls to not think about my own rock-hard cock one touch away from release.

Persephone had been clear about my instructions before I'd even entered the room tonight. *"You don't come without permission. Ever."*

That word echoes in me with each tantalizing thrust from Bryce. *Ever.*

He plants one hand flat on the small of my back and bends his hips, taking a different angle.

Ever.

I whimper, the collar bobbing on my throat, the chain only enhancing my rocking emotions. Bryce tugs on it, making my head arch back; and then he's bending over me, his chest pressing to my back, still balls-deep inside of me. He snakes his metal hand around my throat and squeezes, the slightest pressure.

"Look at them," he tells me, and my eyes instantly go to the crowd.

People are pleasuring themselves with various toys. Others are writhing on each other in mimic of Bryce and I. Desire is ripe on all their faces and I whimper again, my cock aching, sweat dripping down my face with my restraint.

"This is what you wanted, isn't it?" Bryce whispers into my ear. "To let them use you?" When I don't answer—I can't, I don't trust myself to do anything but kneel here, *fuck*—Bryce squeezes my throat again, *hard*, and relaxes. "Isn't it?"

"Yes," I manage, my voice hoarse. Then, I add, "Sir."

I feel Bryce's lips rise into a smile against the side of my face. He pulls back and I exhale, gasping, but he just continues his punishingly slow thrusts.

He was always a master of that. Pulling it out. Holding himself back until I was begging for release. Which was why it was always so utterly satisfying making him come, knowing how much control he had over his body, and knowing that I pushed him over the edge.

I shove my hips back to meet him, and he grunts in surprise. I do it again, and the combined force of that plus his thrusts has me writhing, but this new focus directs me. I will *make* him come. That's why I'm here, after all—for his pleasure.

He pulls on the chain again. "Did I tell you to move?"

There's something in his tone. Something punishing, a little cruel, and it sends a shiver down my spine, tapping directly into that growing place inside of me that *aches* to be treated like this. To be used.

I instantly stop.

He smacks my ass. "Good boy." He tugs the chain, pulling my head to the left—

Piper is walking up the stage.

The straps of her white tank top are already down, revealing her breasts. Her chest is flushed, her cheeks stained pink; the moment my eyes land on her, her lips part in a little huff of breath that makes me dizzy.

Everyone in the audience seems to have a similar reaction. They all pause in their own fucking, staring at the Heroes Org Agent who reaches up and slowly removes first her top, then her gauzy skirt and panties, until she's as naked as Bryce and I.

She can't mean—

She *wouldn't*—

Bryce thrusts again, harsh and deep, and I hiss with sensation.

"You're going to make us both come," he tells me. "Can you do that?"

I nod before I think it through. "Yes, sir."

But fuck, *fuck*, I absolutely *cannot*, not without spilling my load all over this stage.

Piper looks up at Bryce. Her breathing speeds up, chest rising and falling as she crosses the stage to me.

She stops in front of me. Spreads her legs wide.

I haven't been here in ten years. Bryce behind me. Piper in front of me.

A sense of rightness descends over me, familiarity that drops like a blanket, cocooning the three of us on this stage. There's still a crowd; they're all back to fucking again; but suddenly, there is only Bryce and Piper and me.

While Bryce continues his slow fucking of my ass, I balance on one hand and use my other to reach up to Piper's slit. She's wet already, her soft hairs matted with her moisture, and I run my thumb through her lips.

When we'd fucked in my apartment, it'd been fast and basic. I hadn't gotten a chance to savor her, to refresh my memory of her taste and smell and feel.

I do that now. Bryce's slow rhythm sets my tempo, and I part Piper's lips, let her feel my breath roll over her clit and pussy. She shivers, and I peek up to see her eyes closed, her whole focus right where my fingers are, right with me.

I press a long kiss to Piper's clit, sucking until my tongue finds that tender bundle of nerves, tasting the sweetness of her. Her body seizes under my fingers from just that one lick—she's so fucking responsive, arching up against my mouth invitingly. It's so perfect I almost cry out, but I have a task to do—I alternate between ramming my hips back on Bryce's cock and giving Piper's cunt long, slow strokes with my tongue, two fingers curved inside of her and thrusting steadily.

Above, I hear her moan. It makes my balls clench with need.

But this isn't about me anymore. This isn't about my desire. It's about what I can give *them*, how good I can make *them* feel. And with each thrust, each lick, I lay my apologies on them, pouring out everything I've kept pent up for the past ten years.

Piper's whole body starts to shudder. Her fingers grip my collar, holding my face on her clit, her hips bending forward to give me more access.

"Bring her there, Ari." Bryce's order is gruff with his own pleasure and fuck, *fuck*, I'm right on the edge again.

I speed up my attention on Piper's pussy. Three fingers now, crooked to reach her G-spot. I run the flat of my tongue over her clit, over and over, using more force than a normal human could, just enough to push her over the edge. She arches back with a cry, a delicate shiver rippling over her body as she braces herself on my shoulders.

Behind me, Bryce comes, too. He pumps one last time into me and I shove back to meet him, his orgasm coming with a gasping grunt, his fingers digging into my hips.

I feel the tension go out of both of their bodies almost simultaneously. Bryce lowers to his knees behind, easing out of me; Piper matches him, coming down to lift me up level with her.

She kisses me. I fall into it, my tongue exploring her mouth, letting her taste herself on me. Her bare breasts press against my chest and I start to reach for them when hands clamp around my wrists, pressing my fists against my ass.

Bryce bites my ear. "You don't get to touch. Not yet."

Yet?

"Sit back," Bryce tells me. He tugs on the collar, but I understand—I sit cross legged in front of him, and Piper quickly slides onto my lap, her pussy dripping over my cock.

I suck in a breath. My pulse races, my eyes on hers, but Piper's looking at Bryce. Waiting for him to lead. Letting him be in control.

He grabs her throat in that metal hand the same way he'd held me and yanks her face to his, their kiss deep and passionate and so distracting that I cry out in shock when Piper sheaths me with her cunt. They continue to make out over me while Piper writhes her hips on me, not slow, thank god—quick, heady bounces that make her breasts swing in my face. But Bryce still has my hands pinned behind my back. Even though I'm the one with an orgasm building, I still feel entirely like their play toy.

Especially when Bryce bends down to capture one of Piper's perky pink nipples in his mouth. I groan in jealousy, head falling back as Piper's thrusts speed up, her delicate moans making me delirious.

Then Bryce sucks on my neck, and I'm gone.

"Come, baby," he whispers into my skin.

I come with a shout, my whole body seizing as Piper pumps down on my orgasm. She rides out a few more waves before I rock forward, Bryce releasing me, and I grab onto her, head bowing between us as I try desperately to catch my breath. Bryce has his hand on the back of my neck, the three of us crouched on the stage, riding out this high together.

That was—

What did we—
What did *I*—
That didn't feel like penance. Not really.
That felt like...
Home.

13
PIPER

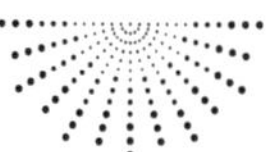

After, sated, Bryce moves both Ari and me to a private room. It happens so fluidly, so easily that I'm not even sure I actually walked here. It feels like a blink, nothing more.

The room itself is a dream. I've been in full spas that aren't as nice as this one room. Gentle ocean colors match the wide bath sunken into the floor, so large that it's more like a pool. Lotus flowers float on the calm surface, bobbing between gently crushed pink rose petals that fill the room with their cloying sweet scent.

Everything in this room is *soft*—a pair of chaise lounges, covered in plump silk with white fur throws, a steady waterfall pouring into the deep end of the pool-bath, thick velvet-like towels draped strategically around the room.

Ari staggers to the pool-bath, slipping into the warm waters and sighing with bone-deep relief. He tilts his head back, exhaustion already closing his eyes, and I know that it was far more than physical exertion that has made him weary. The emotions tugging him one way and another are ripping him apart.

Bryce and I—and everyone in Persephone's sex dungeon, truthfully—used Ari's body. And that's what he wanted—what he needed. There's a release in an act like that, the purposeful removal of self from sex.

I get it.

It's...a type of grief, really. Atonement, yes, and I know that's what Ari thinks he's after, but he's never let himself grieve.

That, I suspect, is Ari's true problem. He thinks he has to make up for his choices and actions and the way things fell apart. But what he doesn't understand is that he's allowed to grieve for the things that happened, even if he's the one that caused them.

Bryce follows Ari into the pool. Ari's body is loose and relaxed in the water, and he drifts easily into Bryce's gentle touch. I step into the water, bringing with me a soft cloth.

We bathe Ari together. Lightly scented soap foams over his hard muscles. My fingers trace the scars on his body—even a superhero can be injured.

Ari's head dips back, resting against the edge of the pool. I float over to Bryce. "I think he's going to fall asleep," I point out.

Bryce smiles. He parts his lips to say something in return, but I can't help it—I lean in for a kiss, soft and warm as water, my body melding into his. We're both nude, both floating, and both flooded with that simple, full feeling of being perfectly satisfied. My body draws closer to his, an anchor in the sea, my hands sliding over his slick skin.

For just one moment, I feel Bryce's hard, firm cock against my thigh, but then he shifts, and I shift, and he's inside me, filling me. It's not a coil of passion that's about to break me under the pressure. It's easy. I glide over his cock, aided by the water, our bodies slipping together as if they were meant to be.

We don't speak.

We ride each other like a wave, accepting the inevitable current that pulls and pushes us. I arch back as his thrusts grow harder, more urgent. He grabs my hips under the water, and I bend, letting him fill me deeply. His release matches mine, hot warmth flooding us both. I drape myself over Bryce's shoulder, letting him keep me afloat.

Behind us, Ari huffs, already asleep.

I chuckle into Bryce's embrace, my smile growing when I feel his chest rise and fall with his own suppressed laughter. When I pull away, the happiness on Bryce's rough lips matches his gentle eyes.

Bryce scoops Ari up in his arms, carrying him to one of the chaise lounges and enfolding him in furs and blankets.

I can't help grinning at the image.

My boys are back.

Naked, warmed with soapy water, I stand in the pool and climb out.

Cold air hits my skin, making my nipples hard. I like it. I like feeling hard when I'm surrounded by so much softness.

Just like I like feeling soft when I'm between my two hard men.

I sit down near Ari's head, pulling him into my lap and finger-combing his hair. Bryce sits at Ari's feet. We both lean against the couch's cushions, our eyes meeting, knowing smiles playing on our lips.

"I can leave," I whisper.

Ari doesn't stir, but I see Bryce shift to face me more fully.

"I'm not a super," I continue, my voice still low. "I'm not important."

"That's not true," Bryce says.

I smile, looking down at Ari's sweet sleeping face. "But I'm not important to Heroes Org. I can leave them. I've..." I pause, realizing the truth even as I say it. "I've considered it before. After you... left... and after Ari... well. It's just a job now, and something I can quit."

Before, I had thought that I was defined by my role as an Agent. I wasn't just Piper, I was Agent Carson. It was *me*, my whole identity.

But it hasn't been that for a long time now.

"It's not as easy for me," Bryce says. His voice is low. I look over to him, and his gaze is full of anguish. "I'm not just an Elysium Operative. I made a deal with Persephone."

He doesn't say it, but he doesn't need to: a deal with Persephone is not easily broken.

"What were the terms?" I ask. "When is your time with her up?"

Bryce snorts bitterly. "A lifetime."

"What?" My voice is so sharp that Ari stirs, almost waking up.

He nods. "My death at Heroes Org for a lifetime with Elysium. Before, it seemed like the right thing to do."

"But it wasn't just your faked death that was part of the deal," I say, half to myself.

His memories.

I peek over at him.

I see the way he absent-mindedly strokes his hands over Ari's legs, not in possession but affection.

His memories are coming back. Softened by time, as warm as the steam rising from the bath.

Ari moves again, and his eyelids flutter open.

"How long have you been awake?" Bryce asks.

"Long enough," Ari says. There's no bitterness in his voice, just acceptance. "Bryce and I—we've made our deals. But you, Piper. You're still free. You can leave us behind."

I bark in humorless laughter. "I could never leave either of you behind." Not when I'm so close to having them back again, fully, as we were.

"You should," Bryce says.

Ari sits up. Now they're both looking at me, eyes full of sincerity.

"We're bad for you, Piper," Bryce continues. He snorts bitterly. "I'm an Elysium Operative working directly for Persephone."

"And I'm just a fucking mess," Ari says.

"We're dragging you down," Bryce says, nodding along with Ari. "You are a shining star of goodness."

"You can only see a star in the dark," I point out. "Don't try to tell me that you're bad for me, when all I do is live for you." I look from one to the other. "You both."

"You can't save us this time," Ari says. "This isn't like one of our old missions when you bail us out."

Bryce laughs at the memories. "She was *always* bailing us out back then."

"I wouldn't have had to if you'd actually followed directives!"

"We were bad at that," Ari concedes.

"Ah, remember Madagascar? Or Budapest?" Bryce says.

"Oh, fuck, Budapest! Wow, did we mess that one up."

"My memories of Budapest are very different from yours," I say, smiling. Yes, the mission had gone sideways in every possible way.

But it also helped lead to us. The full us. All three of us. Together.

Bryce and Ari exchange a meaningful look, one I can read as easily as if they'd spoken aloud. And *that,* more than anything else, fills me with hope.

I lean forward, cupping Ari's cheek. "I'm going to save you," I promise him. I reach further, gripping Bryce's hand. "And you." My eyes dart between them, sure they can see the gravity in my movements. "I'm going to save you both, so that I can save *us.*"

14
ARI

ALL OF MY STANDARD REBUTTALS IMMEDIATELY SPRING UP.

There is no us. *I broke it.*

It's my fault. That's why I'm here. I'm atoning.

What else can I do to pay penance to you?

But I can't say any of it.

I can only look at Piper where I'm twisted to face her on the sofa; and I feel Bryce behind me, his metal arm stretched out along the back of the couch around my shoulders, his other hand resting on my hip.

We're together again. The three of us. Not exactly whole, but far from the broken-beyond-repair mess I'd kept in my head for the past ten years.

Is it possible they've forgiven me?

Is it possible we could be *us* again?

The very thought, the very *idea*, has me gasping, and I have to look away from Piper, my eyes back on that luxurious pool. The water ripples around a few remaining lotuses, the image of them blurring as my eyes sting with tears.

I hadn't let myself want them. Not from the moment I broke us apart. They weren't mine to want anymore, and I punished myself for ten years with refusing to acknowledge the gaping hole this relationship left in my heart.

But having these two back…

Feeling them next to me…

I'm *me* again. I can *breathe*.

I sniff. Without knowing it, I've taken Piper's hand, and Bryce's, but I still can't look at either of them, emotions too raw, hope too fragile.

"What were the exact parameters of your agreement with her, Bryce?" I ask, my voice gruff.

He squeezes my fingers. "She broke me off from Heroes Org. Repaired my body. Wiped my mind. In return, I'm one of her Operatives—" His voice hangs.

"And?" I press, threading our fingers.

He sighs. "And when she wiped my memories, she implanted a special trigger in my brain. With one phrase, I go into attack mode. The perfect weapon."

That makes me look at him, but in horror. "What?"

"She *programmed* you?" Piper gasps.

Bryce's eyes on mine are sad. Still, he manages a small smile. "She's only used it a few times. It was worth it. Entire bases of drug and human traffickers wiped out of her territories with one soldier."

I turn away again, shaking my head, but fuck, it is impressive. And I know Bryce is thinking what I'm thinking, that being able to handle that big of a mission with one soldier means the risk of death to others goes way, way down.

"So why did she let you come to me?" I ask the pool. "When I texted her. Why did she send *you*, when she knows what you mean to me?"

Bryce adjusts to cup my jaw in his hand and pull me to face him. "She wants you here. I don't know why she wants you, what she's got planned, but I couldn't turn down the chance to see you again." He includes Piper with a smile. "Both of you."

"So what now?" I can't help the way my voice hardens. "You and I just go on with our servitude to Persephone while Piper returns to Heroes Org, and we occasionally get together on the weekends or holidays? Fuck that shit."

Bryce's eyebrows shoot up. "You cuss a lot more than I remember."

I fight a smile. This is serious, but damn, his surprise is adorable.

"I want you back," I hear myself tell him.

I turn to Piper. My hand is still in hers.

I lift her fingers to my lips and kiss her knuckles. "Both of you. I want *us* back. I do."

The admission tears apart my soul. A tear slips down my cheek, but I don't dare move, don't fucking breathe, eyes glued to Piper's face, my body pressed against Bryce's.

They have every right to walk out of this room. They got what penance I could give them; they can be done, and leave, and I won't begrudge them that.

But god, I want them to stay.

I *need* them to stay.

I know that now. I need them, Bryce and Piper, if I ever want to be the best version of myself. If I ever want to be the Hero that the world needs, someone who can actually do *good*. I need them at my side.

Piper inches closer to me. Her hands lift to my face, tracing delicate lines down my jaw, and it's only then that I see the tears in her eyes.

"I don't know what it'll mean," I whisper. "I don't know how we'll get out from under Persephone. But I'll never stop trying to figure it out, I swear. I'll never stop—"

Bryce is the one who silences me, his arms coming around my chest, holding me against him.

"That's what you never got, Ari," he whispers into my ear. "We didn't give a shit about what you could do for us. We only ever wanted *you*."

"I didn't wait ten years for you to fix things," Piper says. "I just want you back. Both of you. This isn't about repairing what broke—this is about building something new."

Then she kisses me, breaking off to kiss Bryce too. I twist on the couch until she's on me, one thigh across my lap, the other over Bryce's, her naked body covered by both sets of our roaming hands.

We don't say anything else. We don't need to. This isn't how it was on the stage in the dungeon; this is how it was years ago, when the three of us made love in perfect synchronization, knowing what each other needed without being told.

Bryce and I stand, holding Piper between us. He braces her against his chest while I scramble through the closest box of bath products to find lube. Bryce and I are both rock hard again, and I swipe my hand against Piper's folds to feel she's still wet, her pussy warm and tight as she clenches around my fingers.

Bryce positions her over his cock, her legs wrapped around his ass. She balances herself on his shoulders and starts thrusting on him, guided by his hands on her hips.

Fuck, she's gorgeous. They both are, standing in the soft white light of this spa room, their sweat-slick bodies glistening, eyes lidded in ecstasy.

Mine, I think. They're mine again.

The pain in my chest where grief has been sitting for so long starts to soften. It isn't gone; I still have a lot of guilt to work through; but for the first time in a long, long while, I can see daylight.

I stroke my shaft, coating it in mango-scented lube, and gently glide it into Piper's asshole, inch by inch, not sure how long it's been since she took it like this, but going steadily just in case.

The *moans* she makes.

The sheer guttural *cries.*

I damn near shoot it right then, but I bite my lip, herculean strength overcoming my desire to get off. We need this more than I need to come right now.

Gradually I enter her, and my eyes meet Bryce's over her shoulder when I'm fully submerged. We set a steady pace, never letting her rest for too long—in and out, rhythmic, perfect, Piper's crooning mewls echoing off the high ceiling.

Bryce grabs my neck and yanks my face to his, kissing me, his tongue playing with mine as we build our pace. We ease our free hands down to Piper's clit, taking turns rubbing smooth circles on her tight bundle of nerves until I know we can both feel her tightening, quivering muscles constricting around our cocks.

"Fuck," Bryce cusses into my mouth. "Fuck, baby, I missed this."

I whimper, and it's the only sound I can make—I have Bryce's tongue in my mouth and Piper's breast in my hand and my cock in her ass, and everything is exactly where I've always needed it to be.

15
PIPER

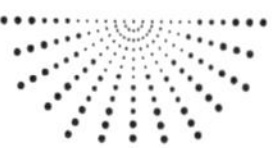

Oh my *god*.

I'm so—so *full*.

Every time Bryce thrusts up, there's Ari, slipping out, but holding on. And when Bryce withdraws, there's Ari, pounding into me from behind. They're—they're fucking *perfect*. They've slipped into the exact right rhythm. Sex is most often a mix of in-and-out, a give-and-release. But this? It's in-and-*in*, give-and-*give*, there is no release, there's nothing but a constant and steady need to be filled, fuller and fuller, overflowing.

I moan, the sound broken up by the way my whole body is being tossed back and forth as I'm rammed from both sides. I can't focus on one sensation—there are too many. I can't focus on anything at all. I can just... I can just *exist*, and barely that.

"Not yet," Bryce mutters as I spasm against his cock. He pulls out as Ari slides into me.

There's a moment there—a blissful, mind-numbing, mind-*blowing* moment where Bryce presses against my inner walls just as Ari presses against me from the other direction.

Time seems to stop. I feel Bryce inside me, pushing against my sensitive G-spot, and I feel Ari inside me, pushing with completely equal force from the other side. I am not just in the middle; that point, that spot of me is in the exact center, with their hot, heavy cocks ramming against me from either side, a perfect pinpoint of desire.

I tip my head back and scream, the primal sound erupting from me. Bryce leans down, claiming a nipple with his teeth, tweaking the nub and swirling his tongue around it. My head is thrown against Ari's chest, and he bites my earlobe, his tongue flicking along the shell of my ear, and *oh god*, I cannot contain it, I *cannot*, I scream again, my whole body writhing with it, warmth washing over, in, and through me.

It's not a wave, it's a fucking *tsunami*.

Bryce's legs steady as he thrusts up into me, and Ari is a solid fucking rock wall behind me. I'm coming apart, I'm turning into nothing but liquid stardust in their arms, but they are strong and firm and hard and filling me up with every bit of them.

My orgasm screams out of me, hitting me from the tips of my curling toes all the way to the roots of every individual strand of hair on my head. My inner walls cling to Bryce as my ass clenches around Ari. I buck back so hard that Ari has to catch me and hold me.

Bryce slides out of me, spent as well, but with a knowing smirk toying on his lips. My legs are nothing but jelly, but thank god Ari doesn't let me go. He holds me, firm and safe, then scoops me up just as Bryce had carried him before.

We slide into the pool together, the warm water soothing my tensing muscles. My breaths still come out as pants. Bryce follows us into the water, his cold metallic hand brushing over my hard nipple, and I scream again, and then he laughs. I splash him, the adrenaline from orgasming so fucking hard making me slip into hysterics.

When I lean back in the water, I expect to feel hard tile.

Instead, I lean into Ari. His arms go around my middle, my breasts floating in the water, barely touching his arms. Bryce drifts nearer us both, and we tangle together.

Bliss.

That's what this is. Bliss.

Because even though they're not inside me any more, I am still full up with both of their love.

I DON'T KNOW how much time passes in the bath house room. Food comes, and we devour it, naked and dripping wet, our skin wrinkled from the pool water, and when Ari laughs at the ridiculousness of us all sprawled, nude, over the tile and cramming pomegranates and apricots and prosciutto into our mouths—when Ari starts laughing, we all do, and then the food is swept aside, our laughs turning to moans, as we each seek to pleasure the others more.

It could be one evening, or it could have been a lifetime. Maybe we lived the remaining decades of our life there in that spa, and died, and were reborn, and fucked some more.

It feels like forever.

It feels like no time at all.

But time can't be ignored for long.

I don't know if Bryce has some sort of internal communication device or if he's just that much more aware of time, but eventually he stands. "We need to confer with Persephone," he tells Ari.

Hope surges within me.

"Do you think she'll release us from her deal?" Ari asks, his eyes flying to mine.

Bryce shakes his head. "No, but we can renegotiate. And we have to. Because I'm not fucking sharing you with anyone else."

Warmth floods me. He means the other Villains in Elysium, perhaps Persephone herself. Sex is sex, but what we have is special, and none of us is willing to share outside our Triad. At least not right now. Perhaps, later, some play, like what Ari had with Doctor Rare and the alien woman—perhaps that could be back on the table. But before that, we need time for each other, just us. And that is not, I think, what Persephone had in mind when she trapped Ari in his ill-begotten deal.

I clear my throat. "I need to communicate to the Magician. I'm tendering my resignation from Heroes Org."

Neither of the boys object, but worry flashes in Ari's eyes. He knows. It's not easy to just walk away from a job like that.

But I'm not as important as they were. And no matter how Heroes Org operates, they can't keep me against my will.

Bryce finds robes for us and wraps me up in fluffy terrycloth. "There's a secure outbound communications link in your villa," he says. "Do you want us to come with you?"

I shake my head. "You two go to Persephone. I can call the Magician on my own." Then I pause, reassessing what Bryce just said. "Is it really that simple? I can just call in to work from here? From *Elysium?*"

Bryce cracks a rare smile. "Oh, you can be sure that when the comm link goes out, it'll be well scrambled. And as soon as the Magician answers, he'll have viruses and hacks trying to break through Persephone's firewalls. But this isn't the first time we've had to call the 'office,'" he says, adding air quotes around the word in a mocking way.

I wonder at that as I head away from Persephone's castle-like fortress and toward the villa. There is no file on Elysium at Heroes Org. Well, that's a lie—there's a file, but it's empty. It's the best kept secret in the world.

And it's nothing like I expected. I'm starting to think that Elysium is far more tied to Heroes Org than either side wants to admit. Persephone targeted Ari with Bryce just like the Magician targeted him with me. And that other thing Bryce said—how Persephone has a code phrase that can turn him into the perfect weapon…

There's stuff like that in Heroes Org records.

I'm not supposed to know about it, but I do. I'm a good agent not just because I'm fucking skilled, but because I know when to not look away, when to dig deeper.

And I saw the files on the Watcher. The experiments that went wrong before.

It's all focused on weaponry.

Which—okay, sure, we're an organization of Superheroes and Elysium is literally a den of Villains. But…

There's something here. I can feel it in my bones. This focus on weapons, this gathering of supers—Villain or Hero—it feels purposeful. I've been in this game long enough to know when I've picked up the traces of a trail worth following.

I don't fucking like it.

Persephone and the Magician are playing a game of chess, and I'm just a pawn. If I'm lucky. I'm only a non-powered Agent—I may not even be on the board. My boys sure as hell are, though.

But there's *something* happening here, something far deeper.

I've worked myself into a right rage by the time I burst into my villa. I quickly change from the fluffy robe into a black tank top and leggings. I twirl my unruly hair into a bun and then reach for my tube of trademark red lipstick.

I slowly swirl the lipstick up.

But then I twirl it back down, capping the tube.

My lipstick is not for him. I'm not wasting it on him.

And I don't need my armor anymore. I'm strong enough without it.

I find the secure comm link easily enough and access the Magician's code. He answers immediately, his image filling the hologram projector.

"Agent Carson," he growls, his fury evident. "It's about time you reported in. You and All-American Man are off the grid. What the fuck is happening?"

"I'm out," I say. His anger made mine disappear—I'm the calm center of the storm.

I am in control.

"Out? What the fuck is that supposed to mean?" he shouts.

"It means I quit," I say. "I don't know what game you're playing. And I'm not playing Persephone's game either. I'm completely out, done with you both."

"What about All-American Man?" the Magician shouts. "Where is he?"

"With me. He's out, too."

"I will send every Super I have to bring him in," the Magician snarls. "And if you're collateral damage—?" He shrugs.

I smile at him coldly, lips pressed together. "You can try," I say. "But I think we'll be just fine."

"Money?" the Magician snaps. "Is that it? You want more for the asset? Fine. Make your demands."

I don't answer.

"Maybe power. You deserve a promotion, Carson. You have for awhile—fucking office politics and glass ceilings and whatnot. I'll make sure you move up the ranks."

I stare at him blankly.

"You can't just fucking quit on me!" the Magician shouts. "Get your ass back to Heroes Org and bring Ari with you!"

"Please don't misunderstand," I say calmly. "This is not a negotiation. It is merely a courtesy. And now it's over."

I reach across the hologram and flick it off.

16

ARI

Bryce and I split up to find clothes. For me especially, it isn't necessary that I go before Persephone dressed, but I don't want to give her the wrong idea.

I find some halfway decent clothes in my apartment, shiny low-cut boots, black slacks, a collared white shirt, and even a tie. I chuck the tie though and opt to just leave the top few buttons of the white shirt undone, chest hairs barely visible.

By the time I get back out in the hall, Bryce is there, looking even more sleek. He's back in his tight black jeans and black t-shirt, one ankle crossed over the other as he leans against the far wall. He's brushed his long brown hair back so it doesn't hang in his face, and when his gray eyes cut up to me, he gives me an unhindered smile.

His gaze drops from my head to my feet and back up, lingering on my half open shirt.

He smirks. "I can't be seen with someone so disheveled."

My eyebrows crease. Other than the buttons, I cleaned up well. I even styled my hair quickly.

"Is this not okay?" I start to reach for the buttons.

Bryce shoves off the wall and grabs my hands. "Don't you dare. I was joking. Because you're usually zipped up so tight a crowbar couldn't pry off your uniform." He strokes a finger into the open gap of my shirt. "This is nice."

He looks up at me, and I can't help it.

I grab the back of his neck and kiss him. I have ten years of absence to make up for. Ten years of kisses I didn't get.

He fists his hands in my shirt, pulling a few more buttons apart—oh shit, they broke actually—but when he tries to shove me against my door, I push back.

"Persephone," I whisper against his lips.

"That's not the name I want you moaning, baby."

I grin. "Later. I swear."

He looks straight at me. The teasing banter fades, and a long moment passes where he just watches me, and I feel my heart thudding in my chest.

We'll get a *later* now.

We'll get a *forever* if we want it.

"Later," he echoes.

Bryce grabs my hard cock through my slacks as he turns away. I hiss, cheeks heating, but I follow him, trying to shake my boner into a more comfortable location.

When Persephone isn't overseeing her harem, she has an office on the highest floor of Elysium. It's the exact opposite of the business-proper glass walls and stark white marble Malcolm harnessed at Heroes Org—this room embodies a castle, with a massive fireplace set behind a huge mahogany desk. Everywhere are dark, decadent trimmings, fur rugs and portraits that have to be centuries old. On the far wall, doors open onto a balcony that overlooks the beach, waves crashing gently down below.

Persephone stands by those doors, her back to us when we enter. Even without her immediate attention on me, I duck my head in deference.

She's in a floor-length gold gown, the slinky fabric hugging every curve like liquid gold was poured over her body. And when she turns, all the breath leaves my lungs at the sight of her bare breasts, the dress cut to show them, each nipple covered by a glinting gold circle and nothing else.

"Thank you for seeing us," Bryce tells her. He nudges me.

"Yes. Thank you," I echo stupidly. This was why it was so easy to make that deal with her—she's hypnotic. That perfectly smooth, dark skin; those curves; that look in her eyes like she knows exactly what effect her body and presence is having, and she will milk out every last ounce of control from us until we're nothing but blithering idiots at her feet.

Persephone tips her head. Her black braids are half pulled back, but a few loose strands shift over her collarbone. "Anything for my Warrior. What do you need to discuss?"

"Our contracts with you," Bryce says.

Her eyes narrow, barely a millimeter difference, but enough that my skin tightens.

She looks at me. "You have barely been here a week, Ari Dodgers. You are unhappy?"

"No," I admit. "But I—" I turn to Bryce. I know the way my face changes is undeniable. "My intentions have shifted."

Persephone looks from me to Bryce and back again.

She blinks. There's no emotion on her face, and it sets me on edge.

"You want out of your contracts," she guesses.

Bryce stiffens next to me. Deep in my chest, I feel something fizz and tighten—that hold she has on me. The invisible tether she enacted the moment I agreed to her deal.

She's reminding me it's still there.

"You know that is not how I operate, Warrior," she says. Her eyes flick back to me. "Least of all with such a valuable asset."

My rising sense of unease sharpens. I step closer to her; Bryce hisses for me to get back.

"Asset? You're hardly using me for anything beneficial," I say.

Persephone bats her hand. "If you no longer wish to serve out your contract in the sex dungeon, I will arrange that. You will be useful on missions, as your Bryce is. But you are mine, Ari Dodgers. You do not get to run back to Heroes Org just because you have reunited with your lovers."

"That's not what this is about," I say, my chest pinching. "To hell with Heroes Org."

She lifts an eyebrow. "Truly? Even now that Malcolm Odyssey is gone? You have not come to the realization that everything you are seeking penance for are actually his sins?"

The way she talks about Malcolm sends a shockwave through me. "You hate him," I guess.

She flinches. It's the first time I've seen her even close to shaken, and I jump on it.

"You hate him more than a Villain to a Hero," I push. I feel Bryce take my arm, trying to rein me in; but curiosity has overridden my caution.

Persephone looks away. "He took something from me." She whips her focus back and now I do stumble away, true fear coursing through me. "So I took something of his."

"Why?" My voice is strained. "How does my being here hurt him now?"

She rolls her eyes, and even that's elegant. "That is hardly the full reason I brought you on. Merely an enticing perk. No, Ari Dodgers—you will remain mine, here, just as you will, Winter Warrior. This is where you are most needed."

"For what?"

"Ari." Bryce's voice is thick with warning. But what can she do? We're already enslaved to her.

"To stand against threats," she says, her voice like ice.

It hits me, then, and I feel like a fool. How did I not see this sooner? "You want me to fight Heroes Org. That's not what I agreed to—I'm here to make up for what I did to *you*, not to attack my—"

She laughs. It's bright and piercing and not at all humorous. "Heroes Org? No, All-American Man—there are far larger threats out there than a single organization linked by misguided honor. You see only one small blip in a universal game."

My eyes narrow. Universal game?

I go utterly still. Persephone doesn't break eye contact, the intensity of her stare settling a weight over me. My years of training, my honed instincts—it all contracts to a single point.

I look out the window, up at the blue sky and, beyond it, a whole universe we've barely scratched the surface of. Extraterrestrials have been popping up more and more in recent years—Simrilians like Yava, humanoid and mostly unthreatening, but others, too. Straight-up monsters who ravaged cities in distant countries that Heroes Org took great pains to keep out of the public eye.

Malcolm feared something like this. It was a big part of why he used his mesmer powers so extensively on us. He'd brought on more and more supers in recent years, always muttering about needing better weaponry, training harder, getting control on Elysium so we'd only have *one problem to deal with*. I thought he meant general alien landings or human crimes against each other —but what if all his prep was for the same thing Persephone's hinting at?

What if all this time, the real enemy hasn't been Elysium or Villains at all—it's been extraterrestrials?

"Something's coming," I guess. I look back at Persephone. "And you're afraid."

She smirks at me, but it doesn't reach her eyes. "Fear can be a useful tool, Ari Dodgers. Now, get out of my office."

I don't move, but Bryce grabs my arm and pulls me for the door. I can't leave; we haven't resolved anything beyond me not fucking other people. Bryce and I are still *hers*. What about Piper? Will she be allowed to stay?

Persephone sits in the stuffed chair behind her huge desk. She drums her fingers on the top, her eyes on the view out the balcony as Bryce opens the door.

"What ever happened to Malcolm?" she asks. "Have you asked that particular question yet?"

Both Bryce and I stop. I look at him. He shrugs. There's something about Persephone's tone that makes me think she knows the answer; she's just testing me to see what I know.

"I'm not sure, honestly," I tell her. "Imprisoned somewhere within Heroes Org, I guess. I didn't stick around long enough to find out."

"Didn't bother staying to clean up the mess?" she mocks.

Guilt flares, but Bryce is immediately there, his hand on my jaw, pulling my focus to him.

I won't spiral. Not anymore.

"No," I admit. "I didn't."

"Hm." Persephone lays her hand flat. "That is the better reason you are here. To stop a mess before it begins."

"WHAT THE *FUCK* WAS THAT ABOUT?" I whirl on Bryce the moment we get into the elevator that'll take us down to the main floor.

He drops back against the wall and stares up at the fluorescent lights. "I have no fucking clue."

"So... that's it. We're just stuck here for whatever vague threat she thinks is coming so she has some kind of army?"

Bryce twists to look at me. His smile is sad. "Is it so bad being stuck with me?"

I take his hands and hold them to my chest.

Then I say the one name I know is rattling in both of our heads. "Piper."

"Piper." He closes his eyes. "Fuck."

17
PIPER

Ari and Bryce find me pacing in my villa. I'm not sure what I expected—Ari and I have no possessions here; we could just walk away. Leave now. But I take one look at my boys and know that it's not going to be as simple as that.

"What's wrong?" I ask, my tone demanding.

"She's not going to just let us out of our deals," Bryce says in a matter-of-fact voice.

Ari looks contemplative. I reach out, rub his forearm until I draw his attention. "What is it?" I ask.

"There's something bigger coming," he says slowly, as if he's still thinking his way through it. "I don't think this is just some power play between Persephone and the Heroes. There's something *else* at hand." He glances at Bryce. "Have you heard anything at all?"

Bryce shrugs. "When I'm sent on a mission as Winter Warrior, my memories are all locked up. It's like those old legends of berserkers. She says the code phrase, I go into fight mode, and I don't stop until the threat is eliminated. When it's over, I don't really remember much. That's part of my deal."

I frown. I *hate* this deal Bryce has made, the way it plays with his memory, punches holes in his mind. But also, if he's had to fight monsters, perhaps it is better he doesn't remember it.

My eyes go to Ari's, and I can tell that he has the same thoughts as me. Something's fishy about that set-up.

"How did it go with the Magician?" Bryce asks me.

I snort in bitter laughter. "He doesn't like to lose," I say.

"What does that mean?" Ari asks, narrowing his eyes.

"I quit, he refused to take my resignation, he pitched a little man-fit at me."

"Man-fit?" Bryce asks.

I roll my hand. "You know, when a man doesn't get his way, and he gets all grumpy."

Ari cocks an eyebrow at me. "The Magician is one of the most powerful Heroes in recorded history, and you're telling me he got *grumpy?*"

I shrug. He may be powerful, but, well, it's hard to be intimidated by anything when you've been fucked by two supers at the same time. Ari and Bryce could kill me in seconds—I'm a glass figurine next to their sheer strength. And rather than hurt me, they fill me, literally, and I can take it. I can take it all, and I love every moment of it.

That's power.

What is the Magician next to that? Nothing but a toddler angry at not getting his way.

"Okay, right, so the Magician is 'grumpy,'" Bryce says, smirking at the word. "But... it means something, right, that he got mad at Piper trying to leave?"

"Oh, he was more mad that I wasn't bringing Ari in," I say. "I'm not important."

"That's not true!" Both boys shout it at me at the same time, and my wide-eyed surprise at their burst of emotion is quickly replaced with a warm smile.

"Okay," I say, grinning, "that's sweet, but let's be real. I have nothing to offer Heroes Org, not really. They want All-American Man back." I glance at Bryce. "And if he knew you were still alive—especially if he knew of your added powers..." I let my words linger between us, my silence speaking volumes.

"You're worth ten of me, Piper," Ari mutters.

I laugh.

"Brains before brawn," Bryce adds, shooting me a look.

Gah, these boys. I can't help but love them.

"But that said," I say, tapping my chin with my finger. "You're right—the Magician was particularly adamant about bringing you back in, Ari."

We've lost supers before. Sometimes to Elysium. It's rare, and the corporation tries to keep it covered up, but it's happened.

Sometimes Heroes just get burnt out or tired and they retire. Being a Hero can be brutal, and while they're always well compensated, all the money in the world doesn't make up for the aching body, the scars, the nightmares. I've worked with enough Heroes during my time at Heroes Org to know that sometimes, we lose the Hero. It happens.

And sure, Ari was All-American Man. The face of Heroes Org. The highest ranking member.

But after the scandal with Malcolm and the leaked footage of Ari being controlled—which made him look scary as fuck, even I can admit that—it wouldn't have hurt Heroes Org all that much to cut our losses and move on. Hell, half of Heroes Org is about the PR. I can think of a dozen ways to spin Ari leaving the organization that would work super well, no pun intended. Even if it came out that he was working with Elysium, it wouldn't be that big of a deal, not from a PR angle.

Everyone loves a fallen hero story.

So the Magician's response... yeah, it was over the top. The more I think about it, the more I'm certain—this was something bigger than just an Agent being sent in to reclaim a rogue Hero.

"There's definitely something going on," I say slowly.

"But all that aside," Ari says, "Bryce and I are stuck here. But you, Piper..."

I shrug. "Is that what you're all worried about?" I glance between the boys. It's clear they both had deep concerns, and it's not about whatever game Heroes Org and Elysium are throwing them into. At least, not *just* that.

"You're a free agent now," Bryce says. I cock my eyebrow at his word choice, and he grins at me.

"But we're stuck here, with Persephone," Ari says.

I laugh, reaching out for both of them. "The solution to *that* problem is really simple, guys." I smile. "I'll just make a deal with Persephone, too. Then I get to stay with you."

18
ARI

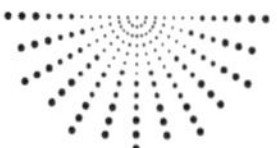

"What?" Bryce and I both say simultaneously.

Piper shrugs, smirking in a way that absolutely guts me. Like this isn't a big issue. Like she's not talking about making a deal with the fucking devil just for *us.*

"Pipes—you can't," I say.

Her grin softens. I hadn't used her nickname in a decade, but after she found me and our past came rushing back to meet us, it feels natural again.

"You're free," I continue. "You can go back to Brooklyn, or Los Angeles, or wherever. We'll find ways to visit, but you're not enslaving yourself to Persephone for us."

"Why not?" Her eyes glint, all sexy defiance. "I'll trade her my skills as an agent for..." She cuts a sly grin between Bryce and me. "Maybe some time in that sex dungeon?"

Bryce and I lurch towards her, but she laughs before we have to say anything.

"I know, I know. But I *can* be useful to her. She'll take me on; you know she will."

"That's not the problem," Bryce says. "The problem is you'd be trapped."

"I'd be trapped with *my boys,*" Piper argues. All her humor vanishes.

"That's not a problem at all. I'll take you however I can get you. And if this is how I get you? Then just call me an Operative."

Bryce's words echo in my head. *Is it so bad being stuck with me?*

I look between them. Piper's dark eyes and full lips to Bryce's gray eyes beneath pinched brows.

And suddenly, all that panic washes away. Because she's right. And he is, too, even if the thought of Piper being bound to Persephone activates our protective responses.

I grab their hands, threading my fingers with theirs. "I stopped imagining a future for us years ago. So if this is the future we get? Yeah, I'll take it."

Piper laughs again and throws her arms around my neck. Her excitement is an effective balm on my worry; I hold her to me, my eyes locking with Bryce's over her shoulder.

He bites his lip. The act is tense but still somehow dead sexy, and I reach for him, one hand on his jaw.

Finally, he relents, his shoulders relaxing. "Fine. But we go to her together."

"Deal," Piper says. She pulls back enough to kiss me, and my cock immediately springs to attention at the feel of her soft lips on mine, the way her tongue darts into my mouth. I'm pissed I'm still wearing the dress slacks. It's been a whole two hours at least since I was naked with them—way, way too long, after everything it took to bring us back here.

I feel Bryce bend closer to us, and Piper turns to kiss him, too.

But before I can set her down to take off her clothes—

Before I can act on the tightening sensation of desire in my gut—

Before I can do anything at all—

A voice slices through our moment like a goddamn machete.

"This is what you left us for?"

Bryce and I act immediately. Identical training takes over—I shove Piper behind me and whirl into a defensive stance that Bryce mirrors, our faces severe, muscles coiled, hands in fists.

Lucas Gardson reclines on the soft white couch in Piper's living room. He's not here casually—he's in his full super regalia, the green-and-gold suit that immediately marks him as the Magician. His black hair is slightly curled on his shoulders, stark against the sheer paleness of his skin. He has his head cocked as he surveys Bryce and me, the angular features of his sharp face taking us in slowly, luxuriously.

His smile is all sin. "I wish I could say I didn't see the appeal."

"What are you doing here, Lucas?" I ask, seething.

"*How* did you get here?" Bryce adds.

Lucas shoves to his feet. A moment of fury ripples over his features before he calms again.

"As if the powers of Elysium could keep me at bay," he says.

Piper shoves between us to face Lucas, and I immediately grab her arm. She whips me a glare that has me relenting.

"Mr. Gardson," she starts. "I don't know what you—"

But he holds up his hand, cutting her off, and the sheer disrespect in it has me lurching forward a step.

"You truly do as she bids, with just a look?" he asks me, not at all fazed. "You, All-American Man, the most powerful super in the world, can be controlled by a single glare from this woman?"

I go rigid. But there's no use denying it.

Both Piper and Bryce control me that way. Fully. Completely. They always have. And I like it that way.

Lucas smiles, the full width of his lips curling up in dark glee. "Well. I was right in sending her after you, then. But this." He points at Bryce. "This obstacle I did not correctly factor in."

"Factor in?" I frown at Bryce before realization makes my blood go cold.

He wasn't at all surprised to see Bryce here. He didn't react at all, in fact.

I place myself in front of Piper again.

But in front of Bryce, too.

"You knew," I guess. The words leave me in a rush. "You knew he was alive."

Lucas lifts one black eyebrow. "I know a lot of things. I know, for instance, that if you do not come back to Heroes Org willingly, I have ways of making you."

"Why?" I spit. "To fight the threat that Malcolm feared?"

Lucas laughs. But it's tense, manic almost. "Malcolm's approach was primitive. You have yet to fully appreciate Heroes Org under my guidance, Dodgers. We will do things Malcolm only dreamed of." He darkens. "But to do those things, you need to be with us. That is your place. It always will be, no matter what petty deals you make with the Villain Queen."

Now it's my turn to laugh. It rips through me, the downright absurdity of Persephone's similar speech from an hour ago, and now Lucas spewing the same kind of vague bullshit.

"You're both fighting the same war, you know that, right?" I tell him. "You and Persephone. You're both after the same goddamn *thing*, and I'm starting to wonder how long, actually, Heroes Org and Elysium have been on the same side but couldn't fucking realize it. But I'm not a pawn anymore."

"Oh?" Lucas's nostrils flare. "Does Persephone know that? How did she respond when you informed her of your ex-pawn status?"

My lips flatten into a line.

Lucas nods. "Thought so. Come back, and I can wipe away her deal with you."

"Fuck this," Piper snaps and stomps for the wall—where a trigger box sits. Likely one of those buttons summons Persephone.

"Ah-ah." Lucas lifts his fingers.

A green fog washes over Piper, freezing her limbs in place.

Bryce and I don't hesitate—we dive at Lucas.

He waves his other hand, and we stop up short, fists raised, faces livid, frozen in his magic.

Lucas clicks his tongue. "I've had my doubts about you for some time, Dodgers. I let the game play out because other parties were *so certain* that they could mold you. But look at you—you're unfit to protect this planet no matter whose banner you do it under. They—" He points from Bryce to Piper. "—have made you soft. Have made you *weak*."

"Lucas—" I manage, my throat constricting under his power. All my strength, all my own abilities, and one wave of his goddamn magic, and I'm frozen.

He taps a finger on his chin. "Let's test that, actually. I want to see just how far you've fallen. Let's see, once and for all, just how far gone All-American Man is."

Lucas turns to Bryce. He gets right up in his face, icy green eyes looking deep into Bryce's.

"You're going to kill him," Lucas tells Bryce. "Initiate code alpha—"

Initiate? That can't be—

Bryce's eyes slide to mine, panicked.

Is this the trigger code Persephone installed? The trigger code that *only* Persephone knew about?

"—gray, seven—"

I strain against the Magician's hold. Every muscle tenses, pushing, *pushing*—

"—tango, magnum."

Lucas steps back, his face serene, almost, as he raises his hands.

"Do your best, All-American Man," he tells me, and then he drops his hold on us all.

My first instinct is to dive at Lucas. There's no way that trigger worked—he's bluffing, trying to distract me.

But I take one step, and a body slams into me, tossing me into the far wall.

Piper screams. "Bryce! Bryce, *stop*—"

He pays her no attention. His entire focus is fixed on me as I peel myself up from the carpet.

His face is completely changed. His eyes are... empty. Wide, all-pupil eyes that see me but don't.

"Bryce," I gasp, one hand out.

My gaze flicks to Lucas, who sits on the couch again, one arm across the back like he's watching a play.

Fury surges up me. Maybe if I take out Lucas, Bryce will snap out of it.

I shove for the couch.

Bryce intercepts me, his metal arm clotheslining my neck. I rebound, but he's there, grabbing my arm and sweeping my legs out from under me to slam my back to the floor. The whole damn villa rattles; the chandelier clanks and shakes; somewhere pictures drop off the walls.

"Bryce!" Piper jumps on his back. "Bryce, this isn't you! Wake up!"

"Piper—*run*," I tell her, but Bryce looks at her over his shoulder.

My whole body hardens. Every beat of blood in my veins. Every nerve ending.

He reaches back for her, and my heart breaks—that she might get hurt, that *he* might do the hurting.

I shove, hard, and flip him off of me. Piper rolls away, tears streaming down her face; but she gets to her feet and scrambles across the room.

Bryce yanks himself up by the fireplace.

"She's right," I try. Maybe I can get him talking. "This isn't you. I *know* you, Bryce. I know I haven't been there in awhile, but I still know you."

He swings at me. I duck it and dodge to the side.

"And I'm sorry," I say. The words soften me, though I know I should stay in a defensive stance. "I don't think I've said it. Not really. I tried to show you; I tried to atone. But I never just said it. I'm sorry I left you. I'm sorry I ruined us."

My eyes go behind Bryce, to where Piper cowers near the end of the sofa, her attention flicking between us and Lucas, his face pinched with disappointment.

"I'm sorry," I say, to Bryce, to Piper.

I drop to my knees.

Bryce advances towards me, his hands in fists, that metal arm glinting as he raises it back.

Fuck, he really might kill me.

Maybe I am broken, like Lucas said. All-American Man is well and truly gone.

Because I'll let him. I'll let Bryce beat me to death, if it means sparing him.

I'm panting, chest tight, cinching even tighter with every step Bryce takes towards me.

"I'm sorry," I say again, holding onto his empty gray eyes. "And I forgive you, for this."

Bryce stops.

His lifted arm holds.

Is that a flicker of recognition in his eyes?

"Bryce," I try. "Baby. *Please.*"

19
PIPER

All I want to do is watch the magic of our love defeat the manipulative magic of that triggering code phrase and the Magician's powers.

But see, that's the thing.

Everyone—Lucas Gardson, Ari—their eyes are glued to Bryce. The way he's hesitating. The way he's straining against his own will to *not* strike Ari.

They're watching him.

Not me.

And that is all the distraction I need to dive for the panic button. My hand slams on it so hard that my arm actually hurts.

Instantly, the air crackles.

The force of it is so strong that it makes my knees buckle. I fall to the floor.

It's as if every single atom in the villa stopped and then jerked to the left. My vision doesn't blur so much as it goes chromatic, the colors off-kilter. My lungs fill with air that burns like electricity.

And *she* is here.

Persephone.

Blue flames lick at her heels, evaporating even as I watch her. Her gold gown flows from her hips like water. My eyes trace up. Her head is tilted, her chin strong, her eyes narrow.

She scans the room. Me, kneeling beside the panic button. Bryce, still poised to strike Ari. It is something else now—Persephone's magic, I think—that has stopped the boys from fighting. They are still in an eerie, statue-like way.

Unlike the Magician, whose eyes are wide as he freaks the fuck out on the couch, fingers clawing at the cream-colored cushions, legs kicking back as if he could scramble away.

"Pers—!" he starts.

Her cold eyes slide to him, and he shuts right the fuck up.

Then she turns, inclining her gaze to me. She strides over to the wall and extends one long, graceful hand. Trembling, I put my fingers in her palm, and she helps me to stand.

"You, Piper Carson, are my guest, and I swore to you that you had my protection as such. Tell me what happened."

"You have no right—" Lucas starts.

Without looking behind her, Persephone flicks her hand in the Magician's direction. He stops mid-sentence, silenced so abruptly that I have no doubt that she *made* him stop, through magic or something else. He claws at his throat, but although he's mute, he doesn't seem in danger of suffocating or anything.

"I want you to tell me what happened. Is this..." She pauses then, raking the Magician with a sneering look of disgust. "Is *he* an invited guest of yours?"

"No," I say, barely able to choke out more.

Persephone's look softens as she takes in the blossoming bruises on my skin, my disheveled clothes, my shaky stance.

"Has he caused injury to come to you?"

"Yes," I whisper.

Without moving her face, Persephone's gaze flicks over to Bryce and Ari, impossibly frozen in place, Ari on his knees, Bryce poised for a killing blow. "Explain," she says.

"He—the Magician—he knew your trigger phrase to activate Bryce's killing mode. He spoke it and ordered Bryce to attack." My words die in my throat, and I swallow down emotion. "Ari tried to protect me. And Bryce—"

Her chin tilts up. "I see."

She turns, the hem of her gold gown brushing across my skin, whisper-soft silk belying the strength of her steps. Persephone makes a movement with her hand, and the strange stillness of Bryce and Ari stops.

Bryce, still under the thrall of the trigger phrase and thrown off from his internal battle that had paused his hand, moves—his arm falls like lightning—straight towards Ari's bent and exposed neck.

I scream.

And Persephone says... *something*. I cannot discern her actual words. It's another language, Ancient Greek, perhaps, or something older, perhaps not even a language humans know. But she speaks, and Bryce staggers back as if pushed by wind. His eyes fill with awareness, and he checks himself, jerking his whole body around so that he won't hurt Ari. And Ari leaps up even as Bryce staggers, reaching for him and catching him.

Bryce is safe in his arms.

And as one, we all turn to face the Magician.

He smirks, one eyebrow raised. He completely ignores the way Bryce and Ari snarl at him, ready to rip him apart limb from limb. He spares me one glance—one appreciative nod, a look of acceptance at my triumph—and then he gives his full attention to Persephone.

"My darling," he says. "You can't blame a fellow for *trying*."

"I tire of your tricks, Lucas," Persephone says. Her tone has almost no inflection at all, but her voice is all the more powerful for it.

The Magician laughs, posing in a way that makes him seem at complete ease.

"If you think you're just going to get away with this—" Ari starts, taking a menacing step forward.

"Oh, of course I am," the Magician laughs.

And then he's gone.

"The fuck!" Bryce exclaims as Ari looks around, shocked.

Persephone sighs, her shoulders slouching just a little, but there's a knowing smile playing on her lips. It disappears almost immediately, but I caught it—

This is a game they've played before, I think. *She knows the Magician. More than just his name, his reputation. She knows the way he is.*

Persephone cocks an eyebrow at me. I wonder again if she can read my thoughts, even though she said she couldn't. I feel laid bare, but I also feel *right.*

"Well," she says, putting her hands on her hips and casting her gaze around the room. "I suspect that it is time to discuss what happens next."

20

ARI

Bryce twists in my arms. I think he wants me to let him go, but I refuse, clinging to him until he faces me.

"I'm sorry," he starts. "I'm sorry, I didn't—"

I silence him with a kiss, one hand on the back of his neck, my tongue lapping up any of his misguided apologies.

I understand him and Piper now more than I had before. How they could so easily forgive me.

There's not a single thing this man or Piper could do that would make me stop loving them.

That's how they feel about me, even if my actions were more intentional. They know me. They know my soul the same way I know theirs, and they probably forgave me a long time ago; I was just too blinded by grief to see it.

I break the kiss, forehead to Bryce's, breathing the same air as him, content to stay this way.

Except for Persephone, watching us, and her words still hanging on the air, thick with intent.

"Let him go," I turn to her. My voice is rough. "If Lucas knows the trigger words, Bryce isn't *your* warrior anymore. You have to let him go."

Persephone purses her lips. She doesn't immediately accept or refuse—and I dive on that.

Hand in Bryce's, I face her, anxiety humming in my chest. "There's a threat coming. Right? Something from... out there." I wave my free hand at the ceiling and, beyond it, the universe. "That's what you're trying to prepare for. That's what Lucas fears, too. Tell me I'm wrong."

Persephone's face is a mask. She gives nothing away for free.

So when she nods, it feels like a massive victory. But that bit of confirmation isn't enough.

"Then I have a new deal for you," I say.

Bryce tightens his hand in mine. Piper, behind Persephone, rushes forward, and I loop my other arm around her waist and hold her to me, ignoring the worried look she gives.

"You let us out of our deals with you. We're not your Operatives anymore. In exchange, we'll serve as your liaisons with Heroes Org."

Persephone's eyebrows vault to her hairline. I've actually managed to surprise her.

"Go on," she says.

"You and Lucas—and Malcolm, I suspect—are all fighting the same war, but you don't get along for reasons I can't guess at, even though you're all way more similar than you think. But I know Heroes Org. Between Piper and me, we know all of the Heroes employed there. And Bryce knows your Villains. So let us be that bridge that finally brings an alliance between Heroes Org and Elysium."

The surprise on her face sharpens as she chews my proposal. "You suggest opening Elysium to your Heroes? Revealing all my secrets?"

"I hardly think you're the type who couldn't keep her secrets hidden even if there were Heroes in your sex dungeon," I say. "Piper and I will convince them to come. We'll be ambassadors, of sorts. And we'll all start building a resistance to whatever this *threat* is—but we'll do it *together*, instead of fruitlessly fighting each other."

Persephone folds her arms under her breasts, still glinting with those gold plates. The look on her face now is impressed, unless I'm totally misreading her. But I don't think she'd let herself be misread.

A long moment of silence passes with Persephone looking only at me. Bryce and Piper are statues at my sides, but having them here infuses me with the strength I need to hold Persephone's eyes and not back down.

Finally, *finally,* she nods. "I accept, Ari Dodgers."

I blow out a breath. The effervescence I'd first felt when I'd made this deal with her lifts, an invisible link unbinding me from her.

I'm...free.

We can truly be *us* again.

Persephone lifts her hand. The air starts to crackle with the heat that'd come when she'd appeared, and I dart forward, eyes wide.

"Wait—did you release Bryce?"

She arches an eyebrow. "I did the moment I saw what Lucas had uncovered."

My chest squeezes. Those words she spoke in that strange language—it hadn't just stopped Bryce in the moment, but broke him of his berserker, mindless warrior mode forever.

Why hadn't she mentioned that before I'd made my plea to her?

She's still in this to get her way, to come out on top.

I'll have to remember that.

"If we're going to start working with you," I say, emphasis on *with*, "we need to know what the threat is. What are you all so afraid of?"

Persephone smiles at me for the first time. It's the pause after a sunset, a deep, rich calmness, the breath in between.

"Oh, Ari Dodgers," she purrs. "That was never part of our arrangement."

Her eyes flick over my shoulder, to Piper and Bryce, then back to me. "You are all welcome to remain in this villa, if you so choose. It will be yours and yours alone."

To me, she gives one last look. It's heavy with the things she knows I know, how she's still in this to win, how she'll keep all her secrets tight to her chest.

But we have cards to play, too. And now, we're free to play them.

She vanishes, the energy of the room contracting before expanding again in a vacuum-like rush.

I stagger in her absence.

But I'm immediately swept up by Bryce and Piper.

Piper clings to my neck. Bryce enrobes us both in his arms.

"That was brilliant," Piper says. Her voice is pinched, either near to tears or maybe from earlier, when she'd screamed Bryce's name.

That memory pierces me, cuts deep into my heart until I start shaking. She'll never scream like that again. Bryce will never get that look in his eyes again, either, nor that wash of horror when he'd woken up and realized what he'd almost done.

We're free now. Free to be here, *this*, as long as we want.

I breathe in deeply, the delicate rose perfume of Piper, Bryce's sandalwood soap.

"Pipes," I nudge her ear with my lips, "you got a bath in this place?"

"No," she says, and I can tell she's smiling now, "but the ocean's right outside."

Bryce presses his forehead to ours, the three of us joined, now and forever.

"I want you both out there, lying on that sand," he tells us, and there's that gravelly, primal twist to his voice again, the one that makes my cock instantly hard, that makes me want to drop to my knees. "Clothes off. Now."

I catch his mouth in mine, nipping at his lip. I know we still have a lot coming. We still have a lot of uncertainties. We will eventually need to go to Lucas and convince him of this alliance; we need to figure out how to reach out to other Heroes and get them to trust us, if not the Villains they've been fighting for years. There is so much to do.

But right now, I could explode with joy.

Right now, I'm lighter than I've been in years.

I'm home again. And I will feel every bit of this happiness.

"Yes, sir," I tell Bryce, and I heave Piper over my shoulder as I race out the door, her squeals of laughter cheering me on.

21
PIPER

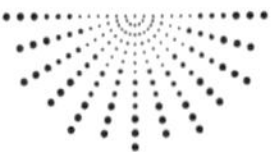

Three months later

I have two monitors open, my eyes darting between each one. A pair of hands wraps around my shoulders, squeezing gently. I close my eyes and lean into the touch. *Ari,* I think. I can do that now—I can tell which of my boys is near by just a touch, nothing else.

I feel brusque lips on the shell of my ear. I keep my eyes closed, a ghost of a smile flitting over my lips. *Bryce.*

I swivel in the desk chair and look up, greeting each of them with a grin. "Good morning," I chirp.

Ari reaches behind him and hands me a cup of coffee from the counter. "How?" he asks as I take the steamy mug and breathe in the scent —freshly ground beans, a splash of almond milk. "How are you so awake in the morning that you can look at—are those *spreadsheets?*"

I sip the coffee. "We need organization!"

"There's a joke in there somewhere," Bryce says, brow furrowing.

"Laugh all you want," I say. "But we're getting to the point where we're going to have to get the Heroes and Villains to schedule time at Persephone's."

Ari, Bryce, and I have been busy at work, spreading the word that Persephone's castle is both an entirely neutral ground, where Heroes and

Villains can exist in safety together, and also, well, a hell of a good time. Heroes find that they can run free from the restrictive rules of Heroes Org in the sex dungeon, and they also know that they can absolutely, entirely, without any doubt be safe there. No cameras. No trails. Discreet portals mean no paparazzi can follow.

I think about the buttoned-up linen shirts and tight pencil skirts I wore at the office, as an official Agent. They served a purpose, I suppose. An image.

But it was so utterly *repressive.*

It was easy for me to find exactly the right Heroes and Agents to bring to Persephone. A chance to completely leave behind the restrictive lifestyle that's omnipresent at Heroes Org? Yes, please. Especially considering that all our legal forms don't apply on this island. Anyone working for the corporation has signed NDAs and morality clauses in contracts and Heroes Org has tied up every legal loophole they can, but none of that applies in the liminal space of Elysium.

The Magician, of course, doesn't know yet. The Heroes who come to Elysium treat it as a neutral territory—as Persephone had hoped—before they return to their regular turf and duties. No one has permanently left Heroes Org after Ari's departure, but we're planting the seeds. Building the trust. And thanks to a bit of portal magic, everything's kept *very* private. Besides, laws don't apply on an island accessed only by interdimensional portals where tech doesn't work unless it's approved by Persephone and the only rule is to protect each other.

It's not just about sex. Some have come here to let loose in other ways. There's a growing fight club that Bryce is handling, allowing Heroes to express their rage without worry of causing harm. You're not allowed to lose your temper in Heroes Org. You always have to be restrained.

It works the opposite way as well. There are Villains who explore creating things in Persephone's castle. They're less restrained than Heroes, not restricted by any set PR rules, but Persephone's safe place means that I once caught Brix the Destroyer knitting a fluffy pink scarf, and there's literally a Villain competition equivalent to the Great British Bake Off happening later this week, and I sure as fuck am not going to miss my chance at tasting Fallon's Victoria sponge.

I frown, turning to my spreadsheet. Fallon is someone to note—he has big beef with Ari. I make a note to remind them both that Persephone's whole island is a neutral zone.

Boundaries have been tested, of course. But both sides see the value of neutrality. And both sides are willing to help with crowd control.

I twirl the bracelet on my wrist. It's tech—made by Scarlet, a mesmer like Malcolm, but also a technological genius. My own personal comm directly to Persephone. I'm the only one in the world with this panic button.

I've not had to use it yet. But once I broke up a skirmish by standing up and making a show of holding up my wrist.

It stopped the fight cold.

No one wants to risk Persephone's wrath.

No one wants to risk a lifelong ban from this paradise.

"A lady in the streets, a freak in the spreadsheets!" Bryce crows, a triumphant look on his face.

Ari and I stare at him.

"I told you there was a joke in the way Pipes like spreadsheets," he says, laughter in his eyes.

"That was so bad," Ari deadpans.

"The worst," I agree. "It's not like I'm really a lady in the streets."

But I glance back at the spreadsheet, then to Ari. "Fallon is coming to the island soon," I say.

"Oh, I like Fallon!" Bryce says. "We've been on missions together. Good guy." Then he remembers the past. "Oh, shit."

Exactly.

We both focus on Ari, the sworn nemesis of the winged Villain Raven, whose real name is Fallon. Ari, under Malcolm's mesmer powers, had brutally injured the Raven more than once. I suspect that part of this was the driving force of repression that needed an outlet, but I know that Ari and Fallon are... not exactly on good terms.

I fix Ari with a stern look. "I know you know the rules, but…"

"It's not me you have to worry about," Ari says.

"I know. I'll have a talk with Fallon, too." I pause. "He's bringing Lillith."

A look—that old, haunted look of remorse—shadows Ari's face. Lillith —known then as Lilly—had been Ari's fiancée. He had nearly killed her while under Malcolm's influence.

"She knows you didn't mean to drive off the cliff," I say gently. "She's already forgiven you."

Ari's jaw is tight. Bryce and I both respond immediately. When one of us hurts, all of us hurt. Bryce rubs Ari's arm while I reach out and grab his fingers, squeezing them, reminding him that we're here for him.

"I know she understands, but... fuck," Ari groans. "Will the atonement ever end?"

"Yes," I say. I wait until Ari looks up at me. "It ends once you learn to forgive yourself. *Fully.*"

"I'm working on it," he says.

"And we're here for you while you are," Bryce adds.

And just like that, there's Ari again, without the shadows of the past haunting him. Grief and forgiveness don't get wiped out quite that simply, but together, we can help each other.

In the meantime...

"We could use some time at Persephone's," Bryce says, reading my mind. "I wonder if there's a free spot for the stage in the dungeon..."

"There's a spreadsheet for that!" I chirp, spinning in my chair and bringing up the stage's schedule.

Behind me, both Ari and Bryce groan, but it's good-natured. "I'm getting her a coffee mug with that on it," Ari whispers to Bryce.

I tap my screen. "No one's using the stage at all this morning," I say. I swivel around slowly. "Why don't we do a little teacher with naughty schoolboys play?" I reach over to a cup of pencils and wind my hair in a tight bun, stabbing it with the sharpened pencils to hold it in place.

Just like that, both Ari and Bryce are hard. God, I love that control I have over them.

"Fuck the stage," Bryce growls. "We can do that right here."

I smirk, knowing full well that my brightly painted red lips are teasing them just as much as my visibly taut nipples under the sheer blouse I'm wearing. "Excuse me, boys," I say in an imperial voice. "I believe I'm the one in charge of this school. Now, to the classroom. Don't be late."

When Ari doesn't move, I swat his ass with an audible smack. He leaps up, laughing, grabbing Bryce's hand, and they race out of the villa and toward Persephone's castle.

I take my time, tucking my gauzy blouse into my short skirt, adding a jacket that buttons tightly just under my breasts, and refreshing my lipstick. I slip into stilettos and grab a ruler, smiling, knowing that my boys have been very naughty indeed.

Time to teach them a lesson.

I don't rush up to the dungeon, letting the anticipation of my arrival do all the foreplay.

Besides, I don't have to hurry.

We have all the time in the world, together.

22

EPILOGUE: PERSEPHONE

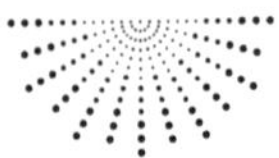

I DO NOT LIKE TECHNOLOGY.

It's too modern, and it sets my blood buzzing. Magic is far better. But this world seems incapable of moving forward without a modicum of tech. At least Scarlet has worked with me to create some forms of communication that aren't as *bothersome* as cheaper technology.

Still, it angers me to be reduced to pixels.

"I'm sorry, Persephone," Fallon says. Behind him, I see Lillith. She seems unaware of the hologram Fallon uses to speak to me; she's wearing nothing but negligee as she hums to herself, cleaning the kitchen at Fallon's base. My eyes drift to her. If we were in a dreamscape, we could be having this conversation truly together, in a place where we could touch.

But Scarlet's busy now, and this is all we have.

"I know you don't like coms or holos, but..." Fallon says, his voice trailing off. Lillith becomes aware of the hologram. She waves, but then exits, giving Fallon privacy.

I am not pleased with this development. I liked seeing her there, like that. I like playing with them together. Her absence furthers my point: tech is the worst.

"What do you need to say?" I demand, growling, letting him feel my ire.

Fallon flinches. "I've seen the way the dungeon on your island's been...

changing," he says. "An Agent—a former Agent from Heroes Org—has contacted me, letting me know of your new rules."

Goddammit. Not this again.

"Do you intend to try to tell me how to run *my* base?" I say in icy tones. "Do you really think whatever petty beef you have with All-American Man is going to limit what *I* choose to do?"

"Petty beef?" Fallon shouts. "The bastard broke my wings! He tried to kill Lill—"

"That is of no concern to me," I bite out.

Fallon looks very much as if he'd like to leap through the hologram and throttle me. I arch my eyebrow at him.

He shakes his head, running his fingers over his hair. "Fine, fine," he says. "That's not what I wanted to talk to you about anyway."

I tilt my chin, waiting. Perhaps this Villain has more to intrigue me with after all.

"Scarlet sent me a weird message," he says slowly. "Told me to pass it on to you."

Interesting. Why couldn't Scarlet reach out to me herself? I don't bother asking. Boys always tell me everything if I leave them only with silence.

"She's helping Watcher recover some of his memories. Apparently they use the dreamscape to analyze the code..." He waves his hand dismissively. "I don't really understand all of it, other than the fact that Watcher's past files have been corrupted, and he can't access the full information."

I lean forward, still not speaking. Hmm. So Watcher and Scarlet are now accessing some of that classified information they'd been unable to uncover before.

When Watcher left Heroes Org so many years ago, he walked out the door with half the corporation's data banks logged into his computerized brain in a brilliant coup. But Heroes Org had encrypted the data so well that it was like untangling a ball of twine in a labyrinth. A part of me has liked his ignorance. However, there's no denying that he's a powerful ally, and an informed ally is generally better.

"Scar's been too tired to do any broader dreamscapes after she's been working with Watcher. She told me to pass along some information to you, but it doesn't make much sense."

He pauses here and doesn't continue. "What's the message?" I ask, annoyed that I have to ask.

"'Niberu is Eris.'" Fallon blinks on the hologram. "Does that make sense to you?"

Fuck. "Yes," I say simply.

"What does that even mean?" Fallon asks. "Scarlet didn't understand it either—she says most of Watcher's code around this is garbled, but since it was the bit that Heroes Org most wanted to keep hidden through encryption and firewalls, she thought you would want to know it, even if it was gibberish." He pauses. "It's not gibberish, though, is it? You know what that means—"

I flick the hologram off.

Steepling my fingers, I stare at the blank space in the wall that had been illuminated by the hologram.

Niberu.

Fuck, fuck, fuck.

Fuck.

I don't want to have to reach out to Malcolm. Ari told me he had no idea where Malcolm was, but I know. I know. And he might be persuaded to tell me about the other part of Scarlet's message... Eris...

I shake my head. No. Scarlet's on the right track. She can keep working on Watcher's mind and the data he hacked from Heroes Org. It'll be more reliable than anything I draw from Malcolm.

Although, perhaps, it is time to implement my ace in the hole.

I tap my chin with one manicured fingernail. Princeton has been a safe place for my secret, but it may be time to pull her out.

A tentative knock sounds at my door. "Yes?" I say. Few would dare disturb me.

Piper Carson stands in the doorway. "I wanted to let you know I updated all the schedules," she says. "And the private rooms you asked me to add. I also contacted those on the list you sent."

"Including—?" I ask. She nods.

"Good."

I bring up the schedules. More tech, but necessary. "Ah," I say, spotting Piper's allotted time on the stage with Bryce and Ari. Beginning now. I turn and inspect her a second time, noting the outfit, the ruler. "Ah," I say again, my voice liquid.

She smiles, her red lips full of invitation. "In case you needed a break from work," she says.

I stand, letting the silver skirt fall over my legs, relishing the feel of it swishing against my hips as I follow the minx down the stairs, to the dungeon.

On stage, Bryce and Ari are waiting. Their eyes go wide at the sight of me, but I don't join Piper on stage with them. I sit in the front row, enjoying the show.

Their excited energy washes over me, roiling inside, filling me with power.

I don't join.

Not yet.

SECRET SANCTUM

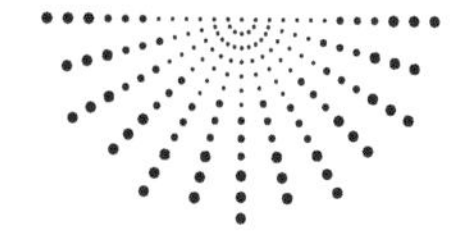

1
ANTHONY

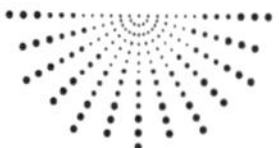

SOMETHING'S NOT RIGHT.

The feeling of wrongness has been plaguing me for a while, truth be told. Longer than I care to admit. It was easier to turn a blind eye when Malcolm was the CEO of Heroes Org. His mesmer powers were like a fog of acceptance over the whole corporation.

But Malcolm's gone now. And the more I start looking at things, the more I realize that something's not fucking right.

It starts with Watcher.

I was there when that shit went down. I realize now it was a set-up. Watcher was born with super healing, making him the ideal candidate to be morphed into a cyborg with a computer for a brain. He healed from the blasts that should have killed him in record time, and the injuries became a part of his strength.

Unlike me.

I press the palm of my hand against my chest. Instead of a heartbeat, I hear only the gentle whirring of my biotech heart pump.

An experiment in my lab led to an injury in my heart that almost killed me. It was only thanks to the advanced tech provided by Heroes Org that I was able to survive.

Well, the tech and my sexy genius brain.

I healed eventually. And then I was able to coalesce that same biotech into something bigger, better. The Steel Soldier suit turns a simple human like me into a Hero. I may not have been born with the mutated DNA that gives me superpowers, but brains before brawn, baby.

Back to Watcher.

Malcolm had wanted to control him, but he couldn't. Watcher went Villain.

But before he did—and this is what no one else knows—he gave me a message. "Look to the stars."

Which, frankly, is kind of a shitty message? I mean, I know my intelligence level, and maybe my gorgeous genius brain isn't a literal supercomputer like Watcher's, but like. That message is fucking useless. C'mon, man, give me something to work with! You *know* how much fucking space and stars are out there?!

So anyway, yeah, that was the first clue, even if it was inconveniently obscure. To put it lightly.

Then it came out that Malcolm had gone rogue with his mesmer powers, using them to influence Heroes and other people in the corporation to bend to his will. As soon as he was gone, it was like a fog had lifted.

And Heroes Org has been *bleeding* Heroes ever since.

Ari Dodgers—that's All-American Man to the public—was first. Agent Piper Carson followed him to the dark side, signing up with the Villain Queen, Persephone.

Since then, the efficiency of the corporation has been sharply declining. The new CEO of Heroes Org—Lucas Gardson, Hero name "The Magician"—has more than once called on a Hero for a mission only for that Hero to be "unavailable."

"Think, Anthony," I tell myself. I probably look deranged to an outsider. If someone walked into my Heroes Org lab right now, they'd see me with my shirt off, biotech heart pump a shining chrome disk in the center of my chest, surrounded by hologram images and charts, trying to connect the pieces.

Heroes going missing.

Malcolm going rogue.

Look to the stars.

What does it all mean? *Something* is up.

Think, Anthony, think. Use that astounding, gorgeous, down-right sexy brain of yours.

I look up, seeing not the holograms around me, but through them, to the window of my lab.

Where the fuck is Malcolm?

Why didn't that question occur to me before? Malcolm went dark, he was arrested…and then he was just *gone.*

I swipe my arm through the holograms, dismissing their glowing images. After tossing on a shirt—making sure it looks nice, I do have standards—I head to the elevator, punching it to the penthouse floor. When the doors slide open, an assistant is standing in the foyer, as if she were waiting for me.

"Mr. Stern," she says, smiling pleasantly.

I may be on a mission to speak to the CEO and demand answers, but that doesn't mean I can't appreciate the way this secretary's blouse is bursting at the buttons over her chest, the way her pencil skirt hugs her curves. "Well, hello there, Penny," I say.

Her pouty pink lips give me a shy smile. "Mr. Gardson is busy right now," she says. "Shall I tell him you…" She clears her throat, a blush rising on her cheeks. "…came?"

My lips twist in a sardonic smile at her last word. I don't know if I'd have noticed the double entendre of the word "came" if she hadn't said it with such emphasis, her eyes dropping to my pants.

What can I say? I have three body parts that are all the rage. My biotech heart pump is a wonder of modern science. My sexy brain is renowned for its genius.

And my cock has a reputation all its own.

Who says I can't be both a brilliant scientist inventor *and* a playboy at the same time?

"Mr. Stern, sir," Penny says, looking up at me through those long eyelashes of hers. "Would you like me to relay a message to Mr. Gardson?"

I walk closer to her. I can see the thrum of her heartbeat in her pale neck, the flush rising from her chest. Science provides physical reactions of the body in response to lust, reactions that can't be denied. And I'm attracted to her, another fact that can't be denied.

But I'm on a mission.

"I'll relay my own message," I tell her in a deep, throaty voice. The tone —full of lust—has delayed the meaning of my words from processing, giving me enough time to slip past her and down the emerald corridor.

Lucas Gardson is at his desk, scowling at his laptop screen. When I burst through his door, Penny appears moments later, eyes wide. "Mr. Gardson, I'm so sorry!" she says.

I shoot her a sympathetic look, but she doesn't meet my eyes. Lucas sighs, folding his laptop shut. "It's fine, Penny," he tells her. Then his scowl turns to me. "What do you want, Stern?"

"Answers," I say breezily. I cross the office and drape myself on the chair across from his desk as Penny leaves, shutting the door behind her.

Lucas rolls his eyes. "You'll have to be more specific."

I eye the man. He's built like a god, muscles unhidden by a suit jacket in a shade of green so dark that it's nearly black. A gold pin replaces his tie, and his dark brown hair is swept into a tight bun at the back of his head. He has all the appearance of a man restraining himself, fitting himself into the box of CEO when he should be out there, fighting with the rest of the supers.

I wonder what an unlimited Lucas Gardson looks like.

The idea both thrills and terrifies me.

"What do you want, *exactly?*" Lucas says, biting off the last word.

I straighten up in the chair. Right. No fucking around. Let's get down to business. "Where's Malcolm?"

"Malcolm?"

"The Hive. The CEO before you. The dick who used his mesmer powers on Heroes. Where is he?"

For just a tick, I notice that Lucas's eye twitches. A barely-there sign that he doesn't want to answer me. But he does. "Imprisoned," he says.

"Well now, that's just interesting," I say. "Because I've checked the prison records of the containment units in Heroes Org. And his name isn't on there."

"You don't have access to every security clearance in this organization," Lucas says coldly. "Trust me. He is secure."

"Oh, I trust you!" I say genially, tossing my hands up. "So, where do I go to see him?" I add.

"Excuse me?" Lucas says. He leans forward, steepling his hands as he stares at me with those ice-jade eyes of his.

"I want to talk to him. He's a prisoner, so I'll have to go to him. Unless you want to bring him to me?" I shoot him my most charming smile.

"He is a mesmer," Lucas says as if I'm simple. "He could control you with his mind."

"I have a helmet for that," I say, dismissing his concern.

"He's off-limits."

"Why?"

Lucas's eyes narrow. "Why are you asking?"

"I'm a scientist, the whole point of my job is to ask questions. And I'm asking. Why can't I see Malcolm?"

"He's off-limits," Lucas repeats.

"Why?" I repeat. The colder Lucas's tone gets, the more cheerful I get.

Lucas growls with frustration. Oh, *interesting.*

"He's...inaccessible right now," Lucas says.

"Is that code for 'you killed him illegally and don't want anyone to know?'" I lean forward. "You can tell me, I won't spill your secrets, pinky promise." I proffer my pinky to seal the deal.

Lucas scowls at it. "He is not dead."

"Good! Then I can talk to him!"

His eyes shift to meet mine. It's like a steel wall descends between us. I know I'm definitely not going to get my way, and I also get the distinct feeling that if I keep pressing, this super is going to take my biotech heart pump out and toss it on the ground.

I slap my knees as I stand. "Right, well, just curious, like I said. You coming to my party tonight?"

Lucas blinks, temporarily thrown off-guard by my change in topic. "Party?"

"It's going to be a banger," I say, grinning. "Literally. They usually descend into brilliant chaos." Code for 'outright orgy.'

"I do not think it will be my type of party." Lucas doesn't get up as I head to his door.

"Open bar," I add, shooting him a grin.

His cold eyes don't at all hide his impatience and fury with me as I leave.

Interesting...

2
GWEN

FRESHMAN YEAR, MY INTRO TO JOURNALISM PROFESSOR GAVE US A SET OF rules.

The first: if we wanted to be taken seriously in journalism, we had to take ourselves seriously.

The second: if we were going to break the law for a story, we had to be fucking *smart* about it.

The third: never play all your cards. Ever.

I think he gave us this list to scare most of us off. And for the bright-eyed kids with dreams of a steady life, it worked, especially the second rule...but not for me.

I fell in love.

And immediately switched my major from business—misguided from the start, really; Dad never gave a shit that I'd been trying to follow in his footsteps—to journalism.

Over the years, I've added my own addendums to the rules.

The first: I would always take myself seriously. Especially as a woman. Especially as a mixed-race woman. Especially as a mixed-race woman in an industry that was slowly, steadily, gaspingly dying beneath waves of internet-fueled blogs and newspaper shutdowns.

The second: I would always know exactly what I was getting into, for Christ's sake. None of this barging into offices in the dead of night and rifling through files without even wearing gloves. I maxed out my schedule with a half dozen minors tacked onto my journalism major in case I ever needed a background in computer programming or forensics or archaeology. My advisor thought I was insane, and it did mean I was taking an ungodly number of hours every semester, but hey, who needs a social life when you have your eyes on a bigger prize?

The third: I learned how to lie. Better, at least. I would be in charge of the story, not the other way around. Not to say that I'd doctor a result if I stumbled on something I didn't like—I wasn't going to be one of those sell-out journalists who got fame and fortune based on ethical questionability. No—what I meant was I wasn't going to let anyone take advantage of me. During an investigation, *I'm* in control. I'm the one who sees the whole picture when my sources are just pieces in the puzzle. I'm the one stringing together leads that crisscross and tangle and create a headache for anyone else but me to make a perfect tapestry. This is my kingdom. My dominion.

I repeat the rules to myself as I sort through my dad's desk.

Take yourself seriously.

I move the chair out of the way.

Be fucking smart.

I crouch and slide under the desk.

Never play all your cards.

There's the hidden compartment I found my first day snooping around. It's so shockingly amateurish I wonder if Dad didn't intend for me to find it all along. In which case, whatever sentiment that might've held is overshadowed with offense. He could've hidden it a *little* harder, damn.

It's been two and a half months since the CEO of Heroes Org got caught using his mesmer powers to control most of the top-level Heroes as well as many of the subordinates. Nothing kinky, thank god—but the fact that my dad used his powers on other people against their will *at all* makes my stomach twist with a sensation I know too well:

Powerlessness.

That feeling pushed me onto a plane. And, days after I graduated and should've been celebrating by applying for jobs like my life depended on it, I found myself in Malcolm Odyssey's abandoned beach house.

No one's come from Heroes Org to commandeer his shit. I realized after the first week that that meant no one at Heroes Org even *knows* about his L.A. beach house, and confirmation that he'd only told *me*, just me, has been sitting like an indigestible lump in my stomach. Like that time he'd tried to make me pancakes after I'd come back from a particularly long stint with my mom, and they'd been barely edible bricks.

Was it possible he'd actually tried to be a good dad in his own way? Was it possible he'd not been just the raging self-centered asshole that immediately springs to my mind?

I fight hard not to answer that question as the hidden compartment pops open. My fingers snag on what I need: his journal.

I climb out from under the desk. The journal's one of those standard college-ruled black-and-white ones. Unremarkable. Unimportant.

The first few pages are nonsense mostly. Secrets he'd been holding over the heads of various Heroes Org employees, and while I've already filed those tidbits away, I move through the journal until I get to the page I want.

Numbers stare up at me.

I drag my finger along them, reading them silently for the thousandth time.

I shut my eyes and repeat them.

Open and double check.

I know them. I have them memorized. Burned into my brain.

Why does my chest still feel too tight? Why can't I take a full breath?

I slam the journal shut. Just first mission nerves is all. It has to be.

But I'm ready. More than ready. It's quite possible I've been training my entire fucking life for this night.

Every day I'd spend in the corner of my dad's office at Heroes Org, bent over homework, pretending not to drool as Hero after Hero breezed in, each more awe-inspiring—and, okay, fucking gorgeous—than the last.

Every year I'd bounce between here and my mom's, growing older and more aware and asking questions no one ever gave a damn about answering.

Every time I'd try to strike up an actual conversation with one of the dozens of Heroes who knew my dad so well, and they'd smile at me and *pat my fucking head* and say shit like, "Sorry, kiddo. Gotta run," or "Are you still into Barbies? How about I pick one up for you when I fly over Paris?"

Every moment I spent in college, determined that if no one was going to give me answers, I'd find them myself.

My dad was a controlling, manipulative dick. He ruled Heroes Org the same way he ruled me in his home—image was everything, not a hair out of place, straight-As or nothing at all, perfect manners, no sass, no back talk, if I catch even a *whiff* of you drinking underage or fucking around with anyone then I swear to god, Gwen—

But it isn't just that. A lot of people have shitty dads.

Few people have a shitty dad who used his superpowers to mind-control dozens of people.

The official story is that he mesmered everyone for power. And yeah, my dad *is* controlling—but he was never gratuitous. He wasn't power-mad. He always had a reason for why he manipulated people, and it usually had to do with image—so I know he wouldn't have risked his whole damn career and standing at Heroes Org just for power.

There's something else here. There's another reason why he mesmered everyone.

And, for the first time in my life, I'm going to get answers.

That was really what drove me to LA from my dingy apartment in Princeton: journalistic instinct. Dad's out of the way, imprisoned somewhere in the bowels of Heroes Org, and while the company will do their best to cover up his indiscretions, now is my time to shine.

He can't stop me from poking around anymore.

He can't use his powers to wipe anything I learn from my mind.

He can't *control me* now.

It only took a few days of searching his house before an actual lead dropped into my lap.

This journal.

These numbers.

They're coordinates. Deep space coordinates that don't show up on any accessible telescope or radar. But they're important enough—and secret enough—that Dad wrote them in his journal.

Forty-two times.

Over and over and over again like he was trying to choke answers out of each number.

The hairs on the back of my neck stand on end. These numbers are important. If I can just get a telescope powerful enough to show me what's out in space here, then I can know for sure whether this has to do with why Dad broke his own code to mesmer his employees.

And if it's something big?

If it's yet another Heroes Org cover up?

Every paper in the country will clamor for this story. I won't need to apply for jobs—editors will come *begging* me to write for them.

I shove up from the desk and cross to the fireplace. A pack of matches sits on the mantle; I toss the journal into the cool ashes and throw in a lit match after it. The dry paper lights instantly, and as it burns, I turn for the door, hands in fists to counteract how they're trembling.

Take yourself seriously.

Be fucking *smart* about the risks you take.

Never play all your cards.

I close the door to Dad's study behind me, leaning all my weight on it until it clicks.

Then I take a deep breath and smooth down my dress. It stops mid-thigh, high enough to be suggestive but low enough to be flirty, with a deep V-cut neckline and long sleeves, all of it in a glittery ivory that sparkles each time I move. My heels are dangerously high, but then again, I never really had a growth spurt, so I need all the help I can get in that department. My hair's already styled, each curl of my short afro perfectly in place, and my makeup's smoky and subtle.

A deep breath in. A deep breath out.

I recount the numbers from Dad's journal again.

Okay. I'm ready.

It's time to go to a party.

3
ANTHONY

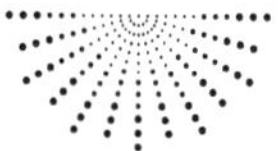

When I first bought the mountain outside of Los Angeles's county border, my friends thought I was mad.

"It's too far out," they said. Nope. Not when you have the Steel Soldier suit to literally just fly wherever you go. Commute's not an issue.

"It's got nothing," they said. Yeah, okay, when I bought it, this low mountain was basically a craggy hill with some scrawny trees. But when you're a billionaire, you can build a mansion wherever you want. Boom, done. A luxurious, sleek mansion perched atop a cliff with gorgeous views, an infinity pool, and an expansive flower garden that shouldn't exist in California's near-desert like conditions. All it takes is money.

"There's no one out here!" they cried. "You don't even have neighbors!"

Yeah, that's the fucking point.

My mansion is in the middle of nowhere, the only house atop a lonely mountain, and that means, quite simply, *anything goes.*

I mean, I'm not an idiot. My laboratory—the stuff I don't want Heroes Org to know I'm working on—is in a very well-concealed and locked-away basement. And my private rooms have enough tech and security to ensure they remain private.

But there's a UN bigwig fucking his assistant on the balcony, and Silicon Valley's biggest computer developer is getting her pussy licked on my kitchen table, and I'm pretty sure an orgy is about to start in my pool.

Like I said, anything goes.

"Brilliant bash, as usual," a man says, clinking his champagne glass against my whiskey tumbler. I turn to see Cliff Barlowe smirking at me.

"Not your usual scene," I say. Cliff and I have an uneasy camaraderie. Like me, he's not a super, but he was a part of Heroes Org's foundation, one of the first vigilantes who turned to the corporation.

But he resisted any biomechanical upgrades. His skills as a sharpshooter are renowned—hell, he even has fancy-ass arrows that can do all kinds of cool shit—but he can't keep up with the big leagues. What's an arrow compared to invincibility and super strength?

Eagle-Eye hasn't been on a mission for years, to be honest, and he's slowly being phased out of the organization.

If I still had my real heart, it would be racing, gearing up for a panic attack. Cliff is my worst fear in the flesh:

Irrelevance.

I didn't choose to have a biomechanical heart. A lab accident ensured I had to cyborg myself, at least with my heart. But the power generator burning in my chest and the Steel Soldier uniform put me back up the ranks with those lucky enough to be born supers.

It kept me in the game.

I'll burn a nuclear reactor in my ribcage for that chance. I'll take sterlinium by-product poisoning for a chance at the immortality being a Hero brings.

Cliff, though—he doesn't seem to mind that Eagle-Eye is nothing more than a collectible action figure on steep discount in the Walmart dollar bins. In fact, he looks more cheerful than I've seen him in a long time.

"So, where have you been, man?" I ask, really looking at him.

A slick smile smears across his face, pulled by the scar on his cheek. "Here and there," he says. "Found myself a little slice of heaven, been going there more and more."

"Really?" I ask. I take a sip of my whiskey. "Where's that?"

"You ever been to the Underworld?" he asks.

I keep my face blank, but my mind's racing. Underworld? Is this where some of the Heroes have been going, a secret club or something that pulls them away from the corporation? Or is this code for something else?

"What's the Underworld?" I ask. I try for a charming smile. *Tell me your secrets, Cliff. At least now you're interesting enough to have some.*

"Oh, I don't think it'd interest a company man like you," he says. He tilts his champagne glass at me.

I make a show of looking around the room. Sure enough, the pool has turned into a very splashy orgy. Clothes are strewn everywhere. The water is making it easy for one partner to slide to another, for positions to easily accommodate multiple partners at once. I take a moment to appreciate the scene—politicians, tech gurus, inherited wealthy elites, Hollywood stars, and various supers are all mingling together, easily meeting each other's basest—and most creative—needs.

Heroes Org is full of morality clauses in contracts and "unspoken rules" that are far from unspoken. Malcolm Odyssey governed the corporation with an iron fist, and although the Magician seems a little more lenient when it comes to what Heroes do in their off time, there aren't that many Heroes here, and certainly none of them top level.

Rules only apply to those who can't pay their way out of them.

Maybe Heroes Org is going to fine me, again, for throwing an absolutely banging bash, but that's nothing more than a pay-to-play fee.

"Holy shit, is that an honest-to-goodness African prince?" I ask, squinting in the pool of frothing water.

Cliff chuckles. "It's a good party, Anthony," he says. "But I'm going to head out."

I arch an eyebrow at him. "Is this too boring for your tastes, Barlowe?"

That *smirk*. What the fuck does this man know that I don't? "It's not that," he says. "But, well. When *you* get bored with..." He waves his hand, as if to indicate everything. "Let me know. I have a contact that can maybe help you see...a different side."

Okay, that for sure as fuck is an indication that Cliff knows something I don't, and maybe this Underworld place is where the missing Heroes go when they get off the grid for days at a time. Before I can press him for more, Cliff sets his glass down on a table, nods at me, and heads toward the hallway.

I blink for a moment, trying to figure out what piece I'm missing when I realize:

That hallway that doesn't go toward the exit.

"Cliff!" I say loudly, but he's already out of sight, and besides, the pulsing music is far too loud for anyone to hear me if they're not standing right beside me. I drop my glass beside his empty one and race down the corridor.

Except—he's gone.

I throw open a few of the doors, but Cliff is well and truly gone. Did he go out a fucking window?

Portals. Shit. As soon as the thought hits me, I know my gorgeous, sexy brain has given me the right answer. There aren't many supers who can use portals, but I know for a fact that one of them works for Persephone at Elysium, according to the most recent files I've gotten my hands on.

Okay, now I'm just pissed. Not only is Eagle-Eye a third-rate Hero at best—I mean, I like Cliff, but come on—but he's got access to some shiny portal tech that apparently is taking him to a better party than mine? Sincerely, that's just fucking rude.

I come out of the corridor. This party is one of my best. The best people. The best music. That K-pop band flew to L.A. just for this party, and they're filling the crowd with an intoxicating beat that seems perfectly timed to the orgy that's rapidly spilling out of the pool and into the gardens.

And he took a portal to some Underworld?

I grab another whiskey from one of the discrete waitstaff I've hired and chug it in one long, fiery burn down my throat.

Well, he's got a point.

Even with an honest-to-god orgy, I'm…bored.

This party isn't that different from the one I threw at New Years, and that was just my Halloween party with confetti instead of costumes.

I don't want a party.

I want answers.

My eyes cast around the room. The same people, the same alcohol, the same fuckery.

Except…

Oh, wait.

That girl's new.

She's rocking a short 'fro and an attitude that screams no-nonsense. Her eyes are sharp, not glazed with alcohol or drugs. Her glittering ivory dress scoops low and draws my focus right to her breasts.

Her eyes meet mine.

A shock electrifies through me with the force of a lightning bolt. I take a step forward, ready to seduce this girl right into my bed.

And she…

She…

Snorts in contempt and gives me such a dismissive look that I stagger back.

She wants something, that's clear.

But it's not me.

4
GWEN

It's his party, in his mansion, so I knew he'd be here.

But still, the sight of Anthony Stern makes me feel like a hormone-crazed teenager again.

He's a good ten years older than I am, which meant he was one of the Heroes who saw me as nothing more than Malcolm's bright-eyed kid daughter clinging to her Wasp Man doll.

I never admitted this to anyone, but of all the Heroes who swaggered into Dad's office while I was there, Anthony was the one I stared at the longest.

He was the one I'd wanted to run into when I got my first bra.

He was the one I was sure would *finally* notice me when my Aunt Val taught me how to do makeup, and I came in with a face full of shaky winged eyeliner and neon purple lipstick over my mouth of braces.

God, my whole body aches with secondhand embarrassment at that memory. What the hell had I been thinking?

That's exactly it, though. I hadn't been thinking. I'd been fourteen and certain I was in love, and Anthony had been twenty-five, insanely rich, viciously confident, and hot enough to melt my adolescent heart.

Now, when he looks at me across the dining room of his mansion, I square my jaw, refusing to gawk, especially when his eyes find mine. I have a whole plethora of excuses ready and waiting to go, but the look he gives me is far from the frown of recognition I'd expected.

His eyes drop down my body.

I can feel his gaze on my skin, dragging across my legs, my thighs, the rise of my breasts under this dress, to the peak where the glittery fabric meets my exposed collarbone. I shiver despite myself. Teenage Gwen positively *writhes* in giddiness at the look on Anthony's face.

There's a smokiness in his eyes with the way he cocks a brow appreciatively. His goatee is perfectly trimmed, of course, his hair a deep mahogany brown that matches his eyes, darkness set against pale skin that's sheened softly. From exertion? From partaking in the orgy happening in his pool? But his clothes aren't mussed, so that can't be it. Does he have that flushed look just because he's looking at *me*?

For a beat, my mind goes completely blank.

Suddenly I'm fourteen again, and I feel a blush rising to my cheeks, the overwhelming urge to duck my head and giggle taking me like a wave.

But *goddammit*, I'm not a kid anymore. I don't have a childish crush on Anthony Stern anymore.

I'm here for a reason.

So I glare at him.

I glare because he doesn't even fucking *recognize me*.

Does he?

Anthony blinks at my glower and jerks back abruptly. He cuts his shoulder to me, his wide eyes saying *Damn, can you believe this girl?* Only there's no one near him to read his exasperated look, and the way he gazes around helplessly for someone to appreciate his response is so pathetic that a little of my confidence returns.

Let him wander off into his party to tell tales of the hot girl who rebuked him.

I have work to do.

I spin on my heels and make my way deeper into the house. There's a huge crystal staircase in the foyer that leads both up and down, but down is barred by a door with a wicked locking mechanism. If there were less people around, I could deactivate it, but there are too many eyes as is.

Gotta try going up.

Luckily, a couple is just now stumbling down the stairs, giggling.

I dart past them. "Bathroom?" I shout over the pounding of the K-Pop band from the veranda.

The man nods at me and points over his shoulder as his woman sucks his neck.

They're going to fall to their deaths if they fuck while walking down stairs.

But I continue.

The second floor is a little quieter, the band and party conversation muffled through the hallway walls.

It's only thanks to that softened drone that I hear the buzzing coming from my clutch.

My phone screen shows seven texts and four missed calls. All from Aunt Val.

Oops.

Tell me you didn't go to that party.

Gwen, answer me.

You have ten seconds before I lose my mind.

GWENDOLYN

Is this why you borrowed (STOLE) my white dress??

GWENDOLYN MARIE ODYSSEY

Don't you fucking spill anything on that dress

I knew I shouldn't have told her where I was going.

But not letting *someone* know where I am goes against Rule #2, and I refuse to vanish simply because I got caught snooping and tossed into some sickos' dungeon.

Not that I'll get caught.

And not that Anthony is a sicko.

Is he?

Ugh, I can't think about this now.

Aunt Val's most recent text stares up at me.

Did you take your meds?

My hand shakes, the phone with it.

She knows me well enough to know that I did. She's asking just to annoy me.

It works.

Of course I fucking took my meds. Of course I counted out the exact number of pills. Of course I double checked I took them because I knew I'd be in a high-stress situation.

"OH MY GOD YES," I type.

Then I think better of it.

Yes. I'm okay, really, I'll call you in half an hour.

I hit send and put my phone on silent.

I slip off my shoes as I creep down the hall so I don't make quite as much noise. I find the bathroom, the whole of that single room bigger than my Princeton apartment, and bypass it, my heart ricocheting against my ribs with each step I get farther from the party. A quick glance behind tells me no one's up on this second floor, but anyone could make a beeline for the bathroom.

I need to be quick.

If I were a Heroes Org keycard, where would I be?

There are two likely places: either in Anthony's underground laboratory—that he thinks Heroes Org doesn't know about, but Dad totally had records of—or stashed away in his bedroom with his other work stuff like phone and keys and such. Since the laboratory is in the basement behind that locked door, the bedroom is my best chance.

Get that keycard, and the device I rigged in my clutch can copy it, getting me into Heroes Org—and, more importantly, getting me access to Heroes Org's deep space telescope.

I repeat Dad's coordinates in my head as I open the first door down the hall: a guest bedroom. The next door: another guest bedroom.

Then: a gym.

Another bathroom.

A…spa room? No, a sauna.

I keep going. The K-Pop group has switched to a thumping, base-heavy song that vibrates the floor, tingling up my bare feet.

A door at the very end of the hall shows another staircase, this one smaller, less ornate. It leads up.

Third floor.

Private quarters?

Bingo.

I check behind me one more time. Empty hall.

And I duck into the stair room, shut the door, and dart up.

The third level feels more lived-in. The floor is carpeted instead of marble, with photos on the walls of Anthony getting various awards or draped over an impressive array of women at parties that look identical to the one happening below my feet.

Whenever I managed to bring up Anthony to my dad in an ill-fated attempt at prying information out of him, Dad would just say something about Anthony's latest conquests or how much of a whore he was.

"You stay away from men like him, Gwendolyn," Dad would say. *"Or I'll keep them away for you."*

It never stopped me from hoping that Anthony would notice me.

And it doesn't stop my chest from squeezing now. I hate that I'm jealous still. That Anthony fucked all these beautiful women, but didn't even recognize me.

I refocus on my goal. No sense dwelling on teenage heartbreak.

Most of these doors are open—a library, a bathroom, a gym —

Ah, finally.

I slip inside what has to be Anthony's bedroom. It's nearly midnight, but there's a soft glow coming from lights embedded in the ceiling's edges. The walls are a deep, rich slate gray and his California King bed stretches low to the ground beneath impossibly fluffy gray blankets. Everything is sleek and polished, not unlike Anthony himself, but the soft, sweet smell of orange musk cologne counteracts it.

I remember that cologne.

I remember he sat on my sweater one time and the fibers smelled like him for a whole month.

Another shiver runs through my body and I find myself inadvertently tightening my legs together against a sudden throbbing.

No way am I turned on by his *smell.*

No. Absolutely not.

I'm just—

It's something else.

Not that.

I scan the room for drawers, a dresser, a closet—but wherever he stores his stuff, it's hidden. Well, I'm rather good at finding hidden shit—

But the moment I step towards the far wall, a hand grabs my arm.

I whirl through the air, shoes and clutch flying from my hand, my toes skidding across the soft carpet. I'm shoved against the wall, the cold bite of it shivering through me where my dress swoops low down my back.

Panic is the exact absence of feeling.

It feels like so much *nothing* that my body can only focus on external sensations, like the feel of the plush carpet and the coolness in the air and the scent of orange musk.

In the middle of that pause, I find myself recounting the meds I took earlier. I took them, I know I did. I *took* them. Everything will be fine.

Still, my heart lodges in my throat. Every limb goes stiff, my pulse freezing as I blink up into Anthony's eyes, his face sculpted by the pale white lights that fog the air like a dream.

"I run the biggest tech company in the world, baby doll," he says. "Do you really think I don't have the best security system in my own *home*?"

His voice is perfectly placid, like he just found me stumbling one door down from the bathroom instead of very clearly in his bedroom.

I swallow. I must've tripped an alert when I came in here.

Admittedly, it was very dumb that I didn't think of that.

But then I realize his hand is around my neck.

His fingers are so soft against my skin that it's more a caress than a threatening grip, but something about it paired with the fire in his eyes has me immobile.

I wonder if he can feel my pulse thudding under his fingers.

I wonder if he can feel the way I'm shuddering, just a little, delicious tremors that feel so good I hate myself.

Can I play this off as a brainless bimbo? Could he think I'm *that* stupid, that I climbed two floors to find a bathroom?

Unlikely.

Then I remember the way he'd looked at me. The lust in his eyes.

It's still there. The twinkle of arousal in the way his focus flicks to my neck, thin and slender in his hand, and back up to my eyes, detouring first to my lips, parted, glossy and inviting.

That's what I can use against him.

"I wasn't sure you'd follow me," I whisper.

Anthony's eyes widen. "Follow you?"

"I thought maybe I was too subtle," I continue. I reach up and thread my fingers, one at a time, around his wrist. "I thought you'd find someone else to occupy your time. Why'd you come after me?"

I lean back, pressing my head to the wall and arching my chest towards him, keeping his hand around my neck.

His wide eyes relax in a smirk. "I came after you because I sensed trouble. Turns out, I was right."

"Oh?" I bite my lip. *You have no idea.*

"What's your name?" The way he asks the question is a purr. A croon that I'm sure has wet the panties of dozens of women worldwide.

I am, decidedly, not one of those women.

No matter what my wet panties imply.

But that question also means I was right—he has no idea who I am.

A bolt of offense surges through me, but I shove it away.

"Name?" I giggle. "I didn't take you as someone who cared about *names*."

Anthony's eyes tighten. He's still smiling though, but he looks hurt.

Shit. That's not what I meant to do.

Keep him distracted. Keep him distracted until I can get out of this room and come back later to find his goddamn keycard.

I do the only thing I can think to do.

I grab the back of his neck, yank him forward, and kiss him.

His lips part for my tongue, accepting it eagerly. He tastes like expensive whiskey, and after a few seconds of letting me explore him, he presses his body to mine and takes my mouth with a growl that rumbles through both of us. His leg slides between both of mine, pinning me to the wall, his hand on my neck now serving as a brace that he uses to hold me in place, exploring every inch of my mouth with his sweet, vicious tongue.

My mind heaves, an explosion of colors and sensations rioting through me.

I'd dreamt of what it might be like to kiss Anthony Stern. I cranked up the setting on my showerhead and imagined what it would be like for him to find me in Dad's office, alone, and put his lips on me.

This is nothing like what I'd imagined.

This is nothing like anything I've experienced.

The man can *kiss*. He kisses with every inch of his body, thoroughly and roughly and devotedly. He kisses so well that when he pulls back, just a beat for the two of us to breathe, I whimper.

He has to know he has that effect. But the look on his face is just as dizzy as I feel, his brow furrowed in a deeply sexy scowl of confusion.

"What the..." he growls but doesn't finish the question.

"What?" I gasp. My lips are swollen. My head is ringing like a struck gong. My pulse is throbbing at a dozen different sensitive points.

Anthony shakes his head. He blinks, and his eyes sweep over my face.

"Tell me what you're thinking," he says.

His voice is hoarse, and it feels like an order.

I'm thinking that all my teenage fantasies just came true.

I'm thinking that I came up here to steal your keycard, but I suddenly don't give a shit about anything except your lips.

"I'm thinking," I start, heart racing, breathless, "that I might incinerate if you don't keep touching me."

He smiles, dragging his nose alongside the side of my cheek. "If you do incinerate, it will be because of the things I do to you."

I whimper again, my whole body seizing up.

What an absolutely *unfair* thing to say— what a downright *cruel,* invigorating, sexy thing to—

He cups my face in his hand, tips my head, and takes my mouth like he's the one burning up with need.

5
ANTHONY

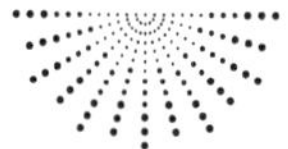

God, I love a mystery.

That's all science is, anyway—a mystery.

Something to be solved.

But even science isn't as sexy as this girl. She's got an innocent mask over sharp eyes that go straight into my soul. And all I want to do is make those eyes soften, fill them with lust, watch her unwind with desire.

Her kiss—

I mean, hot *damn,* that was electrifying.

And the way she looks at me now.

God, I want to *consume* her.

With a growl of lust and desire, I bend down and sweep this girl up in my arms and toss her on my bed. She bounces—those breasts, sweet lord, I'd start a war for them—and she *giggles.*

My cock gets even harder. I know this girl is way younger than I am—but that giggle—holy shit. It fills my veins with every single sexy schoolgirl fantasy I have literally ever had.

Wait—

"You're of age, right?" I ask. "I mean—fuck. I just..." I scan the girl's eyes. She's sober, and I think she's of consensual age.

"Are you going to card me, Anthony Stern?" she asks with a cocky smile.

Naughty schoolgirl. Even fucking better.

God, I'm being ridiculous. I have people checking the gates and doors —no one gets up the mountain much less into the house without being of age. Security details and all that.

I'm shaking. I'm fucking shaking, I want this girl so much.

And she wants me. That desire in her eyes is molten. She doesn't break her gaze from mine as she sits up on the bed, that dress barely containing her, arms behind her and chest forward. "Are you just going to watch, Mr. Stern? Because I'm okay with that, but I think you'd much rather be up here with me."

I rip my shirt off—literally, the buttons pop free and the cloth rips.

I wait a beat for this girl to say something about my biomechanical heart. A silver circle with whirring, glowing lights illuminates the spot where I had to install the unit. It not only keeps me alive, but it powers the Steel Soldier suit.

Ladies love the reminder that, despite being human, I'm a Hero.

But *this* lady? Her eyes are further south. With a smirk, my pants are gone, and I leap up onto the bed. The mattress bounces, and there it is again, that sweetly enticing goddamn *giggle* that goes straight to my cock.

I growl and lean over her body. My hard cock rubs against her thigh, and I know from the slight parting of her lips that she knows exactly what she's doing. But there's a giddiness to her, a wide-eyed wonder, like she can't believe this is happening.

Neither can I.

Look, I've fucked around a lot. No denying that. Women aren't trophies for me, I'm not that much of a dick, but I know what it's like to join in the type of orgy that had my pool frothing, and I know what it's like to invite a stranger to this very bed.

But this girl?

My god.

I've got some of that wide-eyed wonder in me too. That this is happening. That she's real. She's got something magic in her, I think, or maybe the stars are aligned, because this isn't just pheromones or adrenaline. I know my goddamn science, and there's no accounting for that spark of vibrating electricity that goes down my spine and straight to my cock when she runs her fingers up my arm.

Then she bites her lip at me, and it's so fucking innocent, so fucking hot. I swoop down for a kiss—and there's nothing innocent about the way she arches her body up, pressing against me to meet me touch for touch.

My hand fists in that ivory, glittery, slinky material of her dress.

With a little startled sound, she scrambles away.

My mind's reeling—I thought she wanted this? I back away, worried that I misread the whole situation.

"No!" she says, grabbing my arm and pulling me back. "It's not that—I want this—but...I'm going to be in so much trouble if I let you ruin this dress!"

A chuckle builds in my throat—because of course my naughty schoolgirl is worried about getting in trouble. But then she reaches behind her, her deft fingers finding a hidden zipper. She does a little shimmy-shrug, and the whole thing falls off her body.

The laughter dies on my lips and my mind goes fucking blank with lust.

And she—

She *smirks* at me like she knows exactly what she's doing to me.

Oh, I'm going to teach her a lesson she won't soon forget.

I grab her by the ankle and yank her closer to me. Her startled gasp is hot as fuck, but it's even hotter when I slam myself over her body and swallow it up. She's driven my desire all the way up to eleven, and this little girl isn't going to get it easy.

With one hand, I reach for my nightstand and a condom.

"Let me," she says, taking the foil package from my fingers.

She rips it open with her teeth, then positions the condom tip right over my head. She rolls it over my shaft, her touch like fire, but the thing is—she doesn't break eye contact with me. Her hand strokes down my dick, her fingers glide over my balls, and then she trails her touch all the way back up my cock, swirling over my head, and she stares right into my eyes the whole time.

With one knee, I push her legs apart. My hands frame her head, but I raise up on one arm, letting my fingers trail over her body the same way she explored my cock. With the barest touch, I trace down her shoulders, over her firm breasts, swirling her nipple in a way that makes her bite her lip again.

My grin is feral as I swipe down over her flat stomach, dipping my fingers into her. She's wet and hot and so eager that her hips buck up at my barest touch.

I part her lips and notch my cock against her. Before I can steady myself, this girl slams up, taking me in fully. She gasps, her hands bunching in my silk sheets, and her pussy clenches around me. She's so *tight*, sheathing me.

I lift, grabbing her hips with my hands so I can position her better. Her ass clenches under my touch, her breasts bouncing as I glide in and out of her.

"Mr. Stern," she gasps.

Not Anthony. Not Steel Soldier. Mister. Fucking. Stern.

That respect deserves a reward. My hand shifts. She's tight, but there's room enough for me to slide a finger against her clit, rubbing it in slow, smooth circles so that it grinds into my hard cock filling her.

Her gasps pitch up a notch, and her walls clench around me. Her whole body seems to vibrate with desire.

I ram into her, our bodies sliding over the silk sheets. My finger matches my rhythm, driving into that sensitive bundle of nerves. Her whole body clenches, and she's gasping, unable to say anything, but I see my name on her lips even if she can't actually speak, and that's enough to drive me over the edge.

I pulse into her, and her hips rise to meet me, taking all of me in even if she's tighter than I've ever felt before. I press against her clit, and her body spasms, inner walls clenching against my cock, drawing every bit of pleasure out of me and into her.

With a gasping scream of pleasure, her eyes roll back, and she sinks into the mattress, sated. Her legs are liquid as I shift away from her, tossing the condom into the rubbish bin as I stretch out beside her. I trail my fingers up from her slit, tracing her wetness up her smooth, brown skin, and she shivers in pleasure.

"You called me Mr. Stern," I say languidly, a slow smile on my lips.

She giggles. "Force of habit."

Force of…

…habit?

My hand stills.

Her body, under my touch, tenses.

She didn't mean to say that.

Not out loud.

I prop myself up on an elbow, looking intently at her, *really* fucking looking. Her eyes slide away from mine, and her cheeks flush.

Oh, *fuck*. I recognize that blush—the way her eyes dip to the side, jade-green bright and just a little shy.

"You're Malcolm Odyssey's daughter," I say, a wary tone in my voice, as if I can go back in time and warn myself not to follow this girl to my bed, not to fuck her, not to *feel* her.

She doesn't deny it.

Fuck, fuck, fuckity, *fuck*.

6

GWEN

Fuck MY INNER TEENAGER.

She's the reason I let that *"Force of habit"* bit slip. She's the reason I was so consumed in my effervescent fog, tingles like champagne flowing over my body, that I forgot what the *fuck* I am here for, and the only thing I could think at all was *Holy shit, holy shit, I just had sex with Anthony Stern, HOLY SHIT—*

He's staring at me now.

And there's no denying that that's horror on his face.

I shift onto my elbows, breasts stretching between us. It's a testament to the depth of this revelation that he doesn't look down at them—he keeps staring straight into my eyes.

"You're Gwendolyn Odyssey," he says my full name, and it sends a shiver over my bare skin.

I bite my lip and nod.

In a blink, Anthony's on his feet. He taps a bracelet on his wrist—I'd thought it was a watch, but the moment he hits the screen, something detaches from the far wall and flies to him: pieces of the Steel Soldier suit.

A helmet sheaths his head.

A glove folds around his hand.

Still naked but for those two things, he points the glove at me. A glowing orb fills the palm: a plasma blaster.

Everyone in the country has seen the way blasts from that thing can level whole buildings.

I hate that even with that deadly weapon pointed directly at me, I'm still insanely turned on. Maybe next time we have sex, he can wear that helmet—

Next time?

There will *never* be a *next time,* not with the way he's reacting, like I mutated into a pile of snakes in his bed.

He flexes his hand and the plasma blaster whirrs, warming up.

I scramble back across his bed, spine pressing to the headboard, and yank the sheets up to my chin. "What the *hell—"*

"The fuck did you do to me?" Anthony demands. The words are clear even from within his helmet.

"What are you talking about?"

"Do you have his powers? Did you mesmer me?"

I gape at him.

It's so completely the opposite of what I expected him to say that my mind goes blank.

"Shit." Anthony takes my silence as confirmation. He taps on his wrist again, and this time, the whole of the Steel Soldier suit comes flying up the hallway, bursting through the open door and attaching itself to his body.

Fear grows roots and implants itself in my stomach. Fuck, *fuck,* this is the exact worst-case scenario I'd been so certain I could avoid: getting caught by Steel Soldier. I have my rules for a reason, and it's to make sure I don't get myself into situations I can't get out of.

And here I am, on my first mission, not only getting caught, but *fucking the mark beforehand.*

Anthony steps close to the bed the moment his suit's in place. He never let the plasma blaster drop from me.

"Contact Heroes Org," he says, and I hear his suit ping, obeying his command.

"Wait!" I fly onto my knees, keeping the sheet tight to my naked body. "Mr. Stern—*Anthony*—wait!"

"Apologies, sir, but Lucas Gardson is not taking your calls," a robotic voice responds to Anthony.

"The fuck he isn't—override sequence, initiate—"

"Anthony, please!" God, look at me, *begging*—how did I fuck this up so badly? "I don't have my dad's powers!"

"Yeah, like I'd believe that. Override sequence, initi—"

"You know what it feels like for him to control you!" I cut him off again. "Did anything about the past thirty minutes feel like that at all?"

There's a pause. Him thinking it over.

"Fine, you don't have his powers," he relents. "But you're here for him, aren't you? Why else would you be here? Daddy Dearest gets himself in a whole heap of trouble, and that's when you choose to pop up? You could've stayed away, safely tucked up at—what university was it? Columbia?"

"Princeton, sir," his robotic voice says.

"Princeton." Anthony's head tips, his helmet gleaming against the soft lights that rim his bedroom. "But you chose to come here. *Here.* To my *home.*" The plasma blaster whirrs, the light in his palm growing brighter. "Give me one reason why I shouldn't just knock you out and drag your ass to a cell in Heroes Org."

"I hate him!" I scream it. The words rip out of my chest, driven by fear and misery and the past months of stuffing down my true emotions around Dad's betrayal. "He spent my whole life using his powers on me whenever he saw fit. He manipulated you guys for a few years—try living with that for *your whole life*. There are huge gaps in my memory that I'll never be able to fill, so if you think for one second that I'd come flying to his rescue, you're even dumber than I thought."

That makes Anthony pull back. Just a beat.

His head tips again. "You think I'm dumb?"

"Oh my *godddd*—" I drop back, face in my hands, sheet tangling around me.

I hear his plasma blaster whirr again. He's still aiming it at me, and suddenly, it just pisses me *off*.

"Why are you here, then?" he asks again, but his voice is softer.

I glare up at him. My eyes dip down his suited body like I can see beneath it, to the tight abs, the lean muscles along his thighs, the shockingly massive dick that I really shouldn't have been surprised was at all shockingly massive.

"Fulfillment of a lifelong fantasy," I tell him, deadpan.

Finally, his arm lowers to his side. The face mask of his helmet slides up, and his brows are pinched, a little smile playing at his lips.

"Really?" he asks.

"No!" I grab a pillow off his bed and hurl it at him.

He throws his hand up and actually fucking *blasts a bolt of plasma at it.*

It disintegrates the pillow in an explosion of feathers—and disintegrates the ceiling beyond it.

The two of us freeze.

"What the *FUCK?!*" I scream.

"Sorry, occupational hazard." He straightens, not seeming at all bothered by the huge hole in his ceiling. He focuses entirely on me.

"Sir, do you still wish to contact Lucas Gardson?" the robotic voice asks.

Anthony's eyes flick down my body. To my knees bent up against my chest, the sheet wrapped around me, the way I know I must be flushed from being jerked between the best sex of my life and a near-death experience in the span of five minutes.

"No, thanks, Kenneth," he tells it.

That makes me blink dumbly. "You named your robot assistant Kenneth?"

Anthony cocks me a look. "What should I have named him?"

"That's just such an innocuous— It's just a bland— I mean, *Kenneth*." And suddenly, I'm laughing. I can't help it. This whole night has gotten me decidedly nowhere, and I'm still completely naked in Anthony Stern's bed, and wow, I mean just, *wow, what the hell happened?*

I'd come here to get Anthony Stern's keycard. A simple, direct mission. Get the keycard. Break into Heroes Org. Hack their deep space telescope to track the coordinates my dad had. Then use whatever is at those coordinates to write a huge, juicy exposé on what Malcolm Odyssey and Heroes Org have been hiding.

Instead, I let my childhood crush distract me from finally figuring out one of my dad's many, many secrets and landing a career-making article.

I might need to add a new rule to my list. One about not screwing anyone involved in my research.

I bend my forehead to my knees. "Oh, fuck."

There's a rattle of metal.

Then the bed groans.

I peek up to see Anthony kneeling in front of me, all the Steel Soldier suit gone except for the waist down.

I smirk.

He shifts. Is he self-conscious? Fuck, why is that adorable?

"What?" he asks.

"It looks like you're wearing a chastity belt."

He shifts again. "Maybe I am."

"Why?"

"Because you're still..." He looks around, finds my dress on the floor, and hands it to me.

I eye it. Then him.

"You want me to get dressed?" I ask.

Anthony nods. But he winces as he does it.

"You're telling the naked woman in your bed to put clothes *on?*" I clarify.

"You're not a *naked woman*, shit—you're *Malcolm's daughter*," he says with such force that I huff a laugh.

"That means I can't be a woman too?" I start to pull the sheet down, sliding the silk across the mounds of my breasts.

Anthony stares, his cheeks flaring pink, and then forcefully shuts his eyes. "Holy shit, would you please just put some clothes on?"

He waves the dress at me.

I reach forward, bypassing the dress to touch his wrist. My fingertips hover just over his skin, light, but I know he feels me by the way he shivers.

"What if I don't want to?" I ask him, voice low, heady.

God, I want him to take me again. I want him to shuck the rest of that suit and fuck me blind, mission be damned.

That's Teenage Gwen still talking. Her horniness will ruin my life.

But I've already messed this night up six ways from Sunday, so why shouldn't I let Anthony Stern fuck me again?

His entire body is rigid, and I know beneath those armor pants, he's hard. The thought has me reeling, my pussy throbbing to feel him in me again.

He sets the dress against my legs. When he opens his eyes, he looks like he's in pain. I doubt he's ever held himself back from someone like this.

So when he doesn't remove the rest of his suit. When he pulls away from where I'm touching his wrist.

My chest cracks.

And it cracks even more when he licks his lips and says, "Kiddo, I think you need to tell me why you're really here."

7
ANTHONY

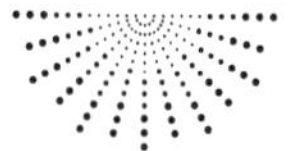

Oh my god, I can't believe I just fucked my ex-boss's daughter. I remember her in goddamn *braces.*

Why is she so hot now?

Why can't I keep it in my pants without literally wrapping my dick up in impenetrable steel?!

I am the worst. A horrible human being who cannot think without his dick making the choices, I am the literal *worst.*

Because even though I demanded answers, all I really want to do is throw her back on the bed and fuck her breathless again.

Ugh, the *worst.*

She's talking.

Oh no, she's *been* talking.

And I've done nothing but think about how horrible I am and how perfect her breasts are, they're right there, just being perfect.

Oh my god, she's still talking.

"I'm sorry," I say, literally covering my eyes and hiding my face because I am the worst, as has previously been established. "Can you please put something back on?"

She blinks at me, all wide-eyed innocence. And then a slow smile smears across her face. She licks those lips and leans down, and her breasts just swing so gorgeously as she shifts her body. "Is something distracting you?" she asks.

Oh, it's *on*. "You keep that smart mouth of yours, and I'm going to have to spank you like the child you are."

Except rather than a threat, that came out like a promise, and from the fire in her eyes, she knows it.

"Oh dear," she says in mock sincerity. "We wouldn't want that."

Rather than answer her, I reach down and touch the button on my nightstand that controls my closets. Part of the wall whirrs back, revealing the hidden panel.

"Fancy," Gwen breathes.

I ignore her, striding to the closet, grabbing a shirt, and tossing it to her. She rolls her eyes but slides it on. As I knew it would, the white cloth goes almost to her knees, covering her more than that slinky ivory dress had. She leaves the top four buttons undone, exposing much more of her cleavage than I should see, but I suspect that if I reached over and buttoned the rest of the top for her, I'd be far too tempted to rip it off her body and fuck her again.

I am the worst, I remind myself firmly.

"Right. Now I'm dressed. Think you can focus?" Gwen asks, her voice dripping with snide laughter she can barely hold back.

"Carry on," I say, waving my hand at her, not quite meeting her eyes.

"So, as I was saying," Gwen says pointedly, "I found my dad's private notes with the coordinates I was looking for."

"Coordinates?"

Gwen rolls her eyes. "Wow, you were really not paying attention."

"I had a couple of distractions," I say, waving at the area of her chest.

And even though the shirt I gave her is ridiculously oversized on her petite frame, the buttons right across her chest strain to break free.

Gwen snaps her fingers, drawing my attention back to her face. "Coordinates," she reminds me. "And if you could just give me your keycard or sneak me into Heroes Org's HQ, we can call this whole thing a night."

I bark in humorless laughter. "You think I'm getting you into the headquarters?"

"Look, it's either break in there or break into one of the NASA controlled research labs with deep-space telescope access, and at least I know my way around the Heroes Org tower."

"Deep...space?"

Look to the stars. That was the clue the Watcher had given me so many years ago, the clue that first had me doubting Heroes Org.

"Yeah. Deep space telescope. Do try to keep up."

Oh, I want to bend her over my knee. And then my shirt on her body would ride up, and she's still not wearing panties, and...

Focus, Stern!

"What's on the other end of those coordinates?" I ask.

"I don't know," Gwen snaps back. "Which is why I need a DST."

Deep space telescope. She's right—outside of NASA, her best bet for accessing a DST is at Heroes Org.

Which...*why* does Heroes Org have a deep space telescope that rivals NASA's? I remember the conference meeting where we were all told about the DST being launched, and the floor at the HQ tower that was requisitioned to showcase the readouts, but...I can't recall the reasoning of *why* we got such an expensive, highly sensitive machine at our disposal. It'd cost billions and—fuck, come to think of it, I helped fund that DST.

And I can't remember why.

"Malcolm," I growl under my breath. Gwen perks up, but doesn't say anything, watching my face shift. I try to school my expression into a neutral look, but I can't.

Malcolm used his mesmer powers to influence me into buying a DST, the type of tech that astronauts use.

But...*why?*

Sure, there have been a few hints at alien life forms out there. I saw the Simrils locked up in the prison; hell, I was back-up for that fight. It's not general knowledge, though, and as I eye Gwen, I wonder if she knows about them.

But the Simrils were mostly peaceful. Pink. But peaceful.

They aren't a threat.

But what if there's another threat...?

Aside from a deep space telescope, I know that Malcolm was also trying to develop some high-grade weaponry. The sort of shit that was hidden not just from the public, but from most of Heroes Org. Stuff I shouldn't know about, such as how the Villain named Watcher was originally a Hero, one that got retrofitted into cyborg parts and who went rogue only after he started piecing together...something.

Something he wouldn't tell me about.

Other than that phrase: *Look to the stars.*

Shit.

A deep space telescope needed to locate coordinates that Malcolm left behind before he went missing after he tried to create a super weapon.

These pieces are adding up, and I am *not* liking the picture they make.

And if Lucas Gardson is going to block me from getting answers, I'll take this route instead.

"Well, thanks for the work you've done so far," I tell Gwen. "Just hand me the coordinates, and I'll look up that info on the DST, and you can be on your merry way, kiddo."

Gwen's jaw hardens. "Do *not* fucking call me kiddo," she growls. "And hell if I tell you what those coordinates are."

"Well, I'm not just handing you my access codes and keycard."

"Fine," Gwen says. "Take me with you. We can see whatever is together."

"I don't work with partners."

"Isn't that the whole point of working at Heroes Org?" Gwen asks. "A team of Heroes that work together?"

"Okay, well, I don't work with civilians. Especially civilian children."

Gwen opens her mouth—smartass quip clearly on the tip of her deliciously naughty tongue—but rather than snap back, she crosses her arms over her chest and glares. "I have the coordinates. You have the telescope access. We work together, or not at all." She states this flatly, no room for negotiation.

I take a deep breath.

If I'm going to do this, I absolutely have to keep my dick in my pants. I want answers more than sex.

Barely.

But still—this is big. Bigger than a one-night stand or a casual fling. I have to focus, goddammit, and that means hands off the ex-boss's daughter, one hundred percent, absolutely no touching. I will *not* think about how soft her skin is, or how sweet her pussy felt clenched around my dick, or those tiny moans of pleasure, or the way her breasts...

Nope. Can't think about *any* of that.

This is work.

Possibly save-the-whole-universe work.

Time to use my sexy, gorgeous brain, and nothing else.

"Okay, you win," I say. "Kiddo."

8
GWEN

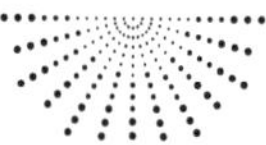

AUNT VAL LIVES ON THE TOP FLOOR OF A SKYRISE NOT FAR FROM HEROES Org's L.A. building. She's made her way being one of the best film agents in the business—she even worked with Dad at Heroes Org once or twice when they adapted various Heroes's stories into film—and every time I got pissed at him or Mom, every time I needed somewhere to hide, this was where I went.

Aunt Val's penthouse is more home to me than any of my parents' places, and when the elevator pings and the doors open, my shoulders instantly relax.

Anthony ordered a car to drive me home. His party was still raging, and he swept me out a side door so no one would see, deposited me in a luxurious town car, and snatched my phone.

"Text me when you're home," he'd ordered as he'd punched his number into my contacts.

When I took my phone back from him, I'd looked up into his eyes in the haloed lights of his driveway. "I don't have to leave."

For a second, I'd thought he'd rethink sending me away.

For a second, I saw him hesitate, lips parted, the dress shirt and pants he'd thrown on rumbled enough that it was obvious he'd just had sex.

But he'd cut me a vicious smirk. "See you tomorrow, eight AM. Parking garage under Heroes Org. Don't be late, kiddo."

"Call me kiddo *one more ti—*"

He'd slammed the car door on me.

Frustration wells as I step into Aunt Val's foyer. The sex had been *good.* Hadn't it? Or had it only been good for me, but for Anthony, it'd been mediocre, then sullied even more once he'd found out who I was?

My stomach bottoms out. Did I misread his reactions? Was it *disgust* that had him fighting to get my clothes on, not arousal?

Shame sets my whole body on fire as I make for the kitchen. Come morning, the open floor plan will show a state-of-the-art kitchen and a sunken living room in front of a gorgeous view of the ocean out a whole wall of windows. All the lights are down now though, and I check the time—nearly two AM.

I kick off my heels in case Val's asleep and tiptoe for the fridge—

Lights flare on.

Aunt Val sits at the counter, drumming her purple fingernails on the marble.

"Hi," I say, giving a little wave with my shoes.

Val is my mom's half-sister, a spitting image of her, just with skin a few shades lighter and eyes a deep, dark brown. She's currently wrapped in a silky dressing robe, her hair in a bonnet, her makeup gone.

"Did I…wake you up?" I guess, though I know from her glare that she's been up all night.

Her eyes go from my matted hair to my rumpled dress.

She bolts off the stool. "Gwendolyn Marie—"

"Oh, don't give me that—"

"Who did you sleep with?"

"Vaaaaal." I drag out her name as I grab a bottle of water from the fridge. "Can we not do this now?"

"You sneak off to *Anthony Stern's mansion* only to come back looking like you—well, shit, Gwen, I know what happens at those parties. I've *been* to those parties. This isn't you."

"Why not?" I whirl on her, frustration welling up. "Because I'm some irresponsible kid all full of innocence? You know I'm not *innocent.*"

She rolls her eyes. "That's not what I meant." But she doesn't clarify what she *did* mean, so I know that *is* what she'd meant.

Fuck, does no one see me as an adult?

"I'm twenty-three years old," I tell her. "If I want to get fucked in an orgy, I will."

Val's eyes flash wide. Is she impressed? "Did you?"

I groan. "I'm going to bed. Your dress is still in one piece, by the way." I wave at the ivory number I'd reluctantly changed back into.

"Wait."

I stop, only because her tone changes. I know that tone.

Shit.

"Your mom called," she says.

Yep.

My back is to her, and I don't turn. "Oh?"

"Gwen. She's worried about you. She wants to make amends."

"That's just it." I turn, finally, every muscle in my body tight. "She *wants*. It's always about what *she wants*. And if she wants to make amends suddenly, there's a bigger plan at work. I'm not falling for it. I won't let her use me."

Val's always been the go-between, and hell, she's committed to that role. She loves both of us, me and her sister, and no matter what shit goes down between us, she's always a neutral party. I want to hate her for still being able to take Mom's side, but that's Val—loyal to the end, to me, too.

"She loves you," Val says. "She's trying. Just—just text her. She's opened that door, but you need to be the one to go through it."

I shake my head. "Val, I—"

"You're in over your head." Her voice goes from coaxing to hard in a split second. "I know you want answers from your Dad, but shit, Gwen, I'm worried. Your mom is, too. Have you been taking your meds?"

"Oh my *god*, yes, okay? I always take them. Always. I have a timer set on my phone. I have reminders. I'm *a grown ass woman,* Val, I don't—"

"You're pushing yourself more than you have before. What if the dosage can't keep you in check? You really need to talk to your mom. She can help—"

"Don't." I throw my hand up, shoes clacking together. "Don't you dare say she can *help* when she's keeping just as many secrets from me as Dad did. I'm finally on track to get *answers,* answers I've been owed my whole life. I'm not stopping. I'll be careful."

"Your rules, right? How'd they work out for you tonight?"

"Fuck off." I spin and vanish down the hall.

"I love you, you asshole," she shouts after me.

I kick into my room and hurl my shoes into the closet. But before I slam the door, I grind my jaw, heat building in my chest.

God, I hate her sometimes.

"I love you too, you bitch," I shout back and slam the door.

I hear her bark of laughter from the kitchen.

My room is still in the tidy state I'd left it in. Clothes arranged by color in my closet. Bed made. Rope lights along the ceiling bathe the room in red.

I should shower and sleep. Eight AM will be here all too soon, and I need to be alert to sneak into Heroes Org with Anthony.

But my chest is too tight still, my brain too loud for me to rest. For a beat, I think I even feel the telltale tingle in my fingertips—an attack, imminent, brewing, and maybe I *did* push myself too hard; maybe Val is right, and my meds aren't strong enough to counterbalance an attack in this new situation—

Deep breath. One in. Hold it for a few seconds. Then out, slowly, long.

Again.

One more time.

The tingling subsides. It isn't an attack. I'm just...*embarrassed.*

That's what it is.

I'm fucking ashamed that I had sex with Anthony Stern tonight, and that for a half second, I thought it'd meant something.

I shimmy out of Val's dress and flop across my bed in my underwear. My clutch spills across the blankets, my phone and lipstick and keys.

When I tap my phone, I see a text waiting for me. From Anthony.

I bolt upright.

The driver dropped you off. And yet, no text from you.

My heart immediately starts thundering. Fingers shaking—anxiety now, not an attack or shame—I unlock my phone and respond.

Then you know I'm home. Why do you even care?

His reply is instant. And the realization that his party could still be going on, and he's texting *me* makes a little smirk play across my lips.

Don't be a brat

It's his whole reply.

Okay. Fuck him.

That's what I should be, isn't it? After all, I'm just a KID, right?

I hit send and bite my lip.
A second passes. Then,

Get some sleep. Kiddo.

Oh, *double fuck him.*

I could've been in your bed, you know. Then you would've been able to make sure I 'get some sleep.'

All the blood in my body is in my face, cheeks on fire. I'm being way more daring than I usually am, especially when I can't see his expression to gauge his reaction.

But I have to know.

Is he actually attracted to me? Or was tonight just another fling for him?

His response comes after a few minutes.

My bed is no place for you. I'll see you tomorrow. 8AM. Heroes Org parking garage.

The fact that he's reminding me, *again,* of the time and meeting point, as if I could've forgotten in the past forty minutes, has me shifting up onto my knees like I could fight him here and now.

"Fuck you, Anthony Stern," I growl at my phone as I punch out a response.

But I stop.

I'm crouched on my bed, in just my silk panties, the red rope lights casting me in a sexy scarlet hue.

My thundering pulse ricochets in every limb as I close the text box and open the camera.

What the fuck am I doing, what the actual living fuck am I doing—

Before I can answer any of those questions, I lean back, finding the best light.

Then I pinch my nipple, and take the shot, making sure to keep my face out of it, you know, just in case. No identifying marks or anything.

That's what I send to Anthony in lieu of a reply.

I huddle down on my bed and watch the image send.

Immediately it flips to *Read.*

The little bubble pops up saying he's replying.

It vanishes.

Pops up again.

Vanishes.

I grin. He's flustered. Even through text, it's sexy.

Finally, after I swear to god a full year, a response pings over.

You're playing a dangerous game, kiddo.

My grin widens.

I know exactly what kind of game I'm playing. And call me kiddo one more time. I dare you.

He shoots back: **You don't give the orders here.**

Me: **And you do?**

Him: **Hell yes I do.**

Me: **Because you're so old and mature.**

Him: **Exactly. Now do what I say, kiddo.**

There's a long pause after he sends that with no real command. I wait, watching the reply bubble as he types.

What comes through sends a full shock through my whole body.

Send me a picture of you fingering yourself.

I press my face to the comforter and squeal into it.

He *is* attracted to me.

He *did* enjoy tonight.

The only reason he held back, the only reason it got weird, was because he found out I'm Malcolm's daughter. That's it. So the attraction I felt, the mind-blowing heat, wasn't just on my side.

I can work with that.

But he made me suffer to get this info. He played ping-pong with my emotions, and something tells me he'll keep on playing as long as I let him.

But I can play, too.

I lay back and stick my hand down my panties, but the picture I take is over top, just the bulge of my hand under the pink silk. A tease.

I send that to him, along with,

You'll get the full picture when you make it up to me.

Then I turn off my phone and bury my head under my pillows and freak right the fuck out, because I had sex with Anthony Stern tonight, *and he liked it.*

9
ANTHONY

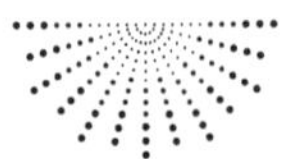

Oh my god, I'm playing with fire, and I'm *going* to get burned—or worse, she is—but I can't fucking stop.

But that little—that little *minx*. That teasing photo. That *second* photo.

And my dumbass said to meet at eight in the fucking morning.

I knew from experience that there was no point in trying to break up a party like the one raging at my place. So I retreated—not to my bedroom, which smelled deliciously of Gwen in a way that had my cock just throbbing with desire—but down, through the high security I'd set up to my basement lab.

Sleep was not going to happen. Every time I closed my eyes, I saw her, spread out before me, the ultimate temptation of a woman I could *not* have. So instead of attempting rest, I stayed up, tinkering, the sounds of the party above blocked thanks to my inches of sound-absorbing tech between rooms. I accomplished absolutely nothing except preventing myself from donning the Steel Soldier suit and flying to Gwen's place.

Which took a lot of concentrated effort, but nothing a little all-night thermodynamics couldn't handle.

It's going to be a Red Bull kind of day.

I ride in the backseat of my Hummer limo from my mountain down to the LA office of Heroes Org, black glasses covering my bloodshot eyes. An entire pot of coffee spiked with espresso is tucked into my thermos.

I close my eyes.

I see her.

I open my eyes and grab my phone. After typing in my security code and scanning my thumbprint, the screen illuminates.

"Nice work, Stern," I tell myself sarcastically, but I don't look away from the screen's image.

Little Gwen sent me a picture of herself, the outline of her hand beneath pink silk panties. There's nothing visible—just the suggestion of what she was touching.

But it's enough.

I go instantly hard.

Check the clock on the phone.

Not enough time.

Groaning, I lean back in the plush seat and turn my phone's screen off. She shouldn't have sent that picture.

I shouldn't have asked for it.

She should not have sent it, though.

I shouldn't have saved it.

Ah, fuck. We're both going to get burned before this is over.

The Hummer slows down, parking in the wide space reserved for my vehicles at Heroes Org. A figure peels away from the shadows, and my heart lurches. Or it would if I had one.

She's dressed all in black, skintight, the picture of inconspicuousness. And she marches up to the driver's side window.

Behind the privacy tinting, I know she can't see inside the Hummer. I press a button, lowering my window. "Back here, kiddo."

I say that last moniker on purpose, watching with poker eyes as the nickname rolls past her. She doesn't say anything, but I can tell it bothers her. Ha. Good.

I open the door, and she steps inside the limo, eyes wide. "You drive a Hummer?" she asks, closing the door behind her.

"It's practical."

She snorts. "This is a gas guzzler."

"No, it's not," I say, leaning back in the seat. "I've altered the engine to be fully operational for a year with one charge." I tap my chest, indicating the biomechanical heart that keeps me alive, hidden beneath my button-down shirt. Her eyes drop down to circle the outline.

"You charge a Hummer limo with the same radiation-based battery that operates your heart?"

"I care about the environment."

"If you got in a wreck and the battery cracked, it could blow the city!"

"Kenneth is a careful driver."

Her eyes widen even more. She scrambles over the back seat, peering through the little window to the driver's side. Sure enough, there's no human driver—the driving operations are fully automated.

"Is that even legal?" she asks.

I shrug.

Gwen shakes herself, as if she's giving herself a refocus. "Whatever. Let's go."

I arch an eyebrow. "Like that?"

She looks down at her outfit. "What's wrong with the way I'm dressed? It's inconspicuous."

"No," I say flatly, "it's obviously an attempt at inconspicuous. You're trying too hard, kiddo."

She grits her teeth. I can't wait to break her.

"Well, I didn't exactly bring a change of clothes with me," she snarls.

"Fortunately, I did."

Gwen gapes at me. I flick my wrist, activating the fold-down seat beside her. The cushion disappears, and a small trunk rises from the floor of the limo. It opens automatically, revealing a miniature wardrobe.

"You brought *costumes?"* Gwen asks, eyes wide.

"Disguises, sweetheart, disguises." She opens her mouth to protest, but I put up a hand. "Look, you've grown up some since the last time I saw you—"

"Some?"

"—but someone inside is gonna recognize Malcolm Odyssey's daughter. Especially when she's dressed up as if she's in *Mission Impossible*."

"I am not—"

"Strip."

I smirk. I knew my command would shut her up.

"Excuse me?" she says.

"Strip." I gesture at the clothes. "I think we'll go for a lab assistant."

Gwen pulls out a white lab coat and starts to shrug it over her black t-shirt.

"Oh, no, sweetheart," I say. "I meant a *complete* costume change." I point to the grey jumpsuit.

Gwen raises her eyebrows at me. "Only interns wear this."

"And you look young enough to be an intern."

"You didn't think so when you had your—"

"Also," I interrupt, "interns don't need eye scans to get in the lab if they're accompanied by a Hero."

Her teeth clack, she shuts her mouth so quickly. I can see the gears working in her mind, trying to poke a hole in my plan. But it's futile. My plan is perfect.

As long as no one recognizes her.

"There's also glasses," I add, pointing. There's a color filter on the lens that will change her green eyes to nondescript brown. "And with a little makeup…" I frame her face with my hands, squinting at her as if I were a director and she was a shot I needed for the film. "This could work."

"Well," Gwen says, a note of defeat in her voice. "Okay. I guess. I can be an intern."

I smile at her charmingly.

A beat goes by.

I don't move.

I know that she expects me to leave the limo for her to change clothes, but I also know I'm not moving my ass until she asks me. Nicely.

She waits another moment, one eyebrow slowly arching.

I blink at her innocently.

And she pulls her t-shirt off. It's quick and fluid, as graceful as a ballerina. She lets the shirt fall to the floor of the limo. The Hummer's got drop flooring, so she can stand easily, but we're close enough that I get a whiff of her perfume as she moves.

Nirvana fills my mind—smells like Teen Spirit. Fuck, I'm going to hell for the thoughts flooding my head right now.

Gwen doesn't break eye contact with me as she undoes the button on her black jeans and slides the zipper down. She shimmies out of her pants with a hip wiggle that has my cock going rock hard. She doesn't look down, but there's a devilish little smirk on her lips that makes me know without a single doubt that she knows exactly what she's doing.

And then she reaches behind her.

The hooks holding her lacy black bra fall free. The straps slide down her shoulders.

Her breasts bounce out.

She's wearing absolutely nothing but a scrap of black lace over her pussy. Her chin cocks up, and she turns her back to me as she bends at the waist, ass inches from me. I could—oh, god, I could absolutely grab her hips and slam her into my lap, make her feel just how hard she's made me.

My hands bunch into fists at my side.

Her ass wiggles a little as she roots around in the trunk wardrobe. She languidly stands up, snapping the jumpsuit out and stepping into it. Still with her back to me, Gwen slowly snaps the closures on the front of the suit.

She turns toward me. The snaps stop just above her naval, her breasts spilling out of the suit. There's not a single goddamn reason for her to have taken off her bra except for tempting me. Her lips twitch with amusement.

She *wants* me to fuss at her. She wants me to tell her to button the jumpsuit all the way up. She wants me to call her a little slut and then spank her the way she deserves.

So I say, "Hurry it up, kiddo, we got places to be."

A flush stains her cheeks, and she grabs the lab coat, throwing it on. Glasses next. The big frames block off her elegant eyebrows and high cheekbones. It's maybe a bit too much Clark Kent, but it works.

By the time I exit the Hummer, she's done up the buttons all the way to her neck. Her eyes slide away from mine.

And then she sees that my knuckles are white, the fists I've bunched my hands into so that I don't rip that dumb intern outfit to shreds.

And she smiles in a way that leaves me panting like a dog.

10
GWEN

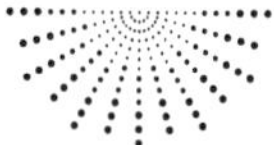

Take yourself seriously.

Be fucking *smart* about the risks you take.

Never play all your cards.

My rules are to keep me out of trouble while investigating stories.

But I think, also, they can work for me in relationships, too.

I follow Anthony into the elevator. He punches the floor for the Heroes Org lobby and the doors slide shut, encasing us in the small metal room, alone.

He tucks himself against the far wall, propped in the corner, trying for a relaxed pose even though I can clearly see his boner through his tight slacks.

He was the one who made me undress in front of him.

I didn't have to take off my bra, but that was my way of fighting back.

I stare at his hard cock until he sees me watching.

Then I slide my eyes up to his.

Neither of us says anything. The elevator whirls past the other parking garage levels, a steady drone of noise as I cock an eyebrow at him, waiting for him to speak first.

The tension arcing between us could power this whole damn building. Every nerve in my body feels like it's been supercharged, throbbing viscerally from the tips of my fingers to the hard nubs of my breasts squeezed into this bodysuit. My clit throbs, too, aching the longer he stares at me, the curiosity in his dark eyes warping to arousal warping to something deeper, something that gives him a heated, animalistic look.

"So, a journalism degree," he finally says.

I smirk. It feels like a victory, that he broke the silence first. "Yeah."

"That, I get." He stretches, shoulders pulling against his tight white t-shirt under a loose suit jacket, the whole ensemble relaxed and sexy yet powerful. "I mean, it's a dying industry, but I can still see the appeal. What I don't get are the *eight* minors you tacked on? Having trouble deciding what you want to be when you grow up, are you?"

I fight a smile. He researched me. "I wanted to be prepared, and I didn't want to stay in school for decades getting degrees in all these things. Seemed like the best alternative." I glare, mischief, and go in for the kill. "Not all of us have daddy's trust fund to roll around in."

Anthony laughs. It's barking and harsh, and I detect a layer of true offense under it.

It's no secret that Anthony's billions came from his dad. It's his dad's company that provides most of the tech for Heroes Org; it's his dad's inventions that power the multinational corporation that supplies everything from weapons to medical tech worldwide. Since his dad died, more than twenty years ago now, Anthony's taken control of everything, but he fell backwards into privilege.

Sure, he's smart. Sure, he's got a better head for business than his father.

But he was still handed everything, and the way he looks at me now tells me that I not only touched a nerve, I awakened a beast.

"Oh, as if Malcolm Odyssey didn't fund your four-year excursion into obscurity," he bites back.

"He didn't. I refused to let him. I got scholarships and took out loans. This degree is *mine*." I owe my parents debts I can't avoid, so I sure as hell wasn't going to give them this, too.

"And the dozens of job offers you have? Also yours? Oh, wait, *yikes*, sorry—no job offers, right?"

"No, no job offers—because I haven't applied anywhere. I won't need to."

"What makes you so sure of that?"

"This. What we're doing. This story will be all I need to go on at any paper I choose."

Anthony's eyebrow lifts, and I think he might be impressed, but he says nothing else, just bites his lip, teeth working the thin skin there as he thinks something over.

The elevator shoots up, up, and up.

Did I give away too much? Don't play all your cards. But it isn't like this is a card he can hold over me—he's not a rival journalist trying to write the same story. This card is nothing to him.

Still. The way he's watching me now makes my heart race, skin too tight, and *fuck,* if he keeps looking at me like that—if he licks his lips like that again—my god, I *cannot* come untouched, not that easily, *fuck him—*

I splay my arms out on either side of the railing that laps the elevator, the bodysuit stretching, cleavage on display.

"Want another picture?" I ask, my voice weak even though I want it to be sultry and sexy. It betrays how close I am to unraveling.

He chuckles, deep and rumbling and heady with his own arousal, and he pushes off the wall, closing the space between us in a single stride.

The elevator keeps moving. Two more floors until the lobby.

Anthony plants his hands on either side of me, pinning me to the wall. He smells amazing. Like expensive cologne, a deep, rich masculine scent that immediately makes me even wetter.

He leans in close, his nose grazing mine, and I inhale sharply at just that small contact.

"You still owe me a *real* photo," he growls. "You didn't follow my orders, kiddo."

I try to get a handle on my breathing. I hold a breath, count to five, exhale slowly.

"You'll get it," I tell him, gasping, "when you make it up to me. I told you. You haven't earned it yet."

"Earned it?" He tips his head, lips just barely brushing down the side of my neck, the heat of his exhale ghosting across my skin. Goosebumps shoot all the way down to my clit.

"Mmm," I manage, and even that sounds desperate.

"Well, I'll tell you what," he whispers into the divot between my neck and shoulder. "You be a good little intern while we're in Heroes Org and do *exactly* what I tell you to do, and maybe, just maybe, I'll *earn* that photo afterwards."

The way he says *earn* liquifies my insides. I can't think. Can barely see. I'm absolutely overcome with desire for this man—I need his hands on me. I *need* him touching me. I wasn't lying when I was in his room last night—if he doesn't touch me, I think I will incinerate.

Oh, fuck—did I take my meds this morning?

Panic zips down my spine. It splashes cold water on my desire as effectively as if Aunt Val had popped into this elevator.

I wheeze and lift a trembling hand to my mouth.

Fucking hell—*did* I take my meds this morning? I did. I had to. I *always* do.

But I slept like shit. I woke up all fogged. I showered and got breakfast and grabbed coffee—but did I *take my fucking pills?*

Anthony pulls back, feeling the shift in me. "Gwen? Are you—"

The elevator door pings open.

Thank *god*.

I duck around Anthony and stumble into the lobby of Heroes Org. The wide-open room is completely rimmed with towering glass windows that let in the brilliant sunrise, all unhindered white and gleaming. The openness counteracts my rising panic.

Breathe. Just breathe.

But my arms won't stop shaking.

It's fine. I'll be *fine*. I can miss one dose. I'm not fragile.

Anthony appears in front of me. He bends down, cups my chin in his strong fingers, and pulls my face up to his.

"One rule in this little game of ours," he tells me, and just hearing him confirm that there *is* some kind of game going on has me right back on the edge of orgasm. "If there's something wrong, you tell me. Immediately. I don't care what the fuck we're in the middle of. Safe word: iron. You got it? Say that, and everything stops. Or at least pauses."

I nod in his hand. His eyes are...kind. Worried, even.

"I got it," I say, and my voice sounds a little stronger, a little more even.

"Good." He drops his hand from my chin and snatches my arm with the kind of cocky confidence only he can pull off. "Now, be a good little intern, remember?"

He leads me across the lobby. The security guard glances up at Anthony but doesn't even spare me a look as we approach. Anthony beeps his keycard, and the doors slide open.

We're in.

Just that easy.

Well, sort of.

Beyond these main doors are various hallways, escalators, and elevators all leading to the myriad of levels in this skyscraper. People already bustle past, busy at work, any normal day in Heroes Org. Most of these are Agents, the low-level workers who keep the Heroes operational. I spot a few upper management.

It's been at least four years since I've been here.

Anthony doesn't gawk around like I do. He pulls us straight for an elevator where another keypad scans his card, and up we go, this time with three other people who get off at other floors.

By the time we reach the lab level, we're alone again.

Anthony exhales when the doors open.

I glance up at him. "Wow, didn't think Steel Soldier could be nervous."

He gives me an exasperated look. "Hardly." Then he grins evilly as we cross the elevator bay and approach the locked lab doors. "I was just thinking about the various ways I can earn that photo."

My breath catches.

He lets the eye scanner read him and punches in a code.

"Welcome, Anthony Stern," a computerized voice says as the doors beep open.

"Both ways would involve my tongue on that hot little clit of yours," he keeps talking as if he isn't sneaking me into one of the highest security labs in the world. "The first way, I'd lick you until you come, and then lick more, until you blackout with pleasure. But I don't want you unconscious, not for what I have planned afterwards."

Oh, fuck me.

I stumble next to him, clinging more tightly to his arm. Thank god the lab is empty—it's still early enough that most techs aren't in yet.

"So, I'm thinking I'll go the second way," he continues. "And lick you slowly, so fucking slowly, until you're screaming my name, begging me to come. And then I'll make you finish yourself while I take that photo you owe me."

We stop by a computer bank, but I'm so dizzy I barely register them. It's all I can do to look up at Anthony, and I see the same delirium on his face.

We should've fucked before we came up here, we're both way too distracted for this.

"Anthony," I gasp his name, breathing ragged.

He bends down to me, pressing his lips to the shell of my ear. "And then I'll stick my cock in you and fuck you until we both come so hard, you'll be ruined for anyone else who might be lucky enough to make it to your bed."

I kiss him. I have to. My body is a spring of need and I cannot possibly wind any tighter, my lips catching his in a searing, manic kiss. It's our first kiss from last night all over again, electricity surging out in vicious waves that weaken my knees and send stars across my eyes.

I've kissed before; I've fucked before; but this, with Anthony—

You can't get this with just anyone. Chemistry is natural, innate, and *shit*, we have it in droves.

Anthony grabs my ass and hefts me onto a table. Something falls to the ground—a cup, pencils spilling everywhere, but fuck, I don't care. I don't even care that this room could fill with lab techs any second. His words, our banter, this game—it's too much. I can't, I fold, he wins, I'm out—I just need him inside of me, *right now*.

His hands go to the top of my bodysuit and when I pull back, his eyes flash to mine. The teasing look on his face is gone. He's fallen into his own words, I realize. That's desperation in the lines on his brow, the fire in his eyes.

We're both burning up, and we can't see anything else through the flames.

His lips find my neck as he undoes the buttons on my bodysuit. I expect him to peel the whole thing off and fuck me on this desk—god, I *want* him to do just that—but he undoes it only as far as he needs to reach into my panties.

He slides his fingers down and in, arching them inside of me, and I throw my head back, hitting the wall.

"Anthony—" I pant his name—no, I fucking *moan* his name, and it's pathetic. "The—lab techs—"

"I reserved the lab this morning. Tapped the security feeds, too," he says into my neck. He lifts, places his mouth on mine, and I can feel his smile. "Had a feeling I wouldn't be able to keep my hands off you."

Oh, shit.

How fucking *dare he*—always with the words that completely unravel any rational thought in my head—

I groan and thrust my hips against his fingers. He starts slowly finger-fucking me, dragging three fingers in and out, then faster, faster. He twists and rubs his thumb on my clit at the same time, creating a perfect rhythm of thrusting and circles that has me arching against him, breasts popping out of the open bodysuit.

Anthony bends and catches one nipple in his mouth. Oh my *god*—the expert way his tongue laps my pebbled nipple, the sensation of his teeth lightly, delicately squeezing down—

I come in a riot of gasps, my hands clamping to his shoulders. "Anthony—*fuck*—"

"That's it, baby." He kisses me, lapping up my cries as I fall apart around his fingers. "Say my name."

"Anthony," I say it again, kissing him as hard as I can, riding the last waves of orgasm. "Anthony."

He's grinning against my mouth. Now *he's* the one who looks like a schoolkid, all giddiness, pleased with himself.

He starts to button up my bodysuit when I grab his hand.

"What about you?"

"What about me?"

I touch his stiff cock through his pants.

He nips at my mouth. "This was all for you, kiddo. Making it up to you, remember? Don't worry—I'll collect what you owe me later."

He finishes rebuttoning my bodysuit. Then he licks his fingers, one by one, cleaning me off him, and it's such an erotic, raw thing to do that I sway.

All this dizziness really can't be good for me in this state, but fuck, I'm addicted. I'm addicted to this man after barely twelve hours with him.

I slide off the table, legs officially gone to jelly. "Okay—we need—we came here for something, right?"

"Something. Coordinates? Malcolm?" Anthony squints, feigned confusion. "Mildly important."

"Mildly. Which computer is the one—?"

"There."

He leads me across the lab to a screen attached to several towering consoles, all blinking and whirring with cooling fans.

"That's…intense," I say, eyeing the set up.

Anthony shrugs and starts tapping into the computer. "This one port is what powers the DST. We need all the juice it can get—had to rewire the whole damn building to support it. Not cheap."

"Why?" I lean over his shoulder, watching as he pulls up the satellite, the box to enter coordinates. "Why did you even set this up?"

My question makes him pause. His hands over the keyboard shake a little.

"I've been asking myself that same question since last night," he says, voice low.

I don't get a chance to pry more. He steps aside and turns the computer over to me.

A wave of severity descends. This is it. If there's nothing out in space, then this lead is cold.

And whatever investigation I have with Anthony is over.

Not to mention my career, this story, etc etc, all that.

I should really care more about the other things, but at this moment, I just want to have more excuses to be around him.

The coordinates run through my head as I punch them in. Now it's my hands that shake.

I hit enter.

The screen flashes, the DST refocusing, targeting those coordinates.

Another flash.

And what fills the screen has me taking a full step back.

"What the—" I can't get more words to come out of my mouth.

Those are—spaceships.

Alien spaceships.

Nowhere on earth do we have tech like that. Knobby, bulbous ships in technicolor. *Thousands* of them.

My whole body starts shaking. Hard. I can't get in a full breath.

"No way," Anthony says and starts tapping on the computer again. He reenters the coordinates, reruns the search, does it all three times, but every time, we get the same image.

An alien spaceship armada.

Just…floating there.

I grab my chest. Breathe, dammit. Take *one breath.*

But I feel it starting. In my fingertips. In my toes. Building up, a steady, cresting rise I know all too well.

I did not take my meds this morning.

"Anthony—" I barely get out his name.

"This can't be real." He's still tapping on the computer, trying to make sense of the senseless. "Those aren't even Simrilians. This is—this is fucked up. And Lucas knows, this is what he's been hiding, isn't it? It has to be—"

"Anthony—" The safe word, shit. "Iron. *Iron."*

He spins around, but it's too late.

My brain *explodes.*

I drop to my knees with a cry as all the sensations I fight so hard to suppress punch right through my walls. My rules, my rigidity—none of it fucking matters without my goddamn meds.

Meds designed by my mom.

Meds designed to keep me from turning into my dad.

I feel everything all at once. Anthony's emotions—he's terrified, and saying my name, calling to me, holding me on the floor.

But beyond that.

Beyond him.

I can… I can *feel* the aliens on those ships.

I can *hear* them.

The language is something foreign, clicks and pops and whizzing that I don't understand. It's the emotion behind it that I absorb, absorb like a fucking sponge—

Anger.

Determination.

Want it back. Want it back. Coming to get it. Want it back.

I don't get those words, not so much. I just get the *intent*, the feel of whoever is on those ships.

Coming to get it. Want it back.

"Gwendolyn! Fuck, baby—" Anthony strokes the hair out of my face.

I hold onto his eyes, the fear pulsing through his whole body, his strong arms around me, the smell of him, that masculine musk.

"Call my aunt," I manage. "Please—she—call her—"

Then my mind surges.

And everything goes black.

11

ANTHONY

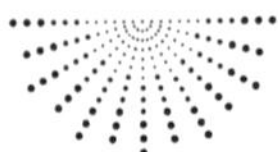

Oh shit. Oh *shit.*

Gwen collapses in the lab, her body crumpling to the floor. "Kenneth," I demand, thanking all my lucky stars that I equipped my personal computer into a microprocessor linked to my biometrics and an earpiece.

"Ready, sir," his comforting British voice says warmly in my ear.

"Do a med scan, now," I command.

In seconds, the data illuminates over my iris. To anyone else, it looks like I'm just staring at nothing, but the information is displaying across a microns-thin lens over my eye.

She's not having any organ failure—no heart attack, no brain trauma. Blood sugar normal; alcohol, drugs, and narcotics levels nil. "What the fuck is wrong?" I growl, kneeling beside her body and checking her pulse. Heart rate is up, but not dangerously so.

When she fell, Gwen bit her lip—a tiny drop of blood rests on the corner of her mouth. "Kenneth, process this," I demand, using a remote vial uplink to send the blood's information to my computer.

While the computing system works, I try to shift Gwen's body. She's light as a feather, and suddenly seems so, so, so ridiculously fragile.

"Sir," Kenneth says in my earpiece, interrupting me. "There are no signs of elevated distress, but I'm seeing a chemical compound that's used to repress superpowers in her bloodstream."

Fuck. She told me she didn't have her dad's powers, but that doesn't mean she doesn't have *any* powers. And supers don't have regular, standard-issue human bodies. There could be…something. Something wrong. And I'm not really a super, I'm a freak with a biomechanical heart and a sexy brain, but that doesn't make me good enough to actually *help.*

"I need someone with medical experience with supers."

"You are currently within the Heroes Org headquarters, which has a full medical unit—"

"Not *here,* Kenneth," I growl.

The computer pauses. "There is also a Villain compound within range that has a fully equipped med center."

Villains? Absolutely out of the question. But so is Heroes Org. That was an entire alien fucking armada just hanging out on the edge of space, and Malcolm Odyssey *knew* about it, and Lucas Gardson has to know now, and neither of them are doing a goddamn thing. If I can't trust them to protect the entire world, I obviously can't trust them to protect Gwen.

"The Villain compound is the residence of a former Hero," Kenneth continues blithely.

"Watcher," I gasp.

"Yes, sir," Kenneth continues. "And Scarlet."

I don't know much about Scarlet—her file has her marked as a mesmer, like Malcolm, and a tech genius, but not as good a one as me, I'm sure. But Watcher? I have history with him.

I *made* him.

A former Hero who got caught in a bad blast in a mission gone south, his superpowered healing made him the ideal candidate for some cyborg tech even more advanced than my biomechanical heart. And while we had a confrontation when he gave up on Heroes Org and abandoned us, he could have taken me down before, and he didn't. He may have gone rogue, and he may no longer have any love for Heroes Org, but I think he may still be a friend of mine.

And to be fair, I'm going rogue right the fuck now, and I'm certainly not sparing any heart-eyes for the organization covering up an entire fucking alien invasion.

Decision made, I scoop Gwen into my arms. "Kenneth, get me a route to this Villain base with Watcher. See if you can ping an SOS to him."

"On it, sir," Kenneth chirps, then he goes silent as he works.

Meanwhile, I plug in a personal emergency code to the closest elevator. A perk of being one of the people who helped design the security systems in the building means that I have an override on the elevators. I've never used it before—once I use this, I know top levels are going to take note and then they're going to ensure that the code doesn't work anymore.

But it's worth it now—an elevator from the laboratory that goes straight to the rooftop launch pad, with all security cameras on the way closed.

In moments, I'm on the roof—also secured and cleared of any cameras or personnel. "Emergency suit 1-H, activate," I say after I carefully lay Gwen's inert body on the cement floor. In moments, the pieces of the Steel Soldier suit I'd stashed within a hidden nearby compartment fly towards my body, automatically aligning with the biometric magnets I'd implanted in my joints for just such an occasion.

I check the time. It's been seven minutes since Gwen passed out.

"Give me that route, Kenneth," I order from behind my Steel Soldier mask.

A map illuminates on the inside of the mask, overlaid through my vision receptors. I carefully cradle Gwen back in my arms.

"Use full thrusters," I say, gripping Gwen and shooting across the sky almost quickly enough to break the sound barrier.

I'M over the California desert, roughly eight more minutes away from the Villain compound with a med unit, when Kenneth interrupts my dark thoughts. "I wanted you to know that I was able to hack into Ms. Gwendolyn's cellular phone," he says.

I glance down at Gwen. Her eyes are still shut—life signs stable, but she's not awake.

"Why did you break into her phone?" I ask.

"Before she passed out," Kenneth says, "she requested that you contact her aunt."

Fuck. I'd—I'd forgotten that, in my panic to just fix everything immediately. "Patch me through."

"I do applaud Ms. Gwendolyn's cyber security methods," Kenneth continued. "It took me rather a long time to break into the phone and locate the correct contact."

"Patch. Me. In."

"Yes, sir."

The sound of the telephone connecting fills my earpiece. I scan the desert ground below for a hint of the base I'm searching for. But the screeching scream that fills my mask's audio unit almost makes me drop from the sky.

"Anthony *Fucking* Stern, what the *fuck* have you done to my niece?!"

"Um. Hi. Yes. Hello. Are you Gwen's aunt?"

"I am Aunt Val, yes, and the only way you're calling me right now is because you did something to my niece. Put Gwen on the line right the fuck now."

I glance down at Gwen's serene face. "Sorry. Can't."

"Fuck!" Val screams in my ear. "It's her meds. Shit."

"Meds? What meds? She seems—sick."

"Tell me what's happening." Val's demand brooks no argument. I speak as quickly as I can, filling her in on how Gwen fainted, but not why.

"So she just randomly passed out?" Val snorts bitterly. "You fucked her, didn't you? You goddamn playboy. Your rep is bad, but even I didn't think you'd go so far to fuck her, or fuck *with* her, or whatever—"

"Excuse me—" I start.

"High emotions!" Val screeches. "High emotions trigger her, and while the drugs help repress her, let me guess—you orgasmed my niece straight into a coma!"

"I—" Did I? I didn't know she had a condition triggered by high emotions. Fuck, I *have* been fucking her and fucking with her, all at the same time, teasing her, purposefully *trying* to get an emotional response—

My god, I'm the worst.

And what's even worse is that this? This little mission with Gwen, this discovery in the lab, and this—this *thing* growing between us—it's the most real I've felt in a long time.

Longer than I can remember.

"Bring her home to me," Val demands.

"Medical unit in sight," Kenneth says, overriding the call.

"Medical unit?" Val screeches, her voice going up an octave.

"Got this covered," I say. I can see someone milling about on the landing pad at the top of a sleek building. There's a flash of yellow eyes—Watcher. He got the message. He's going to help.

"I'll contact you as soon as I can," I say. Val tries to talk over me, but I ignore her. "We're at the medical unit right now. She's going to get treatment. She's going to be okay." I pray silently that the last bit isn't a lie.

Val tries to speak more, but I silence her audio and sever the connection. I land as gently as I can on the pad, Gwen in my arms.

Watcher approaches. He's wary, hesitant.

I lift the Steel Soldier mask.

Let him see the desperation in my eyes.

"Please," I beg. "Help."

12
GWEN

Lights flash beyond my eyelids. Yellow, red—white, blinding white.

"You said your AI detected a superpower repression compound?" a feminine voice asks. I don't recognize it.

But I don't need to.

My powers are awakened now, wild and uninhibited, and I can see deep into her mind whether I want to or not.

Scarlet. Her name's Scarlet.

You're awake, comes her voice, rich and calm.

I flinch.

She can...

She can talk to me.

We're not so very different, she tells me. *Though, my god, aren't you a curious one? What are you, sunshine? You're okay, you're safe here.*

No—safe? *Ha.* If she knows what I am, if she can see into me like I can see into her, then I'm not safe here, I'm not—

But if she's like me.

Then maybe...she's not lying.

I don't lie, she says. *Now, tell me how to help you.*

I want to. I want to—

Everything spins. My mind, my thoughts—

I was in the lab.

The alien armada.

The memory immediately cranks up my heart, and I hear a monitor pinging like crazy.

"Pulse elevated," another voice says.

My powers swivel to him, searching him out, but his mind is a cage wrapped in steel and it sends me quivering back. I whimper; I can't help it. It isn't *me,* though; it's this monster inside of me, the one that demands to be fed, that *writhes* when it's denied.

Why did I think I could control it? I know how I get. I know what I can *do.*

"Compound!" Scarlet snaps out loud. "What was it?"

"I, uh— hang on." That voice, I recognize.

Anthony. He's here.

I didn't scare him away with my…episode.

Oh shit.

Oh shit FUCK.

What did I do? What exactly did my *episode* entail? He's here and talking so he can't be too injured—

My powers channel to him. He's fine. Whole, unharmed, but absolutely pulsating with worry.

I see into his head. I see him flying me here—somewhere in the California desert; I see him calling Aunt Val, who was *pissed;* I see him, fast images from months ago, parties and bars and events, the same emotion breaking through: emptiness. Searching. Loneliness.

"Kenneth—say that again?" Anthony demands. There's a pause. "No way."

"What?" the feminine voice snaps.

"He says the compound he found in her blood was a derivative of sterlinium?"

"Thank you," Scarlet snaps, not sounding at all grateful. "Watcher—get me a syringe of sterlinium. 100 units."

Footsteps hurry away.

"You can't inject her with sterlinium!" Anthony's voice tears, true worry leaching out of him. I've never heard him sound like that. Didn't even know he was capable.

The beast in me rears up. It loves worry. It loves fear and rage and terror; it loves pleasure and desire and need; it loves *everything,* every sweet emotion, ripe for the picking.

Emotions are locks and my power is the key.

"Heart rate is still rising," says the other voice, the man I can't crack.

"Why the fuck can't I inject her with sterlinium?" Scarlet barks at Anthony.

"It's *radioactive—*"

"You've got a chunk of it lodged in your chest."

"As a last resort to keep blood pumping through my body!"

"This is her last resort, too."

It is.

God help me, it is.

Take your meds, Gwen. Did you take your meds? Your mom sent another shipment.

Take your meds—

I'm in elementary school and a kid shoves me down because I refused to get a signed Glory Girl poster for her even though my dad runs Heroes Org. I'd thought the girl had wanted to be my friend; but she spat on me, told me I wasn't good enough to be anyone's friend unless I could get them *nice stuff.*

The moment she turned on me, I screamed.

An aneurysm. That's what the doctors said. It was an aneurysm, and they'd never have been able to detect it; they can lay dormant for years.

I made my dad take me to the funeral. I can still hear her parents sobbing.

I begged Dad to tell me what I did. I *knew* I had done something. No one else blamed me, but I had *felt* it. It'd been my anger at her that had caused her brain to break. *I* had done it.

But Dad had been so certain. "It wasn't you, Gwendolyn. That's not how our powers work."

He'd been trying to train me to be like him. He'd known I was a mesmer since birth.

"But what if I'm like Mom, too?"

"That's not possible."

"Why not?"

"Because it *isn't.* Powers don't combine like that."

"But Dad—a girl is *dead because of me—*"

I'd broken down, inconsolable, unable to leave my bed for days.

A week later, both Dad and Mom had come to me.

I didn't like seeing them together. They always fought.

But this time, they didn't. Mom had sat on my bed, too calm, and handed me a vial filled with little silver pills.

"These will suppress your powers," she'd told me. "As long as you take them, you'll never have an episode again."

Her face was tight. Angry.

She wanted me to be powerful. That was why she let me live with Dad so much—she wanted me to learn to be like him, even though she hated him.

But she was giving me these pills, a way to be…ordinary.

I'd taken the first one right then. I didn't want my powers. I didn't want to be like my parents, never home, cold and angry and so very, very unhappy.

I took my meds.

But the episodes continued, my mom constantly having to adjust them.

In high school, I passed out during a soccer game, and my teammates tried to be supportive. None of them noticed that I'd seen into all their minds, and I felt their anger at me. At my weakness.

In college, at a party. I got drunk. I hadn't known how alcohol would interact with the sterlinium, and when a guy made a move on me, I'd freaked. The entire house—the entire *block*—dropped unconscious. I alone was left standing in a room packed with bodies, alive but out. I'd run home. The police wrote it off as a gas leak.

Little episodes like that my whole life. No other deaths, thank god—but I was on edge enough with just one.

So I took my meds.

I had my rules.

And I would *never, ever* lose control again.

Oh, sunshine, Scarlet's voice echoes in my head, pulling me back to the present.

I realize, with a jolt, that she saw my memories.

She saw everything.

I had no idea, she says, and there's real grief in her voice.

No idea? Why would she have had any idea at all? What—

A sting. The syringe goes right through my bodysuit and into my thigh, and I feel the sterlinium flood my bloodstream, a cool, crisp wave that ricochets out to every limb, every nerve ending.

It's like a switch flips.

One moment, I'm a galaxy of possibility, straining to keep my powers just in *me,* not giving into the push and pull that begs me to unlock Anthony, Scarlet, anyone else within radius.

The next, silence.

Silence so thick I can hear Anthony's breaths grating, tight, panicked sips.

It reminds me that I haven't breathed in a few seconds, and I rocket upright, gasping and arms flailing out for something, anything to hold onto—

Anthony is there. He grabs me, grounding me.

"Hey! Gwen, it's okay," he tells me, even though his face is tight with fear. "It's all right, you're okay."

My mouth is dry. My lips crack as I open them, eyes darting around the room.

It's a little hospital room, stark and white, cupboards for supplies and a few bright operating lights shining down on the stretcher I'm on.

Scarlet stands to one side, a petite woman in a short yellow dress under a white lab coat. Her long tangles of red hair are pulled back in a quick braid that she's slowly undoing, letting the curls fall around her as she smiles softly at me.

The other person is a cyborg. Or some combination of human and machine—his yellow eyes watch me, studious, calm.

"Thank you," I manage to say to them.

Scarlet nods. Her eyes flick to Anthony, her face tightening almost imperceptibly. "We'll give you a few minutes." She hooks her arm with the cyborg—Watcher, she'd called him—and pulls him through a swinging door.

I face Anthony again. He hasn't let me go, his hands tight on my forearms, and he steps closer, my thighs bracketing his slender hips.

His eyes drift out, like he's listening to something far away, and he twitches, groans.

"Oh my god, *fine*—Gwen, your aunt has called *thirty-four times.*" He pulls a bud out of his ear and hands it to me. "Can you please tell her you're okay?"

I take it, hands shaking, and the moment I pop it in, Aunt Val's voice fills my head.

"ANTHONY STERN, I SWEAR TO GOD, I WILL FUCKING *CASTRATE* YOU—"

"Val!" I cut her off with a wince. Anthony rolls his eyes. Even he could hear her screaming without the bud in. "I'm okay, I swear."

"Like hell you are! Where are you? I'm coming to get you."

"No, it's fine. I just…" Shit. I shrink, feeling like a reprimanded child. "I forgot my pills this morning. They're on the counter, aren't they? I don't know how I—"

"No, they aren't."

There's a long pause. I frown at the air.

"What?"

"I saw you take them this morning, Gwen. You were half asleep, but I watched you."

My whole body goes ice cold. Unconsciously, I reach for Anthony, and he's still close, letting me hold onto him.

"What?" the question comes out breathy and scared.

"You had an episode, didn't you?"

"Yeah."

"Gwen..." Val sighs. It's bone deep and exhausted and I know immediately what she's going to say. "You need to call your mom."

"No."

"She can help! You *need* her help. If your dose is off, she needs to adjust it."

"I can't—I don't—" I'm already taking an extremely high concentration of sterlinium. Each pill costs somewhere close to ten thousand dollars. Not that my parents can't afford it, but I *hate* being indebted to them so much.

Shit. How much sterlinium did Scarlet and Watcher inject me with? How much do I owe them?

I lean forward, forehead to Anthony's sternum. "I'm okay, Aunt Val. I promise. I'll call you in a bit."

"Gwendol—"

I sit up and pull the earbud out. Anthony shoves it into his pocket.

For a beat, he just stares at me. Then he frowns, face scrunching up, and I realize—he's uncertain.

Anthony Stern is never uncertain. He's confidence embodied.

Something about this raw side of him is so much more attractive than anything I've seen from him yet.

"Maybe you should lay back down?" he tries.

"No, I—I'm all right." I close my eyes. Take a deep breath.

I twist so I'm holding onto his forearms. The feel of him under my fingers, his muscles tense, strong—I exhale, and a surge of tears washes through me.

"I'm so sorry," I tell him. I can't look up at him, and I just stare at my lap, sight blurred. "I'm so sorry I dragged you into this—"

"Gwen, look at me."

I shake my head. "Did I hurt you? What did I do to you?"

"*Kiddo,* look at me."

I relent, only to give him a flat, unamused stare.

He smirks at me. "Good girl. Now, you didn't do a damn thing to me. I'm okay. What's *not* okay is the fact that *you* are the one who was unconscious and then immediately upon waking you start apologizing for being unconscious? What the actual fuck? Who drilled that into you?"

I flinch. My hands shake against him, and a tear slips down my cheek.

Anthony's whole face changes. Any teasing banter is gone. He looks, suddenly, like he wants to punch someone, but he jerks me into his chest, his strong arms coming around me, holding me to him.

I grab onto him, burying my face in his neck. He still smells amazing, and he feels even better, solid and unwavering, and it's that steadiness that finally lets me relax the muscles that have been so tense for so long. I know he'll catch me.

He rubs circles on my lower back. He doesn't ask me anything. Doesn't say a word.

"I'm a mesmer," I say into his skin. "Like my dad. Only...different. Worse. So I've been taking pills since I was a kid to suppress—"

"Hold up." He pulls back to look at me, keeping his arms around my waist. "You've been taking sterlinium pills *since you were a kid?*"

I nod.

His eyes flick up to the ceiling and he curses. "That's impossible, Gwen."

"It isn't so bad—"

"No, it's *impossible.* That much sterlinium would have killed you. That much radiation? You should be dead."

I blink at him, his words not processing.

Then my focus drifts down to his chest. To the orb, filled with sterlinium, that keeps his body functioning.

I trace a finger down the front of the glowing case. My brain rattles, trying to remember when he transferred over to this cyborg heart. "How long have you had—"

"Six years."

I frown up at him. He shrugs, his eyes bloodshot suddenly.

"I've been looking for alternatives just as long, but sterlinium's properties...there's no replicating it. The things it does...it isn't even an *earth* metal. It lands here on meteors and space debris. What it does, the things it lets me do—there's nothing else. I estimate I have another two years before I start to feel the effects. Three before…game over."

My breath catches. He's dying. He's dying, and he didn't tell me?

Why would he have told me? We've only been…whatever this is…for a *day*.

My fingers shake as I reach up and cup his jaw in my hand. He leans into it, eyes fluttering shut, but when he looks at me again, I sway.

"There's no way you've been taking sterlinium for over ten years and are *fine*," he says again. "Who first gave it to you?"

"My mom." The words are flat. Emotionless.

Anthony nods. "And you're sure it's sterlinium?"

I wave at my thigh, the injection Scarlet and Watcher just gave me.

Anthony nods again. "Fair."

"But my aunt said she saw me take my pills this morning." My throat swells. Damn it, I won't break down again. "So my normal dose—it isn't working anymore."

His brow furrows. "You're not going to increase it?"

"That's what I do. I take it at a dose until it stops working, then I go up."

His face goes gray. "Gwen—how much do you take now?"

"Two thousand milligrams a day."

"Two thousand—" He staggers. Actually *staggers*. I tighten my hold on him until he rights himself.

"I've got just over three hundred and fifty milligrams coursing through my blood at any given time, and that's set to poison me in a few years," he says, "and you're telling me that you swallow *two thousand a day?*"

I never researched it. I didn't want to. I wasn't science-minded, and it *worked*, so I didn't question it. I couldn't even begin to find an alternative that would be safe and guarantee I didn't hurt anyone or myself—besides, Mom refused to let me try other options. Nothing else would work as well, she'd been sure.

Now I see how stupid that was, to just believe her.

Anthony drops his forehead to mine and blows out an exhale between us. I go completely still, just feeling him against me, a calm, quiet moment before he moans.

"I just…don't like the thought of losing you," he whispers.

My whole body lights up, sparks and tingles shooting out to the tips of my toes. "I don't like the thought of losing you, either."

I touch the sterlinium orb in his chest.

He shifts, stroking his fingers up and down my arms, making me shiver deliciously.

"Who's your mom?" he asks. "Maybe I can talk to her. With my sterlinium research, maybe she and I can figure out why you've lived this long with no side effects, and what other options you have. I want you off that stuff. *Now.*"

"You're on a tighter deadline than I am," I say, trying for humor.

He grabs the back of my neck and kisses me. I hadn't even known how badly I needed it; I arch up, arms around his neck, tongue shooting into his mouth with a keening moan.

We pull back. Just a beat for air, and I feel his hands roaming over my body, feel his hard cock between my legs where my thighs cup around him.

I want him to fuck me here, on this table, and feel our connection, our heat. I want to lose myself in his body.

But will it trigger another episode? What will sex with him do to me now that the sterlinium isn't working as well?

No time in the past two days has any of my attraction to him felt triggering. It was only when I was scared—of that alien armada, *shit,* we still need to deal with that—that I lost control.

But with him. With his hands on me. With his mouth on my skin.

I'm fully present. I'm fully in control because I know *he's* the one in control, and it frees my body and mind in a way I've never had before.

But when his mouth trails down the side of my neck, little bites that send electric shocks through me, I turn, pressing my lips to his ear.

He deserves to know.

I'd already withheld who my dad was before our first time—I can't let this continue until he knows exactly who he's sleeping with.

Even if it means he'll never want to sleep with me again.

Dread is a molten ball in my gut. It pricks more tears in my eyes.

"Persephone," I whisper into his ear. "My mom is Persephone."

13
ANTHONY

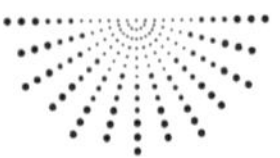

It takes me several long moments to realize she means *that* Persephone. Villain Queen Persephone. The most powerful and notorious super *ever.*

That Persephone.

Who'd apparently had a fling with Malcolm Odyssey and created my Gwendolyn.

Which, frankly, is bullshit—Malcolm had spent his whole career in Heroes Org telling everyone that there was no data on Persephone. And there wasn't. The files were all wiped, and any Hero who got close enough to Persephone to learn anything useful had their mind wiped.

Wait a minute... I think. *Was Persephone wiping their minds or was it Malcolm?!*

On the one hand, image was everything to Malcolm. He *had* to keep the perception of Heroes Org pure.

But even as my rage mounts, I remember Gwen. Her DNA is so fucking powerful that sterlinium is like an ibuprofen for her. She's the daughter of not only two supers, but two of the most powerful supers ever.

Maybe Malcolm was just trying to protect Gwen.

Because...

Holy shit. What kind of powers does Gwen have? Malcolm was a mesmer, able to exert mental influence over the entirety of Heroes Org, seemingly. And Persephone is…something powerful. Powerful enough to lead the Villains's den.

Gwen's mind could blow this whole planet, I bet. She's a nuclear bomb, waiting for a trigger.

But she's also Gwen. And even if I've known her as an adult for a short while, I can't help but think of her as *my* Gwen.

Someone I'll protect, even if I have to protect her from herself.

To my admirable credit—seriously, give me an Oscar already—I keep my shit cool and calm and collected and don't freak the absolute fuck out in front of her.

I give Gwen a back rub and stroke her hair until she falls asleep.

And then I walk out the door, making sure the lights are low and Gwen is truly resting, and I find my way to some amphitheater or something in the center of the base, and *then* I freak the fuck out.

Watcher finds me hyperventilating on the floor.

"Ah, yes, Scarlet mentioned that today's revelations may have a negative impact on you," he says, his voice calm and cool.

"Does she know?" I ask. "Who Gwen's parents are?"

Watcher nods. So he knows, too.

I stare around me, not really seeing anything, eyes just wide and empty. I woke up this morning with nothing on my mind but a sexy picture of a hot girl and a chance at maybe uncovering some Heroes Org secrets. Now I realize I've fucked a girl whose mother could crush me with a look, Heroes Org is hiding an alien apocalypse, and I'm having a panic attack in the middle of a Villain base.

I blink.

There are booths in this room, with a low stage in the middle, and a distinctly…unique layout to the room.

"What is this place?" I ask.

"Scarlet calls it her harem," Watcher supplies helpfully. "It is a place where her mesmer powers can help showcase sexual fantasies."

"What the fuck," I say without any emotion in my voice at all.

Watcher blinks at me with his yellow eye sensors. I helped install them. I helped *build* him.

But, when I probe those memories, that time when Watcher was first being developed after his near-death experience, there are great, gaping holes in my memory.

"Malcolm fucked with my head when we made you, didn't he?" I ask.

Watcher cocks his head at me. "I like to think so."

"You like...?"

He nods. "If he was influencing you with his considerable mesmer powers, then you were not fully aware of how very deeply you failed me as a trusted friend and ally."

His words leave me breathless, a punch right into my gut. I run my fingers through my hair. "Fuck, I'm sorry," I say.

Watcher sits down on the floor beside me. "If it is true that you were not fully conscious at the time, then you have little to apologize for."

We sit in silence for a bit. "Do you remember?" I ask finally, in a low, soft voice. "Before you became Watcher?"

Because I remember. We were friends then.

"No," Watcher says. "Not even my name."

"Oh." I look over at him. "It's—"

He holds up his hand, silencing me. "Do not misunderstand," he says in an even tone. "I am Watcher now. I am not the person you used to know. I do not wish to know my name from before. I do not wish to hear it spoken. I had uncovered some data from the Heroes Org information files I stole before I left the corporation which included information on my past, and I deleted them from my hard drive."

I look down at my hands. "We killed you then, didn't we?" I say. "You had a whole different life. You were a Hero. And we killed you."

"I am the person I want to be," Watcher says. "I do not regret the path that led to my life with Scarlet."

I bite my lip, thinking about Gwen. About how I'm in a Villain base, and I don't care. I don't care about anything, really. This day has been a dividing line—a before time the past I no longer care about, and a future that, I hope, will still be possible.

"I owe you so much," I say. "Not just for the way I..." I pause. I don't want to say that I ruined his life, but I certainly changed it against his will, regardless of how it turned out. "Not just for the way I treated you," I say. "But also for helping Gwen. I contacted you and in moments you opened up your base and provided Gwen with lifesaving medical aid." Sterlinium. Holy shit—that stuff is expensive. "How much do I owe you? You know I can pay."

Watcher shakes his head. "Money is not an issue. And it's not just my base, but Scarlet's."

"I can pay her, too."

"Like I said, money isn't a thing we desire."

I gape at him. But...he's a Villain. And Scarlet, too. This base had to cost serious coin, to say nothing of the amount of sterlinium they had on hand, the doctors they employ…

"What do you want, then?" I ask.

If there's one thing I've learned in this life, nothing—*nothing*—is free.

Wariness claws up my spine. What debt have I made? If money won't pay it, what must be exchanged…?

But Watcher shakes his head again. "You are used to the transactional nature of Heroes Org," he says. "It is possible, Anthony Stern, for people to help others without expecting any kind of recompense."

"What kind of Villain are you?" I ask with what I hope is a disarming smile.

"What I have learned," Watcher says evenly, "is that the lines between Hero and Villain are entirely false."

I cock an eyebrow at him.

"Heroes Org likes to think the world is black-and-white," Watcher continues, blinking at me with his yellow eyes. "But I see things differently. We do our best with what we have, make the best choices we can in each moment. They are not indefinably right or wrong. We just all…" He opens his palms up in his lap, the picture of serenity. "We just all do what we can. To survive. To live. To find a happiness unique to our own hearts."

"Easy for you to say," I quip, tapping my biomechanical pump. "You still have your heart."

"And yet you're the one still called 'human,'" Watcher says.

14

GWEN

It really shouldn't be a surprise that I'm as exhausted as I am, but when I wake up, a shock jolts through me. I slept? How? I don't even know where the fuck I *am*—

Scarlet is sitting on a table across from me, her ankles hooked, heeled feet swinging. She leans forward, giving a not unpleasant view of her ample cleavage in that tight dress, her lab coat gone.

"How are you feeling?" she asks.

I sit up and rub the heels of my palms into my eyes. "Embarrassed."

She laughs. "Whatever for?"

I swing my legs over the bed so I can face her. "I don't even know you."

"Well, that's hardly true." She taps her head. "For as powerful as you are, your grasp of simple mental blocks is abysmal. Did no one train you? I could see all the way back to the day you were *born*."

I blink at her, my cheeks heating. "Oh. Lovely."

She cocks her head at me, and a wave of perfect red curls shifts over her neck. "I don't normally peek so deeply but, sunshine, you—" She sighs. "I'm getting ahead of myself. You're at my base just outside LA. And, believe it or not, I'm actually an...employee...of your mom's."

I flinch. "What? That's not—how did Anthony—"

"Oh, he came here because he knows Watcher. We're all just pawns in this game, aren't we? Fates intertwined." She slides off the table and crosses the space between us, her eyes on me, studious, deep. I get the sense she's reading me, but then she smiles. "You look just like her. I would've known you were hers even if I hadn't seen it."

"I'm not *hers*."

"We're all *hers*, sunshine. Whether we want to be or not."

"Speak for yourself."

Scarlet grins. "I bet getting the two of you together is like watching a tornado go up against a wildfire."

I shiver and tuck my arms around myself. "You have no idea. But," I look at her, "I can't pay you for what you've done. I don't know how much the sterlinium cost, but I—"

Scarlet bats her hand. "Don't worry about it. Like I said, I'm an employee of your mom's. Meaning, if you'd come here, and I'd let you just spiral out into a coma, she'd kill me. So really, you did me a favor by letting me inject you with sterlinium."

I huff a laugh. "Well. I guess, you're welcome?"

Scarlet smoothes my hair back. I must look a mess.

She reads my face—or maybe just that direct thought in my head—and turns over her shoulder. She doesn't say anything, but I get the impression she *is* saying something, to someone I can't see.

A beat later, a short woman with a black bob bustles in, a cosmetology apron tied around her waist. She takes one look at me and immediately whips out a pick and a spray bottle.

"This is Edna," Scarlet tells me. "My stylist."

"You have a stylist?" I cock an eyebrow. "Of course you do. Why not? A personal trainer? A private chef?"

"Ugh, don't mention a *private chef*." Scarlet groans to the ceiling. "I used to have a client who'd cook for me as payment, but he went and got himself a girlfriend—oh, sorry, they're engaged now; *fiancée*—and now he's just *too busy* banging her to make me fettuccine."

Edna doesn't say a word. She just starts working her fingers through my now matted afro, gently spritzing it with what smells like some kind of scented shea butter moisture spray. The act is so tender, so motherly, that I don't protest. It makes my shoulders relax, and I hadn't even realized I'd been so tense.

The room falls silent, just the sound of Edna spraying product, her fingers moving deftly, alternating between fluffing with her palms and the pick.

"I'm sorry," Scarlet says into the stillness.

"For what?"

"That you grew up with her as your mother. Sometimes I think I can count Persephone as a friend. Most of the time, I'm lucky she lets me stay in her sphere alive. I can't imagine there's much maternal love in her."

I make a moan of agreement in my throat. "It definitely wasn't easy."

"She didn't raise you, did she?"

"No. Mostly my dad and Aunt Val."

"Val?"

"Oh, maybe you know her? Valerie Acosta? Mom's half-sister."

Edna moves to the other side of my head.

"Ah," Scarlet says. Her face gives nothing away, but I get the sense that she knows Aunt Val, maybe a little too well. "Yeah, I know of her. Quite the impressive lineage you come from."

"I guess."

Silence falls. I can feel Scarlet thinking, and I wonder—if I didn't have fresh sterlinium in my veins, could I read her mind?

She doesn't make me wait long. "Something triggered this episode. Before you came here. I saw, in your thoughts…"

I go still.

I don't know her. Or Edna, for that matter. They've been kind, sure; but Scarlet herself said my mom is what made her act. What would she do with the information Anthony and I found? How much did she even see?

My heart starts to race. I feel it beating in my neck, tight, quick pulses that have me gasping.

I hadn't really planned beyond finding what was at those coordinates that Dad left. I'd thought it would've been something I could write an exposé on and be set for a career—I didn't think it'd be a whole goddamn *alien armada*.

What the *hell* am I even supposed to do with that?

I don't get a chance to respond—the medical room doors open, and Anthony comes in, followed by Watcher.

The sight of him immediately relaxes me to the point that I laugh at myself, at how quickly I unwind just by seeing him.

He comes over to me and takes my hands in his, eyeing Edna as she packs up her supplies.

Edna holds up a mirror for me. "Better?"

I blink at my reflection. I look sleepless as hell, but my hair is *perfect*.

"Thank you," I tell her, and the surprise in my voice makes her scoff.

"If you need to sleep again, I have bonnets for you to choose from."

Edna eyes Anthony, his hands in mine. "Rough sex will destroy the integrity of the style."

I wheeze and drop the mirror. Edna catches it and tucks it into her apron.

"I—uh—noted," I squeak out, but Edna dips around me and pushes out of the room.

My cheeks are on fire. I somehow manage to look up at Anthony, who is, unsurprisingly, grinning like a loon.

"Rough sex," he mumbles to himself, and his grin widens.

Scarlet backs up until Watcher is behind her, and his arms come around her. Something about the ease of their pose, their bodies entwining like it's the most natural thing in the world, makes me take a second look at how Anthony and I are arranged.

He's between my legs again where I'm still sitting on the medical bed, his hands in mine, thumbs slowly rubbing the insides of my wrists.

Natural. Like this is how we were always meant to be.

I swallow the lump in my throat and look up at him. "Scarlet was asking me about…the um…"

Anthony's eyes widen slightly. "Oh. Yeah. *That.*"

"Yeah." I shrug and try to wordlessly communicate to him that I have no fucking clue what to do.

He, also, looks completely out of his league.

So, what the hell? It's not like this could get a whole helluva lot worse.

"There's an alien armada out in space," I tell Scarlet. "My dad had coordinates to it in his belongings."

Scarlet's eyes bulge. "Excuse me?"

"An alien armada," Watcher repeats to her. "*Alien* here meaning, likely, an interspace creature, not an alien immigrant from—"

"I know what she said, solnishko, *thank you.*" She bats his arm against her waist. "What I mean was—what the *fuck*? What are the coordinates?"

I rattle them off to her.

Her wide eyes go even wider. "No. No fucking way."

"What?"

"Come with me. Now."

She bolts out the door, followed by Watcher.

Anthony and I exchange a look before we trail them.

A few doors down, Scarlet sits in a massive lab in front of a computer hooked up to processors not unlike the one in Heroes Org's lab.

"Damn," Anthony whistles.

She glances back at us when we enter. "Here," she says and waves at her computer screen. "I've been tracking those coordinates for *months*."

"You've *what*?" I squeak, lingering back by the door.

"Let me clarify—*your mother* has had me tracking those coordinates for months." Scarlet looks at her screen and rubs her chin. "But there's never been anything there. I'm looking at blank space. No alien armada."

Anthony ducks around me to bend over Scarlet's shoulder. "What the fuck. That's impossible. Could they have moved on so quickly? But why would Malcolm have had those coordinates if the armada wasn't going to stay there for some set time? Or maybe they did, but they moved on—"

"No, there's never been anything there," she tells him. I can't see the screen. I can't bring my feet to cross the room. "I have a dozen sensors set up to tell me if anything changes. Look—you're seeing this, right? *There's nothing there.*"

My mom knew about Dad's coordinates. They were both tracking this same spot in space.

But there's nothing there now?

That's good, right? Maybe I imagined it. Maybe Anthony and I... both...hallucinated?

My lungs tighten. Each breath aches, grating like fire in my chest, but I force myself to take a step forward.

I need to see the screen myself.

Anthony shifts back to give me room. His face is tight with confusion; Scarlet's too. Watcher just stands aside, but I can hear his machinery whirring, trying to process what's going on.

There's no processing this, though.

The screen I see is blank, just an empty expanse of stars deep in space.

It does nothing to alleviate my growing panic.

Shit. Shit. I need more sterlinium. I need—

I take another step closer.

Something about that proximity. About being close enough to the computer, the servers, the DST—

The screen flashes.

And suddenly, where there had been empty space is now a fleet of alien ships.

Scarlet shrieks. Anthony flinches like someone electrocuted him.

"What the FUCK??" Scarlet screams to her computer and starts rapidly typing.

I can't move.

I can't react at all.

Don't feel it. Don't think. For fuck's sake, just walk away, just go back to the med room and take a deep breath, don't—

Then it comes. Just like it did last time.

Those voices. The ones on the ships.

Want it back. Want it back. Coming to get it. Want it back.

Their determination overwhelms me, the intention in their mind heaving and growing with each passing second.

I cover my ears like that will help. I want to beg Scarlet for more sterlinium. Just get me an IV of it, fill me up—make it *stop, please—*

Anthony grabs my arms. "Gwen, *Gwen*—shit—Scarlet! She's going to pass out again—turn it off!"

"Like hell am I turning it off! There's an armada of alien ships—and they're pointed at *us*. At Earth. They're poised to come *here* the moment someone gives the word. Watcher—get Gwen to the med bay again. This is—"

I kiss Anthony.

I don't know why I do it until my lips are there, grabbing onto his with desperate passion.

He calms me down. He centers me. When I saw him come into the med room, it was like a wave of peace. And that's what floods over me now—intense need mixed with rightness that pulls my focus, soothes my raging emotions and the powers threatening to unfurl.

He must realize what I'm doing, or trying to do—he scoops me up and crushes me to him, kissing me like we're the only two people in this room. His tongue darts into my mouth, his lips harsh and almost painful. I take everything he offers, opening myself up to his control, his desire. Let him take me over. Let him be in charge.

I pull back, panting, and immediately, I feel the difference. My panic is gone. I can still hear—feel?—whoever is on those ships, but it's distant, a background hum.

Scarlet and Watcher stare at us, their faces identical in concern.

Scarlet recovers first. "Emotions, huh? That's what sets you off. Negative emotions."

Still in Anthony's arms, my legs around his waist, I nod. "Every time I've had an episode, it was because of something bad. Some negative emotion. So I figured—a positive emotion might keep me balanced. No sterlinium required."

I say the last bit down to Anthony.

His lips curl up, and I can practically hear the dozens of thoughts racing through his mind. I could, if I wanted to pry with my powers, I think.

"This is going to sound weird," Scarlet starts, "or, maybe not weird, but out of the blue? But I think you two should have sex."

Anthony barks laughter. "Come again?"

"Exactly. But I think it will help Gwen get a handle on her...powers. You've done it before, right?" Scarlet grins at me. She knows we have—she saw, apparently, everything in my head. "This time, when you fuck, focus on those positive emotions. Tap into them. Let them fuel you. It'll help you gain some control over yourself."

"How do you know that?" I ask. Not that I don't want to have sex with Anthony again, but...

Scarlet's cheeks tinge pink. "I've seen someone with similar powers before. Just try it, okay? If it doesn't work, well, you at least both got laid. Watcher explained the harem to you, Anthony?"

Anthony laughs again. "Yeah, he did."

"And you will both be pleased to know that your scans are clean," Watcher says suddenly.

Scans?

His yellow eyes flash. "Miss Odyssey is not on birth control, but she is not ovulating at this moment, so there is no risk of pregnancy."

I have no word for the way my body goes completely stiff.

Then I laugh.

I laugh, and Anthony laughs, and he pivots to give Watcher a look.

"Goddamn," he says. "I could've used you at my parties."

Scarlet claps her hands. "Then it's settled. I'll deal with—" She waves at her computer screen. Her eyes shift to me. "But I think dealing with it will mean getting your mom involved. You okay with that?"

I swallow, but I nod. I've been putting it off long enough. And I seriously have no idea how to deal with what's going on.

I hate it, but I do need her.

Scarlet waves her hand. "I'll set it up."

Anthony starts to turn, carrying me out of the room.

I bend over his shoulder. "Wait! Can you hear them, too?"

Scarlet gives me a horrified look. "Hear who?" She blinks, then points at the screen. "Hear *them*?"

I stiffen. Anthony glances up at me.

"Well, *feel* them, more than anything." I tighten my grip on Anthony's neck. "*Want it back. Coming to get it.* That's all I'm getting from them."

"You can hear them," Scarlet states, deadpan, "and they didn't show up on my screen until you were near it."

I feel my heart start to kick up again. Panic wells in my stomach. It's only because I'm still in Anthony's arms that I don't fall backwards into anxiety.

Scarlet shakes her head. "Go. Go, both of you. Like I said, I'll deal with this. Unless you're an expert on interstellar astrophysics, I can't use you."

"Well, I am, actually," Anthony mumbles into my neck. "But hell if I'm staying here."

He kicks the lab door open and swings me out into the hall. The sheer ferocity of it, coupled with the growl he emits, has me giggling, and my anxiety evaporates.

"Now, come on," he says, nipping at my jaw. "Doctor's orders."

15
ANTHONY

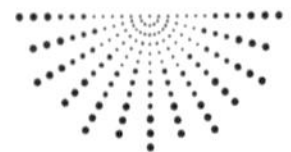

Gwen looks so flushed I'm surprised her clothes aren't melting off her hot skin. From the hallway, my eyes flick past her, to Scarlet, still in the other room and wearing a knowing look as if she can read every dirty thought I'm having.

Oh fuck, I think. *She's a mesmer. She* can *read every dirty thought I'm having.*

I can, Scarlet's voice says in my head. *And my, aren't you the creative one?*

I refuse to show how much that flusters me, but even I feel a stain of red on my cheeks.

Now go on, Scarlet says, her amusement fading to impatience.

I lead Gwen to the harem. A harem. A bubble of panicked laughter escapes my lips. This is all a little much, even for me.

She taps my shoulder until I stop and let her out of my arms in the nondescript white corridor. Her eyes search mine, hope fading to sorrow as she examines my face. "I'm so sorry," she says.

My brows furrow. "For what?" Literally our directive is to fuck, and that is *nothing* to apologize for.

"I'm sorry about…" She gestures to herself.

"It's not your fault you…" I start, but I'm not sure how to finish the sentence. Not her fault for getting sick? But she's not sick—she's superpowered. Perhaps stronger than her father; definitely something way better than anything I've ever encountered before.

"No, I mean, I'm sorry for dragging you into all this," she says, waving her hand weakly.

I bark in bitter laughter. "Last I checked, kiddo, I made my own choices." I see her getting all wound up over my nickname—my god, she's easy to rile, and I love that—but I cut her off before she can protest. "Look, I'm a big boy. I knew I was poking a dragon to go rooting around what Heroes Org was trying to cover up."

"Okay, first of all, quit calling me kiddo—" Gwen growls, and my *god* am I glad to see she has some of her spunk back.

"Sorry, sorry!" I say. My apology throws her off so much that she silences. I smirk. "Sorry for making the moves on you, for letting this get out of control. I had no business hitting on you in the first place." And—well—I did more than hit on her. But I can't quite bring myself to apologize for that. "Anyway, I'm the one who dragged you into my dirty business, not the other way around."

"Hey, I'm a big girl," she says, cocking a sarcastic eyebrow at me. She nudges me in the chest. "I knew I was poking a dragon, too."

"Careful, you may get burned." My grin broadens.

"Maybe I like playing with fire."

Oh my god, Scarlet's voice cuts into our minds, even though she nowhere I can see. *Will you two just fuck and get this over with?*

"That's creepy," I mutter.

Gwen flinches. Fuck.

"I didn't mean mesmer powers in general are creepy. I meant..."

Her face flushes, but her lips twist into a smirk. "We can shut her up by doing what she says."

I shift my hips, hoping my cock will rearrange itself a little, but it's too hard, pressing into my zippered fly in a way that's particularly painful.

"Come on," Gwen says, pulling me down the corridor toward the harem.

I almost ask her—*How do you know where it is?* After all, she's been in a med room for most of her time at this base. But then I remember how her powers surged, how all our minds were probably an open book to her, and knowing the location of a sex harem in Scarlet's base is the least of my concerns.

Gwen opens the door.

Before, when I had my panic attack and Watcher found me, this room was sterile, white, and plain. A stage, some artfully angled booths, bright lights, little more. Watcher had told me that it's usually in use—it's usually crowded, actually—but he and Scarlet had been too focused on work lately to maintain the "harem" as he called it.

But now, instead of a plain white room, there's something more.

Gwen steps through the door, the clacking of her heels on tile silencing as her feet touch soft green moss.

It's a forest. Curated with blossoming bushes lining a path made of pebbles, little flowers interspersed. I can hear the faint sounds of a waterfall. A breeze blows warmly.

"What the fuck is this?" I mutter.

A gift. Scarlet's voice cuts into my mind. *Use it. Help Gwen.*

And then there's silence. Scarlet has left my mind. But she's also left…this.

What had Watcher said before? That Scarlet can make dreamscapes. This must be what he meant—a fantasy come to life.

I look at Gwen, her eyes wide as she turns in a slow circle, looking at the endless sky, the wispy clouds, the flower petals wafting through the air.

She's another fantasy come to life.

"Where are we?" Gwen asks. "Do you know this place?"

"Bit of an understatement," I say.

Because *yeah,* I know this place. Scarlet used her mesmer powers to pluck it right out of my mind, because it's exactly as I remember it.

Gwen looks up with wonder. Pink petals fall like snow around her.

"It was right after I got my biomechanical heart," I tell her. I step closer, wrapping my arms around her. This whole place *feels* so real, yet it must be some sort of dreamscape made by Scarlet's mesmer powers. I should be pissed that we were sent somewhere in a highly personal memory, but I'm not.

"I was coming to terms with the idea of being, you know," I say, tapping the metal implant in my chest. "Had a mission as Steel Soldier to Japan, and after it was done, I…stayed."

"You stayed?"

I nod. "A few weeks. I was mad—I couldn't leave Heroes Org because I owed them literally my life. I had all the money in the world, but it was a little hard getting the parts I needed." Malcolm—Gwen's father—had offered me the needed resources. Among them, sterlinium. Enough to keep me alive. Enough to poison me.

I'd holed up in Japan after the mission because I was pissed. I was so fucking *angry* that I had all my life before me, but also a ticking time bomb implanted in my chest. Sterlinium was keeping me alive, but also poisoning me. Slowly.

But surely.

And the only way to pay back the debt of life Malcolm gave me was by swearing allegiance to Heroes Org and conscripting away the remainder of my years to his service.

"I came to Japan so fucking full of rage," I whisper to Gwen, holding her closer. The scent of the cherry blossoms fills my nose. "But I happened to come here at the height of tourist season. When all the cherry blossoms were blooming."

"It's gorgeous."

"Kyoto in spring is never to be missed," I say.

But it wasn't the tourists that had an impact on me. It was the cherry blossoms. They burst into flower almost overnight and are stunningly gorgeous for just a few days. And then they fall.

They have a short life.

A beautiful life, yes, but a short one.

And, with my newly placed biomechanical heart pump laced with sterlinium whirring in my chest, I needed to be reminded of the beauty that exists in things that don't last forever.

That even if their life was short, the cherry blossoms had a power that could not be denied.

Gwen leans away from me, peeping up at me through her long, dark lashes. I haven't told her what those days, alone in Japan, meant to me. But I think she can guess.

I wonder if she remembers that when I flew back to the office, I'd seen her. I'd had to report to Malcolm, confess that I'd taken too much time in Japan, more than the mission had needed. And she'd been in his office, all precociousness, but with those same big eyes, full of wonder and awe. I wonder if she knows that when I told Malcolm I'd stay with Heroes Org, that I'd see my debt paid, it was her I'd been looking at. Her I'd been vowing to.

And looking down at her now, I think, *I'd swear away all the rest of my days for her, all over again.*

But I can't speak. The cherry blossom petals swirl around us, magic in their effervescence, and Gwen leans up, pressing her lips against mine, sweeter than any flower.

Her arms slip through mine, fingernails gently pressing into my back, pulling me closer to her. Our kiss deepens.

Before, all I felt when I looked at Gwen was urgency. I wanted her *now*. But this moment—it's not about devouring.

It's about savoring.

My mouth drops to her neck, and every little gasp of pleasure that falls from her lips is a balm to my soul. My fingers brush aside the neck of her top, exposing her shoulder. With a growl of impatience, Gwen leans away from me, ripping her clothing off and tossing it to the ground, the material fluttering among the cherry petals.

"So impatient," I whisper as she reaches for me, pulling my own shirt off.

"Hell yes, I'm impatient," Gwen laughs.

I tsk at her, and I can tell she wants to fuss at me for thinking of her as a kid, but she must see in my eyes that I think of her as anything but a child in this moment. Gwen reaches to my pants, tugging the button loose, but I kick them off slowly.

The ground is soft, sun-warmed earth covered in pale green moss, littered with fragrant cherry blossom petals. Gwen's body is splayed across the ground, waiting for me.

And I want her—oh god, I do—and that urgency I'm trying to suppress is rising within me like a tsunami. But I push it down, down.

Some things are worth relishing.

Because nothing lasts forever, but my god am I going to stretch this moment to infinity.

I get on my knees, worshipping her body with a raking gaze of my eyes. I touch Gwen's knee with one hand, and the feeling is electrifying, jolting through both of us, sending shivers over her skin.

But I want to touch much more than just her knee.

I lower my head to her. There's just a moment—a brief little whisper of a gasp from her lips, when Gwen realizes what I'm about to do—and then my lips are on her pussy, my tongue flicking inside of her. She squirms, but my hands go to her thighs, holding her still, holding her open.

She's so wet, so eager for me already, and her hips buck up to meet me. But I force my tongue to go slowly, savoring the taste of her. I lick her clit, swirling it around my tongue, sucking gently, relishing the sound of my name gasping out of her lips. One hand trails down her thigh, and I use my fingers to spread her further open, giving my tongue access deeper inside her. I lick up, claiming her clit again, then push two fingers deep into her, pressing against her walls, finding the exact spot to combine my touch with my tongue against her clit. Her legs seize around me, but I rub my fingers inside her slick passage, and I swirl my tongue against her clit, and I feel the orgasm cresting inside of her, I feel her coming apart under my touch, under my tongue.

"Anthony!" she screams. "Please!"

I raise my head, her taste on my tongue, and Gwen squirms under me, begging. I grab her hips in both of my hands and slide her down, right to my cock, sheathing her bare in one swift, forceful thrust. Her walls clench around my dick, her hips bucking toward me. Her body is still shivering with orgasm as I drive into her, harder and harder.

Gwen's breasts bounce as she slides along the mossy ground, cherry blossoms still falling softly around us. Her back arches, and I reach for her swollen clit with my fingers. One touch, and—like magic—she comes undone, her whole body vibrating with waves of pleasure as she screams my name again, her pussy clenching my cock, squeezing every bit of pleasure from me as she thrusts up, hard, driving me over the edge.

16
GWEN

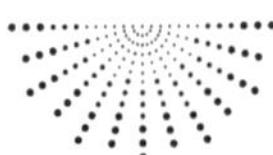

My whole body is *humming*.

Every nerve ending. Every muscle. The tips of my hair down to my toes—everything feels alive with sensation in a way I've never let myself feel before.

Anthony lays on the grass, and I rest across his chest, his hand idly stroking up and down my spine, sending ricocheting waves out to the parts of my body still tingling in the aftershocks of orgasm.

I always have half my mind on controlling the monster inside of me, hoping the sterlinium will hold, hoping I don't have an episode. It never occurred to me that there could be a balance to my powers, that I could harness *good* emotions to not only offset my powers but help me control them.

Thanks to the sterlinium shot, I can't access Anthony's mind or use my abilities; but I feel calmer than I have in days. Months, maybe. And suddenly I want to try again, *without* sterlinium in me, and see if I can use this wash of good emotion to actually *truly* control my powers.

Anthony's sterlinium heart whirs against my chin. The soft blue glow it emits is deceptively pretty—I know now what it's doing to him. What it could cost him.

What it could cost me.

Could my mom have a solution to save him? She knows a lot about sterlinium. More than she ever told me, more than I ever dared to ask.

Could she save him?

Would she?

I haven't really talked to her in…shit. How long? Months? Surely not a year.

Guilt squeezes me. Usually, when I think of talking to her, I can rage somehow with her various sins. But now, I just feel foolish for letting our rift widen, when if I'd fixed it, I'd have the power and support to help Anthony.

I slide up onto him, straddling his waist. He folds his arms under his head and smiles up at me.

The blossom petals still drift lazily around us. Scarlet hasn't pulled us out of the dreamscape yet, so maybe we have time.

Maybe reality doesn't have to find us just yet.

He had his mouth on my pussy earlier, a sensation near to heaven.

"What are you thinking?" he asks, and he bucks his hips slightly under me. He's hard again. I shouldn't be surprised; I'm wet still, too, and aching to have him in me again, always, I'm helpless to the feel of him inside of me.

"Just that it isn't fair."

He frowns. "What isn't?"

I see the answers flit across his face. Our reality, banging incessantly—

"That I haven't gotten to taste you yet," I say. I bite my lip with a fiendish grin and wiggle down until his cock pops up between us.

Then I arch over and take him into my mouth, all the way to the root, in one smooth motion.

He hisses and arches up. "Fuck, Gwen—"

I move in slow bobs, relaxing my throat with each deep thrust. The musky scent of him drives me wild, and I can smell *me* on him too, which only infuses me more, makes me lose myself in the small act of blowing him in this Japanese garden.

I dig my fingers into his hips and lick all the way up his long shaft, then back down again, teasing his head until a drop of pre-cum shines on the tip. I lap it up and go back down again, bathing his cock with my tongue, thoroughly enjoying the chance to make him writhe and moan beneath me. The little helpless noises he makes go straight to my swelling clit; I peek up, and his eyes are half-lidded, his lips parted, forehead wrinkled in concentration.

And when I crawl back up him and sheath his dick in my pussy, he throws his head back into the grass with a groan and anchors on my thighs. We are slower now. This is sensation and longing and possession. He lets me ride him, using his cock however I want, hips rocking until I get him hitting my G-spot perfectly.

Then I slam down, up again, down; *fuck*, my body quivers—

Anthony moves his thumb until he hits my clit. His eyes lock onto mine, and he holds his thumb there, not breaking contact as I ride, rubbing in tight, smooth circles on the little nub of nerves that has me bucking and moaning, control lost. I grab my breasts and run the tips of my fingers over each nipple, the two of us braiding a pattern of thrusting and rubbing and bucking.

But then he pinches my clit between his thumb and finger, and I come apart over him, screaming my orgasm to the high blue skies.

Anthony flies up, grabbing my shoulders, thrusting me down on his cock. He comes too, grunting and cursing, sweat slicking our bodies in delicious release.

Panting, we lean into each other, foreheads together, gasping the same air. His lips find mine, then my jaw, and he leaves a trail of kisses to my ear.

"You're a goddess," he whispers to me, and I only believe him because of the way he worshipped my body.

I thread my arms around him and find his mouth again, just wanting to feel this, *him*, so whatever happens next, I have this memory to anchor onto when all else tries to rip me out to sea.

~

SCARLET HAS a portal ready for us by the time we get back to her lab.

"This will put you right in Elysium," she tells us, tapping away on her computer.

"What?" Anthony's eyebrows shoot to his hairline. "Just…right in Elysium?"

She eyes him, her laptop's screen reflecting in her eyes. "Don't worry. Heroes are welcome there now. Or haven't you heard?"

He swallows and looks at me like I might have answers. I shrug.

Scarlet sighs heavily. "You two have to be the only people associated with Heroes Org who *don't* know, I swear—Persephone has come to an arrangement with Heroes. They get to have free use of Elysium in exchange for their secrecy and obedience."

Anthony rolls his eyes and even I find that hard to believe.

"Just that easy?" I push. "She opened one of her bases to them, no strings attached other than *be nice?*"

Scarlet smirks at me. "Oh, there are a *million* strings, sunshine. But aren't there always? And anyway, most Heroes are more than willing to pay up when the time comes. Whatever that final payment might be. Now, Elysium is the beginning of a truce between Heroes Org and Villains."

Anthony huffs, empty. "Well. Isn't that nice?"

I can't even fake a sarcastic quip like him. A *truce*? Between Heroes Org, the world's largest organization of powered humans, and Elysium, the powered humans who refuse to live by Heroes Org's rules? That rivalry is what fuels Heroes Org. I'd heard the board members rail at Dad over the years—they'd rather pluck out their eyes than ever have peace with Villains.

Villains mean the world needs Heroes.

And if the world needs Heroes, they're willing to pay.

But now that Dad's no longer the head of Heroes Org...maybe Mom really is trying to change things?

Why hasn't she told me?

All those times when Aunt Val pushed me to call Mom back run through my head at once.

Fuck.

Maybe she *has* been trying to tell me.

"Okay," I say, squaring my shoulders. "I'm ready."

Watcher pushes some buttons on a wall panel. A spot the size of a door instantly turns to a heaving, blurry mess of lights and glitter, all of it flashing in purples and blues.

"Step through," he instructs us. "You will be met on the other side."

"Met by whom?" Anthony asks. He takes my hand, threading our fingers together, and I can feel him shaking.

Is he...nervous? I'm the one who should be nervous, right?

But then I realize he's a Hero about to willingly step into the Villain Queen's lair. However she might be professing *peace,* this has to be going against every red flag in Anthony's body.

I slip my arm around his waist and squeeze him to me. "Together?"

He looks down at me. When I smile, his face relaxes, and he brushes his lips across mine. "Together."

17
ANTHONY

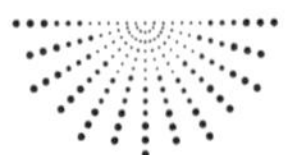

We step through the portal, hands entwined. The sterile lab is replaced with a gentle warm breeze, the scent of saltwater and coconuts filling my nose. "Where are we?" I ask.

"Elysium." I turn at the female voice, familiar enough that I almost recognize it. I blink as I take in the woman before me.

I knew Lilly when she was fiancée to All-American Man. I also saw the raw footage of when Malcolm controlled All-American Man's mind in an attempt to kill her. It was no surprise that she went off-grid, but I hadn't known she'd come *here.*

"Welcome. Scarlet let us know you'd be arriving," she says.

"Lilly? Are you—?" I want to ask if she's okay. The last time I saw her, she'd been engaged to All-American Man. But the question dies on my lips. Because it's obvious that Lilly is more than okay. She's practically glowing with happiness.

"I go by Lillith now," she says, gesturing to a path that leads further up what is very clearly a tropical paradise island. "Persephone thought it'd help if you saw a familiar face, and Piper was busy."

Gwen and I exchange a look, then follow Lillith under the shade of the palm trees. Piper? I only know one Piper... "You mean Agent Carson?"

"Mm," Lillith says, nodding.

Agent *Carson?* Strait-laced, blouse always buttoned to the neck, following people around with a clipboard Agent Carson? I knew she'd gone rogue, but...not like this? However, even as my eyes are popping at this twist, the path is getting more crowded. With...with Heroes. People I recognize from Heroes Org.

I think back to what Eagle-Eye said before, at my party. He knew, too. They all knew. It seems like every goddamned Hero in the world knew about the party at Elysium but me.

Lillith casts a look at me, analyzing my face. "While we have some who came to us first, we have only a few top-level Heroes," she says quietly. "The ones who had been closest to Malcolm, they're the ones we're most...wary about informing."

Ah. There it is. Because Malcolm had his mental claws in my brain for so long, I'm a commodity to fear.

Whatever niggling doubts of anger or worry that worm inside me now fade as we round the corner, and I see something that looks remarkably like a castle. There's a weird disconnect between stepping inside a palace but seeing the highest tech out on the walls. Even I can appreciate the level of detail that goes into this building as Lillith leads us through it.

Although we pass something that looks like a throne room, Lillith doesn't linger there. Gwen has to drag me away, though, because there's a stage in the throne room, a raised platform that is currently being occupied. I see now why Agent Carson didn't greet us herself. And apparently All-American Man has moved on from his broken engagement with Lillith. And also—fuck, is that Bryce? I thought he'd *died*.

"Come on," Gwen hisses, pulling my arm so we catch up with Lillith, who's skirting the edge of the throne room, leading us to a corridor.

Once we're in the more private alcove, Gwen giggles at me. "You're blushing."

"That was—"

"I know," Lillith says. She doesn't seem bothered to see her former lover on stage with two other people in what was clearly more of a sex dungeon than a throne room.

"But that was—"

"Yes," Lillith says. "I *know*."

"You weren't kidding about Piper Carson being busy." I turn to Gwen, eyes wide. Her giggles intensify. "So, the den of the most infamous Villain in history is actually just a cover for a weird orgy party? That everyone knew about but me?"

"Are you more upset that the Villain base isn't some cabal of cackling evil doers, or that you weren't invited to the party?" Gwen asks.

"Honestly, the second thing," I say. "I thought I was the king of parties! What makes her orgy better than mine?"

"It's not a competition," Lillith says.

"But if it *was*, I want to win!"

"You want to throw a better orgy than my mother?" Gwen asks.

"Well, when you put it that way."

"Come *on*," Lillith says, and even though there's a glint of humor in her eye, she moves impatiently.

Right.

There's still the world to save.

The orgy competition can come after.

God, this is weird.

I *love* it.

Lillith takes us to an elevator—anachronistic with the castle-like feel of the building—punches in a code on a keypad, and then steps off the elevator before the door closes, waving at us. I wonder if she's going to go join the orgy party.

Then I glance at Gwen, see the way her fingers are twisting around each other, the tight set to her shoulders.

The sex dungeon makes a lot more sense now that I know Gwen. Positive emotion—and what's more positive than an orgy?—feeds into her power. Persephone could, perhaps, burn the entire world down if she were surrounded by fighting and viciousness. Put her throne in a sex dungeon, and the world's far safer.

I touch Gwen's arm, and she instantly relaxes into my skin.

Gwen—and, I'm assuming, her mother—are like amplifiers. Put them in a happy situation, surround them with joy, fill them with bliss—and they put out a million times more goodness.

I think, then, about the alien armada we saw hanging in space.

And I wonder just how much the world will crumble to ash if Gwen is met with violence.

"Did you hear that?" Gwen mutters, eyes sliding away from mine.

"What?"

Gwen's brows furrow in concentration. "…nothing," she says eventually, the word barely audible.

Before I can say anything else, the elevator stops.

The doors open.

And there, in the corridor directly across from us, is Persephone.

I've never seen her before, but I know her instantly. I know her in the warm depth of her skin. In the clear gaze of her eyes. In the powerful stance, the sharp look, the lilting smile.

I know Persephone because I know Gwen. And the most beautiful parts of Persephone are just an echo of the loveliness Gwen embodies.

Gwen and I step into the corridor, the elevator doors closing silently behind us.

"Anthony Stern," Persephone says. Her eyes slide over my body. She analyzes me with one look, and with another, she dismisses me.

"Gwendolyn." Her voice is filled with a mother's love as she looks at her daughter. I may as well be an annoying fly, buzzing around their happy reunion, and Persephone practically knocks me aside to reach Gwen. She wraps her up in her arms, her attention entirely on her daughter. Gwen, for her part, melts at her mother's touch.

I stand there awkwardly, shifting from foot to foot.

"Mom," Gwen says, her voice muffled in her mother's embrace. "Why didn't you tell me?"

Persephone pulls back, gaze focused on Gwen. "About what?"

"About—about all of it!" Gwen's voice pitches high. "About my powers, about what you were hiding? I mean—what the actual fuck? There's an alien armada waiting to attack Earth?!"

Persephone's jaw tightens. "Yes," she says. She sighs. "To be fair, we weren't entirely sure. I had my satellites pointed to those coordinates, but..."

But it took Gwen to expose the threat.

Just how powerful is she?

"I could hear them," Gwen whispers. "They're so...*angry.*"

Persephone's eyes widen, just a fraction, at that, and I see a flash of worry on her face before she hides it.

"What do they want?" Gwen asks.

"War," Persephone says.

Silence wraps around us.

Persephone sighs, her shoulders sinking. "And we are going to have to face that war."

"War," Gwen repeats, a whisper, horror laced in her voice.

Persephone's eyes widen. "We've wanted to keep this from you, but... we will need your help. I know a mother's job it to protect her child, but—"

"Mom, I can't just ignore this—"

Persephone's head shakes. "Not...not yet. I am happy that you're coming into your powers, but that's just it—you're still new to what your body can do."

"I'm not a child!" Gwen exclaims.

"I know," Persephone says. "But you are also not prepared to fight an intergalactic war. And..." Her eyes slide to me, with such dismissal that I feel nothing but shame.

"This enemy is going to take...finesse. Shooting little plasma blasters at an alien armada will do nothing." Persephone hasn't taken her eyes off me. She wants to protect Gwen, as a mother would want to protect her daughter, but me?

She wants me to know that I'm just not good enough.

"Anthony is the Steel Soldier!" Gwen says, as if her mother didn't know.

Persephone's eyes grow cold. "Oh, I know." She says this as if she were speaking directly to a pile of steaming dog shit. "Your 'reputation' precedes you, Mr. Stern."

Oh my god, oh my god, please sweet lord, do not let this Villain have access to my mind, do not let her see what I have already done to her daughter, do not let her know what I want to still *do to her...*

Persephone's gaze narrows.

Fuck.

She definitely knows.

I look around for a blunt object to bash my own skull in with.

"I doubt you'll be capable of joining us," she says. "But if I allow it, and if you die, at least we can repurpose your Steel Soldier suit, I suppose."

Can I die of shame and awkwardness now? She can have the fucking suit.

I glance at Gwen, who gives me a little thumbs up, as if I weren't the worst human alive.

My smile back to her is a bit more of a grimace than a grin.

But then Gwen's look sharpens. She flinches as if she'd been hit. "Gwen?" I ask, tilting Gwen's chin up to me. "Are you okay?"

Gwen nods, leaning into my touch. When she opens her eyes, she focuses on her mother. "He's here, isn't he?" she asks. "I thought I heard him, and now... He's here."

"Who is here?" I ask.

"My father," Gwen says, her gaze not leaving Persephone. "Take me to him," she says, such command and power in her voice that even the Villain Queen quells before her.

18

GWEN

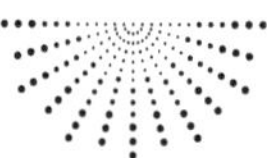

Before I started taking sterlinium, Dad tried to help me learn to use my powers by playing hide-and-seek. He'd hide somewhere in his mansion, and I'd have to find him using my powers—listening for him, feeling his emotions, guiding myself to him. I got really good at it...before my powers flew beyond my control.

But as I stand in the hallway with my mom and Anthony, I feel like that little girl again.

I can't hear his thoughts—no wonder, if Mom has him; she'd have some kind of block on him—but I can feel him. It's a pull I can't really describe except that it's *him*—the man who staged my training sessions as games but made me do them over, and over, and over, for hours, until I was sobbing with exhaustion; the man who never came to a single one of my school functions but always had his car drop me off at his office so I could do my homework near his desk while he worked; the man who rarely got home for dinner but usually had some kind of barely edible breakfast waiting that he'd made himself. The man who rearranged huge chunks of my memories whenever I got too close to uncovering truths he didn't want me to know, but never thought about amending my memories of what an asshole he was to me sometimes.

"You have him here." I stare at Mom, unblinking.

At least she doesn't bother lying. She nods. "It was the only place secure enough."

Anthony makes a strangled sound. "What? Does Heroes Org know?"

Mom flashes him a flat look. He ducks his head, eyes on his shoes, cheeks stained red.

I hate how she talks to him. I hate the energy he's giving off now, something timid and insecure when the man I know is bursting with confidence.

My chest squeezes with shock.

I can…I can *feel* Anthony's energy.

I can feel Mom's, too. She's thrilled to see me, happy in a way that washes over me like a cool breeze on a sweltering day, relief and joy and true, undeniable love. But my feelings for her are as complex as the ones I have for Dad.

Do I love them? Do I hate them? Yes. Everything.

I fist my hands. Mom stares at me a beat longer, a smile playing across her lips.

She knows I can feel her emotions.

"You've grown so much, Gwendolyn," she tells me. "I'm so proud of you. You've come even this far on your own, and I—"

"Not *on my own*." I take Anthony's hand. "And what I *have* done on my own was only because you and Dad refused to tell me what was actually going on. Now, where the fuck is he?"

Mom looks like she might chastise me for speaking to her that way, but she sighs. "Come with me."

We go back into the elevator. She pushes a button and a separate keypad and scanner pops out of the wall. Anthony turns away, but I watch as she types in her keycode and lets the scanner read her hand, then her eye.

Mom looks at me as the elevator starts to move, shooting us down.

"We never meant to hurt you, Gwendolyn."

"Stop." I pinch the bridge of my nose, a headache throbbing behind my eyes. Is it the sterlinium wearing off? Or just general stress and tension? Impossible to tell.

We ride in silence. Anthony angles towards me, his hand still in mine, his thumb rubbing across my knuckles. Each level we descend cranks my heart rate higher until I can feel it thudding in my neck, my wrists, my legs; my lungs stretch, trying to accommodate too-fast breaths.

Fuck. I need to calm down.

Mom is watching me, though. Do I care?

I put my hand on Anthony's chest. He looks at me and immediately reads my panic. Or maybe he's just as nervous as I am.

His eyes flash to my mom before shooting back to me. *She'll flay me alive.*

I flinch.

I…heard him.

I heard him, but his lips didn't move at all.

The sterlinium really is wearing off.

That only makes my heart speed up, my breathing erratic. Damn it, *damn it—*

Please. I don't even know if it'll work, but I send the thought to Anthony.

I see it hit him. I see his eyes widen, his lips part, the worry on his face rippling away when he hears the tension in my voice.

He doesn't hesitate now.

He cups my head and kisses me, body pressing mine against the elevator wall.

Just the touch of his lips stops my breath. The feel of his tongue in my mouth, the way he moans softly into me—the sensations pull my whole focus and send an echoing shockwave through my body, smoothing the rough edges in its wake.

When he backs off, I sway, but I'm far more centered.

"We're here."

Anthony and I whirl around. Mom stands with the elevator door open, her eyes boring into mine.

She doesn't get a chance to look at Anthony; I step in front of him, jaw set, daring her to say anything. She has no right to critique how I'm getting a handle on these powers.

These powers that I am coming to suspect are far more from *her* than they ever were from *Dad.*

She arches an eyebrow but says nothing. I remember, then, what Scarlet said about my mental blocks being abysmal. Can Mom read my thoughts? Can she read Anthony's?

The disapproval on her face remains, but when her head tips, I get my answer.

Yes.

My face flushes. I breeze past her off the elevator, dragging Anthony with me.

We're in a stone room deep under Elysium. It looks every bit a medieval jail, dark flooring and high ceilings with no windows. Only the lights are fluorescent.

Mom walks to the only door in this small room. Another keypad, a scanner, and the door opens, revealing cells on either side of a long stone corridor. They're high tech, panels of bulletproof glass with keypads that beep softly.

The first few cells we pass are dark. I can't see if anyone's inside, or if maybe the glass is just tinted. Can any prisoners within see us? What kinds of people would *Villains* deem as prisoners? I shiver, pulling Anthony closer to me.

Mom stops on the farthest cell down the hall. She hesitates, just a beat, and I can feel the flurry of indecision that churns in her mind.

I get the distinct impression she's only letting me feel what emotions of hers she wants me to feel.

She smirks as her hand reaches for the keypad. "Smart girl," she whispers.

I clench my jaw, refusing to acknowledge the rush of pride I feel. I don't care about pleasing her. I *don't.*

Mom taps the keypad.

The glass panel in front of us turns from pitch black to a smoky gray until, finally, it clears.

Beyond is a cell. Small, but nice. A single cot, even a sitting area with a stack of books on a table, a lamp, a sink and toilet behind a short screen.

And there's my father, lounged in one of the chairs, a book open on his lap.

His eyes flick up. "Back so soon, my love? I didn't think you'd—"

He stops.

His focus hangs on me. He looks older, worn by his time in here, but he's still managed to style his hair and look somewhat respectable in the white prison uniform he's wearing.

Dad comes to his feet slowly, his eyes not breaking from mine. I can't read any of his emotions or thoughts; whatever block Mom has on him is impenetrable, and I'm suddenly glad for it. I don't think I'd survive whatever guilt he's feeling, whatever apology is churning in him, whatever thought is making his eyes tear.

"Gwen," he says.

Finally, he looks at Mom. He straightens. "Have I earned this visit for good behavior?"

"Hardly." Mom folds her arms under her breasts. There's heat coming off her now that she's looking at him. I can't mistake it—she loves him.

The moment I acknowledge it, it vanishes.

She won't look at me. But I see the muscles in her jaw flex.

She's blocking me now. Completely.

She doesn't want me to know she still loves him? I knew that when I was seven. It was never a surprise. But the two of them together are destructive in the worst ways. She might love him, but that love poisons everyone around them.

Mom pivots a little, putting her back to me. "Gwendolyn made a discovery."

Dad's eyebrows go up. He looks back at me. "You found my coordinates?"

I nod.

He grins. "I knew you would. And—" Now he realizes Anthony.

Dad's whole demeanor changes. His eyes fall to our clasped hands, and I'm suddenly grateful for the glass separating us, for whatever block my mom has on his powers.

He looks like he'd kill Anthony if he could.

"What the hell are you doing, Stern?" he growls.

"That's hardly important right now," Mom says. "Gwendolyn was able to penetrate the armada's blocking shield."

That, at least, yanks Dad's attention back. "What?"

"Wait—you knew it was an armada before that?" I ask.

"Of course," Mom tells me. "I could sense them as you could, but their shields..."

She throws me a look, and it's weighted, heartbroken.

"Gwen's stronger than you," Dad exhales. He's at the glass now, one hand on it, like he's trying to reach for me.

"I'm stronger than *her*?" I echo, fury rising through me. "Stronger than *my mother*, even though you let me believe I had *your* powers all these years?"

"It was safer," Dad tries.

"Bullshit. It was a *lie*."

"Yes." He doesn't deny it. "I lied when you first started to show powers because I knew if she—" he points at Mom "—figured out that you were like *her*, I'd never see you again. But if you were like me? I'd get to keep you, to train you, and I wouldn't lose out on you."

My chest deflates. The sincerity on his face batters my weak defenses.

"That's bullshit," I repeat because I can barely talk at all.

Anthony squeezes my hand, wrapping my wrist in his free fingers. I lean into him, breathing deep, grateful that my heart rate doesn't spike.

Dad's glare on Anthony is murderous.

"So you lied to her," I say, "and she really didn't figure it out?"

"Of course I figured it out," Mom snaps. "I recognized the bud of your powers the moment you were born. But I also wasn't a *monster*." She frowns up at Dad. "I wouldn't have kept her from you."

Dad shrugs. "We've had this discussion. I still don't believe you wouldn't have used her against me. I stand by my decisions. This way, I got to keep my daughter, and I didn't have to—"

"Stop!" My shout cuts up and down the otherwise empty hall. "You were both shitty parents, okay? Let's just get to equal footing on that so we can discuss why the *hell* I was able to break through that armada's shields, from *lightyears away*, and also who the hell is leading that armada?"

Dad and Mom share a look. Dad sighs and looks to the ceiling.

"Niberu," he says. "His name is Niberu."

Mom turns away and rubs the back of her neck.

Anthony and I stay silent, holding onto each other.

"He's not from this planet. Hell, he's not even from this galaxy." Dad props one arm on the glass and rests his forehead against it, his eyes closing. "We detected him a few years ago. All the aliens who'd land on Earth came because of him. The breadcrumbs kept leading back to a single puppet master, and it didn't take long to figure out he was coming. We can't defeat him. Not as we are."

"So you used your mesmer powers to control Heroes Org," Anthony says.

Dad flares his eyes open. "Yes," he says, jaw tight.

"How would that have helped? You took advantage of everyone." Anthony's voice wavers between righteous fury and utter terror, and I feel him shaking against me.

What did my dad make him do when he was at Heroes Org? What is he remembering that has him trembling like this?

"We needed a united front," Dad says. His eyes flick to mine, and he clearly doesn't like the way I'm glaring at him, because he shoots another scathing look at Anthony, like it's his fault I've finally seen my dad's shittiness. "We needed an impenetrable army. You have no idea the full threat that's coming. Niberu is the strongest force *in the universe*."

"And you stand by your decisions, right?" I throw his earlier words back at him.

Dad hardens. "Yes," he says, no hesitation.

"So why was I able to break his army's shields?" I whisper the question. The fight is draining out of me; I'm exhausted, I'm terrified, and I just want to curl up on Anthony's chest and rest.

Mom turns back to me. "That," she starts, "is a conversation for the two of us, Gwendolyn." But she hesitates. "The two of us and...someone else."

My mind heaves. "Who else? How is—"

Mom reaches for me, but I flinch back, closer to Anthony. I can see that it hurts her. I don't care.

"You should rest. I need to leave to get—" Her voice hangs. "I'll tell you everything when I get back. I promise. But for now, this day has been enough, I think."

It really has. This morning was when Anthony and I broke into the lab at Heroes Org. Shit, has it really only been a few hours? Good god, no wonder I'm exhausted.

I nod and follow her back up the hall, Anthony trailing me.

"Wait."

Dad's voice makes us all stop.

"I'd like to speak with my former Hero," he says. "Alone."

Anthony goes rigid beside me. When I look up at him, his eyes are wide and glazed.

"No—" I start to say, but Anthony nods.

"It's fine, Gwen," he tells me.

Doubt seizes me. Anthony is clearly unsettled being around my dad, but maybe talking to him will give him some sort of closure.

I look at Mom, who nods.

"Five minutes," she says and gestures for me to come with her, back to the main room. We'll be far enough away not to hear them, though with my powers, I could at least hear Anthony's—

I feel a rush fall over my mind, something soft and tingling and cool.

"It's rude to eavesdrop, Gwendolyn," Mom says.

I glance back at Anthony, who stares after me, and gives one last smile before he turns to my dad.

"That's rich, coming from you. I'm sure you never eavesdrop," I tell her.

She sighs. "You think badly of me. And that is my fault."

I huff.

We reach the main room and the door to the prison hall shuts behind us.

Mom turns to me. She doesn't reach for me again, but she holds my eyes with such ferocity I can't look away.

"I'm sorry, Gwendolyn," she tells me, and my breath catches. "I'm sorry for every strain I put you through. But I hope, going forward, to make it up to you. To be the mother you deserve. I've made far too many mistakes in my life, and with Niberu coming, so much has shifted into perspective."

I hold up my hand to stop her. It's shaking, but I don't try to hide it.

My own perspective has shifted so much, too. I can't find it in me to be mad at her for trying to make amends now. Better late than never.

The door has a little window off to the side, and through it, I can see Anthony talking with Dad. I strain to hear, but I can't catch a word.

My eyes fix on Anthony's profile. The way he stands, his shoulders squared and his chin level even though I know my dad terrifies him.

Better late than never, indeed.

I look back at Mom, whose eyes are wide with hope and promises I never got as a kid. But she's here now.

"I hope so, too," is all I can manage to say to her.

19
ANTHONY

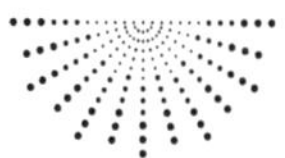

I DON'T WANT TO BE ALONE WITH THIS MAN.

And two days ago, there was nothing anyone could have done to make me stay.

But then I met Gwen.

And knowing she's got my six, I can confront Malcolm Odyssey.

"You ready to face me alone, Stern?" Malcolm says, his voice mocking as soon as Persephone and Gwen are outside and the door is completely closed.

"With Gwen at my back."

"You're such a pretentious asshole," Malcolm snarls at me. "My *daughter* doesn't have your back. She's not *yours.*"

"I know," I say simply. "But she's also not yours. She belongs to no one but herself."

"Cut the bullshit," Malcolm says. I don't know how he can be wearing a prison uniform, kept underneath the Villain Queen's base, and still be so contemptuous. "I know you. I *know* you. And I know you're nothing more than a wannabe playboy who thinks he's important based on the number of people he can get in his bed. Who made the Steel Soldier suit just so he didn't feel weak because his fucking heart was dead."

"Don't," I growl, hands bunching in fists. "If I had the suit right now, you'd know how I actually feel."

"You'd shoot me with a plasma blast?" Malcolm smiles smugly. "You really want to tear me apart, don't you?"

I can't do that. He's Gwen's father, after all. And I'm still a Hero. I…I think.

"But you can't," Malcolm continues.

"Oh, I could." I let myself visualize it. Persephone has Malcolm's mind on lock, but I think from the glint in my eye and the way he flinches that he can guess at the violence I'm imagining right now.

Prison is too good for this man. He claws inside people's minds and makes them do worse than murder. He doesn't deserve this cell.

"If you kill me," Malcolm says, triumph curling his lips into a cruel smile, "Gwen would never forgive you."

That stops me cold.

Malcolm folds his arms over his chest. "I'll never stop being her father," he says. "No matter what you do to me, no matter what happens, I will *always* be her father. But you?" He leers at me, all smug and derision. "You may think you have my Gwen now, you may think you're something to her, but you can be forgotten. Like that." He snaps his fingers, and it's like the crack of a whip across my brain.

I shake my head. "You're wrong."

"I'm not."

"I may have been throwing ragers and partying before, but I've changed."

"In a few days?" He arches an eyebrow.

"Yes." I stare him down. I let him see how little any of my past matters to me. I let him see the full truth of my soul:

I love Gwen.

I have seen her at her strongest, and I have seen her at her weakest. I have seen the fire in her eyes. I have seen the storm in her soul.

And I love her.

And nothing—*nothing*—Malcolm can ever say to me will make me not love her.

There's a grim set in his jaw. I think Malcolm thought he could scare me away from his daughter. Maybe he thought I was just using her body for a good time, using her circumstances for an adventure. But no.

His cold eyes rake over me. He's not happy—I don't need to be a mesmer to see that.

"You think this is Daddy wanting to protect his little girl," he says, ice dripping from his voice. "You completely idiotic asshole. You think that's all this is?"

I grit my teeth together. Let him fill the silence.

"You're going to die, Stern," Malcolm says flatly.

"We all are," I snap back. None of us are gods. None of us are immortal.

Malcolm's bark of laughter is bitter, cruel. "You're dying sooner than any of us. You're poisoned, Stern. You're well past the tolerance point. That thing—" He points to the flat circle of metal poking beneath my shirt. "—has kept you alive. But you're on borrowed time."

I suck in a shaky breath. I know it. The sterlinium that keeps me alive is also killing me. Crueler than chemo, the medicine is a poison. And my body's balancing act is tipping the scales toward the Grim Reaper. I know it. I've known it from the first injection.

"So I'll be with Gwen while I can," I say.

"Exactly." Malcolm smirks like he won a battle. "'There's no point in pretending the truth isn't real.'"

"What *is* your point, Odyssey?" I growl.

"Gwen has enough power in her veins to blow apart the entire Earth." Malcolm's voice is flat, passionless, but his eyes are fire as they bore into me. "And her power feeds off emotion. Persephone's the same way. And yeah, you fucking Gwen helps calm her. For now."

I feel tension tightening my muscles. I force myself to stay still.

"But Stern, goddammit, think for a minute. If you leave her now, Gwen'll be pissed. I'm a big enough man to admit that my daughter likes you, for some unknown fucking reason. And if you leave her, she'll be upset."

"I'm never leaving her."

"But," Malcolm continues as if I'd not spoken, "if you stay. If you let this...entanglement continue. If you let her really know what it's like to love you..."

A future together. Waking up with Gwen in my arms. Her smile the first thing I see when I open my eyes...

"If you let her really fall in love with you," Malcolm continues, his voice cold and hard as steel. "If you stay...think of how it will break her when you die."

My daydream fantasies shrivel up in my mind's eye.

"Think, Stern," Malcolm says. His voice is urgent now. "Think of how Gwen will melt the entire planet in her grief. She'll be sad now, if you go, but if you die in her arms from sterlinium poison? My god. Her grief will kill us all."

I shake my head. No. *No.* Love isn't grief. It's not death.

But...

"You've seen what sterlinium poison does."

I have. I did the research. I will never forget the image of a test subject who died of sterlinium poisoning when that drug was first discovered. The broken body. The shallow hull of a corpse that was left after the drug fully consumed the person.

"You've been a selfish prick the entire time I've known you," Malcolm says, but all the venom is gone from his voice. "But even you have to see that the few moments of happiness you may be able to steal with Gwen are nothing compared to the utter grief you'll cause her in the inevitable end. And Gwen's not in control enough of her power to handle that grief. Are you really willing to trade a few fuck sessions with my daughter at the cost of her sorrow causing a nuclear-like fallout for the entire planet?"

Bile rises in my throat. It's not about fuck sessions. It's not been about the fucking for...I don't know when. I love her.

But does that mean I have to leave her?

No, my entire body rebels at the thought.

But...

I *am* dying.

I've seen my labs. I know the truth.

And I've seen the way Gwen's emotions spiral. She's *not* in control.

Maybe she'll gain that control she needs now? She'll be able to work with Persephone, become strong enough to handle the darkness at my inevitable fate...?

I meet Malcolm's knowing eyes.

He doesn't say it, but I know what he's thinking.

I don't have enough time left for Gwen to learn her powers. By the time she's strong enough to handle the kind of grief my death would cause, it'd be too late.

I'd already be gone.

I turn on my heel and stride out of the prison. Malcolm, to his credit, doesn't laugh at my retreat.

Persephone and Gwen are waiting for me in the entryway, but neither says anything as we get in the elevator. At the penultimate floor, the doors open. Gwen steps out, motioning for me to follow. Persephone stares at the ceiling and huffs a sigh as the door shuts, carrying her to the top floor.

Gwen goes to a door she knows—Persephone must have told her about it while I was speaking to Malcolm—opens it, looks back at me, an invitation to join her. She steps inside the room.

Get it the fuck together, Stern, I tell myself.

But I hesitate, my fists clenching, my jaw tight.

Malcolm was right.

I can't let my doom bring an apocalypse on the world.

But more than that, I can't break Gwen's heart.

I love her.

But she may not love me yet. It's too soon. She's barely had a chance to see the real me, the man behind the Steel Soldier mask.

I have to go before she falls for me.

But I cannot deny myself one last memory of her.

Gwen's on a big bed littered with soft blankets. She changes into a robe made of some flimsy silver material. Her eyes are soft; her body is another invitation.

She opens her mouth to speak, but I rush to her, claiming her lips, silencing her words. If she tells me she loves me, if she asks me to stay—I don't think I could deny her.

So I can't let her use her voice. My kiss is urgent, begging her for a taste of eternity, and she opens her mouth, meeting my tongue and letting me devour her. I had wanted to be soft and slow, but I can't, not now that my decision has been made.

I open her robe as I press against her. Her hands claw at my shirt, my pants, divesting me of clothing in a tumble of tugs and snapping buttons.

And then she's there.

Bare.

Under me.

Her eyes open. Innocent. She's here, fully, in this moment. There's nothing at all between us. There's nothing in existence but the two of us.

And then I push inside of her, and we are one, the only people in the universe, together.

I shift back without pulling out. I want us to be one for as long as we can. I want this to be my forever.

Her body clenches around my cock, claiming me, uniting us. And as much as I want this sensation to last, I cannot help but want to please her more. I reach between us, feeling the spot where we are joined, her wetness slick. My finger glides up, touching her clit.

Her gasp is soft, but she bucks against me, hard, begging for more. I push into her, all the way to the hilt, driving myself as hard as I can and matching the rhythm of our union with my finger on her clit, swirling over the nub, grinding it against my cock.

Gwen is breathless, writhing against me, panting for more, more, and I give her—

Everything.

All of me.

Because, even as we climax together, I know—

This last memory is all I have left to give.

20

GWEN

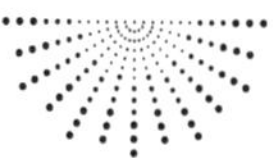

I WAKE UP TO THE SOUNDS OF WAVES LAPPING AT THE SHORE, GULLS CRYING, wind rustling palm trees. For a beat, I think I left some kind of ambient noise machine on—

Then I breathe in, smelling saltwater and sun-warmed air, and I smile, even half awake.

Sure, there's an alien armada barreling toward Earth.

Sure, I have crazy powers I have no idea how to control, and I'm certain my mom still has more information bombs to drop on me.

But right now, I'm curled into bed next to Anthony in some kind of tropical resort paradise that Mom apparently owns, and I will absorb every speck of happiness out of this moment that I can get.

I roll over, pulling the thin sheet with me.

But the bed is empty.

I pat the mattress like it might give me an answer and peek up at the open bathroom door. "Anthony? Are you—"

Movement in the corner catches my attention.

I fly upright, eyes peeling wide. "Aunt Val!"

She grins at me and rushes over, arms extended.

But I pull the sheet closer to my chest before she can hug me. "Um, can you toss me that robe first?"

She hesitates, then complies. She sits on the bed while I tug on the silvery robe.

I throw my gaze around the room again. Where'd Anthony go?

"Gwen." Val is still smiling, but it looks forced now, too big, too bright.

I frown at her. "What?"

She takes my hand. "How are you feeling?"

"…fine?" I remember her panicked voice on the phone. When was it, yesterday? Last she knew, I'd had an attack from my powers. "Oh, fine, really. Anthony helped me, and now—well. I'm finally getting those answers I always wanted out of Mom and Dad. Is that why you're here?"

A cold hand squeezes my stomach.

"Wait. How much do you know about what they told me? About—"

Val reaches over to pull the sleep bonnet off my hair. Her gentle fingers start to pick at my curls. "Your mom wants to talk to you the moment you're ready. You've been asleep for almost two days."

"Two *days*?" But the moment she says that, I feel it—my limbs ache from lying down, but I feel more alert and rested than I have in a long while. I guess I hadn't realized how tired I was. And no wonder Anthony isn't in the room—he's probably off somewhere, exploring Mom's castle.

I suddenly remember that room down below. The booths. The fully-on-display group sex.

My face flushes. "Um—do you know where Anthony is?" Not that I don't trust him. I do. Don't I? We hadn't really talked about…*us*. Are we exclusive? Are we—

Aunt Val's too-wide smile flickers.

"You should get dressed, sweetheart," she tells me and pushes to her feet.

"Aunt Val."

"Your mom is waiting in her office. I'll take you."

"*Val.*"

She pauses. Her eyes are on the floor, and I realize suddenly why her smile is too wide, why something feels *off*.

My powers are awake now, too. Tentative, not wanting to lose control, I reach out to her, to the hall beyond; farther, to the floors of this castle. I feel dozens of people I don't know, can hear brushes of their thoughts.

But there's one I can't find.

"Where is he?" I ask again, my voice low.

Val finally looks at me. She breathes deeply, worrying her bottom lip in her teeth.

I stand, the robe fluttering around me. "Val, if my mom sent him away—"

"He left."

I blink at her. "What?"

"Two mornings ago, apparently. I wasn't here yet." She tells me this the way she used to tell me when Mom had to cancel picking me up or Dad had to extend his business trip; her hands out towards me, her face pinched, all her posture braced like she expects me to fall apart. "He asked for a portal back to L.A. Told someone to pass on the message that he was sorry, but he's done."

"What? No. No way. He'd at least—" I grab for my phone on the bedside table. Thank god it's been charging this whole time.

But when I wake it up, there's nothing. No texts. No missed calls.

"Gwen, I'm so sorry." Val touches my shoulder. "Anthony Stern is... well. You know his reputation. He's never been known to be the kind of Hero who sticks around for the serious things. I think this all just got a bit much for him, you know?"

That's what guts me.

That's what sends me back to the bed, sitting heavily, my head spinning.

A bit much for him.

I got a bit much for him.

But...no. *No.* The way he'd looked at me. The way he'd touched me. It had started as a hot and heavy one-night stand at his house party, sure; but comparing that first time to recently? He was a completely different man. Each caress of his fingers on my skin, each brush of his lips on mine, the way he gazed up at me—I'd never felt so *cherished* before.

No. There has to be a reason he left. There has to be—

"Gwen." Val kneels in front of me. "I know you're hurting, but your mom really needs to see you."

Right. Niberu. The armada. My powers. All the things that could literally decide the fate of the world, and here I am, my heart shattering over a guy I'd been sleeping with for not even a full *week*.

This isn't me. I'm the woman who graduated with honors and half a dozen minors on time while working various jobs. I'm the woman who would've found out all this stuff about my dad's coordinates and the armada and my powers *on my own*—Anthony was just a means to an end.

That's all it was.

He knew it. Clearly.

And this is that end.

I nod at Aunt Val, but I can't look at her, not wanting her to see the tears brimming in my eyes. "Give me ten minutes," I say and shove past her to grab clothes out of a dresser.

They're all my size. My style, too.

Mom had this room all set up for me.

The realization does nothing to staunch the pain rising, and I hurry into the bathroom, slam the door behind me.

I turn on the shower.

Then I sink to the floor, clothes gripped to my chest, begging myself not to cry. I don't know what will happen if I fall apart now that Anthony isn't here to—

A sob grabs me.

No sterlinium to staunch my powers.

No Anthony to calm me down.

I'm alone.

He just…left me here.

~

Mom's office is on the highest floor of this castle, with open doors that show a wide balcony and let in the hot ocean breeze. A massive mahogany desk takes up the middle of the room, with shelves and books and tapestries on the rest of the walls, very medieval chic.

I step through the main door with Aunt Val close behind me. She's still acting like I'll fall apart any second.

I won't.

I definitely *will not.*

Because I won't think about Anthony. Back in his mansion outside L.A. Planning another orgy. Probably already cock-deep in another girl.

Nausea swirls, and I swallow it down, hating the rush of tears that stings my eyes again. The door shuts, closing us in, and I'm so distracted with trying to keep myself distracted that I almost miss the two people in the room.

Mom, of course, sitting at her desk.

And a man, leaning his hip against the edge of her desk, arms folded, piercing eyes locked on me.

It takes me a full second to recognize him. "Lucas Gardson?"

The new CEO of Heroes Org. He's dressed in his uniform, the one that signifies him as his Hero counterpart, the Magician. A master of illusion and mystery.

"What—" I look at Mom. "What is he doing here?" All my nerves seize up, trying to rationalize why Mom's new biggest enemy is *here*. Did he come to get my dad? Did Heroes Org figure out Mom has him, and they're out for revenge?

Mom stands. "Gwendolyn, you've never officially met Lucas, have you?"

"I—"

She licks her lips. It's the only sign she's nervous, and that immediately makes me panic even more.

"This is Lucas Gardson," she says, waving her hand at him like I might not know. "Though you may also know him by his other name."

I nod, almost say *yeah, the Magician*—but she doesn't give me a chance.

"Loki. God of Mischief."

I stare at her. Silence fills the space.

"I'm sorry, what?"

Mom moves out around the desk slowly, her eyes on mine the whole while. "I'm telling you everything now, Gwendolyn. Every answer you wanted as a child. Every secret kept from you. This is it." She tosses a glance at Lucas, but I can't tear my eyes away from her. "He is a god, Gwendolyn. And he's my brother."

He tips his head, shoulder-length black hair glistening in the chandelier's light. "Gwendolyn Odyssey. A pleasure to make your formal acquaintance."

I laugh. It's tight and high-pitched and sounds like I'm drowning. "What?"

"We're not from this planet," Mom continues. "We're from the same galaxy that Niberu is from, only a different world. Certain religions on Earth called it Asgard."

"That was me," Lucas says, grinning. "I gave them that name."

Mom keeps talking like he didn't speak. "More than a century ago, Niberu attacked Asgard as he plans to do to Earth. He destroyed our home."

The sadness in Mom's voice momentarily distracts me from the rest of what she said.

"A century ago?" I repeat. "But you're..."

Mom smiles. It's pained, and I see the answer in her, the agelessness in her eyes.

"Yes, sweetheart. I'm immortal."

My jaw drops open. I have absolutely nothing to say to that.

What the *fuck* is there to say to that, really?

"Lucas and I have been on Earth for a long while," she continues. "Long enough that we thought Niberu had overcome his need for war and forgotten us. But he rallies again, and now—" She exhales, and it shakes a little, and my god, I've never been so terrified in my life. "Now, he's coming for us again."

I want to ask a dozen questions. I can't get my mouth to work.

"Perse, maybe we should sit down?" Val is at my back, her hand on my arm.

She's my mom's sister.

So...she knows. She knows all of this.

I point at Val. Mom reads my question—thank god, suddenly, for her powers—and nods.

"She's a god, too. She was part of the elite fighting force on Asgard."

"And Dad?" The word huffs out of me.

"He knew." Her voice is soft.

"But he's—"

"Human. Mortal."

My eyebrows shoot up. I really wish he were here right now. Maybe I could convince Mom to bring him up just so I'm not the only human in a room of gods—

Wait.

"So if you're...an immortal god...then what am I?"

"That's why your powers are so amplified. You are young, and untrained, and raw, but you have all the similar powers to me. My name on Asgard was Hela," she tells me, "and I was the goddess of death. I took the name Persephone once I came to earth. It felt...fitting."

I sway backwards. Aunt Val still holds onto me. "Death?"

Mom bats her hand. "It's not as gruesome as it sounds. Destruction, more like; but also creation. I know this is a lot to take in right now, but we need to start exploring the full breadth of your powers, Gwendolyn. You seem to be a god, as we are."

"We'll need you once Niberu comes," Lucas tells me. He looks serious for the first time.

"*We*? Who's *we*?"

Lucas smirks. It doesn't reach his eyes. "I've taken Heroes Org in a new direction, darling. Slowly but surely."

"We're merging Elysium and Heroes Org," Mom clarifies. It has me gasping, eyebrows rocketing up. "We've been doing so subtly—and at times with *difficulty*." She glares at Lucas, who grins and shrugs. "But we know it's for the best. The best chance we have against Niberu is a united front. It's what caused Asgard's downfall at his hands. We were divided, driven by conflict. This time, we'll be ready."

"Even if we kill each other first," Lucas grumbles, but he innocently looks at the ceiling like he didn't say anything.

I laugh again. It scratches my throat.

My mother is a goddess from another planet. She's *centuries* old. My aunt is, too; and hey, I also have an uncle I never knew about, because why not?

And oh, I'm also a *goddess.*

And...immortal?

Holy shit.

I shake my head. Shake it again, as though it will stop all of this, change this, *something.*

Anthony—

I turn, instinct driving me to fall into his arms before I remember, with a crack, that he's gone. He left.

"Gwen, sit down," Val prods me. "I'll get you some water."

I push her away, pacing the room, looking for something, something that makes sense, something I can hold onto—

"This is going badly," Lucas says.

"Gwendolyn, please." Mom steps in front of my pacing. I jerk back, and when she reaches for me, I can already feel her powers pushing at me, trying to fight into my mind, to calm me down.

"*No!*" It's reflexive. It rears up from every moment throughout my childhood when she or Dad would do this exact thing, *force* me to calm down when the sterlinium didn't work or when I was just too worked up. I'm not a child anymore; but *shit,* I feel like one, helpless and alone and scared because my whole family has been keeping this massive, world-shattering secret from me, and a boy *left me,* and it *hurts.*

I cup my hands around my face, trying to breathe, but each inhale squeezes my throat tighter. Panic compresses every muscle, my body poised to fight, but there are no enemies here, nothing to attack or run from; just my mom, and Aunt Val, and the CEO of Heroes Org. What will Anthony think when his new boss forces him to work with my mom—and by extension me—anyway?

My chest aches. The pain spreads out, down my arms, up my neck, my mind heaving, throbbing—

"Gwendolyn!" Mom reaches for me again. "Let me calm you down—"

"No." The voice isn't really mine. It's deeper, animalistic, and it terrifies me, but it also centers me—this voice, this woman, will know what to do. "I am not yours."

I throw my head back and scream.

21
ANTHONY

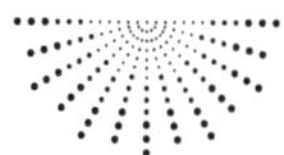

I GO TO MY LAB. THAT'S WHERE I ALWAYS GO WHEN SHIT'S FUCKED UP.

Because science makes *sense.*

It's always been this way. Parents arguing when I was a pimple-pocked pre-teen? Hide in my room and make a battery out of a potato. Nasty break-up of first love? Work on a more efficient self-driving car until every last memory of her was gone. Parents die in a car crash right on the cusp of me making my first million, the best time of my life marred by tragedy? Invent a new chemical compound to neutralize radiation poisoning for astronauts in a lucrative government contract.

Can't get a grip on the idea of dying? Time to invent a superhero suit.

"Fuck!" I shout, throwing a wrench on the table and relishing the way it bounces to the concrete floor with a loud crack.

Somehow, this is worse.

Somehow, leaving Gwen is a problem that not even science can fix.

My brain churns. Memories boil inside me, rising up my throat. The old scars—trauma I've pushed down, PTSD, anxiety—it all comes up.

I'm so fucking broken.

And it's that thought, the thought that I'm dying and it may be for the best, since I'm beyond repair, that finally fills the void inside me with silence.

After all, it's the worst thing I ever did, leaving Gwen that way.

But it was also the best thing I ever did.

The only right thing.

Not even she can fix all that's wrong with me.

And I can't drag her down to my depths.

I take a deep, shaky breath. Right. So, science isn't helping. At all. I reach for my phone. My second coping method was raging orgy parties full of liquor and coke and sex and everything else that will numb my mind.

But I toss the phone to the floor beside the wrench.

I don't want other people.

Maybe some whiskey will help.

I HEAD up to the kitchen, yanking the freezer door open, looking for the whiskey stones I keep there.

Can't find 'em.

Fuck 'em.

I slam the door shut and turn to the bottle on the counter. Don't even need a glass.

I look at the sunrise cresting over the mountains, a gorgeous display of nature through the enormous floor-to-ceiling windows. I salute the sun with the bottle and raise it to my lips.

The burn of whiskey is a direct contrast to the cool glass of the bottle, and I chug it down, relishing the pain. I grab the bottle by the neck, prepared to take it outside and watch the rest of the sunrise from the balcony.

A man's there. And a woman.

The fuck?

Backlit by the sunrise, I can't quite tell who they are, but I know without a doubt that they shouldn't be there. On my highly secure mountain that's entirely mine.

Before I can move, the two people stride across the balcony, ripping open the glass door. There's a shift in the light, and finally I see—

"Watcher?" I drop the bottle on the counter and rush across the room. "What the fuck are you doing here?"

"Hello, Stern," the other person, a woman with medium dark skin and eyes full of rage, says in a cold voice.

I draw up short. I know that voice. It's the woman in Gwen's phone contact, her aunt—Val.

My eyes bounce between Watcher and Val, Gwen's aunt who screamed at me for being a dick. I can't seem to wrap my head around this. The whiskey's barely even reached my stomach yet, and the sun's not fully up, and my mind's already good and fucked.

"We need you," Watcher says. "You may need the Steel Soldier suit."

I shake my head. Missions for Heroes come from Heroes Org. Not Villains and my girl—my ex-girl's aunt.

"Gwen needs you," Val adds.

My eyes widen. "What happened?" I demand. "Is she hurt? Who did it?" I'll rip apart anyone who dared hurt Gwen, I'll paint my suit red with their blood, I'll—

"Gwen needs *you,*" Val says again. "She's...freaking out. She needs you."

Here's the thing. My heart's a motor. It whirrs; it doesn't thud. But as soon as Val says that, I swear it skips a beat.

I shake my head again, slowly, in remorse instead of confusion. "She doesn't need me," I say. I turn my back on them and head to the counter, the whiskey. "She needs anyone but me. I just fuck it all up."

I hear from the footsteps behind me that they're following. I don't care. I made my choice. It was the best—only—choice for Gwen.

"You love her." It's the Watcher's cold, calculating voice that makes me pause, my fingers already wrapped around the neck of the bottle.

"Of course I do," I tell the whiskey.

A sharp intake of breath behind me. Val, I think.

I spin around. "Which is why I left," I say, pointing the bottle at her. "Just like *you* wanted me to do."

"But—" Val starts.

"She has powers the likes of which we can't even begin to comprehend," I snarl. "And I'm a ticking time bomb, waiting to die. I can't hurt her like that."

Watcher stares at me with his yellow optic sensors. I wish I had been a real friend to him at Heroes Org. I wish I had listened to him when he tried to tell me Malcolm was corrupt.

But Watcher escaped. He found Scarlet. He found a life he never had when he was a Hero.

I won't get that chance.

I just get to wait to die.

Alone.

"Get out," I snarl.

Val doesn't back down. She glares at me, her eyes narrow in rage. She *hates* being here. She hates me.

Fine.

I hate me, too.

But—there it is again, the impossible skip in my heart's motor. Because Val glares at me with eyes the exact same shade as Gwen's. Her cheekbones are similar, too, her nose.

"GET OUT!" I shout, hurtling the whiskey bottle. Not at her, but past her, so that it hits the glass window. It's titanium-reinforced glass that can withstand plasma blasts, so the bottle just bounces off, a spray of amber whiskey staining the yellow-red rays of the rising sun on the other side.

Val doesn't flinch. She just strides right toward me.

Just like Gwen would do.

"Gwen needs *you,*" Val says. "And I may not fucking like it, but it's clear that you're something more to her than a playboy asshole with his clock running out."

"Doesn't change the fact that I *am* a playboy asshole," I say.

"No," Val confirms. "It doesn't. But you're not that to *her.*"

"I'm useless," I say. "We're talking about apocalyptic alien armadas, and I just play dress-up as a Hero."

"We don't need you to fight, you fucking idiot," Val says, but her voice is almost kind, despite her words. "We just need you to love the woman who needs to fight."

"And preferably before she completely blows apart Elysium in a meltdown that's reigning destruction on the whole island," Watcher adds.

"Wait, what?" I say, whirling around to him.

"Gwen's lost control. Utterly. The castle is cracking apart—the *island* is cracking apart," Val says. "We can't reach her. She's thrown up this mental shield, and it's destroying everything in its wake."

And that—that—finally breaks through to me.

I can't fight, not against gods and monsters, not like that. I'm weak and useless. That hasn't changed.

I can't fight any of the enemies we're facing now. I can't be a Hero.

But I can be hers.

22

GWEN

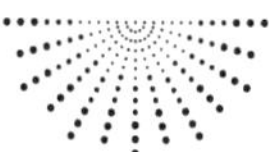

In elementary school, the girl who got mad at me for not using my dad's influence at Heroes Org to get her stuff—her name was Lisa.

And I killed her.

I know that now. I knew that then, even though my parents denied it. I lost control, and my powers manifested my anger at her, and I broke her irreparably.

That's what I'm doing now.

Breaking irreparably.

Everything is heat. Heat and brightness and endless rage, pulsing out of me in wave after wave of beautiful, destructive, terrifying power. I am a bottle uncorked, champagne overflowing in a golden, fizzy waterfall; I am a volcano untapped, lava gurgling up and obliterating everything in its path.

I am life.

I am death.

Mom is death. What did she say? She's the goddess of death and creation.

"Gwendolyn!" she screams my name. Her powers war with mine, but she is a wildfire; I am the sun. "Gwendolyn—*stop*—"

I have a set of rules, Mom. I made a set of rules, and I took my meds religiously, all so I would never have to *stop*. So I would never *start* at all.

This was what you wanted, wasn't it? For me to be your perfect little weapon.

Am I screaming still? I don't know. I can't tell. There is a strange sort of calmness in the epicenter of the storm, like this is where I've always been meant to be: the source of destruction, the eye of the chaos.

Something cracks. Shatters. Glass and stone. Wherever I'm standing, my feet shift, but I don't fall; I readjust, dust raining on my shoulders.

I think, somewhere, people are screaming. Running. From me? They should run.

Take yourself seriously.

I had these rules. I was *so good* about following them.

Be fucking smart.

Because I knew if I ever didn't.

Never play all your cards.

I would end up this. A monster.

My throat is raw, and I do hear myself screaming now. I scream, and I sob, and my heart fucking *breaks*—how was it whole at all? How are there any pieces left to shatter?

I'm alone, and I'm falling apart, and I'm not strong enough to stop this—

"Gwen!"

I drop to my knees, hands to my chest, screaming and screaming, a broken dam. But that voice—

"*Gwen!* Gwen—look at me!"

Is that…?

Fingers touch my arm. Cold, metal fingers, and I jerk back.

Another crack of stone. The floor shifts again.

I'm destroying this building, I think. I'm bringing it all down.

"Shit—Gwen, it's me!" Metal grinds, and then the hand that touches me is soft and strong and real.

I look up. The blinding whiteness of my power clears, focuses—and I see him. In his Steel Soldier suit.

How is he here?

He isn't here.

It's a trick. Is Dad messing with me? Did Mom let him out? I really must be freaking her out, then—but it's that fact that keeps me from giving in.

I want them to suffer for this. Just a little. I want them to feel exactly what they've made me into.

But I also…

Don't.

I tip forward, sobbing, my screams abating.

I'm so *tired*.

I don't want to be a monster. I don't want these powers. I don't want to be their weapon. I just want to be their *daughter*.

And I want so badly for this to really be Anthony that my whole body heaves, wracking sobs pulling up from the pit of my stomach.

"Gwen," he says, and then he's kneeling in front of me. "Hey, Gwen—it's me. It's Anthony. See?"

I look up as he presses a button and his helmet slides back. And there are those teasing eyes, that soft smile, his cheeks tinged pink and his hair a mess. His face is lined with worry, but he forces his smile wider, and leans down to me.

He presses another button and the top half of his suit unfolds, revealing his chest in a tight white shirt, his sterlinium heart glowing.

He opens his arms to me.

"I'm so sorry," he tells me. "I shouldn't have left you. I didn't want—" He pauses, throat working. "I didn't want to drag you down with me. But, baby, I—I need you. I need *you*, Gwen. I know you're in there; I know you can stop this. Please. Come here."

The rawness in his voice, the sorrow in his eyes—

This is real.

He is real.

The waves of my powers keep flowing, rage and destruction, pure white, unadulterated, yanking down stones and breaking windows. Somewhere, the screaming is lessened, and I cast my mind out wide—all the people have gotten out. The building is empty.

I could bring it down.

I could decimate this place with the power of my rage.

But I see only Anthony. His face is pinched with worry and exertion. He's risking his life coming here, putting himself in my path; and I should be furious at him, but I also just want *him*.

He's scared. I'm scared, too.

I heave myself forward, into Anthony's arms.

He envelops me, crushing me to him, and I clamp his mouth with mine. The kiss is searing, a beating of lips and tongues, punishment for him leaving, punishment for what I'm doing.

What am I doing?

"Anthony," I moan his name. Plead for him. "Anthony—"

It's a sob. His hands are in my hair, clinging to the back of my neck, touching me everywhere all at once.

"I'm here, baby," he says into my mouth. "I'm here."

His lips track down my neck, nipping the skin at the base of my ear. I straddle his lap as the bottom of his soldier suit peels away, the whole of his suit folding into a metallic sphere behind him. He's hard between my thighs, bulging against a tight pair of jeans, straining up to my cunt as I twine my body around him.

It's a frenzy.

It's half fight, half consumption.

He drags my shirt over my head. I'm not as kind; I rip his shirt in half and unbutton his jeans, letting his cock spring free, rock-hard and bursting with veins, the tip drenched in pre-cum. My pants are gone, and then I plunge myself down on him, uniting us, connecting us, driving me home.

He's here, he's *mine*, and I don't need anything else.

I ride him, dragging my body up, plunging down. He grips my hips and helps me move hard, driving his full length deep into me, each thrust met with gasps from us both. My nipples scrape across his chest and only add to the electric sensations, my whole body a riot of tingles and friction and need.

"Gwen," he says against me. "Fuck, Gwen—"

He wraps one arm around my waist to keep driving me deep and uses the other hand to grab for my clit. His thumb finds the numb, already swollen, slippery with my own juices, and he rubs hard, brutally, matching our fervor.

I bend into him as the orgasm rises, and when it crests, I scream into his neck, body convulsing around his cock in an iron grip. He comes with a shout, meeting me where I am, the two of us going over the edge together, unified.

"I love you," he says, capturing my lips again. "I love you, Gwen, and I'm so sorry, I—"

I silence him with another kiss. We're both sweat drenched, gasping for breath, but when I pull back, his eyes are clear.

So am I.

My storm is passed. He is all there is, his body against mine, the love in his eyes that has become my foundation.

"I love you too," I tell him, and it comes on a whimper.

He kisses one eyelid, then the other. "I may not have much time left," he whispers, "but what time I do have is yours."

I throw my arms around him, his cock still lodged inside of me, and I cling to him, to this moment.

I still cannot fully accept that he's dying. That there's no way to save him. It's a reality I can't yet—

My focus widens.

I'm still in Mom's office. Only it's destroyed.

The tapestries on the walls are shredded. The furniture, books, windows—all of it is ransacked, like a whirlwind trashed the place. There are even great cracks through the walls and the floor is slightly slanted.

I can only imagine what I've done to the rest of the building. The rest of the island.

But something pushes up through my regret.

I'm *powerful.*

Mom and Lucas were right. They do need me, for whatever fight is coming, for whatever threat the armada represents.

And if I can do *this* without a lick of training? Then god, I can't even imagine what I'll be capable of when I understand what it is I can do.

Anthony shifts under me, still cradling me in his lap.

What time I do have is yours.

I kiss his temple, breathing him in.

War is coming.

Whether it hits me first as Niberu or Anthony's death, I don't yet know.

But I do know that I'll fight either one with every shred of strength I have in me.

23
ANTHONY

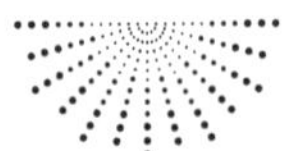

Persephone finds us naked in her office.

Which is….not ideal.

I mean, I know she knows about us, but it's one thing to know your daughter is hooking up with someone and another to walk in on them, *naked* on the floor of *your* office, with drying sweat and fuck-flushes all over their bodies and…yeah.

Not how I should see the mom-in-law.

She looks absolutely wrathful. That's a good word for it. *Wrathful.* She very, very, very clearly wants to smite me for fucking her daughter.

"I love her," I say, somewhat sheepishly.

"Ugh." Persephone waves her hand, and clothes appear on both me and Gwen. She gave me a black jumpsuit that, were it bright orange, would be appropriate as prison garb. Gwen's in a prairie dress that goes up to her neck and down to her ankles.

"Mom," Gwen says flatly.

Persephone heaves a sigh, and we're both in regular jeans and t-shirts.

"So," she says, gesturing her hand first at Gwen and me, then at her office. "This."

Gwen looks around at the debris and chaos with a glint in her eye that's almost proud. "This," she says. "I'm more powerful than I thought."

"You lack control," Persephone says.

"Not with him." Gwen grabs my hand, squeezing it tightly. Persephone opens her mouth, but Gwen cuts her off. "What I really lack is education."

Persephone closes her mouth, lips pursed, eyes narrowed as she takes us in. Slowly, she nods.

"I'm working with Val and Lucas. We're going to get you the education you should have had from the start. But you," she says, lasering her gaze onto me. "Why did you leave in the first place?"

I start to say, *Because I'm not good enough.*

And then I start to say, *Because I didn't want to hurt her, but then fucked up and hurt her even worse.*

But none of my words feel adequate.

So instead I say, "Can you just read my mind? Like, all the way? I know I was a bit of a playboy—"

"A bit," Persephone sniffs.

"—and well, my reputation clearly isn't the best. No matter what I say, the words aren't enough. Can't you just...just look?"

"Anthony," Gwen says in a low voice. "That's a pretty big leap of faith. To open your mind, just grant full access..."

"Can *you* do it, then?" I ask her. "You can have anything in here," I say, putting her hand against my skull. "Anything. I don't care. I want you to know all the truths of me."

Her eyes well with emotion, and she nods. I feel her an instant later, a warm, loving presence in my mind. Gwen steps closer to me, tucking her head under my chin, sifting through my thoughts and emotions so she can know with all certainty just how much she's changed me.

Just how much I'm hers.

With a sigh, she steps back. She looks to Persephone and some sort of silent, mental conversation passes between them. Then Persephone nods in a decisive way.

"Stern, your fear of death almost caused..." She looks around her demolished office. "It *did* cause havoc."

I duck my head, and Gwen squeezes my hand.

"I can see how you have some use. Not in the fights to come. But for my daughter. So—just this once—I will give you a heart."

I blink several times.

"She's the god of death and creation," Gwen tells me.

The motor that replaced my dead heart whirrs.

"What?" I can't wrap my head around any of this.

"Creation." Persephone strides forward. Gwen steps back, and Persephone splays her hand across the hard metal circle that outlines where my heart should be, where the motor is instead. She taps her fingernail over it. "Yes," she says, eyes on the glowing lights that create triangles under the t-shirt. "I can fix this."

"Fix…me?"

"It will hurt. But I don't think you will die."

"Oh," I say.

"Do you trust me?" Persephone asks.

"Not really."

"Do you trust me?" Gwen asks.

"Always, without a doubt."

"I think you should do it."

"Okay," I say immediately.

Persephone waves her hand, sending my t-shirt away in a puff of smoke. Oh, they were serious. Right here, right now, I'm getting a heart.

Or I'm dying.

One or the other.

My hands shake.

Persephone's eyes seem to illuminate with ethereal light. She presses the palm of her hand to the center of my heart's reactor. Her fingers curl over the round edges protruding from my skin. There are scars puckered pink and white around it—I'd been dying when I installed the unit, desperate, my hands unsteady—

Not like Persephone.

She looks at me with cold appraisal, with power, with certainty.

This is what it means to be the goddess over death and life, I think. *This is what it means to not fear mortality and all the damage it can cause to those who are left behind.*

And then her eyes go solid white, and something in a language I don't know erupts past her lips, and her head cocks, and her hands twist, and I—

—die.

I die.

Where there was a heart motor, there is now nothing but a hole. A gaping, bloody, empty hole, right in the center of my chest.

I feel my legs start to crumble; my brain starts to black out. No heartbeat. No oxygen expanding my lungs.

No life left in me.

My eyes shoot to Gwen. She's the last thing I want to see before I'm gone.

"Trust me," she whispers.

And then—

Thud.

Thud.

Thud.

I stagger back. Persephone is no longer touching me, though her sharp-edged fingernails are stained deep red with dripping blood. I look down at my chest, and even as I watch, I see the heart now inside me. It's bloody and veiny and frankly ugly, but it's also *beating.*

My ribcage—sawed up and reinforced with metal to accommodate the motor—grows over the heart, caging it inside me. The bones feel like fiery ice, a contradiction of pain that would have me screaming if I could catch my breath, but I can't—I just have to live through this pain, knowing it will bring me life. Blood and muscle and skin knit over the wound. While my body reforms around my heart, it's excruciatingly ripping through my senses, not just the physical pain but the mental anguish of trying to accept the impossible.

But as soon as it's done, I'm left gasping but clear-sighted. There's a shininess to the skin, like a scar, and when I dare to touch it with a finger it feels sensitive, but…

"I'll be damned," I say in wonder, staring at my own body. My own body that doesn't glow in the center, that doesn't pollute my blood with sterlinium, that's whole and real and not…

Not dying.

Gwen leaps up and throws herself at me, hugging me to her.

And my heart truly does skip a beat to see the love reflected in her eyes.

"I'll give you some time together," Persephone says, watching us. "But Gwen…"

And there it is.

The threat of the future.

Persephone has bought me time, but there's an alien armada waiting to take it away from us.

"I know," Gwen says soberly. "I know I need to train. I know I need to fight."

"And," I add, "well, I'm nothing compared to Gwen. But if you need my suit—I can rebuild it to fit her, maybe, or if you have a better person in mind for it...basically, whatever you need, tell me. I am still a billionaire philanthropist genius, and my sexy brain has got to count for something, surely."

"Surely," Gwen giggles.

"Perhaps," Persephone says regally. But I can tell I said the right thing. Maybe there's something to that whole humility thing people keep telling me I ought to try.

"I'll be in contact," Persephone says. She looks once more around her office, as if she still can't quite believe just how bad the damage is, how much worse it could have been. "In the meantime..."

"You don't have to tell me twice," Gwen says. She grabs my hand and spins me into a kiss.

24
GWEN

Three Weeks Later

I REFRESH the screen for the millionth time.

The armada hasn't moved.

Click.

Reload.

Again.

My bottom lip is caught between my teeth, but I can't help it. It's impossible that the armada hasn't moved *at all.* What are they waiting for?

I close my eyes, stretching my mind, but Niberu must have figured out I can listen in on his crew, because for the last few days, I haven't been able to hear them.

Which is both unnerving and infuriating, considering I'm pretty damn good at breaking down mental blocks now.

I growl at the screen as Anthony kicks into his lab holding a mug of steaming coffee. He hands it to me, and I greedily snatch it.

"This isn't healthy," he tells me and reaches past me to flick off the monitor. "I have alerts set up. Your mom has alerts set up. Scarlet has alerts set up. If anyone on that fleet even so much as sneezes off course, we'll know. You don't have to watch them."

"I know." I blow on the coffee, staring at the now dark screen.

The chair swivels. Anthony swings me to face him, his lips in a thin line.

He runs his fingers over my temple, down my ear. "What's going on in that head of yours?"

I chuckle and take a long drink of coffee. "Oh, butterflies and unicorns, the usual."

He crouches down to me, his hands in my lap. The severity on his face, his worry for me—it immediately refocuses me, and I set down my mug to thread my fingers with his.

"I'm fine, really," I promise and force a smile. "Just…the usual."

"We can cancel today," he says. "You've been training damn near every day for the past month. You could use a break."

"No." I rub my eyes. I *am* tired, but Niberu's fleet could move any day. Any hour. Any minute. I have to be ready. I have to be—

Lips press to my neck. I smile.

"I think," he leaves another kiss, this one lower, on my shoulder, "that you need a different kind of training today."

"Oh? Because we don't train in *that* enough," I say, smirking.

We both know that's a lie. This wouldn't even be the first time we've *trained* this morning. Anthony joined me in the shower after we both ran a few miles in the scraggly desert brush around his mansion.

He hooks his finger into the strap of my tank top and pulls it to the side, kissing lower, brushing the slope of my collar bone.

"Doctor's orders," he says into my skin, and fuck, he's never going to let go of Scarlet telling us *once* that sex would help me. "We don't want you getting overtaxed. Gotta replenish all that good energy, hm?"

His fingers ease one side of my tank top down, exposing my left breast, and I suck in a breath at the brush of cold. My nipple pebbles, achingly hard, and Anthony immediately sets on it, his mouth clamping down. Teeth drag over the tight skin and I throw my head back, writhing on the computer chair.

"I suppose—we could—*god*, Anthony—"

He's wiggling his other hand into my shorts and peeling back my thong. He doesn't hesitate—he plunges three fingers deep inside of me as he sucks my nipple into his mouth, and I mewl.

"Yeah, okay, we'll stay here today," I gasp.

He grins wickedly and moves back to pull my shirt off. I get to work unbuttoning his, and when his bare chest catches in the light, I pause, like

I always do. Checking, maybe, that our miracle really did take. Checking that he's healed, with a beating heart that won't slowly poison him.

My eyes slide up to his, and when he smiles, I don't have to read his mind to know what he's thinking.

Time. We have time now.

At least, until Niberu comes. But I willfully shove thoughts of that threat aside, just for now, and strip out of the rest of my clothes as he does.

I kick off the chair and go to my knees, matching him on the floor. He's fully erect already, his cock bobbing until I clamp it between my thighs.

"Oh no, not yet," he growls and sweeps me into his arms. I squeal until he lands me flat out on the floor.

Reverently, almost worshipfully, he spreads my legs before him. I know I'm dripping wet already—I'm never not around him—and he trails one thumb along the apex of my thigh, staring down at my pussy like it's the most wondrous thing he's ever seen.

Then he flicks his eyes up, holding my gaze, and there's that reverence again, amplified, like part of him is still amazed he gets to be here with me, touch me, make love to me.

I start to sit up—I need to kiss him, I need to feel his mouth on me—but he arcs down and presses that kiss to my pussy. My whole body jolts with a current of desire and I flop backwards, hands to my breasts, rubbing the puckered flesh.

Anthony's kiss deepens, his tongue prodding my folds, taking his time. I start to moan in protest until he licks from my ass all the way to my clit and sucks the tender bud into his mouth.

"Anthony—" I pant his name.

"Yeah, baby?" he asks, his still half lips around my clit.

"Anthony," I say again, and I look down at him, wanting him to feel the reverence from me, too. *I'm* the one who's lucky to be here, with him, after everything. *I'm* the one who will get to have a forever now with him, when it was only ever the far-off dream of a little girl.

I love this man with every piece of my combustible soul.

He runs the flat of his tongue on my clit, his eyes holding mine, and each stroke feels like a promise. As the orgasm builds, he moves faster, covering my pussy in promises, until the pleasure starts to crest and I cry out. He moves his body up to plunge his cock into me, stoking the orgasm blindingly high, rocking his hips into mine in strong, sure thrusts so we're riding this pleasure together.

That's my future now.

Together.

With him.

25

EPILOGUE

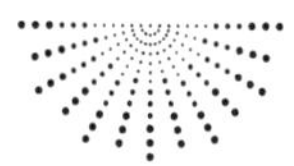

A PHONE ON THE LAB TABLE STARTS TO FLASH, BUT IT'S ON SILENT.

A monitor in a base starts to chirp.

Another on an island starts to wail.

The screen showing the satellite's image of an alien fleet has been the same for weeks. Possibly longer. They couldn't track the image until Gwen—who knows how long Niberu lay in wait before her?

But now.

A single ship among the hundreds dips to the left, just slightly, maybe an engine failed.

That dip recorrects, and the whole vessel turns, vibrating.

It rockets off, deep into space.

Directly towards Earth.

The End

...BUT ALSO A NEW BEGINNING.

With the conclusion of the first Heroes and Villains trilogy, we've shown you just how high those stakes are.

Join us now for the exciting continuation of the series—where Heroes are Gods and the Villains are much, much worse!

THANK YOU FOR READING!

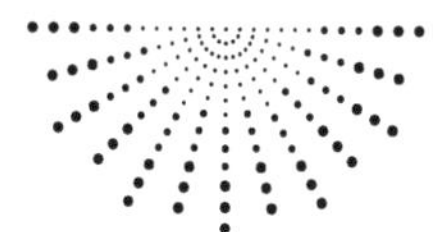

When Liza and Natasha first started writing this series, we had no idea what the future held for us. As the Heroes and Villains universe exploded into being, we got swept up in their stories. We hope that you love them as much as we do, and if so, please consider leaving us some reviews! We would really appreciate it.

Phase Two of the Heroes and Villains Series is already available! Continue with *Magician*, the story of Lucas Gardson (aka Loki, god of mischief) and the girl who falls out the sky and ends up married to the trickster himself!

Sign up for our newsletter at http://thepennandluxe.com for all the latest in our sexy stories. And remember…

Fall in love. Save the World.

ABOUT THE AUTHORS

Liza Penn and Natasha Luxe are a pair of author friends with bestselling books under different names. They joined forces—like all the best superheroes do—for the greater good.

You can keep up with them at their newsletter.

For more information about all their books and extra goodies for readers, check out their website.

ALSO BY LIZA PENN & NATASHA LUXE

THE HEROES AND VILLAINS SERIES:

Prequel Novella Origin (*free for subscribers*)

Book 1: Nemesis

Newsletter short story "Fly With Us"

Book 2: Alter Ego

Book 3: Secret Sanctum

Bundled Box Set of Books 1-3 + Novella Origin

Also available in paperback!

Book 4: Magician

Book 5: Thunder

Book 6: Goddess

...more coming soon!

ALSO BY NATASHA LUXE

Celebrity Crush Series

ALSO BY LIZA PENN:

Hotel Ever After Series

Printed in Great Britain
by Amazon

75937436R00270